A GREAT RECKONING

Louise Penny

~

A GREAT
RECKONING

MINOTAUR BOOKS

NEW YORK

This is a work of fiction. All of the characters, organizations, and events portrayed in this novel are either products of the author's imagination or are used fictitiously.

www.minotaurbooks.com

Grateful acknowledgment is made for permission to reprint the following:

Excerpts from "Half-hanged Mary" from *Morning in the Burned House: New Poems* by Margaret Atwood. In the U.S.: Copyright © 1995 by Margaret Atwood. Reprinted by permission of Houghton Mifflin Harcourt Publishing Company. All rights reserved. In Canada: Copyright © O. W. Toad. Reprinted by permission of McClelland & Stewart, a division of Penguin Random House Canada Limited.

Excerpts from "Herman Melville," copyright © 1940 and renewed 1968 by W. H. Auden; from *W. H. Auden Collected Poems* by W. H. Auden. Used by permission of Random House, an imprint and division of Penguin Random House LLC. All rights reserved.

Library of Congress Cataloging-in-Publication Data

Names: Penny, Louise, author.
Title: A great reckoning / Louise Penny.
Description: First Edition. | New York : Minotaur Books, 2016.
Identifiers: LCCN 2016019580 | ISBN 9781250022134 (hardback) |
    ISBN 9781250022127 (e-book)
Subjects: LCSH: Gamache, Armand (Fictitious character)—Fiction. | Police—
    Quebec (Province)—Fiction. | Murder—Investigation—Fiction. | BISAC: FICTION /
    Mystery & Detective / Traditional British. | GSAFD: Mystery fiction.
Classification: LCC PR9199.4.P464 G74 2016 | DDC 813/.6—dc23
LC record available at https://lccn.loc.gov/2016019580

Our books may be purchased in bulk for promotional, educational, or business use. Please contact your local bookseller or the Macmillan Corporate and Premium Sales Department at 1-800-221-7945, extension 5442, or by e-mail at MacmillanSpecialMarkets@macmillan.com.

First Edition: August 2016

10 9 8 7 6 5 4 3 2 1

For Michael

It strikes a man more dead than a great reckoning in a little room.

—WILLIAM SHAKESPEARE

A GREAT RECKONING

CHAPTER 1

⌒

Armand Gamache sat in the little room and closed the dossier with care, squeezing it shut, trapping the words inside.

It was a thin file. Just a few pages. Like all the rest surrounding him on the old wooden floor of his study. And yet, not like all the rest.

He looked at the slender lives lying at his feet. Waiting for his decision on their fate.

He'd been at this for a while now. Reviewing the dossiers. Taking note of the tiny dots on the upper-right corner of the tabs. Red for rejected. Green for accepted.

He had not put those dots there. His predecessor had.

Armand placed the file on the floor and leaned forward in his comfortable armchair, his elbows on his knees. His large hands together, fingers intertwined. He felt like a passenger on a transcontinental flight, staring down at fields below him. Some fertile, some fallow and ripe with potential. And some barren. The topsoil masking the rock beneath.

But which was which?

He'd read, and considered, and tried to drill down past the scant information. He wondered about these lives, and he wondered about the decisions of his predecessor.

For years, decades, as head of homicide for the Sûreté du Québec, his job had been to dig. To collect evidence. To review facts, and question feelings. To pursue and arrest. To use his judgment, but never to judge.

But now he was judge and jury. The first and final word.

And Armand Gamache realized, without great surprise, that it was a role he was comfortable with. Even liked. The power, yes. He was honest enough to admit that. But mostly he appreciated that he was now in a position not simply to react to the present, but to actually shape the future.

And at his feet was the future.

Gamache leaned back and crossed his legs. It was past midnight, but he wasn't tired. A cup of tea sat on his desk beside a couple of chocolate chip cookies. Uneaten.

The curtains of his study fluttered and he could feel a cold draft coming in through the slightly open window. And he knew if he drew back the curtains and turned on the porch light, he would see the first snow of the season swirling in the light. Falling softly and landing on the roofs of the homes in this tiny village of Three Pines.

It would cover the perennial gardens and leave a thin layer on cars and porches, on the bench in the middle of the village green. It would be landing, softly, on the forests and mountains and the Rivière Bella Bella that flowed past the homes.

It was the beginning of November and this was an early snow even by Québec standards. A tease, a portent. And not enough, yet, for children to play in.

But soon, he knew. It would come soon enough. And the gray November would be transformed into a bright, sparkling wonderland of skiing and skating. Of snowball fights, and snow forts and snowmen, and angels made in snow that had fallen from the heavens.

But for now the children slept and their parents slept. Everyone in the small Québec village slept, while the snow fell and Armand Gamache considered the young lives that lay at his feet.

Through the open door of his study, he saw the living room of the home he shared with his wife, Reine-Marie.

Oriental rugs were scattered about the wide-plank flooring. A large sofa sat on one side of the large stone hearth and two faded armchairs on the other. Side tables were piled with magazines and books. Bookcases lined the walls and lamps filled the room with pleasant light.

It was an inviting room and now Gamache stood up, stretched, and walked out into it, their shepherd Henri following him. He poked the fire and sat in one of the armchairs. His work wasn't done yet. Now he needed to think.

He'd made up his mind about most of the files. Except that one.

When he'd first seen it, he'd read the contents then set it aside, in the rejected pile. Agreeing with the red dot of his predecessor.

But something had niggled at him and he kept returning to that one file. Reading and rereading it. Trying to work out why this one dossier, this one young woman out of all of them, was troubling him.

Gamache had brought the file with him, and now he opened it. Again.

Her face stared at him. Arrogant, challenging. Pale. Her hair jet black, shaved in places, spiked in others. There were unmistakable piercings through her nose and brows and cheek.

She claimed to read ancient Greek and Latin, and yet she'd barely scraped by in high school and had spent the past few years doing, from what he could tell, nothing.

She'd earned the red dot.

So why did he keep going back to it? To her? It wasn't her appearance. He knew enough to look beyond that.

Was it her name? Amelia?

Yes, he thought, that might be it. She shared the name with Gamache's mother, who'd been named for the aviator who'd lost her way and disappeared.

Amelia.

And yet, when he held the file he didn't feel any warmth. In fact, he felt vaguely revolted.

Finally Gamache took off his reading glasses and rubbed his eyes before taking Henri outside for a last walk of the night, in the first snow of the season.

Then it was upstairs to bed for both of them.

The next morning Reine-Marie invited her husband to breakfast at the bistro. Henri came along and lay quietly under their table as they sipped bowls of *café au lait* and waited for their maple-cured bacon with scrambled eggs and Brie.

The fireplaces on either end of the long beamed room were lit and cheerful, conversation mingled with the scent of wood smoke, and there was the familiar thudding of patrons knocking snow from their boots as they entered.

The flurries had stopped in the night, leaving just a thin layer barely covering the dead autumn leaves. It seemed a netherworld. Neither fall nor winter. The hills that surrounded the village and seemed to guard it from an often hostile world themselves looked hostile. Or, if not actually hostile, at least inhospitable. It was a forest of skeletons. Their branches, gray and bare, were raised as though begging for a mercy they knew would not be granted.

But on the village green itself stood the three tall pines from which the village took its name. Vibrant, straight and strong. Evergreen. Immortal. Pointing to the sky. Daring it to do its worst. Which it planned to do.

The worst was coming. But so was the best. The snow angels were coming.

"*Voilà*," said Olivier, placing a basket of warm almandine croissants on their table. "While you wait for breakfast."

A price tag hung from the basket. And from the chandelier above their heads. And the wing chairs they sat on. Everything in Olivier's bistro was for sale. Including, he'd intimated more than once, his partner, Gabri.

"A bag of candy and he's yours," Olivier was heard to offer patrons when Gabri turned up in his frilly apron.

"That is how he got me," Gabri would admit, smoothing the apron he only wore, they all knew, to piss off Olivier. "A bag of allsorts."

When they were alone, Armand slid a file across the table to his wife.

"Could you read this, please?"

"Of course," she said as she put on her glasses. "Is there a problem?"

"No, I don't think so."

"Then why . . . ?" She gestured toward the folder.

He'd often discussed cases with her, before his early retirement from the Sûreté. He was not yet sixty and this was more of a retreat, really. To this village, to recover from what lay beyond the ridge of mountains.

He watched her over the rim of his strong, fragrant coffee, holding the warm bowl between his hands. They no longer trembled, Reine-Marie noted. Or at least not often. She always looked, in case.

And the deep scar near his temple wasn't quite so deep. Or perhaps familiarity and relief had filled it in.

He limped still, sometimes, when he was tired. But besides that, and the scar, there were no outward signs of what had happened. Though she did not need any signs. It was the sort of thing she would never forget.

Almost losing him.

But instead, they'd found themselves here. In the village that managed to be welcoming even on the dullest day.

Reine-Marie had known, even as they'd bought the home and unpacked, that the time would come when he'd want and need to go back to work. The only question had been, what next? What would Chief Inspector Armand Gamache, the head of the most successful homicide department in the country, choose to do?

He'd had plenty of offers. Their study was filled with envelopes marked "Confidential." He'd taken plenty of meetings. From heads of major corporations, to political parties anxious for him to run for office, to police organizations, national and international. Discreet vehicles had pulled up outside their white clapboard home and discreetly dressed men and women had knocked on the door. And sat in their living room, discussing "what next."

Armand had listened politely, often offering them lunch or dinner or a place to stay if it was late. But never tipping his hand.

Reine-Marie herself had found her dream job, after leaving her post at the Bibliothèque et Archives nationales du Québec as one of the head librarians. She'd volunteered to sort years of donations to the regional historical society.

It was a post her former colleagues no doubt viewed as a significant step down. But Reine-Marie wasn't interested in steps. She'd arrived at where she wanted to be. No more steps. She'd stopped. Reine-Marie had found a home in Three Pines. She'd found a home in Armand. And now she'd found her intellectual home, investigating the rich and disorganized collection of documents and furniture and clothing and oddities left to the region in wills.

For Reine-Marie Gamache, each day felt like Christmas, as she sorted through the boxes and boxes. And boxes.

And then, after much discussion between them, Armand had decided on his next step.

For weeks after, while she pored over piles of letters and old documents, he pored over his files, studying confidential reports, schematics, curricula vitae. Across from each other in their comfortable living room, they'd gone through their separate boxes, while the fire mumbled and the coffee perked and late autumn turned into an early winter.

But while she was opening up the world, he was in many ways doing the opposite. Armand was whittling down, honing, shaving, taking out the dead wood, the unnecessary, the unwanted. The rot. Until what he had in his hands was something very sharp. A spear of his own creation. And he'd need it. There could be no doubt who was in charge, and who held the power. Or that he was willing to use it.

He was almost there, she knew. But there seemed one thin obstacle.

They looked down at it now, sitting innocently on the table among the croissant flakes.

Armand opened his mouth to speak, then closed it and exhaled sharply, in irritation.

"There's something that's bothering me about this file and I don't know what it is."

Reine-Marie picked it up and read. It didn't take long. After a few minutes she closed the cover, laying a hand softly on top as a mother might on the chest of a sick child. Making sure of the heartbeat.

"She's an odd one, I'll give her that." She looked at the red dot in the corner. "You're rejecting her, I see."

Armand lifted his hands in a noncommittal gesture.

"You're considering accepting her?" she asked. "Even if it's true that she reads ancient Greek and Latin, that's not much use in the job. They're dead languages. And she might very well be lying."

"True," he admitted. "But if you're going to lie, why do it about that? Seems an odd sort of fabrication."

"She's not qualified," said Reine-Marie. "Her high school marks are abysmal. I know it's difficult to choose, but surely there are other applicants who deserve the spot more."

Their breakfast came, and Armand placed the file on the pine floor beside Henri.

"I can't tell you how often I've changed that dot," he said with a smile. "Red, green. Green, red."

Reine-Marie took a forkful of the moist scrambled eggs. A long thin string of Brie clung to the plate and she lifted her fork above her head for amusement, to see how long the string could stretch before it broke.

Longer than her arm, it seemed.

Armand, smiling and shaking his head, pulled it apart with his fingers.

"There, madame, I set you free."

"From the bondage of cheese," she said. "Oh, thank you, kind sir. But I'm afraid the attachment goes deeper than that."

He laughed.

"Do you think it's her name?" asked Reine-Marie. Her husband was rarely so indecisive, though she knew he also took his decisions seriously. They would affect people for the rest of their lives.

"Amelia?" he asked. And frowned. "I wondered the same thing. But it seems a huge overreaction on my part, don't you think? My mother's been gone for almost fifty years. I've met other Amelias—"

"Not many."

"*Non, c'est vrai.* But some. And while the name will always remind me of my mother, the fact is I didn't think of her as Amelia. She was Maman."

He was right, of course. And he didn't seem at all embarrassed to be a grown man talking about "mommy." She knew he was simply referring to the last time he saw his mother and father. When he was nine. When they weren't Amelia and Honoré but Mommy and Daddy. Going out for dinner with friends. Expected back to kiss him good night.

"It could be her name," said Armand.

"But you doubt it. You think it's something else."

"Oh God," said Olivier, coming over to check on them and looking out the window. "I don't think I'm ready."

"Neither are we," admitted Reine-Marie, following his gaze to the snowy village green, now white. "You think you are, but it always comes as an unpleasant surprise."

"And arrives earlier and earlier," said Armand.

"Exactly. And seems more and more bitter," said Olivier.

"Still, there's beauty," said Armand, and received a stern look from Olivier.

"Beauty? You're kidding, right?" he said.

"No, it's there. Of course, it can stick around far too long," said Armand.

"You're telling me," said Olivier.

"It gets old," said Reine-Marie.

"Gets old?" asked Olivier.

"But having the right tires helps," she said.

Olivier put the empty croissant basket back down on the table. "What're you talking about?"

"Winter, of course," said Reine-Marie. "The first snow."

"What're you talking about?" asked Armand.

"Ruth," said Olivier, pointing out the window at the elderly woman with a cane, and a duck, approaching the bistro. Old, cold and bitter.

She stepped inside and scanned the room.

"Yes," said Olivier. "The right tires would solve that problem."

"Fag," muttered Ruth as she limped by them.

"Hag," muttered Olivier as they watched the elderly poet take her usual seat by the fireplace. She opened the pine blanket box used as a coffee table and took out a handful of papers.

"She's helping me sort through the stuff we found in the walls when we renovated," said Olivier. "You remember?"

Armand nodded. Olivier and his partner, Gabri, had turned an abandoned hardware store into the bistro many years ago, and in updating the electricity and plumbing, they'd opened the walls and found all sorts of things. Mummified squirrels, clothing. But mostly they'd found papers. Newspapers, magazines, advertisements, catalogues used as insulation as though words could keep winter at bay.

Enough heated words had been hurled at the Québec winter, but all had failed to stop the snow.

In the chaos of the renovations, the papers had simply been dumped in the pine blanket box and forgotten. The box had sat in front of the hearth for years, unopened. Countless *cafés au lait*, and glasses of wine, and plates of regional cheese and paté and baguette, and feet, had rested on top of it, until the papers had been rediscovered a few months earlier.

"I doubt there's anything valuable," said Olivier, returning to the Gamaches' table after taking Ruth her breakfast of Irish coffee and bacon.

"How is that woman still alive?" asked Reine-Marie.

"Bile," said Olivier. "She's pure bile. It never dies." He looked at Reine-Marie. "I don't suppose you'd be willing to help her?"

"Well, who wouldn't want to work with pure bile?" she said.

"Once she gets a few drinks in her, she becomes simply nasty, as you know," said Olivier. "Please. Please. It's taken Ruth two months to get the pile down an inch. The problem is, she doesn't just scan, she reads everything. Yesterday she spent the whole day on one *National Geographic* from 1920."

"I would too, *mon beau*," said Reine-Marie. "But I tell you what. If Ruth accepts the help, I'd love to do it."

After breakfast, she joined Ruth on the sofa and started on the blanket box, while Armand and Henri walked home.

"Armand," shouted Olivier, and when Gamache turned he saw the owner of the bistro at the door waving something.

It was the dossier.

Armand jogged back to get it.

"Did you read it?" he asked. His voice was just sharp enough for Olivier to hesitate.

"*Non.*"

But under the steady stare, Olivier cracked.

"Maybe. Okay, yes. I glanced at it. Just her picture. And her name. And a bit about her background."

"*Merci*," said Armand, taking the file and turning away.

As he walked home, Armand wondered why he'd snapped at Olivier. The file was marked "Confidential" but he'd shown it to Reine-Marie, and it wasn't exactly a state secret. And who wouldn't be tempted to look at something marked "Confidential"?

If they knew anything about Olivier, it was that he had no immunity to temptation.

Gamache also wondered why he'd left it behind. Had he really forgotten it?

Was it a mistake, or was it on purpose?

The snow returned by early afternoon, blowing in over the hills and swirling around, trapped there. Turning Three Pines into a snow globe.

Reine-Marie called and said she was having lunch at the bistro. Clara and Myrna had joined the excavation of the blanket box, and they'd be spending the afternoon eating and reading.

It sounded to Armand pretty much perfect and he decided to do the same himself, at home.

He poked the birch log freshly tossed on the fire in their living room grate and watched as the bark caught and crackled and curled. Then he sat down with a sandwich, a book, and Henri curled up beside him on the sofa.

But Armand's eyes kept drifting back to his study, crowded with impatient young men and women, cheek by jowl, staring at him. Waiting for the old man to decide what next for them, as old men had decided the fate of youth for millennia.

He wasn't old, though he knew he'd look old, perhaps even ancient, to them. The young men and women would see a man in his late fifties. Just over six feet tall, he was substantial rather than heavy, or so he told himself. His hair was more gray than brown and it curled slightly around his ears. While he'd sometimes had a moustache and sometimes a beard, he was now clean-shaven, the lines of his face visible for all to see. It was a careworn face. But most of the lines, if followed back like a trail, would lead to happiness. To the faces a face made when laughing or smiling, or sitting quietly enjoying the day.

Though some of those lines led elsewhere. Into a wilderness, into the wild. Where terrible things had happened. Some of the lines of his face led to events inhuman and abominable. To horrific sights. To unspeakable acts.

Some of them his.

The lines of his face were the longitude and latitude of his life.

The young men and women would also see the deep scar at his temple. It would tell them how close he'd come to dying. But the best of them would see not just the wound, but the healing. And they'd see, deep in his eyes, beyond the scar, beyond the pain, beyond even the happiness, something unexpected.

Kindness.

And perhaps, when their own faces were mapped, kindness would be discovered there too.

That's what he was looking for in the dossiers. In the photographs.

Anyone could be clever. Anyone could be smart. Anyone could be taught.

But not everyone was kind.

Armand Gamache looked into the study at the young men and women assembled there. Waiting.

He knew their faces, or at least their photographs. He knew their stories, or at least as much as they were willing to tell. He knew about their schooling, their grades, their interests.

Among the crowd he spotted her. Amelia. Waiting with the rest.

His heart lurched and he stood up.

Amelia Choquet.

He knew then why he was reacting as he was. Why he'd left her behind at the bistro, and why he'd gone back for her.

And why he felt so strongly about her.

He'd shown the dossier to Reine-Marie hoping she'd give him the permission he sought. To do what all reason told him to do. To reject this young woman. To turn his back. To walk away, while he still could.

And now he knew why.

Henri snored and drooled on the sofa, the fire murmured and crackled, the snow tapped the windowpanes.

It wasn't her first name he was reacting to. It was her last. Her family name.

Choquet.

It was unusual, though not unique. The normal spelling would be Choquette.

He strode across to his study and, grabbing her file off the floor, he opened it. Scanning down the pathetically scant information. Then he closed it, his hand trembling.

He glanced at the fire, and briefly considered laying her there. Letting her go up, or down, in flames. A witch for the burning.

But instead he went downstairs, to the basement.

There he unlocked the back room. Where all his files on old cases were kept. And at the very back of the back room, he unlocked a small box.

And there he found it.

Confirmed it.

Choquet.

Logic told him he could be wrong. What were the chances, after all? But in his heart he knew he was right.

Returning upstairs, his feet heavy on the steps, he stood at the window and watched the snow falling.

Children, in hastily unpacked snowsuits smelling of cedar, were running around the village green, chasing and tackling each other into the soft snow. Pelting anyone in their sights with snowballs. Rolling out snowmen. They shrieked and yelled and laughed.

He went into his study and spent the next hours doing research. And when Reine-Marie arrived back, he greeted her with a large Scotch and the news.

He had to go to the Gaspé.

"The Gaspé?" she asked, making certain she'd heard correctly. It was the last thing she expected him to say. Go to the bathroom. Go to the store. Go to Montréal even, for meetings. But the Gaspé Peninsula? Hundreds of miles away, where the edge of Québec met salt water.

"Are you going to see him?"

When he nodded, she said, "Then I'm coming with you."

He returned to his study. Staring through the mullioned windows, he saw the exhausted children falling on their backs, one after the other, into the snow, sweeping their arms and legs up and down.

Then they got up and trudged home, squirming as snow melted down their necks and trickled in rivulets down their backs. It stuck to their mitts and the back of their tuques. Their faces were bright red and their noses ran.

They left behind them angels in the snow.

And in the study, his hand trembling slightly, Armand took a deep breath and changed the dot on Amelia's file. To green.

CHAPTER 2

—

Michel Brébeuf could see the car approaching along the cliff highway for quite a distance. At first he watched through his telescope and then with the naked eye. There was nothing to obscure his view. Not a tree, not a house.

The wind had rubbed the land down to its essence. Some rough grass, and rock. Like a worry stone. Inundated in the summer by tourists and part-time residents who came for the rugged beauty of the area and left before the snow moved in, only a rare few appreciated the glories the Gaspé had to offer the rest of the year.

They clung to the peninsula because they had no desire to leave, or nowhere else to go.

Michel Brébeuf was among the latter.

The car slowed and then, to his surprise, it stopped at the foot of his drive, pulling onto the soft shoulder of the provincial highway.

It was true that he had a particularly spectacular view of Percé Rock, out in the bay, but there were better and safer places to pull over for a photograph.

Brébeuf grabbed his binoculars, sitting on the windowsill, and trained them on the car. It was a rental. He could tell by the plates. There were two people in it. Man and woman. Caucasian. Middle-aged, perhaps in their fifties.

Affluent, but not flashy.

He couldn't see their faces, but quickly, instinctively, surmised this by their choice of rental and their clothing.

And then the man in the driver's seat turned to speak to the woman beside him.

And Michel Brébeuf slowly lowered the binoculars and stared out to sea.

The snow that had whacked central Québec had arrived the day before in the Gaspé Peninsula as heavy rain. The sort of drenching common in the Maritimes in November. If it were possible to render sorrow, it would look like a November gale.

But then, like sorrow, it too passed and the new day arrived almost impossibly clear and bright, the sky a perfect blue. Only the ocean held on to the distress. It churned and broke against the stones of the shoreline. Out in the bay, standing all alone, was the magnificent Percé Rock, the Atlantic Ocean hurtling against it.

By the time he dragged his eyes back, the couple had turned the car into his driveway and were almost at the house. As he watched, they got out. And stood there. The man had his back on the house and stared out to sea. To the great rock with the great hole worn through it.

The woman went to him and took his hand. And then, together, they walked the last few yards to the house. Slowly. As reluctant, it would appear, to see him as he was to see them.

His heart was throbbing now and he wondered if he might drop dead before the couple arrived at his porch.

He hoped so.

His eyes, trained to these things, went to Armand's hands. No weapon. Then to his coat. Was there a bulge there by the shoulder? But surely he hadn't come to kill him. If he'd wanted to do that, he'd have done it before now. And not in front of Reine-Marie.

It would be a private assassination. And one Michel had, privately, been expecting for years.

What he hadn't expected was a social call.

After making sure no blood would be spilled, Reine-Marie had gone inside, leaving Armand and Michel to sit on the porch, wrapped in sweaters and jackets, on cedar chairs turned silver by time and exposure. As had they.

"Why are you here, Armand?"

"I've retired from the Sûreté."

"*Oui,* I heard."

Brébeuf looked at the man who'd been his best friend, his best man, his confidant and colleague and valued subordinate. He'd trusted Armand, and Armand had trusted him.

Michel had been right. Armand had not.

Armand stared out at the massive rock in the distance, its center hollowed out, worn away by eons of the relentless sea, until it was a stone halo. Its heart gone.

Then he turned to Michel Brébeuf. The godfather to his daughter. As he was godfather to Michel's firstborn.

How often had they sat beside each other, as inspectors, discussing a case? And then across from each other, as Michel's star had risen and Armand's had waned? Boss and subordinate at work, but remaining best friends outside.

Until.

"All the way here I was thinking," said Armand.

"About what happened?"

"No. About the Great Wall of China."

Michel laughed. It was involuntary and genuine, and for the brief life of that laugh the bad was forgotten.

But then the laugh died away and Michel again wondered if Armand was there to kill him.

"The Great Wall of China? Really?"

Michel tried to sound disinterested, even irritated. More intellectual bullshit on the part of Gamache. But the truth was, as with all apparently irrelevant things Armand said, Brébeuf was curious.

"Hmmmm," said Armand. The lines around his mouth deepened. Evidence of a very slight smile. "It's possible I was the only one on the flight thinking about it."

Brébeuf was damned if he was going to ask why the Great Wall.

"Why?"

"It took centuries to build, you know," said Armand. "They started it in 200 BC, or thereabouts. It's an almost unbelievable achievement. Over mountains and across gorges, for thousands of miles. And it's not just a wall. They didn't just slap it together. Effort was made to make it both a fortification and a thing of beauty. It kept China safe for centuries. Invaders couldn't get past it. It's an absolutely astonishing feat."

"So I've heard."

"But finally in the sixteenth century, fifteen hundred years after it was started, the Manchus broke through the Great Wall. Do you know how they did it?"

"I'm thinking you're going to tell me."

But the veneer of weariness and boredom had worn away, and even

Michel could hear the curiosity in his voice. Not simply because he wanted to know about the Great Wall of China, something he had not spent a moment thinking about his entire life. But because he wanted to know why Armand was thinking of it.

"Millions of lives were lost building the wall and defending it. Dynasties went bankrupt paying for it and maintaining it," said Gamache, looking out to sea and feeling the bracing salt air on his face.

"After more than a thousand years," he continued, "an enemy finally broke through. Not because of superior firepower. Not because the Manchus were better fighters or strategists. They weren't. The Manchus breached the Great Wall and took Beijing because someone opened a gate. From the inside. As simple as that. A general, a traitor, let them in and an empire fell."

All the fresh air in the world surrounded them, but Michel Brébeuf couldn't breathe. Armand's words, their meaning, clogged his passages.

Armand sat with apparently infinite patience, waiting. For Michel to either recover or pass out. He would not hurt his former friend, at least not at the moment, but neither would he help him.

After several minutes, Michel found his voice. "A man's foes shall be they of his own household, eh, Armand?"

"I doubt the Manchus would quote the Bible, but it does seem universal. Betrayal."

"Have you come all this way to taunt me?"

"*Non.*"

"Then what do you want?"

"I want you to come work for me."

The words were so ridiculous Brébeuf couldn't understand them. He stared at Gamache in undisguised confusion.

"What? Where?" Brébeuf finally asked.

Though the real question, they both knew, was why.

"I've just taken over as the commander of the Sûreté Academy," said Armand. "The new term starts right after Christmas. I'd like you to be one of the professors."

Brébeuf continued to stare at Armand. Trying to grasp what was being said.

This was no simple job offer. Nor, he suspected, was it a peace offering. There'd been too much war, too much damage, for that. Yet.

This was something else.

"Why?"

But Armand didn't answer. Instead he held Brébeuf's eyes, until Michel lowered them. Then Gamache shifted his gaze back out to the view. To the vast ocean and the massive rock it had worn down.

"How do you know you can trust me?" asked Michel, to Armand's profile.

"I don't," said Armand.

"You don't know, or you don't trust me?"

Armand turned then and gave Michel a look he'd never seen before. There wasn't loathing there. Not quite. It wasn't quite contempt. But it was close.

There was certainly knowing. Gamache saw him for what he was.

A weak man. A Percé man. Hollowed out by time and exposure. Worn down and misshapen. Pierced.

"You opened the gate, Michel. You could've stopped it, but you didn't. When corruption came knocking, you let it in. You betrayed everyone who trusted you. You turned the Sûreté from a strong and brave force into a cesspool, and it has taken many lives and many years to clean it out."

"Then why invite me back in?"

Armand got up and Brébeuf rose with him.

"The weakness in the Great Wall wasn't structural, it was human," said Gamache. "The strength, or weakness, of anything is primarily human. Including the Sûreté. And it all starts at the academy."

Brébeuf nodded. "*D'accord*. I agree. But again, even more so, why me? Aren't you afraid that I might infect them?"

He studied Gamache. Then smiled.

"Or is there already an infection there, Armand? That's it, isn't it? Did you come all this way for the antidote? Is that why you need me? I'm the antivirus. The stronger infection sent in to cure the disease. It's a dangerous game, Armand."

Gamache gave him a hard, assessing look, then went inside to get Reine-Marie.

Michel accompanied them back down the drive. And watched them drive away, back to the airport and the flight home.

Then he went inside. Alone. No more wife. No more children. No grandchildren. Just a magnificent view, out to sea.

On the flight, Gamache looked down at the fields, and forests, and snow, and lakes and considered what he'd done.

Michel was right, of course. It was dangerous, though it wasn't a game.

What would happen, he wondered, if he couldn't control it and the anti-biotic, the virus, went viral?

What had he just sent in? What gate had he opened?

Instead of going back to Three Pines when they landed, Armand drove to Sûreté headquarters. But first he dropped Reine-Marie at their daughter's home. Annie was four months pregnant with her first child and was showing now.

"Coming in, Dad?" she asked from the door. "Jean-Guy will be home soon."

"I'll be back later," he said, kissing her on both cheeks.

"No rush," called Reine-Marie, and closed the door.

At headquarters, Armand pressed the top button in the elevator and was swept up to the office of the Chief Superintendent.

Thérèse Brunel looked up from her desk. Behind her, the lights of Montréal spread out. He could see three bridges and the headlights of cars filled with people heading home. It was a commanding view, and behind the desk was a commanding presence.

"Armand," she said, rising to greet her old friend with an embrace. "Thank you for coming in."

Chief Superintendent Brunel indicated the sitting area and they both took seats. In her late sixties now, the slight, elegant woman had come to policing late in life and had taken to it as though she had been born to investigate crime.

She'd risen fast through the ranks, passing her old professor and colleague Chief Inspector Gamache, until she could rise no further.

Her office had been redecorated in soft pastels since the former chief superintendent had been, what? "Replaced" was not really the word.

While she'd been promoted beyond Gamache, they both knew it was a function of the politics within the Sûreté, and not competence. But still, she held the rank and commanded the office and the force with confidence.

Armand handed her his dossiers and watched as she read. He got up and poured them both drinks, giving her one and taking his to the wall of glass.

It was a view that never failed to move him, so much did he love Québec.

"There's going to be hell to pay, Armand," she finally said.

He remained where he was but turned and saw that while her face was serious, stern even, there was no criticism. It was simply a statement of fact.

"*Oui,*" he agreed, and turned back to the view as she returned to the documents.

"I see you've changed some of the students," she said. "I'm not surprised. The problem will come from the faculty. You're replacing at least half of them."

Now he walked back to his chair and sat, placing his almost untouched drink on the coaster and nodding. "How could there be significant change if the same people are in charge?"

"I'm not disagreeing or arguing with you, but are you prepared for the blowback? These people will lose their pensions, their insurance. And they'll be humiliated."

"Not by me. They've done it to themselves. And if they want to sue, I have the proof." He looked not at all concerned. But neither was he triumphant. This was the tail end of a tragedy. And there was a sting in it.

"I doubt they'll sue," she said, replacing the last file on the pile. "But neither will they go without a fight. It simply won't be in public, or in the courts."

"We'll see," he said, sitting back. His face grim and determined.

Armand watched as she turned to the final stack of dossiers. These were the files on the men and women he planned to invite to teach at the academy. To replace the men and women he was about to fire.

Showing the list to Thérèse was a courtesy on his part. Chief Superintendent Brunel had no authority over the academy. The academy and the Sûreté were two separate entities, connected theoretically by a common belief in the need for "Service, Integrity, Justice." The motto of the force.

But the previous head of the school had commanded in name only. The reality was, he bowed to, then bent and finally broke under the demands of the former head of the Sûreté, who ran the school as his personal training ground.

But Chief Superintendent Francoeur was no longer the head of the Sûreté. No longer with the force. No longer on this earth. Gamache had seen to that.

And now Gamache was cleaning up the *merde* the man left behind.

The first step was to establish autonomy, but also a courteous collaboration with his counterpart at the Sûreté.

Commander Gamache watched as Chief Superintendent Brunel made her way down the pile of proposed professors, occasionally making notes or small comments, mumbling to herself. Until she reached the final dossier. She stared at it, then, without even opening it, she looked up at Gamache and held his eyes.

"Is this a joke?"

"No."

She looked back down but didn't touch the manila file. It was enough to see the name.

Michel Brébeuf.

When she looked up again, there was anger, bordering on rage, on her face.

"This is madness, Armand."

CHAPTER 3

Serge Leduc waited.

He was prepared. All morning his iPhone had buzzed with text messages from colleagues, other professors at the academy, to say that the new commander was going to visit them.

At eight in the morning they'd assumed it was a courtesy call. Armand Gamache was making the rounds to introduce himself and perhaps ask their opinions and advice.

By nine o'clock a slight pall of doubt had descended, and the texts became more guarded.

By eleven, the stream of information had become a trickle as fewer and fewer messages appeared in Professor Leduc's inbox. And those that did were curt.

Have you heard from Roland?

Anyone know anything?

I can hear him coming down the corridor.

And finally, by noon, Leduc's iPhone had fallen silent.

He sat in his large office and looked at the books lining his walls. On weapons. On federal and provincial regulations. On common law and the Napoleonic Code. There were case histories and training manuals. The wall space not taken up with textbooks was allocated to his citations and an old etching of the parts of a musket.

A small man in his mid-forties, but still powerfully built, Leduc had been moved to the academy after he'd been caught with drugs stolen from the Sûreté evidence locker.

Leduc had nursed a slight suspicion that Chief Superintendent Francoeur had engineered the whole thing. Not that he wasn't guilty. Leduc had been skimming from the mountain of seized drugs for years, selling them on to crime syndicates. What struck him as suspicious was that he'd suddenly been caught just as an opening for the number two position at the academy had come up.

Francoeur had presented Inspector Leduc with a choice. Become second-in-command at the academy or be fired.

Serge Leduc had navigated the realpolitik of the Sûreté by being a pragmatist. If this was what the Chief Superintendent wanted, then so be it. It was unhelpful and unhealthy to nurse a grudge or to fight the inevitable. Especially against Sylvain Francoeur. Leduc himself had been an enforcer long enough to know what being fired by Francoeur might mean.

That had been almost a decade ago, and with his transfer a new era had dawned. Though not, perhaps, an Age of Enlightenment.

On Francoeur's orders, Serge Leduc had reshaped the academy. Picking and choosing the recruits. Changing the curriculum. Guiding, nurturing, and whipping the young men and women into shape. And the shape they took was that of Serge Leduc.

Any recruit who resisted or even appeared about to question was marked for special treatment. Something guaranteed to create an attitude adjustment.

The actual head of the academy had protested feebly but was just going through the motions. The Commander excelled at form without function. He was an impressive figurehead, a relic kept in place to calm worried mothers and fathers who naturally, though mistakenly, believed the primary danger to their children was physical.

The Commander inspired confidence with his gray hair and straight back, in his dress uniform on entrance day when he smiled at the eager recruits, and on graduation when they smiled at him smugly, knowingly. The rest of the time he cowered in his office, afraid of the phone, afraid of the knock on the door, afraid of the night and afraid of the dawn.

And now he was gone. And Chief Superintendent Francoeur was gone. "Fired," as it were, in an irony not lost on Leduc.

And now Professor Leduc waited for the knock on the door.

He wasn't worried. He was the Duke. And all this belonged to him.

Armand Gamache walked down the long corridor. They'd torn down the old academy, where he himself had trained, a few years earlier and relocated to the South Shore of Montréal to this new glass and concrete and steel structure.

Gamache, while appreciating tradition and respecting history, had not mourned the loss of the former academy. It was only bricks and mortar. What mattered wasn't what the building looked like but what happened inside.

Two Sûreté agents walked behind Gamache, personally chosen for this detail and lent to him by Thérèse Brunel.

He stopped at the door. The final one on his list. And without hesitation, he knocked.

Leduc heard it and despite himself gave a tiny, involuntary spasm. And he realized that a small part of himself never thought the rap on the door would ever really come.

But still, he wasn't worried.

He got up, and turning his back on the door, he folded his arms across his broad chest and looked out the floor-to-ceiling window at the playing field below, covered in a layer of undisturbed snow.

Gamache waited.

He heard the agents beginning to shuffle and grow restless behind him. He could almost see them shooting glances at each other and frowning.

But still he waited, clasping his large hands behind his back. No need to knock again. The man inside had heard and now was playing a game. But it was a game of solitaire.

Gamache was declining to play. Instead, he used the time to think about the best way to implement his plans.

Serge Leduc was not an issue. He was not even an obstacle. He was, in fact, part of the plan.

Leduc stared out the window and waited for the next knock. A sharper rap. An impatient little tattoo on his door. But none came.

Had Gamache left?

Sylvain Francoeur had always declared that Chief Inspector Gamache was a weak man who hid it well behind a thin façade often mistaken for wisdom.

"His one real talent is fooling others into believing that he has talent," the head of the Sûreté had proclaimed more than once. "Armand Gamache,

23

filled with integrity and courage. Bullshit. You know why he hates me? Because I know him for what he is."

By this time, Francoeur was usually a few Scotches in and had become voluble and more than usually aggressive. Most subordinates knew enough to excuse themselves and get the hell out after the third drink. But Serge Leduc stayed, excited by this game of chicken and because he had nowhere else to go.

Francoeur would lean across his desk, looking past the bottle of Ballantine's, to whoever was left. His face suffused with blood and rage.

"He's a coward. Weak, weak, weak. He hires the goddamned dregs, you know. The agents no one else wants. The ones better men have thrown out. Gamache picks up garbage. And you know why?"

Leduc knew why. He'd heard this story before. But just because the familiar words came out in a miasma of Scotch and malice didn't make them untrue.

"Because he doesn't like competition. He surrounds himself with sycophants and losers to make himself look better. He hates guns. Afraid of them. Fucking coward. Fooled a lot of people, but not me."

Francoeur would shake his head and his hand would creep to his own handgun in the holster on his belt. The gun that Armand Gamache would one day use to kill him.

"This isn't a 'police gentle,'" Francoeur liked to say at convocation, when the students graduated from cadets to agents, streaming into the Sûreté like water through a cracked hull. "It's not a 'police kindness.' It's a police force. It's called that for a reason. We use force. We are a force. And one to be reckoned with."

That always brought wild applause from the students and slight unease from the families gathered in the auditorium.

Chief Superintendent Francoeur didn't care. His words weren't for the parents and grandparents.

During the term, Francoeur would visit the academy once a month, staying overnight in the lavish quarters reserved for him. After dinner he'd invite a select few to join him for drinks in the large living room overlooking the vast playing field. He'd regale the wide-eyed cadets with harrowing tales of great danger, of investigations wildly perilous, expertly leavened by the odd story of ridiculous criminals and silly mistakes.

And then, when Francoeur judged the time was right, he'd insinuate the real message into his stories. That the Sûreté du Québec wasn't there to be on guard for the population, but to be on guard against them. The citizens were the enemy.

The only ones the recruits could really trust were their confrères in the Sûreté. And even then, they had to be careful. There were some intent on weakening the force from within.

Serge Leduc would watch the unlined faces and wide eyes, and over the course of the months, the years, he'd see them change. And he would marvel at the skill of the Chief Superintendent, who could so easily create such little monsters.

Chief Superintendent Francoeur was gone now but his legacy remained, in flesh and blood and in glass and steel. In the cold hard surfaces and sharp edges of the academy and the agents he'd designed.

The new academy itself appeared simple, classic even. It was placed on land appropriated from the community of Saint-Alphonse, the Sûreté's needs judged far greater than the population's.

It was designed as a quadrangle, with a playing field in the middle, enclosed by gleaming buildings on all four sides. The only way in was through a single gate.

It gave the appearance of both transparency and strength. But in actuality, it was a fortress. A fiefdom.

Serge Leduc stared out at the quadrangle. This was, he now suspected, his last day in that office. This was his final view of those fields.

The knock on the door had confirmed that.

But he would not leave meekly. If the new commander thought he could walk in there and take over his territory without a fight, then he wasn't simply weak, he was stupid. And stupid people got what they deserved.

Adjusting the holster on his belt and putting on his suit jacket, Leduc walked to his door and opened it. And came face-to-face with Armand Gamache. Though Leduc had to tilt his head back a little.

"May I help you?"

He'd never met the man in person, though he'd seen him often enough at a distance and in news reports. Now Leduc was surprised by how solid he was, though unlike Francoeur, Gamache did not exude force.

But there was something there, something unusual about him. It was probably the scar at the temple, Leduc thought. It gave the impression of strength, but all it really meant was that the man was plodding and hadn't ducked quickly enough.

"Armand Gamache," said the new commander, putting out his hand and smiling. "Do you have a moment?"

At a subtle signal, the two large Sûreté agents stepped back across the corridor, but the man himself didn't move, didn't walk right by Leduc and lay claim to the office.

Instead he stood there, politely waiting to be invited in.

Leduc almost smiled. It would be all right after all.

Here was the new commander, no better than the old one. One relic replaced by another. Put Gamache into a dress uniform and he would look impressive. But blow and he'd fall down.

But then Serge Leduc met Gamache's eyes, and in that instant he understood what Gamache was really doing.

The new commander could, especially with the help of the large agents, force his way into Leduc's office. But what Gamache was in fact doing was much more cunning and far more insidious. And for the first time, Serge Leduc wondered if Francoeur had been wrong.

Gamache had killed the Chief Superintendent with Francoeur's own gun. It was an act that was both final and symbolic.

And now Serge Leduc looked into those calm, confident, intelligent eyes and he realized Gamache was doing the same thing to him. Not killing him. Not physically anyway. Armand Gamache was waiting for Leduc to invite him in. To voluntarily step aside.

Because then the defeat would be absolute.

Anyone could take something by force, but not many could get someone to surrender without a fight.

So far, Armand Gamache had taken the academy without a fight. And this was the last hill.

Professor Leduc moved his left arm, so that his wrist felt the butt of the handgun through his jacket. As he did that, he lifted his right hand and shook Gamache's. Holding the man's hand and his eyes. Both of which were steady, and displayed neither anger nor challenge.

It was, Leduc realized, far more threatening than any overt show of force could ever be.

"Come in," said Leduc. "I've been expecting you. I know why you're here."

"I wonder if that's true," said the new commander, closing the door behind him and leaving the Sûreté agents in the corridor.

Leduc was confused, but he remained confident. Gamache might have his plans, his charm, even a degree of courage. But Serge Leduc had a gun. And no amount of courage could stop a bullet.

Serge Leduc knew that he did not care all that much about the academy. What he hated was someone taking what was his. And this office, this school, belonged to him.

Leduc waved toward the visitor's chair and Gamache took it, while Leduc sat at his desk. He was about to speak. His hand, unseen below the desk, had moved over to the holster and removed the handgun.

He would be arrested. He would be tried. He would be found guilty, because he would be guilty. But Leduc knew he would be considered a martyr by many former students. Better that than going quietly, as everyone else had. And besides, he had nowhere to go except out into the cold.

But before Leduc could say anything, Gamache placed a manila file on the large desk. His hand rested on it for a moment, as though giving it final consideration, then he wordlessly pushed it toward the professor.

Despite himself, Leduc was curious. Resting the gun on his lap, he pulled the dossier toward him and opened it. The first page was simple, clear. In bullet form it listed his transgressions.

Leduc was not surprised to see the ones from his days at the Sûreté. Old news. Francoeur had promised to destroy the files, but Leduc hadn't believed that for a moment. But he was surprised to see the others. From the academy. From the land appropriations. The building contracts. The negotiations no one else knew about, supposedly.

Clear, concise, easy to read and easy to understand. And Serge Leduc understood.

Closing the folder, he once again lowered his hand to his lap.

"You're predictable, monsieur," he said. "I was expecting this."

Gamache nodded, but still didn't speak. His silence was unsettling, though Leduc tried not to show it.

"You're here to fire me."

And now Gamache did something completely unexpected. He smiled. Not broadly. Not smugly. But with some amusement.

"I can see how you'd expect that," he said. "But in fact, I'm here to ask you to stay on."

The handgun hit the floor with a thud.

"I believe you've dropped something," said Gamache, getting to his feet. "You will not be my second-in-command, of course, but you will continue as full professor, teaching crime prevention and community relations. I'd like your course outline by the end of the week."

Serge Leduc sat there, unable to move or to speak, long after Commander Gamache's footsteps had stopped echoing down the hall.

And in the silence Leduc realized what Gamache exuded. It wasn't force. It was power.

CHAPTER 4

───

"What've you found?"

"Piss off," said Ruth, and turned her bony back to protect what was in her hands. Then she shot a sly glance over her shoulder. "Oh, it's you. Sorry."

"Who did you think it was?" asked Reine-Marie, more amused than annoyed.

She'd been sitting beside Ruth every afternoon for almost two months, going through the documents in the blanket box, as Olivier had asked. Most afternoons, like this one, Clara and Myrna also came over and helped, though it never felt like a chore.

The four women sat around the fireplace, sipping *cafés au lait* and Scotch, eating *chocolatines* and examining the mass of papers Olivier and Gabri had pulled from the walls of the bistro twenty years earlier, while renovating.

Reine-Marie and Ruth, and Rosa, her duck, shared the sofa, while Clara and Myrna took armchairs across from each other.

Clara was taking a break from her self-portrait, though privately Reine-Marie wondered if when Clara said she was painting herself, she didn't mean it literally. Each afternoon Clara showed up with food in her hair and dabs of paint on her face. Today it was a shade of bright orange and marinara sauce.

Across from Clara sat her best friend, Myrna, who ran the New and Used Bookstore next door to the bistro. She'd wedged herself into the large chair, enjoying every word of her reading and every bite of her *chocolatine*.

A hundred years ago, when the papers were first shoved into the walls as insulation against the biting Québec winter, the women of the village would have gathered for a sewing bee.

This was the modern equivalent. A reading bee.

At least, Clara, Myrna, and Reine-Marie were reading. Reine-Marie had no idea what Ruth was doing.

The old poet had spent the previous day and this one staring at a single sheet of paper. Ignoring the rest of the documents. Ignoring her friends. Ignoring the Scotch gleaming in the cut glass in front of her. That was most alarming.

"What are you looking at?" Reine-Marie persisted.

Now both Clara and Myrna lowered the pages they'd been studying to study Ruth. Even Rosa looked at the elderly woman quizzically. Though Reine-Marie had come to understand that ducks rarely looked anything but.

Reine-Marie had fallen into a relaxed routine of sorting through the township's archives in the morning, then heading to the bistro in the afternoon.

On weekends, Armand would join her, sitting in one of the comfortable armchairs, nursing a beer and going over his own papers.

Though the pine blanket box looked a little like a treasure chest and had yielded many fascinating things, none could remotely be considered treasure, not even by an archivist who saw gold where others saw insulation.

When Ruth had started this project, the leaves outside had been bright amber and red and yellow. Now Christmas had come and gone and the trees were heavy with snow. A thick layer lay on the village so that the only way to get from one place to another was via trenches dug out by Billy Williams.

It was now early January. A peaceful time of the year, when the cheery lights and wreaths were still up, but there was no longer the pressure of the season. Their fridges and freezers were full of shortbread and fruitcake and turkey casseroles. Their own form of insulation against the winter.

Sitting in front of the bistro fire, looking from the snow outside to the stack of old documents, Reine-Marie felt a deep peace and contentment, marred only by the look she sometimes caught on Armand's face.

His first term as commander was just days away now. She knew the changes he'd implemented were controversial, even revolutionary.

Against all logic, and advice, he'd kept on the most senior and corrupt professor, Serge Leduc. He'd gone to Gaspé and tracked down the quisling Michel Brébeuf. He'd brought in sweeping changes to the curriculum, and gone through each and every application for admission, changing many of the dots from green to red, and vice versa.

He'd instituted a policy of allowing the community access to the magnificent facilities at the new academy, as well as an obligation for the students and staff to volunteer as coaches, as drivers. As visitors to the lonely and readers for the blind. As Big Sisters and Big Brothers. They would deliver meals where needed, and dig out driveways after blizzards. They would be at the disposal of the mayor of Saint-Alphonse in times of need. The mayor and the new commander would work together.

The mayor had met these suggestions with a marked lack of enthusiasm, bordering on disdain.

The community had, after all, greeted the arrival of the Sûreté Academy a few years earlier with unalloyed delight, helping them find an appropriate site on the outskirts of Saint-Alphonse.

The mayor and the council had worked closely with Serge Leduc. Right up until the moment the mayor had received the notice that the academy would not be moving to the edge of town after all. Instead, it would be appropriating land right in the center. The plot Serge Leduc knew was reserved for their much-longed-for recreation center.

The mayor could barely believe it.

It was an act of betrayal not easily forgiven, and never forgotten. And the mayor, not being a stupid man, wasn't going to be fooled again.

The community didn't want anything to do with the academy, the deceitful bastards. The professors didn't want anything to do with the community, the great unwashed.

In that they were in agreement.

"All the more reason to reach out, don't you think?" Gamache had said to Jean-Guy Beauvoir, his former second-in-command and now his son-in-law, as they'd sat together one evening at the Gamaches' home in Three Pines.

"I think you go out of your way to find mountains to climb," said Beauvoir, who was reading a book on a particularly disastrous Everest ascent.

Gamache had laughed. "I wish it was a mountain. At least they're majestic. Conquering them brings some sense of triumph. The Sûreté Academy is more like a great big hole filled with *merde*. And I've fallen into it."

"Fallen, *patron*? As I remember it, you jumped."

Gamache had laughed again and bowed his head over his notebook.

Beauvoir watched this, and waited. He'd been waiting for months now, ever since Gamache had told Jean-Guy and Annie about his decision to take over the academy.

While some had been surprised, it had seemed the perfect move to Jean-Guy, who knew the man better than most. It had also seemed perfect to Annie, who was relieved her father would at least, at last, be safe.

Jean-Guy had not told his pregnant wife that the academy was, in fact, the last shit pit in the Sûreté. And her father was in up to his neck.

Beauvoir had sat in the study, quietly, and then taken his book on Everest into the living room and read, in front of the cheerful fire, of perilous ascents. Of oxygen sickness and avalanches and great jutting shards of ice ten stories high that sometimes toppled over without warning, crushing man and beast beneath.

Jean-Guy sat in the comfortable living room and shivered as he read of bodies left on the mountain where they fell. Frozen as they reached out, for help or to drag themselves one inch closer to the summit.

What had they thought, these ice men and women, in their final lucid moments?

Would their last thought be why? Why had this seemed a good idea?

And he wondered if the man in the study would one day ask himself the same thing.

Inspector Jean-Guy Beauvoir knew that his mountain analogy with Gamache had been wrong. If you died on the side of a mountain, it was in the middle of a selfish, meaningless act. A feat of strength and ego, wrapped in bravado.

No, the academy wasn't a mountain. It was, as Gamache had said, a cesspool. But it was a task that needed to be done. As went the academy, so went the Sûreté. If one was *merde*, the other would be too.

Chief Inspector Gamache had cleaned up the Sûreté, but he knew his work was only half done. Now Commander Gamache would turn his attention to the academy.

So far, while firing former professors and hiring new ones, he had not named a second-in-command. Everyone assumed he'd approach Jean-Guy. The younger man had assumed that too, and waited. And was still waiting. And beginning to wonder.

"Would you take it?" Annie had asked one morning over breakfast.

Never a petite person, she had blossomed with pregnancy, which was one way of putting it. All Jean-Guy cared about was that she and the baby were healthy. He would kill if he had to, to get her that last tub of Häagen-Dazs.

"Do you think I should?" Jean-Guy had replied, and seen Annie smile.

"You're kidding, right? Give up your position as inspector in the homicide division, one of the most senior officers in the Sûreté, to go to the academy? You?"

"Then you think I should do it?"

She'd laughed in that full-hearted way she had. "I don't think 'should' has ever entered your thinking. I think you will do it."

"And why would I?"

"Because you love my father."

It was true.

He would follow Armand Gamache through the gates of Hell, and the Sûreté Academy was as close as Québec got to Hades.

Reine-Marie sat in the bistro and looked out at the darkness and the three great pines, visible only because of the Christmas lights festooned on them. The blue and red and green lights, luminous under a layer of fresh snow, looked as though they were suspended in midair.

It was just five o'clock but it could have been midnight.

Patrons had begun arriving at the bistro, meeting friends for a *cinq à sept*, the cocktail hour at the end of the day.

Armand hadn't joined her, preferring the peace and quiet of the study as the first day of term approached. She looked across the village green, past the cheerful trees, to their home, and the light at the study window.

Reine-Marie had been relieved when she'd heard his decision to take over the academy. It seemed a perfect fit for a man more inclined to track down a rare book than a murderer. But find killers he'd done, for thirty years. And he'd been strangely good at it. He'd hunted serial killers, singular killers, mass murderers. Those who premeditated and those who meditated not at all, but simply lashed out. All had taken lives, and all had been found by her husband, with very few exceptions.

Yes, Reine-Marie had been relieved when, after reviewing all the offers and discussing them with her, Armand had decided to take on the task of commanding the Sûreté Academy. Of clearing up the mess left by years of brutality and corruption.

She'd been relieved, right up until the moment she'd surprised that grim look on his face.

And then a chill had seeped into her. Not a killing cold, but a warning of worse to come.

"You've been looking at that for a day now," said Myrna, breaking into Reine-Marie's thoughts and gesturing toward the paper in Ruth's hand. The old poet held it delicately, at the edges.

"May I see it?" Reine-Marie asked, her voice gentle, her hand out as though coaxing a lost dog into a car. Had she had a bottle of Scotch, Ruth would've been wagging her tail on the front seat by now.

Ruth looked from one to the other, then she relinquished it. But not to Reine-Marie.

She gave it to Clara.

CHAPTER 5

"It's a map," said Armand, bending over it.

"What was your first clue, Miss Marple?" asked Ruth. "Those lines? They're what we call roads. This"—she placed her knotted finger on the paper—"is a river."

She spoke the last few words slowly, with infinite patience.

Armand straightened up and looked at her over his reading glasses, then went back to studying the paper on the table under the lamp.

They'd gathered at Clara's place this wintery night for a dinner of bouillabaisse, with fresh baguette from Sarah's boulangerie.

Clara and Gabri were in the kitchen just putting the final ingredients into the broth. Scallops and shrimp and mussels and chunks of pink salmon, while Myrna sliced and toasted the bread.

A delicate aroma of garlic and fennel drifted into the living room and mingled with the scent of wood smoke from the hearth. Outside, the night was crisp and starless as clouds rolled in, threatening yet more snow.

But inside it was warm and peaceful.

"Imbecile," mumbled Ruth.

The fact was, despite Ruth's comments, it wasn't obvious what the paper was.

At first glance, it didn't look like a map at all. While worn and torn a little, it was beautifully and intricately illustrated, with bears and deer and geese placed around the mountains and forests. In a riot of seasonal confusion, there were spring lilac and plump peony beside maple trees in full autumn color. In the upper-right corner, a snowman wearing a tuque and a *habitant* sash, a *ceinture fléchée*, around his plump middle held up a hockey stick in triumph.

The overall effect was one of unabashed joy. Of silliness that somehow managed to be both sweet and very affecting.

This was no primitive drawing by a rustic with more enthusiasm than talent. This was created by someone familiar enough with art to know the masters, and skilled enough to imitate them. Except for the snowman, which, as far as Gamache knew, had never appeared in a Constable, Monet, or even Group of Seven masterpiece.

Yes, it took a while to see beyond all that, to what it really was, at its heart. A map.

Complete with contour lines and landmarks. Three small pines, like playful children, were clearly meant to be their village. There were walking paths and stone walls and even Larsen's Rock, so named because Sven Larsen's cow got stuck on it before being rescued.

Gamache bent closer. And yes, there was the cow.

There were even, faint like silk threads, latitude and longitude lines. It was as though a work of art had been swallowed by an ordnance map.

"See anything strange?" asked Ruth.

"Yes, I do," he said, turning to look at the old poet.

She laughed.

"I meant in the map," she said. "And thank you for the compliment."

Now it was Gamache's turn to smile as he went back to studying the paper.

There were many words he'd use to describe it. Beautiful. Detailed. Delicate yet bold. Unusual, certainly, in its intersection of practicality and artistry.

But was it strange? No, that wasn't a word he'd use. And yet he knew the old poet. Ruth loved words and used them intentionally. Even the thoughtless words were used with thought.

If she said "strange," she meant it.

Though Ruth's idea of strange might not be anyone's. She thought water was strange. And vegetables. And paying bills.

His brow furrowed as he noticed the celebrating snowman seemed to be pointing. There. He bent closer. There.

"There's a pyramid." Armand's finger hovered over the image.

"Yes, yes," said Ruth impatiently, as though there were pyramids everywhere. "But do you notice anything strange?"

"It's not signed," he said, trying again.

"When was the last time you saw a map that was?" she demanded. "Try harder, moron."

On hearing Ruth's querulous voice, Reine-Marie looked over, caught Armand's eye, and smiled in commiseration before going back to her own conversation.

She and Olivier were discussing the blanket-box finds that day. A layer of *Vogue*s from the early 1900s.

"Fascinating reading," she said.

"I noticed."

Reine-Marie had long marveled at how much you could tell about a person by what was on their walls. The art, the books, the decor. But until now she had no idea you could also tell so much by what was in their walls.

"A woman who loved fashion obviously lived there," she said.

"Either that," said Olivier, "or a gay man."

He looked into the kitchen where Gabri was gesturing with a ladle as though dancing. Voguing, in fact.

"Gabri's great-grandfather, you think?" asked Reine-Marie.

"If it's possible to come from a long line of gay men, Gabri's done it," said Olivier, and Reine-Marie laughed.

"Now," she said, "what about the real find?"

They looked over to where Armand and Ruth were huddled.

"The map," said Olivier. "Some marks on it. Maybe water damage. And dirt, but that's to be expected. But being in the wall also preserved it. No exposure to sunlight. The colors are still vivid. It must be the same vintage as all the other stuff. A hundred years old or so. Is it worth anything, do you think?"

"I'm just an archivist. You're the antiques dealer."

He shook his head. "I can't see selling it for more than a few dollars. It's fun and the art is good, but basically it's a novelty. Someone's idea of a joke. And too local to be of interest to anyone but us."

Reine-Marie agreed. It certainly had a beauty to it, but part of that was its silliness. A cow? A pyramid, for God's sake. And the three spirited pines.

Dinner was announced, if Gabri shouting, "Hurry up, I'm starving," could be considered an announcement. It certainly was not news.

Over the scallops and shrimp and chunks of broth-infused salmon, they discussed the Montréal Canadiens and their winning season, they discussed international politics and the litter of unplanned puppies Madame Legault's golden retriever had had.

"I'm thinking of getting one," said Clara, dipping a slice of toasted baguette, spread with saffron aioli, into the bouillabaisse. "I miss Lucy. It would be nice to have another heartbeat in the home."

She looked over at Henri, curled in a corner. Rosa, forgetting her enmity for the dog in favor of warmth, was nesting in the curve of his belly.

"How's the portrait coming?" Reine-Marie asked.

Clara had managed to scrape the oil paint off her face, though her hands were tattooed with a near-permanent palette of colorful dots. Clara seemed to be morphing into a pointillist painting.

"You're welcome to take a look," she said. "But I want you all to repeat after me, 'It's brilliant, Clara.'"

They laughed, but when she continued to look at them they all, in unison, said, "It's brilliant, Clara."

Except Ruth, who muttered, "Fucked up, insecure, neurotic and egotistical."

"Good enough," laughed Clara. "If not brilliant, I'll settle for FINE. But I have to admit, my focus is being undermined by that damned blanket box. I actually dream about it at night."

"But have you found anything valuable?" asked Gabri. "Daddy needs a new car and I'm hoping to turn that old pine box into a Porsche."

"A Porsche?" asked Myrna. "You might get into it, but you'd never get out. You'd look like Fred Flintstone."

"Fred Flintstone," said Armand. "That's who you—"

But on seeing the look of warning on Olivier's face, he stopped.

"Baguette?" Armand offered the basket to Gabri.

"That map?" asked Gabri. "You all seemed interested in it. It's got to be worth something. Let me get it."

He hopped up and returned, smoothing it on the pine table.

"This's the first time I've looked at it," he said. "It's quite something."

But what, was the question.

"It's both a map and a work of art," said Clara. "Wouldn't that increase its value?"

"The problem is, it's both and it's neither," said Olivier. "But the main problem is that map collectors tend to like maps of a specific area, often their own, or ones of some historic significance. This is of a small corner of Québec. And not even a historic corner. Just villages and homes, and that silly snowman. It might seem charming to us because we live here. But to anyone else, it's just a curiosity."

"I'll give you fifty for it," said Ruth.

They turned to her in shock. Ruth had never, in their experience, offered to pay for anything.

"Fifty what?" asked Myrna and Olivier together.

"Dollars, you dickheads."

"Last time she bought something, it was with licorice pipes," said Myrna.

"Stolen from the bistro," said Olivier.

"Why do you want it?" asked Reine-Marie.

"Does no one get it?" demanded Ruth. "Don't any of you see? Not even you, Clouseau?"

"It's Miss Marple to you," said Armand. "And see what? I see a beautiful map, but I also understand what Olivier's saying. We're probably the only ones who value it."

"And do you know why?" Ruth demanded.

"Why?" asked Myrna.

"You figure it out," she said. Then she looked at Myrna closely. "Who are you? Have we met?"

Ruth turned to Clara and whispered loudly, "Shouldn't she be doing the dishes?"

"Because a black woman is always the maid?" asked Clara.

"Shhh," said Ruth. "You don't want to insult her."

"Me insult her?" said Clara. "And by the way, being a black woman isn't an insult."

"And how would you know?" asked Ruth, before turning back to Myrna. "It's all right, I'll hire you if Mrs. Morrow lets you go. Do you like licorice?"

"Oh, for God's sake, you demented old wreck," said Myrna. "I'm your neighbor. We've known each other for years. You come into my bookstore every day. You take books and never pay."

"Now who's demented?" said Ruth. "It's not a bookstore, it's a library. Says it right on the sign." Ruth turned back to Clara and whispered again, "I don't think she can read. Should you teach her or would that just be inviting trouble?"

"It says *librairie*," said Myrna, giving it the French pronunciation. "'Bookstore' in French. As you very well know. Your French is perfect."

"No need to insult me."

"How is calling your French perfect an insult?"

"I think we're going in circles here," said Armand, getting up and starting to clear the table. Years ago, when he'd first heard exchanges like this, he'd been appalled. But as he got to know them all, he'd seen it for what it was. A sort of verbal *pas de deux*.

This was how they showed affection.

It still made him uncomfortable, but he suspected it was meant to. It was a form of guerrilla theater. Or maybe they just liked insulting each other.

Reaching for more dishes to take to the sink, he looked down at the map. In the candlelight it seemed to have changed.

This wasn't just a doodle, made by some bored pioneer to while away the winter months. There was purpose to it.

But there was another slight change he was noticing now. One he might even be imagining.

The snowman, who appeared so jolly in daylight, seemed less joyous by candlelight. And more, what? Anxious? Was that it? Could a *bonhomme* be worried? And what would he be worried about?

A lot, thought Gamache, as he ran hot water into the sink and squirted detergent. A man made of snow would worry about the very thing the rest of the world looked forward to. The inevitable spring.

Yes, a snowman, however jolly, must have worry in his heart. As did the work of art. Or map. Or whatever it was they'd found in the wall.

Love and worry. They went hand in hand. Fellow travelers.

Going back to the table to get more dishes, he saw Ruth watching him.

"Do you see it?" she asked quietly as he bent for her bowl.

"I see an anxious snowman," he said, and even as the words came out, he realized how ridiculous they were. And yet the old poet didn't mock. She just nodded.

"Then you're close."

"I wonder why the map was made," said Armand, looking at it again.

He didn't expect an answer, nor did he get one.

"Whatever the reason, it's not for sale," said Olivier, looking at it wistfully. "I like it."

While Armand and Myrna did the dishes, Olivier got dessert out of the fridge.

"Are you looking forward to the first day of school?" Olivier asked as he served up the chocolate mousse, made with a dash of Grand Marnier and topped with fresh whipped cream.

"I'm a little nervous," Gamache admitted.

"Don't worry, the other kids'll like you," said Myrna.

Gamache smiled and handed her a dish to dry.

"What're you worried about, Armand?" Olivier asked.

What was he worried about? Gamache asked himself. Though he knew the answer. He was worried that in trying to clean up the mess at the academy, he'd only succeed in making it worse.

"I'm worried I'll fail," he said.

There was silence, broken only by the clinking of dishes in the sink, and the murmur of voices as Clara took Reine-Marie into her studio.

"I'm worried that I've undervalued what's in the blanket box," said Olivier, putting a dollop of whipped cream on a serving of mousse. "But what I'm really worried about is that I don't know what I'm doing. That I'm a fraud."

"I'm worried that the advice I gave to clients years ago, when I was a therapist, was wrong," said Myrna. "I wake up in the middle of the night, afraid I've led someone astray. In the daylight I'm fine. Most of my fears come in the darkness."

"Or by candlelight," said Armand.

Myrna and Olivier looked at him, not sure what that meant.

"Do you really think you'll fail?" Olivier asked, putting the coffee on to perk.

"I think I've made some extremely risky decisions," said Armand. "Ones that could go either way."

"When I'm afraid, I always ask myself, what's the worst that can happen?" said Myrna.

Did he dare ask that? Armand wondered.

He'd have to resign and someone else would take over the academy. But that would be the very best outcome, if he failed.

The worst?

He was bringing Serge Leduc and Michel Brébeuf together. For a reason. But suppose it backfired? There would be a conflagration, he knew. And one that would consume not just him.

It was a very dangerous sequence of events he'd set in motion.

"I wouldn't recommend it," said Clara.

"What?" asked Reine-Marie.

They were in Clara's studio, surrounded by canvases and brushes in old tin cans and the smell of oil and turpentine and coffee and banana peels. In the corner was a dog bed where Lucy, Clara's golden, used to sleep as Clara painted, often into the night. Henri had followed them into the studio and was now fast asleep in the bed.

But what held Reine-Marie's attention, what would grab and hold anyone's, was the canvas on the easel. Close up it was a riot of color, of bold slashes in purple and red and green and blue. All the tiny dots on Clara's hands were splashed there, large.

But take a step back and what appeared from the confusion was a woman's face. Clearly Clara.

"I wouldn't recommend doing a self-portrait," said the woman herself, sitting comfortably on the stool in front of the easel.

"Why not?" Reine-Marie asked, though she seemed to be speaking to Canvas Clara.

"Because it means staring at yourself for hours on end. Have you ever seen a self-portrait where the person didn't look just a little insane? Now I know why. You might start off smiling, or looking intelligent or thoughtful. But the longer you stare, the more you see. All the emotions and thoughts and memories. All the stuff we hide. A portrait reveals the inner life, the secret life of the person. That's what painters try to capture. But it's one thing to hunt it down in someone else, and a whole other thing to turn the gun on ourselves."

Only then did Reine-Marie notice the mirror leaning against the armchair. And Clara reflected in it.

"You start seeing things," said Clara. "Strange things."

"You sound like Ruth," said Reine-Marie, trying to lighten the mood. "She seems to see something in that map that no one else can."

She'd sat down on the sofa, feeling the springs where no spring should be. The portrait, which had appeared stern when she'd first seen it, now seemed to have an expression of curiosity.

It was an odd effect. How the mood of the portrait appeared to mirror the mood of the actual woman. Clara too was looking curious. And amused.

"She saw W. B. Yeats at one of her poetry readings last year," Clara remembered. "And this past Christmas she saw the face of Christ in the turkey. That was at your place."

Reine-Marie remembered it well. The fuss Ruth had made, trying to get them to not carve the bird. Not because she believed the Butterball was divine, but because it could be auctioned on eBay.

"I think 'strange' and Ruth are fused," said Clara.

Reine-Marie took her point. The woman, after all, had a duck.

Now the portrait's expression changed again.

"What're you worried about?" Reine-Marie asked.

"I'm worried that what I see might actually exist." She gestured at the mirror.

"The portrait's brilliant, Clara."

"You don't have to say that." Clara smiled. "I was just joking."

"I'm not. It really is. It's far different than anything else you've done. The other portraits are inspired, but this?"

Reine-Marie looked again at the canvas, and the strong, vulnerable, amused, afraid middle-aged woman there.

"This is genius."

"*Merci*. And you?"

"*Moi?*"

Clara laughed, imitating her. "*Moi? Oui, madame. Toi.* What're you worried about?"

"The usual things. I worry about Annie and the baby, and how Daniel and the grandchildren are doing in Paris. I'm worried about what Armand is doing," Reine-Marie admitted.

"As head of the Sûreté Academy?" asked Clara. "After what he's been through, it'll be a breeze. He's facing spitballs and paper cuts, that's all. He'll be fine."

But of course Reine-Marie saw more than Clara. She'd seen the visit to the Gaspé. And she'd seen the expression on Armand's face.

While they'd been at dinner, the front had moved in, bringing thick flurries. Not a blizzard, but constant heavy flakes that would need shoveling in the morning.

At the door, after putting on all his outerwear, Olivier shoved the map into his jacket and zipped up.

After saying good night to Clara, the friends walked through the large flakes, along one of the paths dug across the village green, their feet sinking into the new snow. Gabri walked beside Ruth and held Rosa, cradling the duck to his chest.

"You'd make a good eiderdown, wouldn't you?" he whispered into what he assumed were her ears. "She's getting heavy. No wonder ducks waddle."

Trailing behind, Myrna whispered to Reine-Marie, "I've always liked a man with a big duck."

A puff of laughter came out of Reine-Marie and then she bumped into Armand, who'd stopped at the intersection of paths, where Myrna veered off to her loft above the bookstore.

They said their good nights, but Armand stayed where he'd stopped, looking up at the pine trees, the Christmas lights jiggling in the slight breeze. Henri stood looking up at him, his shepherd's tail wagging, waiting for a snowball to be tossed.

Reine-Marie obliged, and the dog sailed into a snowbank, headfirst.

"Come on," said Reine-Marie, linking her arm in Armand's. "It's late and cold and you're beginning to look like a snowman. You can stare at the trees from our living room."

At the path to their home, they parted ways with the others, but once again Armand stopped.

"Olivier," he called into the darkness and jogged over to him. "Can I borrow the map?"

"Sure, why?"

"I just want to check something."

Olivier brought it out from under his jacket.

"*Merci*," said Armand. "*Bonne nuit.*"

Reine-Marie and Henri were waiting for him, and farther ahead Gabri was slowly walking Ruth and Rosa home. At her own path, Ruth turned and stared at Armand. In the light of her porch, she looked amused.

"You asked why the map was made," she called. "Isn't the better question, why was it walled up?"

The next morning, Armand phoned Jean-Guy and asked if he would be his second-in-command at the academy.

"I've already sharpened my pencil, *patron*," said Jean-Guy. "And I have new notebooks and fresh bullets for my gun."

"You have no idea how that makes me feel," said Gamache. "I've spoken to Chief Inspector Lacoste about this. Isabelle will put you on leave for a term. That's all we have."

"Right," said Jean-Guy, all humor gone from his voice. "I'll come down to Three Pines this afternoon and we can discuss your plans."

When Jean-Guy arrived, shaking the snow from his hat and coat, he found Gamache in his study. After pouring himself a coffee, Beauvoir joined his father-in-law. Instead of studying the curriculum or staff CVs, or the list of the new cadets, Gamache was bent over an old map.

"Why did it take you so long to ask me to be your second-in-command?"

Gamache took off his reading glasses and studied the younger man. "Because I knew you'd agree, and I'm not sure I'll be doing you any favors. The academy is a mess, Jean-Guy. You have your own career. I don't think being my second-in-command at the academy will advance it."

"And you think I'm that interested in advancement, *patron*?" There was an edge of anger in his voice. "Do you know me so little?"

"I care for you that much."

Beauvoir inhaled and breathed out his annoyance. "Then why ask me now?"

"Because I need help. I need you. I can't do this alone. I need someone there I can trust completely. And besides, if I fail I need someone to blame."

Jean-Guy laughed. "Always glad to help." He looked down at the map on the desk. "What've you got there? Is it a treasure map?"

"No, but there is a mystery about it." He handed it to Jean-Guy. "See if you can figure out what's strange about it."

"I'm assuming you know the answer. Is this a test? If I solve it, the job's mine?"

"The job is hardly a prize," Gamache pointed out, and left Jean-Guy to study the worn and torn and dirty old thing. "And it's yours now, like it or not."

A while later, Jean-Guy joined Armand and Reine-Marie in the living room, only to find another worn, torn and dirty old thing on the sofa.

"Well, numbnuts, I hear Clouseau has finally asked you to be his second-in-command," said Ruth. "I always knew you were a born number two."

"Madame Zardo," said Jean-Guy, making her sound like a Victorian medium. "As a matter of fact he has asked, and I've accepted."

He sat beside her on the sofa and Rosa waddled onto his lap.

"Did you figure it out?" asked Gamache. "What's strange about the map?"

"This. Three pines," said Jean-Guy, circling his finger over the illustrated trees. "Three Pines. The village isn't on any official map, but it's here."

He'd put his finger on it. And once seen, something else became obvious. All the roads, the paths, the walking trails led there. They might pass through other communities, but they ended at the three pines.

Armand nodded. Jean-Guy, with his sharp mind, had seen through the clutter to what was most extraordinary about it.

It wasn't a map of Three Pines, but a map to it.

"How strange," whispered Reine-Marie.

"What's really strange isn't that it's on this map," said Jean-Guy. "But that the village doesn't appear on any other. Not even the official ones of Québec. Why is that? Why did it disappear?"

"*Damnatio memoriae*," said Reine-Marie.

"Pardon?" said her son-in-law.

"It's a phrase I came across only once," she explained. "While going

45

through some old documents. It was so extraordinary I remembered it, which is, of course, ironic."

They looked at her, missing the irony.

"*Damnatio memoriae* means 'banished from memory,'" she said. "Not simply forgotten, but banished."

The four of them looked down at the first, and last, map to show their little community, before it vanished, before it was banished.

CHAPTER 6

Amelia Choquet folded her arms across her chest and leaned back at her desk. She was careful to make sure the sleeves of her uniform rode up, exposing her tattoos, and as she did she played with the stud in her tongue, shoving it up and down. Up and down. In an unmistakable display of boredom.

Then she slumped down and observed. It was what she did best. Never participating, but always watching. Closely.

At the moment she was watching the man at the front of the classroom. He was large, though not fat. More burly, she supposed. Substantial. And old enough to be her father, though her own father was even older than this man.

The professor wore a jacket and tie and flannels. He was neat, without being prissy.

He looked clean.

His voice as he spoke to the first-year students wasn't at all lecturing, unlike many of the other professors. He was talking to them, and his attitude seemed to be that they were free to take in what he was saying, or not. It was their choice.

She clicked the stud against her teeth and the girl in front turned and shot her an annoyed look.

Amelia sneered and smiled and the girl went back to scribbling notes, apparently taking down what the professor was saying verbatim.

So far they were a week into the term and Amelia had only taken down a handful of sentences in her brand-new notebook. Though, to be honest, she was still surprised to be there at all.

She'd shown up at the Sûreté Academy the first day expecting to be turned away. Told that some mistake had been made and she didn't belong there. Once through the door, she then expected to be ordered to remove her piercings. Not just the one through her tongue, but the ones in her nose, through her lip, her eyebrow, her cheek, all over her ears like a caterpillar. Had they known about the others, the ones they couldn't see, she'd definitely be told to get rid of them too.

She was expecting to receive, in the weeks before the academy started, warning that dyed hair and body art would not be tolerated.

But all she'd received was a reading list and a box.

When the letter and box arrived, Amelia had locked the door to her bedroom in the rooming house where she lived, and after scanning the reading list she tore open the box.

Inside was a uniform, neatly folded. New. No one had worn it before. Amelia brought it to her face and inhaled.

It smelled of cotton and cardboard. Fresh and clean. And unexpectedly soft.

There was even a cap, with the Sûreté Academy insignia on it, and some words in Latin.

Velut arbor aevo.

Amelia had slowly lowered the hat onto her spiky black hair and adjusted it. She wondered what the words meant. Well, she knew what the Latin translated into, but not what they meant.

She'd stripped down and put on the uniform. It fit. Then she stole a furtive glance in the mirror. A young woman stood there, a woman who lived in a whole different world from Amelia. One that could've been hers, had she turned left instead of right. Or right instead of left.

Had she spoken or remained quiet. Had she opened the door, or closed it.

She could've been the girl in the mirror. Shiny and neat and smiling. But she wasn't.

As she tossed the hat on her bed, Amelia heard a footfall outside her door and her eyes zipped to the lock, making sure.

There was a sharp rap and then a sweet voice.

"Just checking to see if you got the package, *ma belle.*"

"Fuck off."

There was a pause, then the footsteps receded and with them a soft chuckle.

On Amelia's first night in the rooming house, the landlady had suddenly opened the door and peered in. Amelia had just managed to shove what she held in her hand under the bed. But not before raising the interest of the flabby landlady, who stank of smokes and beer and sweat.

"I heard noises and thought you might be sick, *ma petite*," she'd said, the scent of urine, soaked into the carpet in the hallway, wafting in with her.

Her small eyes scanned the room.

Amelia had closed the door in her face, seeing the plump cracked lips, the veined and bulbous nose, the blotchy complexion. And those runny eyes. Filled with guile and plans.

Since then, Amelia had been sure to lock the door as soon as she entered, and whenever she left, even if it was a quick trip down the hall to the toilet or the shower.

Amelia despised the landlady. And she knew why. As soon as she'd walked through the door of the rooming house, Amelia had the instant and over-whelming certainty that she would never leave.

The landlady was her.

And she was the landlady.

Amelia suspected that the woman had also been young, slender, in from the country. Looking for a job in Montréal. A typing course certificate in one hand, a small suitcase in the other.

She'd taken a temporary room there, not realizing that she'd crossed a threshold. And there was no going back.

She'd never left. She'd rotted there.

And Amelia would too. It had already begun.

After four months of applying for all sorts of unskilled jobs and not getting them, Amelia began lowering her sights to just above blow jobs on rue Sainte-Catherine. Until she'd finally taken the pail the landlady held out.

That became her job. To clean the toilets. And showers. To unclog the drains, pulling out stringy hair and other things.

Some nights she sat on her knees in the men's shower and wept into the drain. Her life, she knew then, was as good as it was going to get. At twenty, the best was behind her.

She began numbing herself with dope, bought from the ragged man down the hall in exchange for blow jobs. She'd promised herself never to stoop so low, and now she wondered how low she was going, and where the bottom might be.

So far she'd resisted crack and heroin, but only because she couldn't afford them and wasn't yet prepared to do what was necessary in exchange.

But finally the need to numb had overwhelmed all barriers. The weed wasn't working anymore. In what she knew was her last act of self-respect, and recognizing how ludicrous it was, she'd showered and put on clean underwear, before going out. The point of no return was right in front of her. She would at least cross that line smelling of soap and baby powder, though she suspected the scent of stale urine followed her everywhere now, like a vestigial tail.

She walked down the stairs she'd only just scrubbed.

They were cleaner than they'd been since she'd arrived. As were the toilets and showers and carpets. The other residents began to notice and some even started cleaning themselves.

But it would always be a losing proposition. The filth of the place was not on the surface. It could never be disinfected. The rot went too deep.

"Where're you going?" the landlady had called through the crack in her door.

"None of your fucking business," said Amelia.

"Don't swallow," said the landlady, laughing, sweaty legs spread wide on her Barcalounger. "But you know that, little one."

Her television was on and there was a report of a murder in a village south of Montréal. First the body of a boy had been found, thought to be an accident and now known to be murder. And then a second death.

Amelia had paused, and through the crack in the door she'd watched. And seen a youngish woman being interviewed. They identified her as the head of homicide for the Sûreté du Québec.

Amelia took a step closer.

The woman wore a nice suit. A skirt and light blue top and a jacket that draped. Not at all masculine. A feminine cut. Practical, yet attractive. Simple.

There was a badge on a string around her neck and a holster on her hip.

Large men in uniform stood behind her. Respectfully.

The landlady twisted in her chair, her naked legs squealing on the Naugahyde as she moved.

"What do you think she had to do to get that job?"

The plump lips glistened with spittle and the laugh followed Amelia down the hall and out the door.

Amelia found the answer to that question that night.

But not on rue Sainte-Catherine. She found it in the apartment of her only friend, a gay man from the same village she came from. He'd come to

50

Montréal a year ago and was dancing in a male strip club. It was a good job and he could afford his own small place.

"What the fuck are you doing?" he demanded, handing her a spliff and leaning over her as she tapped on his laptop. "You're googling the cops?"

Amelia didn't answer.

By the time she returned to her room she had a sheaf of papers, each explaining the entrance requirements for the various police schools. The next day, as she scrubbed, she composed the letters. The résumés she'd send off.

They were not, of course, completely accurate.

"They'll never take you, you know," her friend had said. "Look at you. You're on the wrong side of the prison bars. You're the one they're trying to arrest."

They'd both laughed at that, knowing it was true. But unlike her friend, Amelia thought maybe she could get to the other side. And be the one with the nice suit and clean hair. With large men behind her, not leering at her ass but there to follow her orders.

Maybe she could be the one with the power. And the gun.

That was before the rejections started. First the Montréal Police College rejected her. Then the Sherbrooke Police. Then the Quebec City Police. And even the tiny private college, apparently in some fellow's barn in Rivière-du-Loup, didn't want her.

The Sûreté Academy didn't even bother to reply. Of course.

She'd gone back to the floors, and down the drains. And one cold night she found herself on rue Sainte-Catherine. There, behind a strip joint, she'd done the very things she'd sworn never to do. And worse.

And with the money she'd bought cocaine. And then heroin.

She'd had two hits in two days, and while it freaked her out, the goal wasn't to enjoy it. It was to end the pain.

One more, she suspected, and there would be no going back. There was nowhere to go back to anyway. And no forward.

And then, as the snow began to fall, the letter had arrived.

Inviting her to the Sûreté Academy for the winter term. And saying that she had a full scholarship. For her knowledge of Latin. It was all paid for.

"*Futuis* me," she muttered, sitting on the side of her bed. Clutching the letter and staring into space.

She'd put the letter in her pocket and carried it with her as she cleaned and scrubbed. Not daring to read it again, in case she'd got it wrong. But finally, in the men's shower, she'd brought it out, and read it. Sinking onto her knees, she'd wept into the drain.

And now here she was. Late January. Sitting in a classroom, shoving the stud up and down in her tongue, clicking it against her teeth. Arms tight across her chest. Staring at the professor under half-closed lids.

Feigning boredom, but taking it all in. Every word, every action. Everything.

The keen young man beside her, with bright red hair and a gay vibe even the blackboard could feel, tsked at her.

"Jealous of my stud?" she hissed in English.

When he turned a violent red, she wondered what he was more ashamed of. Being gay or being an Anglo.

She liked him. He was different, though clearly fighting hard not to be.

"Pay attention," she said, pointing to the front of the class, and saw him huff in annoyance.

The commander of the academy himself was teaching this course, though it was far from clear what the course was about.

Not target practice, that much was obvious. They hadn't yet got their hands on a gun, though Commander Gamache had made some passing reference to the "aimed word."

"I didn't feel the aimed word hit," he'd said when a student had asked when they'd get some weapons. The professor's voice was deep and quiet and calm. *"And go in like a soft bullet."*

He'd smiled at them and then turned and wrote a phrase on the blackboard.

That had been the first day. And every day after that he'd written a new phrase, erasing the previous one. Except that first. It had stayed at the top of the chalkboard, and was still there.

Amelia wondered if this man with the graying hair and thoughtful eyes had any idea that he'd quoted a poem by her favorite poet.

I was hanged for living alone,
for having blue eyes and a sunburned skin.

Amelia could quote the whole thing. Had lain in bed, memorizing it. And when the wretched landlady had surprised her by suddenly opening the door that first night, Amelia had shoved the book under the bed.

Not food. Not dope. Not some stolen wallet.

Something far more precious, and dangerous.

The poetry book had joined the others hidden under there. Books in Latin and Greek. Poetry books and philosophy books. She'd taught herself the dead languages, and memorized poetry. Among the filth. Shutting out the sounds of sex, the mutterings and shouts and screams of other boarders. The flushing toilets and obscenities and stench.

All erased by poetry.

> *Oh yes, and breasts,*
> *and a sweet pear hidden in my body.*
> *Whenever there's talk of demons*
> *these come in handy.*

The landlady was afraid of rats and cops.

But what she really should have been afraid of was words, ideas. Amelia knew that. And she knew that that was why drugs were so dangerous. Because they blew the mind. Not the heart. But the mind. And the heart followed. And the soul followed that.

Amelia leaned forward and, while the professor's back was turned, she hurriedly wrote down that day's phrase.

It is the chiefest point of happiness, she scribbled quickly, before the Commander could see, *that a man is willing to be what he is.*

Amelia stared at the words and then, feeling eyes on her, she looked up and saw him regarding her.

She put her tongue out, exposing the stud, and shoved it up, and down. For him to see what she was.

He nodded, and smiled. Then turned to the rest of the class.

"Who here knows the motto of the academy?"

"When're we getting guns?" a kid yelled from the back. Then on seeing the look on the Commander's face, he added, "Sir."

Amelia snorted to herself. Be insolent or not. But don't do it, then suck up in the same breath. It was pathetic. Either commit or don't do it.

"I am giving you weapons," said the Commander, and Amelia snorted again, louder than she meant to.

As she watched, the professor turned his considerable attention to her.

It was like seeing a mighty ship in a storm. Steady, strong, calm. It would survive not because it was anchored in place, but because it wasn't. It could adjust. In that calm there was immense self-control. And with that, she realized, came power.

He was more powerful than anyone she'd ever met because he wasn't at the mercy of the elements.

Now he stared at her and waited and she knew he was capable of waiting forever.

"*Velut arbor aevo*," Amelia mumbled.

"That's right, Cadet Choquet. And do you know what it means?"

"*As a tree with the passage of time.*"

It was the most she'd spoken since she'd arrived.

"*Oui, c'est ça.* But do you know what it means?"

She was about to make something up. To say something either clever or, failing that, crude. But the fact was, she didn't know and she was curious.

Amelia looked at the board behind the Commander, and the words he'd written there. About the chiefest point of happiness.

She shook her head. "No, I don't."

"Would you like to know?"

Amelia hesitated, sensing a trap. But she gave one curt nod.

"Let me know when you figure it out," he said. "And see me after the class, please."

Well, fuck him, she thought, sinking down in her chair and feeling the other students' eyes on her. She'd exposed herself, shown ignorance and worse. She'd shown interest.

And he'd told her to go figure it out for herself.

Well, he could go fuck himself and fuck the academy while he was at it.

He was about to kick her out, she knew. For insolence. For her tattoos, her piercings, the stud in her tongue.

> *Whenever there's talk of demons*
> *these come in handy.*

He was about to toss her overboard.

And she realized then, watching him at the front of the class, listening closely to some student drone on, that he wasn't the ship. This apparently calm man was the storm. And she was about to drown.

At the end of the class, Amelia Choquet gathered her books. When the other cadets had left, she went to the front, where Commander Gamache was standing behind his desk, waiting for her.

"*Mundus, mutatio; vita, opinion,*" he said slowly.

She cocked her head to one side and stopped fidgeting with the skull ring on her index finger.

"My Latin isn't very good," he said.

"Good enough," she said. She understood perfectly. "The Universe is change. Life is opinion."

"Really?" he said. "That's not what I meant to say. I thought I said, *Our life is what our thoughts make it.*"

He brought a thin book out of his satchel. Studying it for a moment, he extended his hand, offering her the tattered volume.

"What we say and what we mean can sometimes be two different things," he said. "Depending on what we want to hear."

"Yeah, right."

"The quote came from here," he said. "I'd like you to have it."

She looked at the book in his hand.

Marcus Aurelius. She read the tattered cover. *Meditations.*

"No thanks. I already got the message."

"Take it," he said. "Please. As a gift."

"A parting gift?"

"Are you leaving?"

"Aren't I?"

"I asked you up after the class to invite you to join me and a few others for drinks in my rooms tonight."

So that was it. She could stay, but there would be a price. Amelia could guess who the "few others" would be.

She'd pay off the scholarship one way or another. She dropped the book on the desk. Amelia wanted no further debt to this man.

Commander Gamache picked it up and placed it in his satchel. As he left the classroom, he pointed to the very first quote he'd put on the blackboard.

The one that stayed, even as the others came and went.

It was from some Buddhist nun. The other cadets had snickered at that, but Amelia had written it down. They were the very first words in the very first notebook.

Don't believe everything you think.

CHAPTER 7

A fire was laid and lit in the rooms Commander Gamache kept at the academy.

Most nights he drove home to Three Pines. It was only an hour away, and a pleasant drive. But a blizzard was forecast, and so he'd decided to stay the night. Reine-Marie had driven in with him, bringing with her a box of her own work and a package wrapped in brown paper.

When they got into his rooms at the academy he pointed at the parcel. "A new chair?"

"You are a detective," she said with exaggerated admiration. "Actually, it's a pony."

"Ach." He shook his fist in frustration. "I was going to say that."

She laughed and watched him walk down the corridor to start the day.

Reine-Marie spent her day going through old documents from the archives while he taught and saw to administration, of which there was a staggering amount. The former commander had ignored most of the paperwork, and Serge Leduc, the second-in-command, had had his own agenda, which did not seem to involve the effective running of the Sûreté Academy.

But mostly what Armand Gamache had to manage were the personalities of the remaining professors and the senior cadets. To say they were resistant to the changes he'd brought in would be a gross understatement.

Even those happy to see the old guard go were overwhelmed by the scale of change.

"Maybe you should do it more slowly," advised Jean-Guy.

"*Non*," said Professor Charpentier. "Give bad news swiftly, and spread out the good news. Machiavelli."

Charpentier was one of Gamache's recruits and taught tactics, for which

57

Machiavelli's *The Prince* was compulsory reading. It was, in effect, a course not so much on tactics as manipulation.

Beauvoir looked at the boyish man with deep suspicion.

Charpentier was perspiring freely, as though each word had been wrung out of him. He was young and thin and frail and often relied on a wheelchair to get around.

"We make the changes at once. Swiftly," Commander Gamache had decided, and had called a staff meeting to announce them.

And so began the term, and so began the struggle.

They were a week into it now, and while a rhythm and routine had been established, his authority was being challenged every hour of every day. Commander Gamache was seen not as a breath of fresh air, but as a willful and ignorant child knocking over building blocks, even by those who admitted the blocks were rotten.

"Give it time," he told Jean-Guy at the end of a particularly trying day.

"Time, *patron*," said Beauvoir, shoving books into his case, "is one thing we don't have."

It was true, thought Gamache. And Jean-Guy didn't know the half of it.

But that evening, the end of the first week, might help change the charged atmosphere. At least, he hoped so.

As soon as he returned to his rooms, Armand got out of his suit and into slacks, an open-necked Oxford shirt and a cardigan. Reine-Marie was in a cashmere sweater with a silk scarf and a skirt that fell to just below her knees.

Sitting on the Eames chair and putting down his mug of tea, Armand reached for the parcel.

"Do you know what it is?"

"I don't," said Reine-Marie. "Olivier gave it to me this morning as we were leaving. Said it was for you. Please don't shake it."

He always shook parcels, for reasons she could never understand. Surely not to make certain it wasn't a bomb, since that would set it off.

He shook it. Listened to it. Sniffed it.

By now Reine-Marie was pretty sure he was doing it for her amusement.

"It's not a pony," he announced with regret.

"If only your students knew what a fine mind was teaching them."

"I think they suspect."

Opening the package, he stared at it for a moment.

"What is it?" she asked.

He turned it around and she smiled.

"Dear man," she said.

"*Oui*," said Armand.

It was the old, odd map they'd found in the wall of the bistro. Olivier had had it framed. Attached to the back was a card.

So you'll always find your way home.

The card was signed by Olivier, Gabri, Clara, and Myrna, and Ruth had added in her scrawl at the bottom, *When you inevitably fuck up, again.*

Armand smiled and, taking a deep breath, he rocked himself out of the comfortable chair and put the picture on a side table before walking to the huge window.

His rooms were on the top floor of the academy, commanding a spectacular view through the wall of windows. At least it would be spectacular, had the blizzard not arrived and the night not fallen.

Now all he could see was his own reflection. The snowstorm had swallowed the town of Saint-Alphonse, lights and all.

Saint-Alphonse was one of the first places settled by the French centuries ago, because it was flat and fertile. But the very elements that made it so inviting in summer made it especially brutal in winter.

There was absolutely nothing to stop the wind and snow as they howled down from the mountains and along the riverbanks and burst out across the flatlands. The only thing that eventually stopped them was the town of Saint-Alphonse, which took it in the face.

Out of the darkness, a white fist thumped the thick glass window, as though to remind Gamache it was still out there. And not happy.

He didn't flinch. But Gamache was aware that they were fortunate to be inside while it was outside.

There was a knock on the door and Jean-Guy entered.

"Since when have you knocked, *mon beau*?" asked Reine-Marie, getting up to greet her son-in-law.

"I wasn't sure if anyone else had arrived," he explained, his eyes scanning the room.

Jean-Guy suspected the other staff members knew of his relationship with the Gamaches, but the students probably didn't yet. He had no intention of letting anyone see an act of friendship and intimacy.

Beauvoir's sharp eyes took in his surroundings. Always alert for any threat. Like a gunman, or an open poetry book.

These were very different quarters from any other home the Gamaches had had.

This space in the academy was modern. Mid-century modern, he'd learned. With odd-shaped chairs with names that did not include La-Z-Boy, and did not look at all comfortable. At first he'd assumed the place had come furnished, someone else's taste, and then he'd found out that the Gamaches had bought the stuff themselves.

He didn't like it.

Walking across the thick shag area rug, he warmed his hands at the fireplace, then grabbed a Coke from the drinks table.

There was a knock on the door and the first of the guests arrived. Within twenty minutes they were all there. A group of carefully chosen cadets, and a group of equally carefully chosen professors.

They chatted, and helped themselves to food and drinks.

The initially stiff atmosphere softened with the help of the cheerful fireplace, the storm outside, the drinks, and the ease of their hosts, Commander and Madame Gamache.

Amelia Choquet wasn't fooled.

She stood in a corner, wedged between a bookcase and the wall of windows. She could feel the cold glass against her sleeve, and every now and then there was a scratching from outside, as a particularly savage gust of snow hit the glass and slid down.

From there she surveyed the room.

And the room surveyed her. When one set of eyes stopped staring at her and looked away, another set jumped in. Like a visual tag team. Or cage match.

Amelia had shown up, expecting something else entirely. What she had not expected was a cocktail party.

Madame Gamache had greeted her at the door, leading her to the drinks table where Amelia poured herself a Canadian Club and ginger.

In her soft sweater and scarf, smelling of soap and roses, the Commander's wife was as alien to Amelia as Amelia was to the rest of the room.

She could see it. She either revolted or frightened, or amused, the other cadets. And the professors simply dismissed her.

Except one. He was middle-aged, short and stubby, but not fat. Amelia could sense taut muscles beneath the casual sweater and wondered if he took steroids.

The man kept looking at her, but not with a critical eye. Not after that first sharp glance. It had evolved. She interested him. She could see it. Not, she thought, sexually. She had a pretty good radar for that.

60

This was something else. He was assessing her.

It was, from what she could see, a strange group. At first she'd thought those invited must be the most promising, the most intelligent, the natural leaders. Though that didn't explain her presence.

But now, watching the other students more closely, she knew that wasn't true. There were both men and women. Some clearly Anglos, most Francophones. Most white, but one was Asian and there was one black man. And one of the guests was in a wheelchair. She couldn't tell if he was a student or a professor.

None of them seemed remarkable.

The Asian woman approached Amelia.

"Huifen."

"What?"

"That's my name. I'm a third-year cadet. You're a freshman?"

She was looking at Amelia expectantly. This woman, thought Amelia, did not have good survival instincts.

"What?" demanded Amelia.

"Who are you?"

"None of your fucking business."

It wasn't exactly the sparkling cocktail party conversation Amelia had read about in books.

Huifen nodded, as though Amelia had given her valuable information. It was a gesture Amelia found disconcerting.

"He's new, you know." Huifen was looking through the crowd toward Commander Gamache, who was standing with a drink and listening to some students.

"He looks used," Amelia said.

Huifen laughed.

"That man"—Huifen gestured toward the professor who'd been staring at Amelia—"is Professor Leduc. The Duke. He used to run the place."

Huifen looked from Leduc to Gamache, then she leaned closer to Amelia, who bent away but not before she heard Huifen whisper, "Stay away from him. He's interested in you, I can see. Stay away."

Then Huifen stood up straight and laughed, as though one of them had said something clever.

Amelia looked at Leduc, then at Gamache. Not at all sure which "he" this senior cadet meant.

"I wonder why he's here," said Huifen, and this time it was obvious that she meant Gamache.

"Either way"—Huifen returned her gaze to Amelia—"this should be interesting."

She raised her brow and smiled, then drifted, apparently aimlessly, across the room. But Amelia soon noticed there was a destination. After meandering about, Huifen stopped next to Leduc. The Duke.

He looked, Amelia thought, not at all like a duke. There was nothing remotely regal about him. He radiated raw energy. In this genteel gathering, there was something primitive about him.

He was both repellent and attractive. Not in a personal way, but in the way that power attracts. And she wasn't the only one to feel it.

There was a tight knot of students around him.

Whoofa, or whatever her name was, was speaking with him. And then, slowly, he turned his head. And looked at Amelia.

This was the second time Leduc had stared at her. It was a long, thoughtful, assessing stare. It was the way a person might judge a puzzle piece.

Would it fit or not? Was it useful, or not?

And Amelia wondered if Whoofa had come over to speak to her on his orders. And she wondered what she'd reported back.

And then the moment passed, the connection broke, and Amelia was set adrift once again.

She sipped her CC and ginger and watched the ebb and flow of the gathering. It came to her attention that someone else was also quietly observing the party. An older professor.

He'd slipped in late, long after everyone else had arrived. Amelia hadn't seen him before. Not in the corridors, not in the classroom or even the dining hall.

He was new, and old.

He stood alone by the door, elegantly holding a glass of Scotch and scanning the room. His eyes met Amelia's, and for a moment she thought he might smile. Or, even worse, gesture her over, to keep him company.

But his sharp eyes traveled over her, and through her, and beyond her.

Amelia wondered if he was one of the old guard or a new professor brought in by the Commander.

Surely the old guard. He looked exactly that. Old. And on guard.

She watched him for a few moments. Long enough for him to know he was being observed. Amelia did it just for fun, and because she liked playing with razor blades, and needles, and knives.

Then she turned her attention elsewhere.

To the Commander and his wife. She saw the Commander smile, then laugh at something one of the students said. They were sitting now by the fireplace and there was a warm glow in their faces. There was an ease about him. About the way he looked over at Madame Gamache. About the way he listened and didn't feel the need to dominate.

She shifted her gaze and noticed that Professor Leduc had broken away from the small group around him and walked over to the new arrival. Shaking the old man's hand. Smiling. The two exchanged a few words, then the Duke glanced over at the Commander.

It was not a friendly look.

She kept her eyes, then, on Gamache.

Anyone who produced such loathing in another human being was worth watching.

Yes, she thought, taking another sip of her drink and hearing the clinking ice and the scratching of the blizzard outside, it might not be fun at the academy, but that Asian cadet was right. It was going to be interesting.

What Cadet Amelia Choquet didn't know, couldn't know, what no one in that room knew, was that before the snow melted one of them would be dead. And one of them would have done it.

"Interesting" didn't begin to describe what was about to happen.

CHAPTER 8

—

"Don't look now," Beauvoir bent down and whispered in Gamache's ear. "Brébeuf and Leduc have found each other."

Jean-Guy watched Leduc place a friendly hand on the older man's arm. *Confrères*, Beauvoir thought. Brothers. Two of a kind.

Commander Gamache didn't turn to look. Instead he gestured toward a chair recently vacated. Jean-Guy considered it. It was black leather and looked like a mouth about to snap shut.

Resigning himself to it, he sat down, sliding to the back of the seat.

"*Merde*," he whispered.

It was, without doubt, the most comfortable chair he'd ever sat in.

It was just one of a number of unexpected things in the room.

So much had happened so quickly when Jean-Guy accepted the post as second-in-command, he hadn't had a chance yet to ask Gamache about keeping Leduc on. And bringing Brébeuf back.

Either decision would be considered ill advised. Together they seemed reckless, verging on lunacy.

Putting them on the same campus was bad enough, but inviting them to the same party? Then giving them alcohol?

Beauvoir wondered, in passing, if either man was armed. Gamache had forbidden firearms among the staff, even the Sûreté officers on loan to the academy. And so Jean-Guy, against his will and instincts, had left his pistol locked up at Sûreté headquarters.

As Beauvoir watched, the two men grew more and more chummy. Leduc animated, and Brébeuf more contained, nodding. Agreeing.

Michel Brébeuf, the former superintendent of the Sûreté, had been one of the most powerful officers in the force before his disgrace.

Serge Leduc had been the most powerful presence in the academy, turning out hundreds of cadets, giving them weapons even as he took away their moral compass.

To see the two heads bowed together was deeply disturbing.

"Should I go over there?" Jean-Guy asked, preparing to haul himself out of the spectacularly comfortable chair.

"Why?"

"To stop them," said Beauvoir. "To break it up."

"If they don't talk here, they'll talk somewhere else," said Gamache. "At least they're doing it in plain sight."

"This isn't some teenager learning to drink, *patron*," said Jean-Guy, trying to keep his tone civil. "These men are . . ." he searched for the word.

"Merde?" asked Gamache with a smile. Then the smile faded and his face grew serious. "Though I think the word you're really looking for is evil."

"I wasn't," said Beauvoir, quite truthfully. He didn't think in terms of good and evil. He didn't even think in terms of good and bad.

Jean-Guy Beauvoir's thinking was very clear and very simple. Did someone need to be stopped? Did their actions need to be arrested? Were they breaking the law, causing harm, intentionally or not?

And for those two men, no action would be unintentional. Every act was well considered.

But the same could be said, Beauvoir knew, about Armand Gamache, who had intentionally, Beauvoir now realized, placed his back to the door. To Brébeuf and Leduc.

As though to invite attack. Or to send a message.

Armand Gamache wasn't just in command, he was in total command. He was invulnerable. Serge Leduc and Michel Brébeuf could do their worst, and it would never overwhelm Gamache's best. He wasn't worried.

It might be the message Gamache was sending, but Jean-Guy Beauvoir knew it wasn't the truth. And he suspected Gamache knew that too.

The back, turned on evil, was symbolic. But nothing more.

Serge Leduc had greeted the former superintendent of the Sûreté with no sign of censure for what Brébeuf had done.

And Brébeuf? He'd know perfectly well what Leduc had done, and was capable of doing.

He greeted the Duke as a king in exile welcomed a loyal subject.

"You might not care, *patron*," said Jean-Guy, "but what about them?"

Gamache turned in his chair to see a clump of students standing behind the two professors. Waiting to be tossed a crumb of attention.

Commander Gamache turned back to Jean-Guy.

"I didn't say I don't care. I care very deeply. That's why I'm here."

His voice, while calm, carried a gravity and even a censure that Beauvoir didn't miss.

"*Désolé*, of course you care. But shouldn't we do something?"

"We are doing something, Jean-Guy."

Gamache focused on the cadets who'd joined him and Madame Gamache and Jean-Guy around the fireplace. And Armand Gamache tried not to show his unease.

Michel Brébeuf had not been invited to the party. He wasn't even expected at the academy until the following day.

Yet here he was. Out of the storm. And into the arms of Serge Leduc. It wasn't, perhaps, surprising. But it was disappointing.

And then some.

He'd brought these two men together for a reason, but he thought he had some control over them. Now he saw he almost certainly had less than he thought.

As he turned back to the bright hearth, Gamache felt the hairs on the back of his neck rise.

Most of the staff and students had left and Amelia was heading for the door when she noticed the brown paper folded on the side table, with a picture on top. She picked it up.

"What do you think of it?" Commander Gamache asked, and Amelia started, then made to put the picture down, but it was too late.

He'd caught her.

She shrugged.

"You can do better than that," he said, holding out his hand. She gave him the painting.

"It's a map," she said. "Somewhere in Québec." She pointed to the snowman with the hockey stick. "But what's with the pyramid?"

Gamache's eye never left her. Amelia Choquet had found the strangest thing in a strange picture.

"I have no idea."

"I like the card," she said. "Your friends expect you to fuck up?"

"Always."

The ring piercing her lip twitched, betraying amusement.

"Again?" she asked, pointing to the word hanging off the end of Ruth's sentence.

"You don't get gray hair without having messed up a few times," he said. "You know?"

He held her eyes, and for the second time that day she saw intelligence there.

He was, she told herself, just another large, white, middle-aged man. She'd had her fill of them. Literally.

"Have you figured out what the academy motto means?" he asked.

"*Velut arbor aevo.* 'As a tree with the passage of time.' It means you have to put down roots."

She was wrong, she knew. The motto might mean that, at a superficial level, but there was more to it. And more to this man.

She'd noticed something else in his gaze. A shrewdness, as though he knew her better than she knew herself. As though he saw something in her, something she didn't think he altogether liked.

"Well, that was interesting," said Reine-Marie after they'd cleaned up and could finally collapse into the seats by the fire. "Did you happen to notice a slight tension?"

It was asked with wide-eyed innocence, as though she could be wrong.

"Maybe just a little," said her husband, joining her on the sofa.

"Want some?" asked Beauvoir. He'd gone down into the kitchens and grabbed a tray of sandwiches, which he held with one hand while eating with the other.

Now he offered the tray to Armand and Reine-Marie, who each took one.

"I don't like it," said Beauvoir, sitting in the Barcelona chair, which he now claimed as his own.

"What?" asked Reine-Marie.

"This whole thing," said Beauvoir. "Socializing with cadets."

"The lower orders?" asked Reine-Marie. "You seemed to be enjoying yourself."

"Well, maybe a little," he admitted. "What's with that Goth girl? How did she get in? She doesn't seem to even want to be here. Some of the cadets might be a little soft, but at least they're eager. She's just . . ."

He looked for the right word, then turned to his father-in-law.

"No, not evil," said Beauvoir, before Gamache could.

"I wasn't going to say that."

"Then how would you describe her?" Beauvoir asked.

"Adrift," said Gamache. Then he paused. "No, not adrift. Drowning."

"Troubled, certainly," said Reine-Marie. "Why did you admit her, Armand? When last I heard, she'd been rejected."

"What?" Beauvoir struggled to sit forward on the chair. "She'd been rejected and you changed that? Why?"

"I went over the application for every first-year cadet," said Armand. "They're all here because I saw something in them."

"And what did you see in her?" Reine-Marie asked, getting in before Beauvoir could ask the same question, though not, she knew, with the same tone.

"A last chance," he said. "A lifeline."

There was a knock on the door and he got up.

"This isn't a reform school," Beauvoir called after him. "The Sûreté Academy isn't a charity."

At the door Gamache turned, his hand on the knob. "Who said the lifeline was for her?"

Armand opened the door and came face-to-face with Michel Brébeuf.

Reine-Marie stood up and walked to her husband's side.

"Armand," said Brébeuf, then turning to her, "Reine-Marie."

"Michel," she said, her voice curt but courteous. She could smell the Scotch on his breath but he didn't seem drunk.

"I'm sorry I showed up uninvited to your party." He gave her an embarrassed, almost boyish, smile. "I didn't mean to. I came in a day early because of the storm and wanted to drop by to let you know I was here. I walked right in on the party. I came back to apologize."

"I'm a little tired," Reine-Marie said to Armand. "I think I'll go to bed. Michel."

She nodded toward him, and he smiled.

As Reine-Marie left the room, Jean-Guy caught a look pass between the Gamaches.

She was angry, livid, at this further incursion into their private space, their private time. Jean-Guy had rarely seen his mother-in-law angry. Armand knew it too and acknowledged it with a quick squeeze of her hand before she walked into the bedroom and closed the door. Firmly.

"You know Jean-Guy Beauvoir, of course," said Armand, and the two shook hands.

"Yes, Inspector. How are you?"

"Fine," said Beauvoir. "As are you, obviously."

Superintendent Brébeuf had also been Beauvoir's boss, but so far up the ladder that they rarely met. And now here they were, as though equals. As though nothing had happened.

They were all playing the game. The charade.

One word. Sounds like hypocrisy.

But Beauvoir also knew there was more to it than that. Yes, the Gamaches were pretending to be civil. But there was history there. Not just of hurt, but of deep affection.

Would the affection win? Should it? Was such a thing even possible? Beauvoir wondered.

Jean-Guy watched as Gamache invited Brébeuf in. The former super-intendent stood in front of the fire and waited for Armand to invite him to sit.

It was a long, ripe moment.

And then Armand gestured, and Michel sat.

And Beauvoir left, taking the sick feeling in his stomach with him.

CHAPTER 9

⌐

"Help yourself," said Armand, waving toward the sideboard and the bottles lined up there.

Without waiting to see what Brébeuf did, he went into the bedroom and over to Reine-Marie, who was hanging up her clothes.

"You okay?" he asked, watching her fluid movements, her back to him.

Then she turned around and he could see she'd been crying.

"Oh," was all he managed, taking her in his arms.

After a few moments, she pulled away and he handed her a handkerchief.

"It's just upsetting," she said, waving the handkerchief as though to clear the air. "When I see Michel, and hear him, for a moment I forget. It's like nothing has happened. And then I remember what happened."

She sighed. And looked toward the closed door.

"Do you know what you're doing?" she asked, dragging his handkerchief under her eyes to wipe away the mascara.

"Michel Brébeuf is no threat," he said, holding her hands and holding her eyes. "Not anymore. He's a paper tiger."

"Are you sure?"

He nodded. "I'm sure, *ma belle*. Are you all right? Do you want me to ask him to leave?"

"*Non*. I'm fine. I have some reading to do. You go back and entertain that shithead."

Armand looked at her with surprise.

She laughed. "I seem to be channeling Ruth. It's quite liberating."

"That's one word for it. After I get rid of Michel, I'll call an exorcist."

He kissed her and left.

At one in the morning, Reine-Marie turned out the light. Armand was still in the living room with Michel. She could hear their laughter.

"Oh my God, I'd forgotten that," said Michel.

The bottle of Scotch had been moved from the drinks table to the coffee table, and the level had moved down considerably.

"How could you forget Professor Meunier?" said Armand, reaching for the bottle and pouring them each another shot. Then sitting back, he put his slippered feet on the footstool. "He was like something out of a cartoon. Barking orders and throwing chalk at us. I still have the scar."

He pointed to the back of his head.

"You should've ducked."

"You shouldn't have provoked him. He was aiming at you, as I remember."

Michel Brébeuf laughed. "Okay, I remember." His laughter slowed to a chuckle and then silence. "Those were the longest three years of my life. The academy. I think they also might have been the happiest. We were so young. Is it possible?"

"Nineteen years old when we entered," said Armand. "I looked at the kids here tonight and wondered if we were ever so young. And I wondered how we got so old. It seems no time has passed. Came as a surprise that we're now the professors."

"Not just professors," said Michel, raising his glass in salute. "But the Commander."

He drank, then looking into the glass, he spoke softly.

"Why . . ."

"*Oui?*" said Armand, when the silence had stretched on.

"Leduc."

"Why did I keep him on?"

Brébeuf nodded.

"You two seemed to hit it off tonight. You tell me."

"He invited me back to his rooms after the party," said Brébeuf. "He's a cretin."

"He's worse than that," said Gamache.

"Yes," said Brébeuf, studying his companion. "What're you going to do about him?"

"Ahhh, Michel," said Armand, crossing his legs and raising his glass to his eyes, so that he saw Brébeuf through the amber liquid. "You worry about your side of the street. There's enough mess there to keep you busy. I'll worry about mine."

Brébeuf nodded, eating a stale sandwich as he thought. Finally he asked, "Have you told the cadets about Matthew 10:36 yet?"

"*Non*. I'll leave that up to you."

Michel tried to get up but couldn't. But Armand did. He stood up and stood over Brébeuf, large, solid, almost threatening. No longer under the influence, it seemed.

Putting out his hand, and with more strength than Brébeuf expected at that late hour in the day and in their lives, Armand hauled him to his feet.

"Time you left. You have a job to do."

"But what job? Why am I here?" Michel asked, his eyes bleary, looking into Armand's familiar gaze. "I need to know."

"You do know."

As he left, one bony hand like a claw brushing the wall of the corridor to keep him on course, Michel Brébeuf knew there were probably many reasons Armand had gone all the way to the Gaspé and brought him back. From Percé Rock. From the dead.

Armand had always been the more clever of the two. And there was cleverness at work here.

From that first visit, Brébeuf had known he wasn't going to be simply a professor. He would be the object lesson, the walking warning to the cadets. What happened when you gave in to temptation. When you listened to the fallen angels of your nature.

But after tonight he suspected there was even more to it than that. More expected. Armand had other things in mind.

If Armand wasn't going to tell him why he'd invited him to the academy, Michel wasn't going to tell him why he'd accepted.

And there was another question, just as tantalizing.

Why was Armand really there?

Gamache closed the door and, leaning against it, he brought a hand to his head. It was all he could do not to slump to the floor. It had been a long time since he'd drunk that much. And a long time since he'd dredged up all those memories.

Pushing off from the door, he turned off the lights and carefully made his way to the bedroom, wondering which hangover would be worse in the morning. The one from the alcohol or the emotions.

Over the following weeks the Sûreté Academy fell into a comfortable rhythm of classes, hockey practice, and meals. Of rigorous exercise and volunteering in the community.

Mind, body, and spirit, the cadets were told. Over and over.

It was a structured life, with just enough free time to get the trouble-makers into trouble.

After a while the cadets, new and old, came to know what was expected.

The freshmen settled in more quickly than the older students, who found it difficult to adapt to the new set of rules and expectations that were at once more firm and more forgiving than those of the old regime.

It was made clear by the new commander that there were no harsh pun-ishments, but there were consequences. Over and over, the cadets were made aware that actions had effects. Swift and decisive and in proportion to the act. Something that seemed to come as an unpleasant surprise to many of the older cadets, who were used to currying favor.

The new reality won Commander Gamache many supporters, and many more detractors.

Once a week, Reine-Marie would drive in with Armand and that night they'd host a gathering of cadets. It was a chance to air, in confidence, griev-ances. To ask questions.

They discussed, around the fireplace, old cases, difficult cases. Moral un-certainties, the place of policing in a free society. About when to take a stand, and when to step away.

Issues most of these young people had never considered, but now must.

As the days and weeks progressed, friendships were made. Groups were formed. Allegiances solidified. Rivalries flared. Enemies were made. Lov-ers attached, and detached.

And Amelia Choquet remained alone. By choice. A class by herself.

Except for the gatherings in the Gamaches' quarters. It had not been her idea to go. She'd been invited, and she took the invitation as not really optional.

"What is it?" asked Huifen one evening.

She stood beside the Goth Girl, who'd been staring at a small framed picture by the door.

"What does it look like?" asked Amelia.

The Commander could command her to be there, but not to like it, or the other cadets.

"A map," said Huifen. "Hey, Jacques, look at this."

Jacques Laurin walked over. He was the head cadet, chosen the year before by Leduc and kept in place by Gamache.

Amelia had never spoken to him, though she'd seen him drilling his squad. Jogging around the frozen quad. He was tall and attractive, with an air about him someone charitable might call assurance. Amelia saw it as arrogance.

And yet, she noticed, he deferred to the small Asian girl.

"So?" he asked.

"It's kinda neat," said Huifen.

"It doesn't make sense," said Jacques. "There's a snowman and a rose? The two don't go together."

Another cadet had joined them, standing slightly off to the side. The gay kid with the red hair from class, Amelia knew. Nathaniel Something.

"I like it," he said, and the other three looked at him, and Jacques gave a small, dismissive snort, then turned away from the freshman. The gay Anglo freshman.

But Amelia continued to look at Nathaniel. Who had either the courage, or the stupidity, to contradict the head cadet.

Amelia returned her gaze to the map.

She had no idea why it had such a hold on her. When she'd seen it, that first evening, she'd thought, like Jacques, that it was ridiculous. But every week, during these gatherings, she found herself in front of it.

Was it the cow? The snowman? Those trees that looked like children?

It was silly, but it was also sad. It was, she thought, strange. Maybe that's why she liked it.

Gamache noticed the group and, walking over, he took the map off the wall. He stared at it, then looked into their expectant faces.

"There's a mystery about this," he said. "Any idea what it is?"

He handed it to Huifen, who looked at it more closely and passed it around.

"Why do you have it on the wall?" said Jacques. "I don't see anything great about it."

"Then why are you looking at it?" Gamache asked.

The head cadet was as tall as the Commander, but not yet filled out. Not yet substantial.

"There's no shame in showing curiosity," said Gamache. "In fact, it's sort

75

of a prerequisite in an investigator. The more interested you are in things, in people, the better you'll be at your job."

Commander Gamache looked down at the map. "This shows the place where Madame Gamache and I live. It was a gift from friends."

Then, making up his mind, he turned it over and carefully removed it from the frame.

"I have an assignment for you," he said to the four of them. "Solve the mystery of the map."

"But it's not a crime," said Nathaniel. "Is it?"

"Not every mystery is a crime," said the Commander. "But every crime starts as a mystery. A secret. Some hidden thought or feeling. A desire. Something not yet illegal that evolves, with time, into a crime. Every homicide I've investigated started as a secret."

He looked at them, as serious as they'd ever seen him.

"You all have your secrets. You might be surprised how many of them I know."

"And you, sir?" asked Huifen. "Do you have any secrets?"

Gamache smiled. "Lots. I'm a warehouse of other people's indiscretions."

"She meant your own," said Amelia.

"I certainly have things I keep private, and yes, I do have a few secrets." He turned from her to the other three. "Most of our secrets are pretty benign. Things we're ashamed to tell others because they make us look bad. But there are a few that fester, that eventually consume us. Those are what we look for, as police. We investigate crimes, but first we investigate people. The things they don't want others to know. Secrets aren't treasure, you know. Secrets don't make you powerful. They make you weak. Vulnerable."

He looked down at the painting in his hands.

"The skills you'll need to investigate a crime are the same ones you'll need to solve the mystery of the map. I want you to work together, as a unit, and come up with the answers."

"Together?" said Jacques.

"Maybe we can split into teams?" suggested Huifen. "The seniors versus the freshmen?"

"Wait a minute," said Nathaniel. "That's not fair."

"Why not?" demanded Amelia, though she knew the answer.

"How about guys versus girls?" asked Nathaniel.

"There is no 'versus.' You'll do it together," said Gamache. "As a unit. In the Sûreté, we can't choose our colleagues. They're assigned. Get used to it."

"Is this for credit?" Jacques asked.

"No, it's for experience. If you don't want to do it, just excuse yourself from the exercise. It's all the same to me."

Jacques looked at the map, and despite himself, he wanted to know.

"I'm in."

"*Bon*. I'll have copies made and dropped off to each of you before the end of classes tomorrow."

The rest of the evening was spent with the students huddling, working out strategies.

The next afternoon, copies of the map were handed to the four cadets, and the day after that there was a knock on the door of Commander Gamache's office.

"*Oui*," he called, and looked up from his desk.

Huifen, Jacques, Nathaniel, and Amelia entered. He took off his reading glasses and gestured toward the sitting area.

"We've solved the mystery," said Jacques.

"Well, you didn't do much," said Amelia.

"I was busy."

"Yes, being head cadet. I've heard."

"I did most of the work," said Nathaniel.

"How can you—" Huifen began before the Commander raised his hand and silence descended.

He turned to Jacques.

"And?" he asked.

"And this place doesn't exist." Jacques gestured dismissively toward the painting. "It can't be your home, unless you live in a hole in the ground or a tree trunk. There's no village there. Nothing. Just forest and mountains. We checked on Google Maps and GPS."

"I even found some old paper maps of the Townships," said Nathaniel. "Williamsburg is there, Saint-Rémy. Cowansville. But not the village, the one the map is designed around."

"Three Pines," said Gamache.

"You lied," Jacques repeated.

"Be careful, cadet, with your words," he said softly.

"That's the mystery though, isn't it?" said Huifen. "It's a map to a fictional place. Why would someone do that? Isn't that what you really want us to find out?"

Gamache stood up and, walking to the door, he showed them out.

They stood in the hallway, looking at the closed door.

"We fucked up somewhere," said Amelia, clicking her stud up and down.

"Calling him a liar didn't help," said Huifen. "Why would you do that? He's the Commander."

"In name only," said Jacques.

"Isn't that enough?" asked Nathaniel.

"You wouldn't understand."

"Back to the map," said Amelia. "We were right, weren't we? The place doesn't exist."

"And yet the Commander said he lives there," said Huifen.

"He's fucking with us," said Jacques. "Like the Duke said he would."

"Well, I know one way to find out," said Huifen.

Armand looked in the rearview mirror. They were still there.

It was early evening and already dark. He'd spotted them as soon as he turned out of the academy parking lot to drive home.

At first he thought there was just one car, but after a few kilometers he noticed a second, hanging further back.

He nodded approval. Someone had been paying attention in class.

It was early March and winter still had its grip on Québec. His head-lights caught the ragged edges of snowbanks on either side of the sec-ondary road. He drove through the clear, crisp evening, the two cars still behind him.

And then he lost them. Or, more precisely, they lost him.

Sighing, Gamache pulled over into a Tim Hortons outside Cowans-ville. Parking under the lights, he waited. One of the cars circled once, twice, and on the third time, they spotted him and turned in, parking well away.

The second car had managed to follow him and had pulled off the road a hundred yards beyond the doughnut shop.

Huifen, he suspected. With Jacques, maybe. But he wondered why they hadn't just called the others in the first car when they pulled over.

They needed, perhaps, another lesson on what teamwork meant.

As Gamache drove out of the parking lot the first car pulled right out, determined not to lose him again. The second hung back.

Yes. There was more skill there. And confidence.

He decided to take the scenic route home.

"Where's he going?" asked Huifen.

"I don't know," said Jacques, bored and hungry. "It doesn't make sense."

"Maybe he's lost," said Amelia.

"Maybe he can't find the door back into the parallel universe," said Nathaniel.

It was difficult to tell when he was serious.

"Has anyone been taking notes on where we're going?" asked Amelia. "I'm lost."

"That was your job," said Huifen.

"Mine? I'm in the backseat. I can barely see."

"Well, I'm driving."

They argued some more until the road ahead went dark. Very dark. No streetlights. No taillights. No car.

"*Tabernac,*" said Jacques. "Now where'd he go?"

Gamache shook his head.

"I'll be a little later than expected," he said into the Bluetooth.

"Lost them again?" said Reine-Marie. "Well, I'll set more places at the table. They'll be hungry when they finally find you again."

"*Merci.*"

He put his car in gear and started looking for the cadets, finally finding them parked in a service station. He pulled in, and though he didn't need any, he decided to gas up. Just to see them scramble. And also to explain his own presence there.

"Shit, there he is," said Amelia, sliding down in the backseat. "Get down."

By now they'd gotten so well into the exercise, they'd almost convinced themselves their lives, and those of others, depended on following this man.

79

They got down. So far down they missed it when the Commander pulled out.

Gamache sighed and paused at the exit to the service station, his blinker on. He all but honked to get their attention.

First thing in the morning, he thought, *I'm going to call Professor McKinnon and get her to take the students out and refresh them on trailing a suspect.*

Tiring of the exercise and wanting his own dinner, Commander Gamache drove straight home. A motorcade behind him.

"Don't lose him," said Jacques.

"I'll make a note of that," said Huifen. She was starving and they still had to figure out how to get back to the academy after this. By that time, they'd have missed dinner and would have to break into the kitchens or do with the crackers they had stashed in their rooms.

Up ahead, the Commander's car disappeared from sight, as though he'd driven off a cliff.

"What the hell just happened?" asked Jacques.

Huifen slowed down and edged the car forward. Then she stopped.

"Holy shit," she whispered. Behind her Amelia and Nathaniel sat up.

Below them, in the middle of the dark forest, was a radiant village.

Huifen turned off the car and the cadets got out, walking forward. Their boots crunching on the snow and their warm breath coming out in puffs.

They stopped at what felt like the edge of the world.

Amelia tilted her head back, feeling the fresh air raw on her cheeks.

Above them, a riot of stars formed horses and birds and magical creatures.

And below the stars, the village.

"It does exist," whispered Nathaniel.

Gamache's car drove slowly by old brick and fieldstone and clapboard homes.

Light spilled from mullioned windows and glowed on the snow.

At the far end of the village, the cadets could see people coming and going from what looked like a brasserie, though the view was obscured by three huge pine trees grown up in the very center of the village.

"We should go." Nathaniel tugged at Huifen's coat, but the older girl just stood there.

"Not yet. We need to know for sure."

"Know what?" he asked. "We followed him and found the village. This is the mystery. Not that it doesn't exist, but that it does. Let's go before we get into trouble."

"Aren't you curious?" Amelia asked him.

As they watched, the car came to rest in front of a two-story white clapboard home, all lit up. Smoke came out of the chimney into the crisp night air. Puffs. As though the home was breathing.

The Commander got out of the car, but instead of walking up the path cut through the snow to the sweeping front veranda, he turned in the other direction. And walked away from the home. Toward them.

"Oh, shit. Don't move," whispered Nathaniel. "He'll see movement. He'll hear us."

At the bottom of the hill, the Commander stopped and peered.

"Be quiet," Nathaniel whispered. "Be quiet."

"You be quiet," hissed Amelia.

"Dinner's on," Gamache called into the darkness. "*Boeuf bourguignon*, if you're interested."

Then he retraced his steps. Followed shortly by the munching of tires on snow. He stopped and watched as a car made its way down the hill and around the village green. A single car. He looked up and saw a very faint glow approach the edge of the hill. And recede. It crept back until there was complete and utter darkness up there.

Armand Gamache walked slowly along the path to his home. Thinking. And realizing he'd been wrong.

The cadets were all in one car.

So who was in the other?

CHAPTER 10

———

"Are you mad at us?" asked Nathaniel.

"Mad?" asked Armand, passing him the basket of fresh rolls. "Why would I be angry?"

"Well, we followed you," he said, taking a warm roll and holding it in his still chilled hands.

"After a fashion, yes. I'm not angry about the fact you did it, just the way you did it."

"And we doubted you," said Huifen. "We thought you were lying when you said you lived in the village."

Her voice petered out as she watched Madame Gamache ladle huge spoonfuls of beef stew onto plates of egg noodles.

The young people stared as though they'd never seen food before.

Except for Amelia, who was engaged in a staring contest of her own with the other person at the table.

A broken-down old wreck. And her duck.

Commander Gamache smiled. "Doubt is never a bad thing in a Sûreté du Québec agent. You did exactly as I'd hoped. You didn't take me at my word, you looked for proof."

"But why doesn't this place show up on any map?" asked Jacques, speaking into his fork of *boeuf bourguignon*.

"There're way smaller villages that're on the maps," said Huifen, managing to look at Gamache. "We didn't believe you lived here because, well, there is no here, here."

That brought a smile to Reine-Marie's face as she held out her hand for Nathaniel's plate. He'd wolfed down the first helping at a speed that would put Henri to shame, and now she spooned out more chunks of tender beef and onions and carrots along with the rich, fragrant broth.

The food in the academy dining hall had improved since the contract had been taken from a national chain and given to a local chef. But it wasn't this.

Amelia had finished her dinner quickly, putting her head down and scooping the stew into her mouth, barely chewing. Wiping the gravy up with the rolls, she'd cleaned her plate, then sat back, her arms across her chest.

The elderly woman also sat back, and crossed her arms. Amelia had the impression that if the demon duck could have crossed its wings, it would have.

The woman, who'd been introduced to them as the Gamaches' neighbor, Ruth, seemed to be intentionally mirroring Amelia's actions. When Amelia reached for a drink, so did the creepy old lady.

Only, Amelia's glass held Coke. The old woman's was Scotch.

When Amelia ate, she ate. When Amelia sat back, she sat back.

And now they were in a staring contest.

"Well, you found the village," said Gamache. "And solved the first mystery. And now you've come face-to-face with the second mystery. Why isn't it on any map, except that one?"

"Even Google Maps doesn't have it," said Huifen. "And the GPS thinks we parked in the middle of the forest."

"The middle of nowhere," said Jacques.

"It's still recalculating," said Nathaniel. "She seemed quite concerned for us."

Huifen picked up the old map from the pine harvest table and examined it again.

"And you don't know the answer to that question?" she said, looking from the Commander to Madame Gamache and back again. "Why the village only shows up here but nowhere else?"

They shook their heads.

"What gets me is that this shows things a normal map never would," said Huifen.

"Like the snowman and the cow," said Jacques, leaning toward her. "Why a snowman? It can't possibly be a landmark since it would melt away."

"Then there's the pyramid," said Nathaniel.

"Maybe it was just an exercise, to pass the time," said Huifen. "Like those old embroideries. What were they called?"

"Samplers," said Madame Gamache.

"That's not a sampler," said Amelia, keeping her eyes on the wretched

84

old wreck in front of her. "All those little lines. They're contours. Showing elevation. It's a real map."

"Why was it made?" asked Huifen.

"And that's the third secret this map has yet to give up," said Gamache. "What's its purpose?"

The map had seemed almost laughable when they'd first seen it hanging on the wall of the Commander's rooms, but now it was ripe with intrigue.

"It's sort of nice that Three Pines isn't on any official map," Reine-Marie admitted. "It means we won't be disturbed."

"Too late," said Amelia, gesturing to Ruth.

Armand said nothing, remembering the glow on the hill.

Someone had found them.

"So where did the map come from?" asked Amelia, breaking eye contact with the crazy old lady.

Throughout dinner, the kitchen had been filled with the scents of cinnamon and brown sugar, mingling and mixing with the earthy aroma of the *boeuf bourguignon* and rolls.

Now Armand got up and brought something out of the oven, and the fragrance became even more pronounced.

Taking off the oven mitts, he turned to Amelia.

"It was a gift from the person who found it. He could see how much I'd admired it."

"Olivier didn't find it," snapped Ruth. "I did."

They were the first words she'd spoken, besides the "Fuck off" to Huifen when she'd tried to help the frail old woman to the table.

"True," said Reine-Marie. "But it belongs to Olivier. Not sure if you noticed the bistro when you arrived. He and his partner Gabri own it."

"But where did he find it?" asked Amelia. "It wasn't drawn yesterday, it must've been lying around for years."

"It was in a wall," said Ruth. She too had broken eye contact and was looking down at the copy of the painting on the pine table.

The duck, however, continued to glare at Amelia, winning the contest.

"It'd been walled up," said Ruth.

"What?" asked Nathaniel. "Why?"

"Why?" asked the Commander, putting bowls of warm apple and raspberry crisp with melting Coaticook vanilla ice cream in front of them. "That's a very good question."

He could tell by their faces that the cadets were beginning to appreciate that an investigation wasn't linear. It was like the map, with contour lines and winding roads. And obstacles. And every now and then you came across something completely unexpected.

"Why put a map into a wall?" Gamache asked.

"It was waiting," said Ruth.

"Now, Ruth," said Reine-Marie. "Don't play mind games with our young guests."

"It's no game. There's something strange about that map. I feel it. And I know you do too."

She'd spoken to Armand. After he gave a curt nod, the old woman turned to Amelia, resuming the staring contest.

"And so do you."

"I feel nothing. None of this matters. It's an exercise," said Amelia. "An assignment. Nothing more. And not even a very interesting one."

"Then why're you here?" asked Ruth, struggling to her feet. This time no one helped her. She walked to the door, followed by Armand.

"Some things disappear for a reason, Armand," she said, then turned back to the cadets at the table. So young. Trying to be unmoved by this creepy old woman. But their wide eyes betrayed them.

"You asked what the map was waiting for. Maybe it was waiting for you," said Ruth. "You found the village, maybe that's enough. Maybe you should stop now. *Sneak home and pray you'll never know/the hell where youth and laughter go.*"

"Now there's a woman who knows an exit line," said Huifen as Ruth left. Even Amelia laughed. Though she expected to see her breath in the suddenly chill air.

Through the kitchen window, they saw Commander Gamache supporting Ruth, keeping her upright on the icy road. He cradled the duck close to his body to keep it warm.

"Alzheimer's?" asked Huifen.

Reine-Marie shook her head. "Poetry."

"*Bonne nuit*," said Armand when Ruth had opened her unlocked door and he'd handed Rosa back to her.

"Yeah, right," said Ruth, moving to close the door in his face.

"Wait," said Armand, putting out a gloved hand to stop the door. "Why did you just quote Siegfried Sassoon?"

"Why do I say anything? It's anyone's guess really."

And then she did close the door and he walked back home, pausing to marvel at the stars. Many of which no longer existed. Just their light.

His gaze dropped to the village. That did, and did not, exist.

The map had been walled up. To become part of the building. To act as insulation, protection. Helping to keep the cold winds at bay.

But it had been removed, and the cold winds were howling, were baying, again.

He pulled his coat tighter around him, and as he passed the kitchen windows of his home, he stopped and looked in. Reine-Marie had her chin on her hand and was listening to the cadets. She was so beautiful. And they were so young.

The Gamaches invited the cadets to stay the night, and while Reine-Marie got them fresh pajamas and toothbrushes, Armand called the academy to let them know not to worry about the students.

He spent a few hours in his study, going over coursework and making notes on upcoming meetings with professors and community leaders, while Reine-Marie sorted more archival material in the living room.

The cadets, after sitting quietly in the living room for a nanosecond, decided to head over to the bistro.

Just after midnight, Armand heard the front door open. Reine-Marie had gone to bed and he was waiting up.

The cadets paused at the doorway into the study where he sat, legs crossed, reading glasses on and a dossier open.

"Good night, sir," said Nathaniel.

"Thanks for the dinner," said Huifen, "and for letting us stay."

"Did you have fun at the bistro?" he asked.

"The owner showed us where the map was hidden," said Jacques. "But he couldn't tell us any more."

Amelia just kept walking, stomping up the stairs to bed. The others followed, and after finishing his reading, Gamache got up, locked the front door and checked the back door and windows. Though he knew if there was any danger, it probably wasn't lurking in the snow-covered garden. Like the Great Wall of China, most threats were already inside.

Armand was awoken in the small hours by the creak of old wood.

He sat up, alert. Listening.

Then he put on a dressing gown and crept to the top of the stairs, and crouched down.

From there he could see a figure enter the living room from the kitchen.

Was it the person in the second car? The one who'd followed them there, then disappeared? Only to reappear at two in the morning?

The shape moved about the living room. The embers in the fireplace were almost out. There was just enough light to see the shadowy figure, but not enough to see who it was.

Until they turned the light on, and Gamache almost fell onto his bottom. Standing in the living room, eating a chicken leg, was something that looked like a science experiment gone bad. Or mad.

The head of a pierced and tattooed Goth was grafted onto a pink and frilly body. Amelia was wearing one of Reine-Marie's flannel nightgowns, and rifling their home.

Gamache made another mental note, to contact Professor McKinnon and ask her to go over how to do a clandestine search.

Number one: get a search warrant.

Number two: do not turn on a lamp.

He shook his head before remembering the numbskull things he and Michel Brébeuf had done. Though they had never included rummaging through the Commander's home.

Amelia studied the books on the shelves and picked up photographs of the Commander's family. Her fingers, greasy from the chicken leg, left smudges on the photos. Finally she came to a wedding picture. A woman who was obviously the Gamaches' daughter, now grown and gowned, and beside her was her new husband.

Amelia clicked her stud against her teeth.

Armand knew exactly what she was looking at, though he couldn't see the expression on her face. He'd wondered, when the cadets had arrived, whether he should hide the pictures, but decided against it. They were private, but not secret.

And he was curious to see if any of them noticed.

The living room went dark, and Armand prepared to withdraw as soon as he heard her foot on the bottom stair. But that creak didn't come. Instead he saw another light go on. In his study.

This was going too far, and he walked downstairs and found her sitting in his chair. Staring at another photo.

"Put that down," he said, and saw her jerk in surprise.

He stood framed in the doorway, in a dressing gown and slippers.

She put the black-and-white picture down.

"Exactly as you found it," he said.

She adjusted it, noting the smiling man in the old-fashioned hat and winter coat, and the woman in a neat cloth coat and gloves and hat. She held a child in her arms, bundled up so well against the Québec winter it looked like she was holding a hamper of clothes. Only a tiny hand was visible, gripping her finger.

For a moment, Amelia assumed it was Monsieur and Madame Gamache, but then she realized it was far too old.

"Your parents?" she asked.

"You've taken advantage of our kindness," he said.

"I was just looking for a book to read."

"You could have asked."

"At two in the morning? I didn't want to disturb you."

"This room is private. The things in it are personal, as you know very well."

"Personal," she asked, getting up. "Or secret?"

"Please leave."

Upstairs in her room, under the duvet, Amelia pulled out the book she'd found in the shelves downstairs.

I'm FINE, by one of her favorite poets, Ruth Zardo.

She read the subtitle and laughed.

Fucked-up. Insecure. Neurotic. Egotistical.

Burrowing deeper into the bed, she ate the last of the cookies she'd taken from the kitchen and flipped through the poems. Some she already knew. Some she didn't.

> *You were a moth*
> *brushing against my cheek*
> *in the dark*
> *I killed you*
> *not knowing*

you were only a moth,
with no sting.

She splayed the book against her knees and wondered what the academy had been like before Gamache. When Professor Leduc was in charge.

Jacques said it was way better, and that Gamache was undermining it, making it and the Sûreté weak. She knew he was just parroting what the Duke was saying, but she wondered if there was truth in it. And while Huifen didn't agree, neither did she disagree with what Jacques said.

There had been no commendations in Gamache's study. No photographs of him in uniform. Leduc said Gamache was a disgrace, that he had been forced to "retire." And there were rumbles around the academy about some corruption case.

She found it hard to reconcile these rumors with the man himself, but Amelia knew that people were not always what they appeared.

She reached for her iPhone to google Armand Gamache, something she'd been meaning to do since she'd arrived at the academy, but more pressing things kept occupying her. Like getting through each day.

No connection. She tossed the iPhone on the bed in frustration. She'd forgotten. There was no Internet coverage here. Not only had mapmakers forgotten this place but so, apparently, had time. And technology.

She pulled the duvet up higher and wondered who Armand Gamache really was. And if he knew that Huifen and Jacques and even Nathaniel quietly visited Professor Leduc regularly.

The Duke met with a few select students. And she wondered if Gamache knew that she was among those selected.

Sides had been chosen, allegiances declared, the game of Red Rover was over.

Finally, eyes heavy with sleep, she went to turn off the light. Only then did Amelia notice the inscription at the front of the well-thumbed volume.

For Clouseau, who will be just FINE one day. Ruth.

Ruth?

Ruth?

She sat up in bed and stared at the book, then out the window at the village. That appeared and disappeared and contained all sorts of secrets within its thick walls.

CHAPTER 11

Another week passed and by then they were deep into the term.

Some of the older students still grumbled, but less and less. Not necessarily, Gamache knew, because they were coming to terms with the realities of the new regime, but because they were kept too busy to complain.

He was in his rooms early one morning, talking with Reine-Marie on the phone. He'd had late meetings and decided to stay the night at the academy.

"Did I tell you that Clara got a new puppy yesterday?" she asked.

"From that litter she talked about? That was a while ago."

"No, Billy Williams found these ones in a garbage can."

He inhaled deeply and exhaled the word "people." Not so much an indictment as in wonderment. That there could be so much deliberate cruelty and so much kindness in one species.

"Clara took one. A little male she's called Leo. Adorable. But there is something—"

And that's as far as she got. Even down the phone line, she could hear the shouting. Reine-Marie couldn't make out the words, but she could hear the panic.

"I have to go," said her husband, and the line went dead.

Gamache threw a dressing gown over his pajamas and was out the door in moments, the shouting hitting him in the face as he ran toward it.

One voice. A man's. Young. Frightened. The terror bounced off the marble floors and walls, magnifying.

"Help," the voice was screaming. "Help." The single syllable elongating. "Heeeeelllll-p." More a sound than a word.

Other professors came out of their rooms, joining in behind Gamache. As he ran past Jean-Guy Beauvoir's door, Gamache gave it a single pound with his fist, but kept going.

Behind him, he heard the door open and the familiar voice, groggy.

"What the—Jesus."

Up ahead, the screaming had stopped. But the hallway was still clogged with fear.

Gamache rounded a corner and there, back to the wall, stood Nathaniel Smythe. On the ground in front of him was a tray, with broken glass and china and food.

Stepping in front of the boy, to break his line of sight, Gamache looked quickly, expertly, over him.

"Are you hurt?" he asked.

Nathaniel, eyes wide and not quite focusing on Gamache, shook his head.

"Look after him," Gamache said to whoever had arrived right behind him. "Take him to my rooms. Don't let him out of your sight."

"What's happened?" Jean-Guy Beauvoir asked, skidding to a stop beside Gamache.

Other professors were arriving and craning to see. But the Commander was blocking the open door, and their view.

He himself had yet to look, but as Nathaniel was led away, he turned around.

"Call the police," he said, speaking to Beauvoir but still staring into the room. Then he looked at Jean-Guy. "Call Isabelle Lacoste."

"*Oui, patron,*" his voice betraying none of the surprise he felt. Though shock would be a better word.

He knew what that meant. What Gamache was seeing.

Jean-Guy ran back down the corridor to his rooms to call. As he went, he was met with worried and excited faces all asking, "What's happened?"

More professors were arriving, and behind them, staff. And behind them, the first of the students.

"Lock the doors to the academy," Gamache told two other professors. "No one gets in or out."

They took off down the corridor.

The other professors were crowding around, trying to see what could possibly be in the room. But Gamache blocked their way.

"The head of each year," he said, scanning the now-crowded corridor. Three professors stepped forward.

"Here, Commander."

"Make sure the cadets are safe. Get them into the dining hall and do a head count. Keep them there. Give them breakfast, but no one leaves until I say so."

He held their eyes. "Understood?"

"Understood."

"Quickly, then. If someone is hurt or missing, we need to know."

The professors split up, shepherding reluctant students back down the hallway.

Commander Gamache still had not entered the room.

"Professor McKinnon, take a couple of teaching assistants and gather up the staff. Secretarial, grounds, maintenance, kitchen. Everyone. Take them into the dining hall as well. Ask the head of operations to confirm everyone is who they say they are, and that no one is missing."

"*D'accord*, Commander." And she hurried down the hallway. Leaving just one other professor standing there.

"What would you like me to do, Armand?"

"Nothing," came his curt response.

Michel Brébeuf stepped away and watched as Gamache stared into the room.

"Actually, there is one thing you can do," said Armand, turning back to Brébeuf. "Get the doctor."

"Of course."

Brébeuf walked quickly down the corridor, though he knew he'd been given the least urgent, the least important, of the tasks. He knew by Gamache's orders and actions that there was no real need of a doctor.

"Isabelle's on her way," said Beauvoir, arriving back at Gamache's side and marveling at the now-empty corridor.

He looked at his watch at the same moment Gamache did.

It was six twenty-three in the morning.

There was silence now. Except for a tiny sound like a squeal. Both Gamache and Beauvoir looked up and down the corridor. It was still empty. But still the sound came closer.

Then around the corner came Hugo Charpentier in his wheelchair.

"What's happened?"

Professor Charpentier's progress stopped when he saw Gamache's face.

"As bad as that?"

Gamache didn't move.

"Where're the others?" Charpentier asked.

"Securing the building. The staff and students are being taken to the dining hall."

"And they forgot about me," he said. He started to wheel forward. "Can I help?"

"*Non, merci.* Just join the others, please."

As he turned back down the hall, Gamache also marveled that they'd forgotten Professor Charpentier. He felt slightly ashamed, but mostly he tucked that information away. How easily overlooked that man was. And he thought about what an invisible man could get away with.

He also noted the squeal of Charpentier's wheelchair, as he withdrew. Something Gamache had never noticed before.

And then he turned his attention to the doorway and what lay beyond.

Who lay beyond.

Serge Leduc was crumpled on the floor.

It was all too obvious what had happened. By the body, and the blood. He'd been shot in the head. The gun still lay by his side.

And while it was also clear, by the glaring eyes and open mouth, and the pallor, never mind the wound, that he was dead, Gamache still bent down and felt for a pulse, his hand coming away with a bit of blood, which he wiped off with a handkerchief.

Jean-Guy's practiced eye swept the scene, then he looked toward the bedroom.

Gamache gave a brief nod and Beauvoir covered the ground swiftly.

"Nothing," said Jean-Guy a moment later.

"That's enough," said Gamache from the bedroom door, when Beauvoir opened a drawer in the nightstand. "I doubt the murderer's in the drawer. Let's leave it for Lacoste and the Scene of Crime team."

Beauvoir closed the drawer, but not before Gamache saw something Jean-Guy had not.

What was inside that drawer. Even from a distance, it was unmistakable.

"As tempting as it is to start the investigation, we need to wait. Call

Isabelle back, Jean-Guy, and report in more detail. She should be here soon with the homicide team. Can you please go to the main door and show her up here?"

"Now?"

"Is there a better time?"

"Don't you want me to help here?"

"There's nothing we can do to help. I just need the doctor to confirm he's dead. You know the drill. Then I'll lock the door and wait for you to return with Chief Inspector Lacoste."

Beauvoir looked down at the body.

"Suicide?"

"Maybe," said Gamache. "Does something strike you as strange?"

Beauvoir examined the scene more closely.

"*Oui.* The gun. It's on the wrong side. If he'd killed himself, it'd be on the same side as the entrance wound."

Gamache nodded, lost in thought.

Beauvoir left, stopping at his own rooms to throw on some clothes.

When he walked back down the corridor, the door to Leduc's rooms was closed and Gamache was nowhere to be seen.

Armand stood over the body of Serge Leduc, careful to avoid contaminating evidence more than he already had.

His eye took in the placement of furniture, the curtains and books. The ashes in the hearth.

But his eye kept returning to the body, and the weapon. As Jean-Guy had said, on the wrong side of the body, for suicide.

Yes, it was odd that the weapon was there. But what was odder still was that the murderer must have placed it there.

For this was murder, Gamache knew. And there was a murderer. And instead of trying to make it look like suicide, as any reasonable killer would, this one had made sure there was no doubt.

Serge Leduc's death was deliberate.

That's what struck the former head of homicide as strange. Very strange. Not the body. Not even the fact Serge Leduc had been killed. But the behavior of his killer.

Gamache stood staring. But not at the body. Now his attention had turned to the bedroom. Knowing he shouldn't, but doing it anyway, Gamache walked swiftly into the bedroom and opened the bedside drawer.

As he looked down, his face grew as grim as when he'd gazed at the body.

There was an electronic whirring, then a clunk, and the door to the academy opened. Chief Inspector Lacoste stepped inside quickly. Not because there was so much urgency to the case, but because it was so damned cold.

A damp wind was sweeping across the flatlands, carrying moisture from melting snow and ice, for hundreds of miles, and depositing it in their bones.

The initial message from Inspector Beauvoir had been brief. Simply that there'd been a death at the academy. Not who. Not how. Not even if it was murder, though the fact the call had been made to her, the head of homicide, was in itself a fairly significant clue.

She also knew the victim had not been Commander Gamache. Beauvoir would have told her, in words, but also in his tone.

Once in the car, an agent at the wheel and the Scene of Crime van behind, Isabelle Lacoste received another call from Beauvoir.

"Tell me what you know," she'd said.

On the other end, Jean-Guy gave a brief smile. He wondered if Isabelle realized that was exactly how Chief Inspector Gamache had begun each and every homicide investigation.

Tell me what you know.

He told her what he knew, and as she listened she took notes on her tablet. But then she stopped and just listened.

"The killer?" she asked, when he finished his report.

"No sign of him," said Beauvoir. "The cadets and staff are in the dining hall. The academy is on lockdown and they're doing a head count."

"And the body?"

"Commander Gamache is with him, waiting for the doctor. He'll lock up and wait for you once death is confirmed."

"I've called the coroner. She'll be arriving soon too."

"*Bon.* On first inspection, no one is missing and no one appears obviously guilty. No blood-stained hands."

It was not a joke. There would be blood on someone's hands, and then some. To place a gun at Leduc's temple like that, and fire.

Beauvoir had questioned the night guards and staff, but not too closely. Just enough to find out if they'd seen anything that needed immediate action.

They had not.

Which led to an obvious conclusion.

The killer hadn't left, and hadn't arrived. Because he was already there, hidden within these walls.

Isabelle Lacoste walked beside Jean-Guy Beauvoir down the deserted halls. The Scene of Crime team was behind them, their feet clacking on the marble floor.

It was her first time in the new academy and she was curious. She'd heard rumors of extravagance. Of the project being wildly over budget.

And then quieter whispers, of kickbacks and bribes and contract fixing. But nothing had ever been proven. Most likely because the Sûreté and the Québec government had bigger and more immediate messes to clean up.

But those piles of *merde* were now under control. Those caught up in the corruption scandal within the Sûreté and the government were dead, in prison, or had been fired. And slowly, she suspected, the spotlight was turning toward the academy.

Did that explain Armand Gamache taking over as commander?

Did that explain the murder?

She realized she'd linked the two, and now she stopped herself. Far too early for speculation.

They turned the corner and saw a man standing outside a door. At his feet was a tray and shattered glass and china.

As she drew closer, Isabelle Lacoste recognized him.

Not Armand Gamache. It was Superintendent Brébeuf. And she checked herself yet again. Just plain old Brébeuf now. No longer a superintendent. Though she was so used to seeing him as that, it was her automatic reaction. Old habits, she thought. Very dangerous. As was he.

Brébeuf was alone in the middle of the wide corridor, looking like a man lost, or abandoned.

Isabelle felt her disgust growing with each step. She didn't think it showed on her face, but it must have. He backed up slightly and nodded to her but didn't offer his hand. Not wanting, she suspected, to risk her rejecting the offer in front of so many witnesses.

"Chief Inspector Lacoste," he said. "This is a terrible business."

"Yes."

He'd aged in the few years since she'd last seen him. Lacoste knew that the former superintendent of the Sûreté was the same age as Gamache, but he looked ten, fifteen years older. And while never a robust man, there'd been a sort of wiry vitality about him that many had admired. Including herself.

But now he seemed desiccated. Withered.

"Commander Gamache is inside with the body."

"So I understand," said Chief Inspector Lacoste. "And why are you here?"

He bristled slightly, but only slightly. The instinctive reaction of a once great man, reduced.

"Monsieur Gamache asked me to get the academy doctor from the infirmary. I did. He confirmed that Professor Leduc is dead."

"Is the doctor still in the room?"

"No, he left as soon as death was confirmed."

Isabelle Lacoste continued to stare at him, while her team stood behind her, kits at the ready.

Those who knew who this man was, and once was, were watching with open curiosity.

Brébeuf squared his shoulders, but somehow it only made him look more pathetic. And a thought drifted into her mind. Lacoste wondered if he knew that was the effect. And did it on purpose.

And the purpose was obvious.

It was easier, natural even, to dismiss those who were pathetic. Not to take them seriously, and certainly not to see a threat. There was even an instinctive desire to get out of their company. People who were pathetic were natural targets for the vicissitudes of life. And if you were standing beside one, you might get hit too. Collateral damage.

"I stayed in case he wanted something else," said Brébeuf.

And now, before her eyes, Michel Brébeuf evolved into something else. Not a man disgraced, but a once beloved old mutt, waiting for attention from his master. A smile, a pat. Even a kick.

Anything.

In a very subtle way, Brébeuf seemed to be positioning himself as a loyal servant, and Gamache as a brute. It didn't work on her. She knew the truth. But she suspected some might be taken in.

"And that?" She pointed to the tray and toast and broken glass.

"A cadet found the body," said Beauvoir, stepping forward to answer the question. "He dropped the tray. We left it there."

"I'll take samples," said one of the forensics team, and he did, while another looked for prints and DNA on the door handle, and still another took photographs. And Lacoste wondered at this transformation in Michel Brébeuf.

A leopard might not change its spots, but the former superintendent of the Sûreté had never been a leopard. He was then, and always would be, a chameleon.

When the technician gave the all-clear, she stepped across the threshold, relieved to be away from him. A dead body was preferable to a living Brébeuf.

Though prepared for what she'd see, violent, deliberate death still surprised Isabelle Lacoste. And it had clearly surprised Serge Leduc.

CHAPTER 12

"The academy doctor confirmed the death," said Gamache, standing to one side as the Scene of Crime team got to work.

"I'm assuming the cause is obvious," said Lacoste.

She stood next to her former chief, with Beauvoir on the other side of him. It still felt natural to be on either side of Armand Gamache. It felt safe. Though there was now a sense of nostalgia. Like going back to a childhood home.

Gamache simply nodded.

"We'll have to wait for the coroner to give us the official cause of death, but yes," said Beauvoir, looking down at Serge Leduc. "It would be hard to miss."

"When was he last seen alive?" asked Chief Inspector Lacoste.

"He was at dinner in the dining hall," said Commander Gamache. "That's the last I saw of him."

"Me too," said Beauvoir. "That would be about eight o'clock."

They looked around. There was no evidence that Leduc had entertained anyone in his rooms the evening before.

Neither Gamache nor Beauvoir had ever been in these rooms, the private territory of the Duke.

The apartment was the same layout as the Commander's, only the mirror image. A living room led to a bedroom, with an en suite bath. But while Gamache's was furnished in a modern style that suited the building and managed to make it inviting, this room felt stuffed, stifling.

The furniture was heavy, Victorian. Dark wooden sideboard, massive horsehair sofa upholstered in a deep purple crushed velvet. It felt oppressive, but also vaguely effeminate. A contrast to the stark, linear world beyond his front door.

It was like stepping into a boudoir, or a stage set.

And yet Gamache had the feeling this was not staged. It was a reflection of who this man really was. Or at least an element of him. Much of the furniture, Gamache suspected, had been inherited, passed down within the family, perhaps for generations.

Serge Leduc had wrapped himself in tradition. Even as he broke rule after rule.

But then, the Victorians had revered the Great Man model. A single extraordinary individual for whom the normal rules didn't apply. Great Men should rule and others should revere them. Leduc lived as though he believed it.

"What sort of a man was he?" asked Lacoste.

"What sort would you guess?" asked Gamache. "Judging by what you see."

"Fussy," she said immediately. "Rigid. Probably pedantic and officious."

She looked down at the dead man, still in his street clothes. A jacket and tie. Neat. So at odds with what lay above the collar.

"Am I close?"

"Inspector Beauvoir, how would you describe Serge Leduc?"

"A brute and a bully," said Beauvoir. "Cunning and stupid. A weasel and a rat."

"Both the hunter and the hunted. An uncomfortable position," said Gamache, looking around.

"I would've thought he'd have lots of leather chairs," said Beauvoir. "And antlers on the walls. Not this."

"I wonder if he was happy, when he stepped in here," said Gamache. "He was clearly not happy outside these rooms."

"Well, not since you arrived, anyway," said Beauvoir.

Isabelle Lacoste took that in with interest.

"It wasn't suicide," she said. "He was shot in the right temple, but the gun's on the left side of the body. Now why would that be? Is that his weapon?"

"I don't know," said Gamache. "I ordered that there be no firearms within the academy, except those locked in the armory."

"Does he have a key?"

"He did, when he was second-in-command. But I took it from him and changed the locks. I have a key and the weapons instructor has one. It takes both to open the armory."

"Any ideas who could have done this?"

"He was a divisive figure," said Gamache, after considering for a moment. "Admired by some. Most of the professors who admired him are gone. A lot of the senior class looked up to him. But that, I think, was more fear than respect. This room might look like it belonged to a Victorian gentleman, but the Duke was really from the Dark Ages. He believed in swift and brutal punishment and that you could shape young people by battering away at them, as though they were horseshoes."

Isabelle Lacoste turned her full attention to Gamache. A man who was the antithesis of what he'd just described.

"You didn't like him?"

"No, I did not. You're not thinking . . ." He waved toward the body.

"I'm just asking. The thinking will come later."

He smiled at that. "I neither liked nor trusted him."

"Then why—"

"Did I keep him on? You're far from the first to ask."

"And the answer?"

"To keep an eye on him. You're aware of the rumors of bribery and price fixing and even money laundering associated with the awarding of the contracts for this building?"

"Yes, but not in detail."

"That's because there are no details. Just a whole lot of suspicions. Circumstantial, but no hard evidence."

"You were trying to gather it?" she asked. "Did he know?"

"Yes, I made sure he knew. When I met with him before term started, I showed him what I had."

"Why?" both Lacoste and Beauvoir asked, astonished.

"To shock him."

"Well, it just shocked me," said Beauvoir to Lacoste.

"While looking for corruption in the Sûreté, I kept coming across references to strange dealings at the academy," said Gamache, his voice low so that no one else could hear. "But even more disconcerting than suggestions of corruption in the academy was the behavior of the recent graduates. You must have noticed."

Both Lacoste and Beauvoir nodded.

"There's a brutality about them," she said. "I won't have any in my department."

"Reconsider that, please, Isabelle," said Gamache. "They need decent role models."

"Indecent," she said. "That's the word for them. And I'll consider it. That's why you came here?"

He nodded. "As goes the academy, so goes the Sûreté. I wanted to find out why it was graduating so many cadets steeped in cruelty. And to stop it."

"And have you?"

He sighed. "*Non*. Not yet. But I knew Serge Leduc was at the center of whatever was happening."

"You called him the Duke," said Lacoste. "Why?"

"A nickname the cadets gave him," said Beauvoir. "From his name, obviously. He seemed to like it."

"Not surprised," said Lacoste. "So you showed the Duke what you had on him?"

"Yes. I needed to shake him up. Show him how close I was. Make him do something stupid."

"And did he?"

"I think he did," said Gamache, glancing down at the body. "And so did someone else."

Isabelle Lacoste's eyes shifted over to the gun. "A strange choice of weapon. I can see now that it wouldn't be from the armory. You wouldn't have a handgun like this there, would you?"

Gamache shook his head. "Not even for history class. We only have weapons the cadets need to train on. Ones they'll use in their jobs. No Sûreté agent would have used a gun like that in decades."

Lacoste bent down and took a closer look. "I've never seen one close up. A revolver. Used to be called a six-shooter, didn't it?"

"*Oui*," said Beauvoir, joining her.

She bent closer. "Still five bullets in the chambers."

Lacoste looked across the room, where some of her team were following the spray of blood. Trying to find the sixth.

"On the way down, I was trying to work out why no one heard the shot. Now I know." She used a pencil to point. "It has a silencer."

Lacoste stood back up, but Beauvoir remained on his haunches.

"I didn't think revolvers could have silencers," he said.

"Silencers can be fitted onto anything but they're not usually effective on revolvers," said Gamache.

"The cadet who found the body," said Lacoste. "Where is he?"

"In my rooms," said Gamache. "With one of the professors. He's a freshman. Nathaniel Smythe. Would you like to speak to him?"

"I would." She turned to Jean-Guy Beauvoir, who was still looking at the gun. Then he stood and turned to her.

"Trying to decide whether to invite me along?" he asked. "Am I a suspect?"

"*Oui*. As is Commander Gamache. For now."

Gamache seemed completely unfazed by her statement. He'd come to that conclusion early on.

He was still in his dressing gown and slippers, his hair mussed from sleep, stubble on his face, waiting to be shaved off.

Lacoste wondered if he realized he was in that state. But it didn't seem to matter.

"I'd like you with me, Inspector," she said, then turned to Gamache. "Can you take us to him, please?"

"Of course, Chief Inspector," said Gamache, ushering her out of the room, followed by Beauvoir. Once in the hall, their manner became less formal.

As they walked down the corridor, Isabelle Lacoste had the odd sensation they were not actually making any progress. Each corner they turned led them to a hallway that looked exactly like the one they'd just left.

The old academy, where she'd trained, had been a confusion of narrow corridors, with portraits and pennants and sporting trophies going back generations, with dark wooden staircases and worn carpets muffling the shouts and laughter and conversation of the cadets. The rumor among the students was that the building had once been an asylum. She could believe it. It either housed the insane or drove them there.

It had taken almost the entire three years for her to confidently make her way to the women's toilet, and she privately suspected they moved the women's bathroom every now and then, in protest at even having to have one.

But the new academy was just as confusing, in its own way, because of its utter lack of character and landmarks.

"Did Professor Leduc have any family?" she asked Gamache.

"Not that I know of, but I'll look at his personnel file. If there is family, will you contact them, or shall I?"

They'd arrived at the Commander's rooms, though the door looked like any of the other twenty or so they'd already passed. It struck her as interesting that Gamache's suite was about as far from Professor Leduc's as possible.

And she wondered whose decision that had been.

"Do you have a preference?" she asked.

"I'll do it, if you don't mind," said Gamache. "He was in my employ and was my responsibility."

She nodded.

"You have no idea who might've killed him?" Lacoste pressed, looking from one man to the other.

"*Non*," they both said, but when Gamache reached for the door handle, she stopped him.

"But there is something," she said, studying him.

How well she knew that face, those mannerisms. His ability to hide his thoughts and feelings behind a wall of calm. Even now. It wasn't what was written on his face that had given her pause, but rather his earlier actions.

"Why did you stay in the room?" she asked. "Why not leave and lock the door, once the doctor had confirmed death?"

Jean-Guy had been wondering the same thing and was waiting until they were alone to question Gamache. But Isabelle had gotten there first. He felt a wave of both pride and annoyance.

He'd helped train her. And now he wondered if he'd done too good a job.

"I didn't want him to be alone. Serge Leduc might not have been a good man, and he certainly was no friend. But he does deserve some common decency."

Lacoste studied him for a moment. It was, she had to admit, the sort of thing Armand Gamache would do. And yet . . .

"And you felt he would, if he could speak, prefer that you stare at him in that condition, rather than simply lock the room and leave him in peace?"

She was pushing it, she knew. But if Gamache had been any other man, she'd have asked these same questions. And not let his answer go.

"I did," he said simply. "And I wasn't staring at his body."

"Then what were you doing?" she asked.

Gamache cocked his head slightly and regarded her.

"I was noticing the details of the room." He smiled. "Training and ex-perience."

Then his smile disappeared and he looked stern.

"You're the head of homicide and I respect that. But I'm the commander here, and everyone and everything under this roof is my responsibility. A person not only died, he was murdered. And yes, I chose to use my exper-tise. Do you have a problem with that?"

"You know I do, sir. It wouldn't be tolerated in anyone else. And you, above all, know the importance of keeping a crime scene as clean as possible."

"I do. Which is why I touched nothing. I looked and I breathed."

His voice was curt. Not exactly chastising her, but pushing back.

"I'm sorry if what I did upset you, Chief Inspector. It was only meant to help." Then his voice softened. "Do you really think I killed Serge Leduc?"

Isabelle Lacoste visibly relaxed. "No, I don't."

"Good," he said, smiling. "Because I sure wouldn't want you on my tail."

"And I hope you know that I do respect your position here, Commander. But I'm in charge."

"I do know that, Isabelle. I'm not trying to take over. But I do need to be a part of this investigation. I should tell you that I'll be calling the mayor of Saint-Alphonse to report what's happened. As well as their chief of police."

"Sounds reasonable," she said.

Beauvoir was watching and listening, following closely what was being said, and not said. Mostly he watched Gamache.

While he'd deflected the question, Armand Gamache had not, in fact, properly answered it. And it was the same question he himself had.

Why had Gamache stayed in the room with the body? Lacoste was right. The appropriate action, by an experienced investigator, would have been to leave, lock the door, and await the forensics team.

But Gamache had not done that.

"Right now," said Lacoste, "I need to speak to the cadet who found the body."

"*D'accord*," said Commander Gamache, and opened the door to his rooms.

Nathaniel sat on the edge of the sofa, nervously answering their questions. He seemed to grow more and more agitated as they went on, no matter how benign the question or how gently they were put to him. Though, it must be admitted, the interview had not started well.

"Your name?"

"Nathaniel Smythe."

He'd given it a French pronunciation, though it was obviously an English name and he himself was English. It came out as Nataniel Smite.

"Nathaniel Smythe?" asked Isabelle Lacoste, giving it the proper English pronunciation.

Nathaniel colored. His red hair and fair complexion made the blush immediate and vivid.

Here was a young man desperate to fit in, to pass as Québécois, thought Lacoste. Though his name and coloring would give him away immediately. And while he had not actually lied right out of the gate, he had misled. Tried to pass himself off as something he was not.

It was a small, but telling, detail. And Chief Inspector Lacoste knew murders were built on tiny, almost imperceptible things. They were almost never provoked by a single massive event, but rather by an accumulation of small insults, slights, lies. Bruises. Until the final flesh wound proved fatal.

She looked at young Cadet Smythe. Who'd just tried to pretend he wasn't Anglo. And now she was getting another sense from him.

He's gay, she thought with dismay.

Gay was fine. Anglo was fine. Anglo and gay was fine. Anglo, gay, and in the Sûreté Academy was something else. No wonder this young man's instinct was to hide.

She looked over at Gamache, still in his dressing gown and pajamas, sitting at ease on one of the Eames chairs. She wondered if he had also picked up on it, and she thought he probably had.

"Cadet Smythe is in my class," said the Commander. "And you sometimes come to the gatherings in these rooms."

"*Oui.*"

"Tell us what happened," said Lacoste. Her voice matter-of-fact.

"I was taking Professor Leduc his morning coffee and toast. I knocked on the door, and when there was no answer I tried the handle. It was unlocked, so I opened it."

This raised a number of questions, but Lacoste held off until he'd finished.

"I saw him right away, of course."

He blushed again with the effort of holding it together. Keeping down the emotions, and the vomit.

"And what did you do?" she asked.

"I backed away and yelled for help." He looked at the Commander. "I dropped the tray."

"Naturally," said the Commander. "I would have too."

"Did you go into the room?" Chief Inspector Lacoste asked.

"No."

"Even a little bit? A few steps?" she pressed, her voice suggesting it would be understandable if he had, but the cadet shook his head.

It was the last thing this young man had been tempted to do.

"Why were you taking coffee to Professor Leduc?" Beauvoir asked.

"We do it every morning. Amelia Choquet and I take shifts. A week at a time."

There was a slight movement from Gamache, and an inhale.

He's surprised, thought Lacoste.

"Do you know the practice of freshmen serving meals to professors was stopped when Commander Gamache took over?" Beauvoir asked.

"Professor Leduc told us that, but said it was tradition. That it helped establish respect and order and a chain of command. He said Sûreté Academy traditions were there for a reason and important to uphold."

He said it apparently without understanding the insult to Commander Gamache. It was another small, but telling, detail. It spoke about this student. But mostly it spoke of Serge Leduc and his disdain for the new commander.

And Leduc's willingness to pass his opinions on to the cadets.

Beauvoir didn't look over at Gamache, but watched him in his peripheral vision. His face was again one of calm attentiveness. But his posture had changed. It was more tense.

"Not all traditions are good," said Beauvoir. "That one belittles freshmen. You're agents in training, not servants. I hated it when I was a freshman. I'm interested to see that you don't seem to mind."

"Professor Leduc explained that Amelia and I were specially chosen."

"And did he explain what was special about you?" asked Lacoste.

"We were the most promising."

"I see," she said.

Lacoste turned to Gamache, but he shook his head to say he had no questions, though he was listening intently and watching the young man closely.

"The door to Professor Leduc's rooms was unlocked," Lacoste said. At that moment her iPhone vibrated, but she ignored it. "Was that unusual?"

"No. He often unlocked it first thing in the morning, so we could get in."

"And what did you do, once in his rooms?" asked Lacoste.

"Put down the tray and left."

"And the times he was there?" asked Gamache, finally speaking.

"He'd thank me, and I'd leave."

Chief Inspector Lacoste, after quickly checking a text, got up. "*Merci*, Cadet Smythe." She turned to Gamache and Beauvoir. "Dr. Harris is here. Would you like to come?"

"I think now would be a good time to shower and change," said Gamache. "I'll be along in a few minutes."

He turned to Nathaniel.

"Wait here, please. Pour yourself a coffee, if you'd like."

Gamache pointed to a coffee maker with a full carafe on the sideboard. "I'll be out soon."

Lacoste and Beauvoir left Nathaniel pouring coffee, while Commander Gamache went into the bedroom, closing the door.

He emerged a short time later, shaved, showered, and in a fresh suit and tie. On seeing the Commander, Nathaniel got to his feet.

Gamache waved him to sit back down and, pouring himself a coffee, he joined the cadet.

The sun was up, illuminating a bleak March landscape. Through the floor-to-ceiling windows, they could see patches of snow and patches of gray scrub. A month earlier it had been a wonderland of fresh, clean snow, cut across by trails left by cross-country skis and snowshoes. In another month, it would be alive with spring wildflowers and trees in fresh green bud.

But for now it was a sort of zombie landscape. A living dead.

"So, Cadet Smythe, what did you find out about the map?"

He'd asked the question in flawless English, with just a hint of a British accent, and gestured toward the framed painting on the wall.

Nathaniel hadn't been expecting that question, or the language, and he blushed again.

"*Pardon?*" he asked, in French.

Gamache smiled. "It's okay to be English, you know. If you're not true to yourself, how can you ever recognize the truth in others? I was asking about the map. You and three other cadets were looking into it."

"We stopped," said Nathaniel, still in French. "We got sorta bogged down in coursework."

They were in the odd position, as sometimes happened in Québec, where the Francophone was speaking English and the Anglo was speaking French.

"And what did you do with your copy of it?" he asked.

"The map? I don't know. It's around somewhere, I suppose."

Commander Gamache leaned forward slightly. Enough to be just inside Cadet Smythe's personal space.

"I'm not asking to make conversation, young man. Everything I ask has a purpose, and never more so than now. This is a murder investigation, not a get-together for coffee."

"Yessir."

Nathaniel had switched to English, and his eyes had widened.

"Good. Now, let's try again. What did you do with your copy of the map?"

"I don't know."

On seeing the Commander's face, he blushed again.

"Really, I don't remember. I don't think I threw it away. It's probably in my desk in the dorm."

"Go and find it, please," said Gamache, getting up. "But I do have one more question."

"Yes?"

"Were you ever in Professor Leduc's bedroom?"

"What do you mean?"

"You know what I mean, cadet. There's no fault to you. No law broken, moral or legal. At least on your side. But I need to know."

"No, sir. I was never in his bedroom."

Gamache studied the young man, who now looked as though his head was on fire.

"What was your relationship with Professor Leduc?"

"What do you mean?"

"I know you're afraid. And you have reason to keep your private life private, especially here. This has not been, in the past, the most tolerant of institutions. I think you're very brave to come here."

"I don't know what you're talking about."

Gamache smiled. And nodded. "Just remember, this is now a murder investigation. Your secrets will come out. I'm giving you a chance to tell me quietly."

"There's nothing to tell."

Gamache lowered his voice, even though they were alone in the room.

"I will understand," he said. "Trust me. Please."

Nathaniel Smythe looked into those eyes, and caught the slight scent of sandalwood and rosewater, though he could never have named the actual aromas. He knew he liked it. It was calming. As were the eyes.

But then he remembered Professor Leduc's warnings. About Commander Gamache.

And then he remembered Professor Leduc's body.

"Should I return to my dorm?" he asked, reverting to French. "I can look for the map, if you'd like."

Gamache held his eyes for another moment, then nodded. "In a minute."

He picked up the phone and placed a call.

Before long, there was a knock on the door, and a professor stood there. "Please take Cadet Smythe back to his room, then on to the dining hall."

"What should I tell the others?" Nathaniel asked at the door. "About Professor Leduc? Everyone will want to know."

"Tell them the truth."

When the door closed, Gamache looked at it for a moment, then shifted his gaze to the framed map on the wall.

The smears of brown that might be mud, or not. The wear and tear. The fine contours, like the lines on a weather-beaten face. The rivers and valleys. The cow and pyramid and three tiny pines. And the snowman, his arms raised in victory. Or surrender.

Gamache exhaled a long breath he didn't know he'd been holding.

The map had been hidden for a reason, Ruth had said. Walled up for a reason.

Gamache took his coffee to the window and stared out.

He thought and he thought, then he called the mayor and the chief of police.

And then he returned down the deserted hallways, to Serge Leduc's murdered body.

They'd have found it by now. What he'd seen in Serge Leduc's bedside table.

A copy of the map.

CHAPTER 13

Dr. Sharon Harris had seen worse in her time as coroner. Far worse. Horrible, horrific things. As far as disfigurement went, this was fairly tame. If she didn't turn him over and look at his full head. And if she didn't turn her own head, to see where the rest of his had gone.

Which, of course, she did.

Dr. Harris got to her feet and, peeling off the latex gloves, stepped away from the body of Serge Leduc and joined Jean-Guy Beauvoir and Isabelle Lacoste.

"He was dead before he hit the ground. Probably just before midnight. Single shot to the temple and no other wounds. Looks like the bullet was a hollow-point. What used to be called a man stopper, for obvious reasons."

They did not need to refer to the body to know the reason.

"Have they found the bullet yet?" Dr. Harris asked.

"No," said Beauvoir. He waved toward the opposite wall. "They're looking."

Just then there was a knock on the door and Armand Gamache entered. He and Dr. Harris greeted each other as old friends, having consulted on many cases in the past.

"I was just saying that the cause of death is not in doubt," she said. "And his death was fast, almost merciful."

"It seems Professor Leduc just stood there and let it happen," said Isabelle Lacoste. "No sign of a struggle at all. Now why was that?"

"Because he didn't believe the murderer would actually pull the trigger?" asked the coroner.

"Maybe he didn't think the gun was loaded," said Lacoste. "Maybe the murderer had no intention of killing Leduc and ran away, terrified at what he'd done."

Beauvoir walked over to the Scene of Crime investigators, happy to get away from all the maybes and talk facts.

He knew that motive was important, but often they never really got to the heart of the matter. Never learned the real reasons someone took a life. Those were often too shrouded, too complex for even the killer to understand.

But good, solid evidence? That's where a murderer was found and trapped. In lies and DNA. In secrets revealed and in fingerprints found.

Still, years of working with Chief Inspector Gamache had rubbed off on him, and he grudgingly admitted that feelings played a role in creating a murderer. And could, perhaps, play a role in finding him. Just not as big a role as the facts.

Isabelle Lacoste now joined him in discussing progress with the Scene of Crime agent in charge, leaving the coroner and the Commander with the body.

Dr. Harris looked from Gamache to the homicide victim, then back to Gamache. And on her face there grew a look of surprise, even wonderment.

"You didn't like him, did you?" she said.

"Is it that obvious?"

She nodded. It was more what wasn't in his expression than what was. Compassion was missing.

"I kept him on," said Gamache, almost under his breath. "I could have fired him."

"Then you didn't dislike him?" asked Sharon Harris, having difficulty following. But she, more than most, knew that emotions were far from linear. They were circles and waves and dots and triangles. But they were rarely a straight line.

Every day she dissected the end result of some untamed emotion.

Gamache knelt beside the body, staring at the wound on Leduc's temple. And the much larger exit wound. Then he followed the remains of Serge Leduc, which were fanned across the room, to where agents were combing for the bullet.

"Found it."

But the voice didn't come from one of the Sûreté agents Gamache was watching. And the find was not the bullet.

They turned and saw an agent standing at the door to the bedroom.

"In the bottom drawer, under some dress shirts," she said as she led Chief Inspector Lacoste and the others into the bedroom.

There, under the neatly folded and laundered shirts, was a leather box.

The agent had opened it, and inside was red velvet covering a precise mold. Of a revolver. There was another space for the silencer, and empty slots for six bullets.

"So it was his," said Lacoste, and straightened up.

They looked from the empty case through the door into the living room, each trying to figure out how the revolver got from one place to the other. Had it been taken there by Leduc, or his killer?

"*Excusez-moi*," said an agent, looking into the room. "You called the Saint-Alphonse police chief, I understand, sir."

The agent was speaking to Gamache, who nodded. "And the mayor."

"They're both here," said the agent. "We've put them in your office."

"*Merci.* I'll join them in a few minutes."

"Fucking Leduc," muttered Beauvoir. "Keeping a loaded gun in his rooms. Unlocked. In a school. Stupid, stupid man."

"Either Leduc brought the gun out, or the murderer did," said Lacoste. "In which case, the murderer must have known Leduc well enough to know there was a gun and where it was kept."

"There's something I need to show you," said Commander Gamache.

Amelia Choquet sat at the long table, empty chairs between herself and the cadets on either side.

They'd been moved into the dining hall so that a search of their rooms could be conducted. Around her conversation buzzed, and far from dying down after the first flush of news, it had grown as speculation spread.

> Rumor was loose in the air,
> hunting for some neck to land on.

The cadets were shocked. And excited. Some were frightened and trying to hide it inside bravado.

Every now and then, there was a glance in her direction. She could tell what they were thinking. If there had to be a killer, let it be the weird one.

The easiest target. The one no one would defend.

Amelia shoved the sleeves of her uniform up to her elbows. Showing them the images and words etched into her skin, like a birthmark.

Their pink and perfect faces frowned in disapproval.

She was sticking her neck out, she knew.

Professor Leduc was dead. Murdered.

And she wondered how long it would be before they came for her.

"Can I sit down?"

She looked up, and there was Nathaniel, a soft white hand on the back of the chair next to her.

A *fuck off* caught in her throat, but instead she nodded.

"No one wants to sit with me," he said. "Once I told them everything I knew. I think they think I did it and sitting close to me would make them look guilty too."

"They're afraid," said Amelia.

"I'm afraid," said Nathaniel. "Aren't you? Look at what happened. How it happened—"

"Be quiet," she warned, and deeply regretted letting him join her.

"Commander Gamache was asking about the map," he whispered, leaning close to her. "He wanted me to find mine."

He brought out a piece of paper and smoothed it on the table, but she swept it off.

"Get away from me."

But it was too late.

With him joining her, the hunt for a neck to land on was over. She could tell. Not by the way the other students looked at her, but the way they looked away.

Gamache reached out and, using a pen, he pulled open the drawer of the bedside table.

"This was almost certainly already seen by your agents," he said, replacing the pen in his breast pocket and putting his hands behind his back. "But the Scene of Crime team couldn't know its significance."

"And what is its significance?" asked Lacoste.

"I've seen it before," said Beauvoir, bending closer. "It's a map."

Like Gamache, he held his hands behind his back.

For years, he'd assumed it was a mannerism of the older man, but as the investigations piled up, Inspector Beauvoir came to appreciate it for what it really was.

In holding his hands behind his back, Chief Inspector Gamache was less likely to instinctively reach out and touch something that should not be touched. From there, it became a mannerism. But the root of it was practical.

There was, Beauvoir was beginning in his late thirties to understand, a purpose for every action. From the blaring act of murder to the subtle grasp of one hand in the other.

Now Beauvoir turned to Gamache.

His mentor, his boss, his father-in-law. But still, in so many ways, a mystery.

"You saw it when we first found the body," he said. No use hiding that fact, even if he'd wanted to. "When I opened the drawer. You suggested we leave, and so I closed it without even looking. But you saw. That's why you hustled me out. Why didn't you say something then?"

"I needed to think," said Gamache.

"About what?" asked Lacoste. She too was surprised that Armand Gamache should conceal evidence. That might be overstating it, she knew. He didn't so much hide the map as fail to point it out as soon as he himself had seen it.

"This is a copy." Gamache waved toward the paper. "I have the original, here in my rooms."

"You do?" asked Lacoste. "Then why . . . how?"

"Yes," said Gamache. "Why. How. Jean-Guy is right. I saw the map when he opened the drawer, but it was fleeting and from a distance. I needed to make sure."

"You didn't touch it?" asked Lacoste.

"*Non.*"

"But why didn't you tell us right away?"

"I used the map as an assignment for four of the cadets," he explained. "I gave them each a copy. Nathaniel Smythe was one of the cadets."

"And you thought—?" she asked.

"I wondered if he'd given his to Leduc," said Gamache. "But he claims to still have it. He went back to his dorm to look for it."

"So four copies were made?" asked Lacoste.

"Five. I made one for myself."

"Do you have yours?"

"It's in Three Pines."

"Three Pines," said Lacoste, staring down at the map in the drawer. "That's what the map is of." She looked closer. "Huh. I've never seen a map of the village."

"That was the assignment. To find out why this one was made. But also to try to find out why Three Pines disappeared from every other map of the area."

"And?"

"Nathaniel says they put the assignment on hold," said Gamache. "It wasn't for credit, just to hone their investigative skills. They were overwhelmed with actual coursework."

"And do you believe him?" asked Lacoste.

Armand Gamache looked at her, then at the map, and sighed. "I don't know."

"You want to, though."

"Nathaniel Smythe was one of the applicants who'd been rejected by Leduc. I accepted him. I thought he showed promise. It is, I have to admit, disappointing to know he'd grown close to Serge Leduc."

"The question," said Lacoste, "is how close."

"*Oui.*"

She called a technician over and asked that the map be sent to the lab and given special attention.

They watched as the agent placed it in an evidence bag.

"The question isn't just who gave Leduc the map," said Beauvoir, following it out of the bedroom. "But why Serge Leduc wanted it, and chose to keep it."

"And keep it so close," said Lacoste. "There's something intimate about a bedside table."

Beauvoir was fidgeting. Another nettle had dug into his skin. Perhaps not the largest of thorns, but an irritant nonetheless.

"You've had time to think," said Lacoste to Gamache. "Any conclusions?"

"No, but something strange did happen. Shortly after I gave the cadets the maps and the assignment, someone followed me home."

"To Three Pines? Why didn't you say something?" asked Beauvoir, immediately alarmed.

"Because I didn't want to alarm anyone," said Gamache with a smile. "And I don't know who it was, or why. Nothing came of it."

"You think it was Leduc?" asked Lacoste. "And that the map has something to do with all this?"

"I don't see how," Gamache admitted. "The murderer couldn't have been looking for it, since Leduc didn't exactly hide it and the place doesn't seem to have been searched. I don't think the map has anything to do with his death."

"But it worries you?" said Jean-Guy.

Armand Gamache nodded, very slowly.

"It worries me because one of my students must've given him the map, and it worries me because Serge Leduc kept it. Which leads me to believe he valued it for some reason."

Gamache turned to Isabelle Lacoste.

"Please believe me. If I thought for a moment that map had anything to do with the murder, I'd have said something immediately."

"I do believe you, *patron*," she said. "But we still have to make sure. Can you give me the names of the other cadets who had copies?"

"Besides Nathaniel Smythe, there were two seniors, Huifen Cloutier and Jacques Laurin. He's the head cadet. And another freshman, Amelia Choquet."

"The other cadet who served him coffee in the morning?" Lacoste glanced down at the dead man.

"Yes. When you analyze the paper, can you tell me what you find?" asked Gamache.

"Of course," said Lacoste.

"With your permission, I'd like to invite those four down to Three Pines."

"Now?"

"Yes, immediately," said Gamache.

"Why? If the map's of no real importance?"

"What it does tell us is that one of those four had a close relationship with Professor Leduc. Close enough for them to give him the map, and close enough for him to keep it. For whatever reason. Whoever that was might know more than they realize about his death."

"Or might know more about his death, period," said Lacoste.

"Yes."

"Are you taking them away to protect them, or to protect the rest of the academy?"

"I'm taking them away because I can't answer that question," said Gamache. "There's a killer here. Someone who put a gun to the head of an unarmed man, and shot. Do you think that person would hesitate to do the same thing to a student, if that young man or woman became a threat? The sooner they get out of here, the better."

Isabelle Lacoste nodded but was far from certain if, in removing the cadets to Three Pines, Gamache wasn't also removing the murderer. To Three Pines.

"I'll tell them the map might figure in Professor Leduc's death and ask them to restart their investigation," said Gamache. "That'll explain it."

"I have no objection. Inspector?"

Jean-Guy Beauvoir also shook his head.

"I've spoken with Cadet Smythe," said Lacoste. "We'll need to interview the other three before they can leave. The students' rooms are being searched now."

"I'll get the agents to be extra thorough with those four," said Beauvoir, and stepped away to speak to one of the investigators, who left the room.

"I'm going to address the school," said Gamache, looking at his watch. It was only ten in the morning, though it felt like midafternoon. "Can you assemble the students and staff in the auditorium?"

One of the agents nodded and left.

"*Bon*. While he does that, I'll go to my office to see the mayor and the police chief." Gamache turned to Chief Inspector Lacoste. "There's something else we need to discuss. Can you come by my office in an hour?"

"Of course."

"Let me walk you out," said Beauvoir to Gamache. Once in the corridor he asked, "Do you really think that map has nothing to do with Leduc's murder?"

"I don't see how it could."

But he looked uncertain, and as Beauvoir watched Gamache walk purposefully down the corridor, he squirmed slightly, rolling his shoulders to relieve the tension and the prickling sensation between his blades.

CHAPTER 14

⌐

Silence fell over the student body as Commander Gamache walked onto the stage.

He stood at the very center and waited. Only when he had their complete attention did he start to talk.

He told them what had happened. He spoke simply, clearly. Neither minimizing the horror of having a professor murdered on campus, nor turning it into a melodrama.

He gave them just enough information to stop much of the more lurid speculation, but not so much as to compromise the investigation.

He did not mention the revolver. He just said that Professor Leduc had been killed by a single shot to the head.

He said nothing about the map.

"Are there any questions?" he asked when he'd finished.

A hundred hands went up.

"That are not 'Do we know who killed Professor Leduc?'" he clarified, and most of the hands went down. "Or 'Do we know why he was killed?'"

Most of the rest of the hands went down.

"Yes, Cadet Thibodeau." Gamache pointed to a third-year student, who stood up.

"When will we be allowed back in our rooms?"

Gamache considered him for a moment. "Are you asking if what we find in your rooms during the search will be held against you? Dope, for instance. Or booze. Or stolen exam papers."

There was shifting in the seats.

"We will have a quiet word about what we find, but it will be kept internal unless there's a particularly grievous breach or it's evidence in this crime."

Cadet Thibodeau nodded and sat down, clearly concerned but relieved.

There were a few other questions, about procedure, and classes, and what they could say to family and friends.

"Tell them the truth," said Gamache. "Some of you will be questioned by Chief Inspector Lacoste and her homicide team. Mostly those of you who were students of Professor Leduc or who met with—"

"Liar."

Gamache raised his hand to his forehead, to better see who had spoken. But the person remained hidden in the crowd.

"If you have something to say, stand and face me," said Gamache, his voice deep and calm, carrying to the very back of the room.

The cadets turned in their seats and looked around the auditorium.

At the front of the room, Gamache waited. When no one stood up, he continued as though there'd been no interruption.

"You'll be allowed back in your rooms within the hour. If you know anything that could be helpful, however trivial you think it is, keep it to yourself until you can speak to one of the investigators. Unfortunately, you now have a chance to see a homicide investigation from the inside. It is not attractive. It is not exciting. A lot will be revealed that people had hoped to keep hidden. And not simply the contents of your rooms."

Nervous laughter met that comment. And when it died down, the Commander continued.

"Make no mistake, it will all come to light. Far easier if you volunteer than that it be dragged out into the open."

"Hypocrite," the same voice yelled.

Now there was an audible murmur in the room as students reacted. Some with shock. Some with nervous amusement.

Commander Gamache stared into the gathering of cadets and slowly they grew silent. The room waited for his response, bracing for the explosion.

After a few very long moments, Commander Gamache did what none of them expected.

He smiled. Very, very slightly. And then the smile faded and he spoke. Softly, but the words penetrated each and every person in the room.

"Be careful. This is a time of menace. There's a murderer among us. Almost certainly in this room." He paused, and then he looked at them with such caring that a few sighed, breathing out lifelong tension. "It's too easy to feed the anger. Too cowardly to stoke the hate. You must look inside yourself and decide who you are and who you want to be. Character is not created in times like these. It's revealed. This is a trying time. A testing time. Be careful."

Then Armand Gamache walked off the stage.

"Coward," the voice pursued him.

The word hit, then glided off Commander Gamache's back. He didn't pause, didn't hesitate, his stride unbroken.

Amelia sat forward, leaning toward the stage. Even after the Commander had disappeared. She stared at the empty space once occupied by him.

Commander Gamache had spoken those words to each and every cadet, including herself. But his eyes had lingered on one young man. And that was when his expression had changed. And that look of almost aching caring had settled there.

He knew exactly who had shouted those words, shot those words, at him. And Gamache had spoken directly to the young man. Be careful.

"Huh," she murmured.

"What?" said the cadet beside her.

"Screw off," she said, though her heart wasn't in it. She was thinking.

Chief Inspector Isabelle Lacoste, standing at the back of the room with Jean-Guy Beauvoir, inhaled sharply.

"Don't they know?" she whispered.

"Who he is?" asked Beauvoir. "They either don't know or don't care. Serge Leduc successfully poisoned the well before Gamache arrived, and added shit for the past couple of months."

"And he couldn't fight it?" asked Lacoste.

Around them the room had erupted in speculation. About the murderer, and about the words hurled at the Commander.

"He chose not to," said Beauvoir. "He said it was a deliberate distraction and there was too much to do to waste time waging war on the Duke."

"They're fools."

"Not all of them."

While it looked, quite understandably to Lacoste, as if Gamache might have lost control of the academy, Jean-Guy Beauvoir saw something else in that room.

Like her, he'd heard the open insults to Gamache. But Beauvoir now saw pockets of quiet as some of the cadets contemplated what had just happened. And began to evolve their thinking.

"You're a fool," hissed Huifen.

"What? Everyone was thinking it," said Jacques.

"Not everyone. Not anymore anyway."

Her keen eyes took in the activity around them. And in some cases, the inactivity. The quiet that had come over more than a few of her fellow cadets.

Then she studied him. So handsome. Fine, intelligent features. Muscular. From rock climbing and rowing and hockey. His body contained a strapping energy she found almost irresistible. She dreamed of running her hands over those taut muscles, even as she was doing it. She dreamed of wrapping her arms and legs around him, even as she was doing it.

But now, and not for the first time, she wondered what else was contained in that fine body. In that mind. And what would happen if those straps ever broke.

When Huifen got back to her room, she found a woman waiting for her and an agent searching her belongings.

"Cadet Cloutier?"

"*Oui.*"

"I'm Chief Inspector Lacoste, of homicide. Have a seat, please."

Huifen sat on the edge of her bed and watched the agent go through the dresser drawers.

Lacoste took the desk chair and crossed her legs, comfortably.

"Where were you last night, between ten and two in the morning?"

"Here. In bed."

"Alone?"

"Yes."

"Did you get up at all, to go to the bathroom? Get a drink?"

"No, I was asleep. Between classes and all the activities and sports, it's pretty exhausting."

Lacoste smiled. "I remember. What was your relationship with Professor Leduc?"

"I was one of his students. And I suppose you could call him a mentor."

"Did he choose you, or did you choose him?"

Huifen regarded the Chief Inspector. It was an insightful and uncomfortable question.

"He chose me. When I was a freshman, he invited me to bring him his morning coffee. Then, after a while, he began inviting me to his rooms in the evening."

"What for?"

"Talks. We weren't alone," Huifen hurried to reassure her, "if that's what you think. It wasn't like that. He just spoke to us, about policing, about the Sûreté. He took an interest in certain cadets."

"His death must be a shock."

And yet it was clear to Lacoste that this young woman wasn't at all shocked. And certainly not saddened. But she was nervous.

"It is," said Huifen.

"You're just a few months away from graduating and becoming an agent in the Sûreté. You know how this works. Any idea who did this?"

"I think you should ask the Commander."

"Really? Why?"

"They hated each other. It was obvious."

"How so?"

"By what they said about each other."

"What did Professor Leduc say about Commander Gamache?"

"That he was weak, and was weakening the academy and the Sûreté. That he was a coward."

Lacoste pressed her lips together for a moment before she could speak again.

"And what did Commander Gamache say about Professor Leduc?"

Huifen opened her mouth, then slowly shut it again as she racked her brain. What had she heard him say about the Duke?

She looked at Chief Inspector Lacoste, who was nodding.

"Nothing, right?"

Huifen nodded.

"You won't make a very good agent if you take gossip as fact, Cadet Cloutier."

The agent searching the small room leaned down and spoke into Lacoste's ear and handed her something. She looked at it and thanked him.

"Please pack up a few things," she told Huifen, getting to her feet. "Overnight things. And please bring this with you."

She handed the stunned young woman the map of Three Pines, and left.

Down the hall, Inspector Beauvoir was just leaving Jacques Laurin's room.

"I'm pretty sure he's the one who insulted Monsieur Gamache," said Beauvoir, as the two investigators fell into step.

"Why?"

"Why do I think it, or why would he?"

"Both."

"Because he's one of Serge Leduc's Mini-Mes. Was his servant, as a fresh-man."

"So was Cadet Cloutier." She waved toward Huifen's rooms. "Did you find the map?"

"Yes. He still has it."

"So does Cadet Cloutier. That's two accounted for."

"I told him to pack an overnight case and bring the map with him, but I didn't tell him where he was going. The little shit looked pretty scared."

"But if Professor Leduc was their mentor, and they respected him, they almost certainly didn't kill him," said Lacoste.

"Well, I wouldn't rule it out," said Beauvoir. "Worship can turn to hatred pretty fast in young people. If Leduc found new favorites."

"Like the other two cadets," said Lacoste. "The freshmen."

"Maybe."

"You take the young woman," said Lacoste. "I'll speak to Nathaniel Smythe again. See if he's found his map."

Nathaniel produced the map.

"*Bon.*" She studied it, then handed it back. Three down. "When you met with Serge Leduc in the evenings, what did you do?"

"How do you know I met with him?"

The young man turned an outrageous color.

"I've spoken with other cadets, you know."

"There were a bunch of us," said Nathaniel. "We didn't meet often, just when the Duke invited us over."

"And were there always others? Were you ever alone?"

"Never."

"And last night?"

"I had dinner, then hockey practice, then came back here and did home-work. We had to design a step-by-step investigation of a break-and-enter."

"When did you go to bed?"

"About eleven, I guess."

"From what you saw, did anyone particularly dislike Professor Leduc?"

"Well, he wasn't the most popular professor," said Nathaniel. "But people respected him."

"Respected or feared?"

Nathaniel remained silent.

"You? Which did you feel?"

"I respected him."

"Why?"

"I— I—"

"You feared him, didn't you?" she asked quietly.

"Never. I was grateful he chose me."

Lacoste nodded. That might actually be true. With the Duke as his mentor, the other cadets might leave him alone. But Leduc must have known this young man had been one of his rejects, and that Commander Gamache himself had reversed that decision.

Is that why Leduc had adopted him? Because Gamache had favored him? He wanted to sour anything and anyone special to the Commander?

"Please pack some things for a few nights away," she said, getting to her feet. "And bring the map along."

Nathaniel also rose. "What? Why?"

"Have you been taught to question orders?"

"No."

"Then do it, please."

She left, shaking her head. She could see what Monsieur Gamache was up against in his new post.

"It's here somewhere," said Amelia.

First the Sûreté agent and now she herself searched the entire room while Jean-Guy Beauvoir watched.

It didn't take long. There was a single bed, a desk. A chest of drawers and a small closet, with a school uniform hanging there.

The chest of drawers was empty aside from one drawer of socks and underwear and bras.

But there were books. Stacked on the shelves above the desk, and sitting on the floor, lining the walls. Amelia had created a makeshift bookcase using bricks and old two-by-fours.

She opened each book, shaking it. But nothing fell out.

"Give it up," said Beauvoir. "The map's not here."

He indicated the bed, and she sat. He pulled the desk chair close, and after sitting down he leaned toward her and quietly asked, "Where is it?"

"I don't know."

She seemed genuinely perplexed.

While Beauvoir didn't much like what he saw when he looked at Amelia

Choquet, he had to admit since the beginning of the term Cadet Choquet had never pretended to be anything other than what she was.

It was refreshing and alarming at the same time.

But that did not mean, Beauvoir knew, that she wasn't capable of lying.

"Did you give it to Professor Leduc?"

"What?" she asked. "No, of course not. Why would I?"

"When did you last see it?" Beauvoir asked.

"I don't know."

"Try, cadet."

Up until then, this somewhat attractive professor had been just that to Amelia. A professor. He taught Scene of Crime management and techniques. He was also, she knew, Commander Gamache's second-in-command.

And his son-in-law. She'd learned that from the photo she'd seen in the Commander's home. But it was a secret she was hoarding, to be used at the *moment juste*.

But Amelia had not thought of him as a full-blown inspector within the homicide department, and one of the more senior officers in the Sûreté. Didn't even know he was that.

Until this moment.

Before her eyes, the professor became the senior inspector.

Amelia shook her head and lifted her hands in resignation.

"I don't know where it is."

"Professor Leduc asked you to be one of his servants," said Beauvoir.

"He didn't ask," she said. "He told. And he didn't describe it as a servant. It was an honor, an opportunity."

"Did you see it like that?"

"I didn't think I had much choice. I just did it."

"You don't sound like you liked the man."

"I don't like anyone," she said.

"Did you dislike him?"

"I don't dislike anyone."

"Really?" he said. "You're above all that nasty human stuff?"

"Look, I'm here to learn how to be a Sûreté agent. Not to make friends."

"You do know that the people you meet here will be your colleagues for many, many years to come? Perhaps you'd better learn to like, or even to dislike, them."

"Yessir."

Beauvoir watched her, and in her eyes he saw intelligence. And if not fear, then worry.

She had reason, he knew, to be worried. She even had reason to be afraid.

Her map was missing. Either she gave it to the dead man, or someone took it and planted it there. Either way, attention was focusing on her. Cadet Choquet was in the crosshairs. He knew it. And clearly she knew it too.

"Pack up a few things, please. You'll be going away for a few nights. An agent will escort you out."

"Why? Because of the map?" Amelia called after him, but got no response.

"May I come in?" Lacoste asked, knocking once and opening the door. "You've had your meeting with the mayor and the police chief?"

Gamache got up from behind his desk and greeted her, motioning to a chair by the sofa, while he took the other one.

"*Oui.* That poor man. I feel for him. I've tried for the last few months to regain the mayor's trust. He finally, against the wishes of his councilors, endorsed the volunteer program with the academy at the last town meeting, only to have this happen."

"But the two aren't connected," said Lacoste.

"No, but it puts the academy in a very bad light, wouldn't you say? When one of our own professors is murdered? How can the mayor now say it's safe for kids to come and use our pool or the hockey rink?"

"I see," she said, and saw that Gamache was genuinely saddened. But not, she suspected, by the brutal murder of one of his colleagues. He was saddened that a good man like the mayor, and the children of the community, were being hurt, once again, by Serge Leduc.

"The chief of police was more sanguine," he said. "Offering to help."

Isabelle Lacoste straightened the crease in her slacks, then looked up at Armand Gamache.

"I had no idea this was such a hostile environment, *patron.*"

He smiled. "Nor did I, to be honest. I expected resistance when I first arrived, and God knows, I found it. I expected Serge Leduc to try to contaminate and control the feeling on campus. Which he did. I expected that the third-year students would be a lost generation. Which they are. Almost."

He looked at her and considered for a moment.

"Do you know why the armed forces recruit eighteen-year-olds?"

"Because they're young and healthy?" she asked.

"Healthier than a twenty-three-year-old? No. It's because they're malleable. You can get an eighteen-year-old to believe almost anything. To do almost anything."

"The same could be said for street gangs and terrorist organizations," said Lacoste. "Get them young."

The thought set her back. The words had come out casually, but their meaning took a moment to sink in. Serge Leduc had essentially turned the Sûreté Academy into a terrorist training ground.

Within a few short years, he'd soured a once fine institution. Not just the academy—from here his cadets would become Sûreté agents. And rise through the ranks. No, not would. Had. They were already inside the Sûreté.

And worst of all, these young men and women wouldn't see anything wrong with what they did. Or were about to do. Because they'd been told it was right.

Armand Gamache had chosen this post for a reason. To right the balance. And to do that he had to stop Serge Leduc.

She watched as Commander Gamache got up and walked to his desk.

An alertness stole over her. The sort that came to highly trained, finely attuned officers.

Serge Leduc had been stopped. Utterly and completely.

But it wasn't Monsieur Gamache's doing, she told herself. He had nothing to do with it. He had nothing to do with it. Nothing.

She watched as Gamache picked up a dossier and returned to his chair.

"You could've fired him, *patron*," she said. "You might not have been able to arrest him for corruption, but at least that would stop him from doing more damage."

"Firing Leduc would solve nothing. The problem would simply be shifted onto someone else. The Leducs of this world will always find fertile ground. If not with the Sûreté, then with another police force. Or a private security firm. No. Enough was enough. It had to end, and the people he'd already corrupted, here and in the Sûreté, had to see that his philosophy would no longer be tolerated."

"And how did you intend to do that, sir?"

He looked at her closely now, quizzically. "Are you saying what I think you are? Are you suggesting I might have stopped him with a bullet in the small hours of this morning?"

"I need to ask," she said. "And you need to answer. I'm not making small talk."

"No, and neither am I," he said, sitting back in his chair. "You think I'm capable of cold-blooded murder?"

She paused, holding his eyes. "I do."

That sat between them for a very long moment.

"For what it's worth, I think I am too," she said.

"Under the right circumstances," Gamache said, nodding slowly.

"*Oui.*"

"The question is, what are the right circumstances?" said Gamache.

"It must have become clear to you, *patron*, that Serge Leduc was winning. He'd already polluted the third-year cadets. You yourself said they were beyond redemption—"

"I said almost beyond. I haven't given up on them."

"Then why not teach a third-year class yourself? You only take the freshmen."

"True. I gave the seniors someone better. Someone with more to teach them than I ever could."

"Jean-Guy?" she asked, not even trying to disguise her doubt.

"Michel Brébeuf."

Isabelle Lacoste sat very still. As though something horrible had entered the room and she didn't want to attract its notice.

Finally she spoke.

"A known traitor?"

"An example," said Gamache. "A powerful example of what corruption will do. It robbed Michel Brébeuf of everything he cared about. His colleagues, his friends, his self-respect. His career. His family. He lost everything. Serge Leduc was promising the cadets power and rewards. Michel Brébeuf is the reality check. What really happens to corrupt Sûreté officers."

"Does he know that?"

"He knows he's been given this chance to redeem himself. To close the gate."

Isabelle Lacoste cocked her head slightly, missing the allusion.

"And suppose he doesn't try to redeem himself?" she asked. "Suppose he sees this as his chance to get back in? Suppose he's gone back to his old ways and has found his own fertile ground. Aren't you worried that putting Michel Brébeuf, Serge Leduc, and a school full of impressionable cadets together will be a disaster?"

"Of course I am," he snapped, then quickly reined himself in. He looked at her, his eyes sharp and the anger just below the surface. "You can't possibly think I don't worry about that every moment of every day. But how do you put out a wildfire? With another fire."

"A controlled burn," said Isabelle Lacoste, then lowered her voice. "Controlled."

"You think I've lost control?"

"There's a body being taken to a morgue, and you were heckled by the cadets." She sighed. "I do think you've lost control. And please know, I say that with the greatest respect. If anyone could have solved this problem, it would've been you."

"But you think I've made it worse?"

She opened her mouth, then closed it.

"I'm not going to sit here and tell you the murder of Serge Leduc was part of my plan," said Gamache. "Or anything I thought remotely possible. But I won't back down. You've never run away, Isabelle. Even when you could have. Even when you should have, to save yourself."

He smiled at her now, with those same deep brown eyes that had looked up at her as he lay dying on a factory floor and she was desperate to stanch the blood. As automatic weapons fire hissed overhead and the walls around them exploded with bullets and the air was thick with dust and shouting and the screams of mortally wounded men and women.

She'd stayed with him. Held his hand. Listened to what they both knew would be his last words. *Reine-Marie.*

He'd placed those words into Isabelle Lacoste. And with them all his heart and soul. All his happiness, and an apology. *Reine-Marie.*

Gamache had survived, of course. And Isabelle had not had to deliver that final message.

"And I won't run away now," he said. "We stay the course."

"*Oui,*" she said.

"We've seen worse, haven't we, Isabelle?" he said.

She smiled. "We have. At least the cadets aren't armed and shooting at us. Yet."

Gamache gave a single gruff laugh. "I've asked the chief of police to quietly take all the ammunition from the armory. The weapons will stay, but there'll be nothing to fire."

Her smile disappeared. "I was joking. But you're seriously expecting trouble on that scale?"

"I was not expecting a murder," he said. His face as serious as she'd ever seen. "The cadets must be safe. The only thing more dangerous than a killer is a killer trapped. He is now trapped inside the academy. Best not to have an armory at his disposal."

"Or an army," said Lacoste, remembering the reaction in the auditorium. "Serge Leduc had a lot of supporters."

"Yes, but did you see any grief?"

That set Lacoste back, and after thinking for a moment she shook her head. "No."

"No," said Gamache. "The problem with the breath of kings."

"The breath of kings?"

"Who float upon the tide of state," said Gamache. "I only wish Jean-Guy was here to appreciate this."

"Another poem?" she asked, knowing full well it must be.

"Hmmm, Jonathan Swift."

He handed her the dossier he'd retrieved off his desk.

"What's this?"

"The gun I held to Serge Leduc's head," said Gamache. "Read it and tell me what you think."

She took it and got up. "*Merci.* I will. Is there an office I can use?"

"There's a boardroom across the hall."

"Perfect."

Though she was on her feet, Gamache himself had not risen. And so, taking the cue, Lacoste sat back down.

"There's more?"

"Of a political nature, nothing that will help solve the murder, I'm afraid," said Gamache. "There are some considerations in running a department. Especially one with as high a profile as homicide."

"Yes?"

"Justice must be seen to be done."

"I agree."

It was an old adage, a cliché even, and Gamache was not given to spouting clichés. So when he did, it must be particularly apropos.

" 'Not only must justice be done,' " she quoted, " 'it must also be seen to be done.' What are you saying? That I need to hold a news conference?"

"Well, that might not be a bad idea, but my thoughts run to something more nuanced. This is the Sûreté Academy. The professors are all former officers or those on leave, like Inspector Beauvoir, or people who do contract work with the Sûreté. I'm the former head of homicide. Your former boss."

Chief Inspector Lacoste got it then.

"In effect, it's the Sûreté investigating the Sûreté."

"In a murder case," said Gamache.

She nodded, considering. "You think I should call Chief Superintendent Brunel and ask that an outside agency take over?"

"*Non*," he shook his head. "Not take over. You must fight against that. Simply ask that an outside investigator be sent. Someone who can vouch for the fairness of your investigation."

She sat thinking. Her thoughts were not happy ones. "Have you ever had to do that?"

"Twice. It was not pleasant. But it had to be done. And better to have it come from you than be imposed. I suspect Chief Superintendent Brunel is contemplating it even now."

Lacoste pulled out her iPhone and punched in the number for the head of the Sûreté. "Is there someone I should ask for specifically?"

"No," he said, getting to his feet. "That would taint it. You have to take what comes. I'll leave you to it."

Gamache stepped into his outer office just as Jean-Guy arrived.

"They're heading down to Three Pines, *patron*."

"Good. *Merci*."

Now, close up, Beauvoir could see how stressed Gamache really was.

"There is something," said Jean-Guy. "One of their maps is missing."

"Whose?"

"The Goth Girl's."

"Amelia?"

Beauvoir raised his brows at the familiarity.

"Cadet Choquet, yes."

"What did she say?"

"She seemed surprised. She denied there was any special relationship with Professor Leduc, aside from taking him coffee in the morning and gathering for the odd meeting with others in his rooms."

"So it's true," said Gamache. "She was one of them."

Gamache took a deep, deep breath, then on the exhale he looked out the door and down the empty hallway that had once teemed with cadets and was now completely devoid of life.

He muttered so quietly as to be almost inaudible, "What have I done?"

CHAPTER 15

—

"You've kidnapped us."

"That's a little harsh, wouldn't you say?" said Armand Gamache later that day as he stood in the bistro and looked at the four cadets. "Hardly a prison."

"You know what I mean," said Jacques.

"Oh yes, Cadet Laurin. I heard you."

Amelia wondered if Jacques had picked up on what the Commander was really saying. But he seemed too intent on his own message to hear anyone else's.

"Why're we here?" Huifen Cloutier asked, her tone more polite, though the edge was still noticeable.

It was midafternoon and the bistro was filling up, but their table was private. At Gamache's request, Olivier had given them a place in the corner, tucked between the wall and the window. When Commander Gamache walked in, they'd stood up, but now he waved them to their seats and grabbed a chair for himself from another table.

Amelia found herself at home in the faintly familiar surroundings. It didn't smell of urine and cigarettes, like the rooming house. It didn't sound hollow, like the academy. Instead, it smelt of wood smoke and coffee, and she could hear the fire crackle in the grate and the murmur of muffled conversation nearby, spiced by laughter. Not the loud, often jarring, bursts of laughter that reverberated down the halls of the academy. This was a low rumble. An undertone of good humor.

After being marched out of the academy, she'd been taken to an unmarked Sûreté vehicle, already running, with Nathaniel waiting in the backseat and two plainclothes agents in the front seat. As they'd been driven deeper and deeper into the wilderness, away from the academy and way away from Sûreté headquarters, her disquiet had grown.

The car had turned off the main road and taken progressively smaller back roads. Then, finally, a dirt road.

"Where're you taking us?" she demanded, just as the car slowed and crested a hill. "Where are we?"

"Well, we're not in Kansas anymore," said one of the plainclothes agents, turning around.

It was Gabri. And Amelia immediately recognized the village.

"Three Pines," she said. "But why?"

"Honestly," said Olivier, as they pulled up to the bistro, "I have no idea why Monsieur Gamache wants you back. But he does."

The cadets were shown to the table reserved for them, and Olivier explained that Commander Gamache had asked that they wait there for him.

They'd been joined shortly after that by Huifen and Jacques. The two women who'd driven them down, the bookstore owner and the artist, left them at the table. The artist woman went home, but the bookstore owner found a table across the room, ordered a beer and a sandwich, and watched them.

The cadets had had lunch, and then endless cups of coffee, waiting. And then the Commander had arrived.

"Why're we back here?" Jacques repeated Huifen's question when Commander Gamache sat down.

Armand asked Olivier for a double espresso, then turned his attention to the cadets. "I had my friends bring you here because secrecy is vital. Chief Inspector Lacoste and Inspector Beauvoir know you're here. But no one else. I didn't even want agents to drive you down. No one must know where you are."

They moved forward then, drawn toward the Commander.

Huifen and Nathaniel immediately asked, "Why not?"

But Amelia and Jacques did not. And Gamache wondered if they knew. They were suspected. Of being the killer. Or being the next victim.

As he looked at their young, troubled faces, he saw the village beyond and the hill they'd driven down. And he remembered the headlights up there, that first night the cadets had visited.

The lights, like eyes, had stared down at them, then had slowly, slowly withdrawn.

Gamache had no idea who was in the car, and he'd assumed whoever it was had been following him. But now he wondered. And now his worry increased.

Suppose he wasn't the target? Suppose whoever was in the car had been following the cadets?

All of them.

Or just one of them.

"Why are we here?" Huifen asked, almost demanded.

"I brought you here because I have a job for you."

"Let me guess," said Jacques. "You want us to shovel your walk and cook your meals."

He'd spoken loudly, and the tables immediately around them shot glances their way before returning to their own business.

"I think you're mistaking me for someone else," said Gamache, his voice reasonable. Not taking offense. A bird of prey unbothered by a moth. "No. In fact what I'm going to ask you to do is quite difficult and very important. And needs to be kept quiet. I hope it will help in the investigation of Professor Leduc's murder."

He could not have put together a string of words more potent for the young men and women. Even Jacques grew quiet and attentive, and Amelia sat forward.

So very young, he thought. So young they don't know it.

"A copy of this map was found in Professor Leduc's night table," said Gamache as he placed the map on the table.

Only Nathaniel noticed the blood seep from Amelia's face. Already pale to begin with, she now looked translucent.

"No one outside of the homicide investigators knows that," the Commander was saying. "We don't yet know how he got it, or why he had it."

"Whose is it?" asked Huifen.

"Others are looking into that question," said Gamache.

Amelia was staring at him, though she said nothing.

"Is that why they told us to find our copies?" asked Jacques.

"It is. I hope you brought them, because I need you to find some things out."

His eyes, as always, came to rest on Amelia.

He'd been watching her progress since the first day.

She was top of her class. Top of the entire freshman intake, in fact. By a long shot. But she hadn't chosen a volunteer assignment, belonged to no clubs or sports teams, and sat alone at meals.

This afternoon, just before leaving to come down here, he'd looked at the report on the contents of her dorm space. No drugs. No alcohol. Some chocolate chip cookies, hoarded from the kitchens.

There were no photos. No letters or cards. Nothing from her father. Or her mother.

It was as though she'd been birthed in the academy. A twenty-year-old newborn. Though Armand Gamache knew different. He knew exactly where she'd sprung from. He knew her bloodline.

In his peripheral vision, he could see the duffle bag beside Amelia's chair. It was bulging, the canvas sticking out at awkward angles.

He could guess what was in it. Some clothing and toiletries. But mostly it was crammed full of the only things Amelia Choquet valued.

Books.

He wondered if the small volume of poetry by Ruth Zardo was in there. The one she'd taken from his home. He hesitated to call it "stolen," still hoping she'd return it one day.

The cadets had lifted their eyes from the map and were looking at him.

Out the window Gamache could see a car arriving, one he recognized.

Lowering his voice, he spoke quickly, urgently.

"I need you to continue what you started," he said. "To find out everything you can about this map. Who drew it. Why. Was there a purpose? Is there some message in it that made it valuable to Professor Leduc?"

Gamache saw the car draw up to his home.

He rose to his feet, but continued to talk. They also got up.

"Why, after someone put such time and effort into drawing it, was it then walled up?" he asked. "I have to leave, but I'll be back in a few minutes. Stay here."

He got up, put his copy of the map in his pocket, and left.

Amelia watched him go, walking just a little more quickly than a relaxed man might. Once outside, he took long strides around the village green to his home, where a man and a woman had stopped partway up the path to his front door and were waiting for him.

Amelia didn't recognize the man. Middle-aged, he had graying hair and slightly soft features. But the most striking thing about him was that he was in uniform. Not a Sûreté uniform. This one was a deep blue with gold buttons and insignia. He wore a cap with a broad gold ribbon and he stood straight, almost at attention, as Gamache approached. He didn't quite salute, but close.

And once again, Amelia wondered about the Commander. He must have been someone, once. To command such respect from such a senior officer. And she wondered what terrible thing Gamache had done to have been shuffled off, away from active duty. To the flat plains of Saint-Alphonse and the Sûreté Academy.

As the two men shook hands, Amelia looked more closely at the woman.

She was in plain clothes. Blond. Petite without giving the impression of being small. Just the opposite. There was something formidable about her, even at a distance.

And then Amelia's eyes opened wide.

"Holy shit."

"What?" asked Huifen, following her glance out the window. "Who're they?"

"How should I know?" said Amelia.

It was the homicide chief. The one she'd seen interviewed on the news, while the drunken slop of a landlady spread her legs on the La-Z-Boy in front of the TV.

Amelia got up and headed for the door.

"Stop."

Everyone in the bistro stopped. Including Amelia.

"Come here."

Amelia turned around. When they realized the target was the young woman, everyone else averted their eyes from the inevitable carnage.

Ruth was pointing a crooked finger at the empty armchair at her table. After a moment's hesitation, Amelia went over and sat.

"Didn't he tell you to stay put?" Ruth demanded.

"You're Ruth Zardo, the poet," she said.

"I hear there was a murder at the academy. Did you do it?"

The demented old poet glared at her with eyes so sharp Amelia felt she must be bleeding.

Beside Ruth, the demon duck was nodding and muttering, "Fuck, fuck, fuck."

Amelia's mind went blank. Except for one line from that book the Commander had offered her. She'd refused his gift, but had subsequently found a copy in the used bookstore next door and bought it. Marcus Aurelius.

The object of life is not to be on the side of the majority, but to escape finding oneself in the ranks of the insane.

Amelia knew she was deep in the ranks of the insane.

CHAPTER 16

As he walked across the village green, Gamache could see the insignia on the visitor's uniform. The crown above three Bath Stars, from the ancient order of chivalry.

This man was a high-ranking Mountie. An assistant commissioner in the RCMP.

Isabelle Lacoste opened her mouth to introduce them, but the man was already stepping forward to meet Gamache, his hand out, a smile on his face.

It was a restrained smile, one of greeting rather than happiness. It was, after all, a tragedy that had brought them together.

"Commander Gamache," he said. "I'm sorry for the circumstances, but can't say I'm sorry to finally be meeting you."

"This is Deputy Commissioner Gélinas," said Isabelle Lacoste. "He's here to help with the investigation."

"Help" was, of course, a euphemism. For all his courtesy, Deputy Commissioner Gélinas was there as a watchdog. Watching them. Dogging them.

"Paul Gélinas," said the Deputy Commissioner.

"Armand Gamache," said Gamache. "A pleasure."

The RCMP officer's handshake was firm, but not crushing. There was no attempt, or need, to show force. It was assumed.

"The Deputy Commissioner was visiting the RCMP headquarters in Montréal from Ottawa when Chief Superintendent Brunel called with a request for oversight," said Lacoste.

"Well, that was fortunate," said Gamache.

"*Oui*," said Gélinas. "I asked that the three of us meet as soon as possible. Though I didn't expect it to be here." He looked around. "Pretty."

It was polite, but it was also clear Monsieur Gélinas would not be moving down to Three Pines anytime soon.

"*Désolé*," said Gamache. "I had to come back here briefly, but I'll be returning to the academy as soon as possible. Sorry you had to come all this way."

"Well, to be honest, it's even better for me," said Gélinas, walking beside Gamache as they made their way up the path to his home. "Nice to get away from the city, and the truth is, these situations are always awkward. Inserting myself into someone else's investigation. I did it once before. Not my favorite thing, but needs to be done. I always find it's easier to have the initial talk away from the scene of the crime. More private. Fewer distractions and interruptions. Chief Inspector Lacoste and I had a chance to talk on the drive down."

"And now you'd like to talk to me?"

"Yes. Privately, if possible."

Gamache gestured for the RCMP officer to go ahead of him up the porch steps. "Have you been to the crime scene?"

"I have, and I scanned the preliminary report on the way down."

"Then you probably know more than I do."

"Oh, I doubt that, Commander."

It was said with warmth, and yet Gamache thought he detected a subtext. Perhaps even a warning.

Don't believe everything you think, he reminded himself. But still . . .

A face suddenly appeared at the door. With bright eyes and ears that started in the frame of the mullion and looked like they ended close to the ceiling.

Gamache laughed. Seeing Henri standing on his hind legs, eager face at the window, tongue lolling, body swaying as the tail wagged the dog, always made him happy. Then he heard the familiar voice and the familiar words, always the same.

"Oh, Henri. Back up. Off the door. You know he can't get in with you leaning on it. Good boy. Sit."

Armand mouthed along to the words, *Good boy. Sit.* Unperturbed by witnesses.

But then other, unfamiliar, words followed.

"Now, Gracie. Here, it's okay. It's okay. Please don't. Oh."

Gracie? thought Gamache.

He opened the door to find Henri sitting, tail wagging furiously, his mouth open in a smile, his satellite ears pricked forward. About to explode with happiness. And behind him, Reine-Marie, smiling.

Apologetically.

"You might want to . . ." she waved toward the puddle on the wide plank floor.

"Oh," said Armand, looking down at it. But that was not the most disconcerting thing in the room.

Something was squirming in Reine-Marie's arms.

"Come in." He turned to their guests. "But you might want to . . ." He too gestured and saw both Lacoste and Gélinas first grimace, then smile politely, as though the puddle was a welcome mat.

They stepped carefully across it, into the room.

"Here." Reine-Marie thrust whatever was in her arms at her husband, then left to get something to clean up the moisture.

"Ohhhh," said Lacoste, approaching Gamache. "Now who's this?"

"I have no idea," he said. He could feel it trembling violently. "But its name seems to be Gracie."

"It's so small," said Gélinas, also approaching. "May I?"

He reached out and, when Gamache nodded, stroked its head. "And soft."

Reine-Marie had returned with a sponge and soapy water. And a disinfectant spray.

"May I help, madame?" asked Gélinas.

"*Non, mais merci.* Sadly this isn't the first time in my life I've done this. Not even, to be honest, the first time today."

"Is there something we should talk about?" Armand asked.

Gracie had stopped struggling in his arms, and slowly he could feel her relax. Her trembling eased as he stroked her. From nose to tail. She was about the size of his hand, so they were not long strokes.

"I'll explain mine, if you explain yours." Reine-Marie gestured with the sponge toward their guests.

Both Gélinas and Lacoste laughed.

"Isabelle I know, of course," said Reine-Marie, peeling off the kitchen gloves and leaning in to kiss her. "Welcome, *ma belle.*"

"This is Paul Gélinas," said Armand, as the two shook hands.

"*Un plaisir,*" said Gélinas. "I'm sorry to barge in like this."

"RCMP," said Reine-Marie. "The Mounties are always welcome." She turned to Armand. "What have you done now?"

"Deputy Commissioner Gélinas is here to help us investigate the murder of Professor Leduc," said Isabelle.

"I see."

Armand had already called to tell Reine-Marie about it, so it was no surprise. She did not, they noticed, offer the usual words of grief and shock and sadness. No need to add hypocrisy to an already complex situation.

"Your turn." Armand looked down at Gracie, now asleep in his arms.

"Remember when I told you this morning that Clara had gotten her rescue puppy?"

"And this is it?" asked Armand with relief.

"Well, no."

"What have you done now?" he asked her. "And what is it?"

It did not, in all truth, look like a puppy.

"It looks like a groundhog," said Isabelle Lacoste.

"I think it might be one of those teapot pigs," said Gélinas.

"Oh, God, don't tell me," said Armand.

"Some detectives," said Reine-Marie with a smile, taking Gracie from him. "She doesn't have trotters. She isn't a pig."

"Well, Ruth doesn't have cloven hooves," said her husband, "but we all know . . ."

"She's not a teapot pig," Reine-Marie assured him.

"Then what is she? Not a puppy."

"Ummm," said Reine-Marie. "We think so."

"You think?"

"She hasn't been to the vet yet. The litter was found in a garbage can by Billy Williams, out Cowansville way. He called around and—"

"At least it's not a skunk," said Isabelle. "Is it?"

"A ferret?" asked Gélinas.

Reine-Marie put Gracie in the cage by the fireplace, soft towels and small chew toys keeping her company.

The four adults and Henri bent over her, like surgeons examining a complicated case.

She was so tiny it was difficult to tell what she was. She had rounded ears and a long thin tail, and paws with sharp nails. She was bald except for patches of black hair, not yet long enough for a combover. Her eyes opened and she looked back at them.

"She's a puppy," Gamache declared and straightened up.

"Don't you need to say it three times for it to be true, *patron*?" asked Lacoste.

"You don't believe it?" he asked.

"I reserve judgment."

"Smart," said Deputy Commissioner Gélinas. "I myself will stand by ferret. *Désolé, madame.*"

"Not at all," she assured him. "I admire you for standing behind your conclusion, however misguided."

There was no mistaking the subtext, or the warning.

Gélinas nodded. He understood. Mess with her family, you messed with her. And she had a ferret at her disposal.

"We should talk," said Gamache, after pulling the towel up around Gracie to keep her warm, and resting his hand on her.

"*Oui*," said Lacoste. "And I need to get back to the academy. You're returning?"

She held his eyes and saw a very slight nod.

The cadets were here, in the village. Somewhere. Out of sight. Even from the Deputy Commissioner. And he wanted to keep it that way, for now.

"Yes, later this afternoon," said Gamache. "I'll drive Monsieur Gélinas back after filling him in."

Isabelle Lacoste left and Madame Gamache offered them a late lunch. "You probably haven't eaten much today."

"True," said Gélinas. "But I don't want to put you out. I noticed a bistro in the village . . ."

"Probably best to have a more private discussion," said Armand, leading him into the kitchen where he sliced fresh bread from Sarah's boulangerie and Gélinas helped him grill sandwiches of Brome Lake duck, Brie and fig confit.

"Your wife is very caring, monsieur," said Gélinas, as they worked side by side. "And not just of the ferret—"

"—puppy."

"You're a lucky man. I miss this."

"A puddle of pee at the front door?"

"Even that." Paul Gélinas was looking down at the sandwiches as he sliced them. "My wife was a lot like Madame Gamache. Always bringing home strays. Animals. People." Gélinas's hands paused and he grunted in surprise. "She died three years ago. Sometimes it seems like she's been gone forever. And sometimes I still smell her perfume and hear her footsteps and look up, expecting to see her. And then I remember."

"I'm sorry," said Armand.

"When a job came up at the embassy in Paris after she died, I took it. Needed to get away. A change. I came back a few months ago."

"Did it help?" asked Gamache. "Paris?"

"It didn't hurt," said Gélinas, smiling.

Gamache smiled back and nodded and turned the sandwiches over in the pan. There was nothing to say that didn't sound trite, or hollow.

Paul Gélinas, roughly Gamache's age, was living his nightmare.

But Gamache knew something else.

Deputy Commissioner Gélinas had not been seconded to Paris to serve canapés at diplomatic soirées. This man had been in the intelligence service. He'd almost certainly spent the last few years as a spy.

And now he was here. Invited into the investigation, to spy on them.

"You have a nice home here, monsieur," said Gélinas as they took their sandwiches to the harvest table. "The Sûreté Academy must have held some powerful attractions, for you to leave this for that."

It was said pleasantly. A guest making polite conversation. But both men knew that, while polite, it was not simply conversation.

"I left to clean up the academy," said Gamache. "As I suspect you very well know."

Gélinas took a huge bite of his sandwich and nodded approvingly. "Delicious," he managed to say as he chewed. Finally swallowing, he said, "Sometimes, to clean up a mess, we have to make an even bigger one. It gets worse before it gets better."

Gamache put down his sandwich and looked across the pine table at the RCMP officer.

"Is this going somewhere?"

"I think you'd do just about anything to protect your family, your home."

Gélinas glanced at the kitchen, then looked in the other direction, to the woodstove and comfortable chairs next to the windows looking out to the village green.

"Are we talking about the death of Serge Leduc, or something else?" asked Gamache.

"Oh, we're still on topic. The Sûreté Academy is an extension of your home, isn't it? And the cadets are extensions of your family, just as the homicide division of the Sûreté once was. You are a man with a protective instinct. To care that deeply is a blessing. But like most blessings, it can also be a curse."

Now Gélinas also carefully, regretfully, returned his sandwich to his plate.

"I know."

"And what do you know?"

"I know how much it hurts when someone we care about dies, or is threatened."

"I did not care for Serge Leduc."

Deputy Commissioner Gélinas broke into a smile at that. "I wasn't referring to Leduc. From all I hear, he was a nasty piece of work. *Non.* I meant the academy."

"It's true that I care about the academy," said Gamache. "But it's an institution. If it disappeared tomorrow I'd be sad, but I wouldn't move to Paris."

Gélinas nodded and gave a small grunt. "Forgive me, but are you being intentionally obtuse, Commander? By academy, I mean the cadets. The flesh-and-blood young men and women who are your responsibility. While Leduc was in charge, there was misconduct, misappropriation of funds. Perhaps even abuse. I hear the rumors too, you know. But within months of you taking over, there was a murder."

"Who's worse? Is that what you're saying?"

"I'm asking," said Gélinas. "I've followed your career, Commander Gamache. I know what you're capable of doing. And believe me, I have only the greatest respect for you, for your choices. Doing what others could not. It's only because of that respect that I am being this open with you. You must know why I'm here."

"I do," said Gamache. "You're not investigating the murder of Professor Leduc, you're investigating me."

"Wouldn't you? Who had it in for him from the very beginning?"

"But I kept him on. I could have fired him."

"And isn't that in itself suspicious, monsieur?" Gélinas wiped his mouth with his napkin, then placed it carefully on the table.

"You've been open with me," said Gamache. "Now let me be open with you. I detested Leduc, but I did not kill him. And you are here because I asked for you."

For the first time since they met, Gélinas showed surprise.

"For me personally?"

"*Oui.* I called Chief Superintendent Brunel just before Isabelle Lacoste placed her call. I asked for you."

"But Chief Inspector Lacoste didn't mention that."

"She doesn't know."

The RCMP officer cocked his head slightly and examined Gamache. "Why me?"

"Because I wanted to meet you."

"Why? And how did you even know about me?"

"I spent some time in retirement, you know. Recovering. Deciding what to do next. Figuring out what I really wanted to do."

147

"Yes, I'd heard."

"In that time, there were a number of job offers. Including from the RCMP."

"For Paris?"

Gamache shook his head.

"To head up the Québec detachment?"

Gamache shook his head.

"Ottawa?"

Gamache sat still while Gélinas's mind followed that path. Then stopped.

"The Commissioner? You were offered the top job? He's to retire in the next few months."

"I declined. Do you know why?"

"To take over the academy?"

"That was, actually, the major reason. But I also declined after doing a great deal of research."

"And what did you discover?"

"That there is a better person for the job. You. This morning, when it was clear we needed an independent observer, I realized it was an opportunity to meet you. To see if I was right."

"I'm not one of your protégés," said Gélinas. "And this is a murder investigation, not a job interview."

"No one knows that better than me," said Gamache, also placing his napkin, like a flag of truce, on the table. "Now. Let me tell you about Serge Leduc."

CHAPTER 17

⁓

"*Oui, je comprends*." Though Olivier sounded unconvinced. "Are you sure?"

On the other end of the phone, Armand Gamache spoke swiftly, softly, not wanting to be overheard. He stepped from his study, out into the living room, and could see Gélinas and Reine-Marie still in the back garden of their home.

Then he turned and looked through his study window, to the bistro. He could see movement in the window and wondered if it was the cadets.

And he willed them to stay there. To stay put. To not leave the bistro.

"I wish people would stop asking me if I'm sure," he said.

"They will, *patron*, once you stop making almost incomprehensible decisions." He was whispering too, to match Gamache's voice, though he had no idea why.

"I'll do my best. Can you keep the cadets there, Olivier? Just until we leave?"

"Fortunately, I have a whip and a chair. Don't ask."

"I'm assuming it has something to do with Ruth," said Gamache, and heard Olivier chuckle softly, and then it stopped.

"What's this about, Armand? Are they in danger?" There was a pause. "Are we?"

"I'm trying to prevent something terrible happening," said Gamache, though something terrible had already happened.

In bringing the cadets to Three Pines, he was trying to prevent something worse.

"Okay," said Olivier, standing at their table. "Monsieur Gamache just called and said he couldn't rejoin you after all."

"Just fucking great," said Jacques, throwing himself back in his chair. "He drags us down here, away from the action, then just leaves us here? What's he doing? Napping?"

"What is wrong with you?" asked Olivier. "Is it just him or are you rude to everyone?"

"You don't know him," said Jacques. "You think you do, but you don't. You know the nice neighbor. You don't know the real man."

"And you do?"

"Professor Leduc did. He told us all about Gamache."

"Really? And what did he say?"

"That he was caught up in the corruption scandal. That he resigned one step ahead of being fired. That Gamache is a coward. He ran away from the mess he made and now he's trashing the academy."

"Enough."

Behind them, the old poet and the bookstore owner had risen to their feet. But it wasn't Ruth Zardo who'd spoken. It was Myrna.

"It's all right, dear," said Ruth. "They don't know what they're saying."

Beside her, Myrna was so angry she was actually shaking. Her face so filled with rage, she was almost unrecognizable.

Jacques stood abruptly and faced her.

"You'd defend him? Do you know how many agents died while he was Chief Inspector? Do you know he murdered his own superior? You think we don't know that he killed Professor Leduc? Of course he did. A shot to the head of an unarmed man. It has coward written all over it. It has Gamache written all over it."

"You stupid, stupid man," was all Myrna could get out, while Ruth's hand held her arm. The human contact, if not her strength, restraining Myrna from going further.

"You—" said Jacques. Huifen had gotten to her feet and put her own hand on his arm, stopping him from saying what everyone in the room heard anyway. It throbbed out of him. What he was thinking. What he was seeing.

A big, fat black. Not a woman. Not a person. Just a black. Though he was clearly longing to shoot another word at her.

And now Myrna did step forward, and Ruth went with her.

Jacques Laurin glared and dared them to go further.

Myrna Landers had seen that look many times. When stopped for traffic tickets. While walking in civil rights marches through Montréal. She'd seen it in reports of riots and police shootings. She'd seen it in color and in black and white. In recent news reports and in old newsreels. And archival photographs. Of the Deep South. And the enlightened North.

And now it was here. In Three Pines.

He didn't just loathe her. He dismissed her, as subhuman.

And in just a few months, Myrna knew, he'd have a gun and a billy club and permission to use them. On anyone he wanted.

"Well," said Olivier. "That little contretemps makes this even more difficult."

"What?"

"Monsieur Gamache has handed out billeting assignments."

"Aren't we staying in the B and B?" asked Huifen.

"All of you at our place?" said Olivier. "I don't think so."

"Then where're we staying?"

Amelia looked over at Ruth Zardo.

Please, let me stay with her.

Ruth sneezed and wiped her nose on Myrna's caftan.

Please let me stay anywhere else.

"Cadet Huifen Cloutier will be billeted with us in the B and B."

Huifen smiled and looked at her fellow cadets, who didn't even pretend to be happy for her.

"Cadet Amelia Choquet—"

Ruth. Not Ruth. Please, please, not Ruth. Please, Ruth.

"—with Clara Morrow."

Amelia looked at Ruth. Did the old poet seem surprised? Maybe even a little disappointed?

Ruth scowled at her and gave her the finger.

Perhaps not.

"Cadet Nathaniel Smythe will be staying with Ruth Zardo."

"Oh, shit," they both said at once.

"Now, Cadet Laurin." Olivier turned to Jacques. "Can you use your superior skills to work out where Commander Gamache has billeted you?"

Jacques looked at him. In the background, Myrna was staring wide-eyed at Olivier.

"He didn't," she said, and saw Olivier nod.

"Cadet Laurin will be staying with Myrna Landers."

"I won't do it," said Jacques.

"It's either that, or that." Olivier gestured toward the bench on the village green, glistening with melting snow.

"Or I could leave. We don't have to stay."

"Absolutely," said Olivier. "I can't imagine anyone here trying to stop you. But it's a long walk back to Saint-Alphonse."

"Now who's the coward?" asked Myrna. Her horror had turned to a certain satisfaction.

He squared his shoulders. "I'm not afraid." Then he turned to Huifen and whispered, "Can we trade?"

Huifen shook her head.

"Nice," said Myrna.

"Yeah, like you wouldn't trade me in an instant."

"Trading isn't what I have in mind for you."

"Why do I get him?" Ruth demanded. "He's like a hole in the room."

She pointed a gnarled finger at Nathaniel.

"Hey," said Nathaniel. "I'm a great guest."

"Right, if I want to play an endless game of hide and seek. Come out, come out, wherever you are."

"What's that supposed to mean?" Nathaniel demanded.

"Oh, go fffff—"

Now it was Myrna's turn to lay a hand on her arm.

"Who's Clara Morrow?" asked Amelia.

"The artist," said Huifen, and gestured toward her head, mimicking abandoned hair. "She drove us down. Seems nice."

Olivier, somewhat more helpful, gestured out the window to where Clara was walking her new puppy, though it looked from a distance like she was dragging an empty leash through the thin layer of snow on the village green.

Amelia sighed. Nice. In her world, it was code for dim-witted.

Armand Gamache waved at Clara, who picked up the puppy and walked over.

"Who's that?" asked Gélinas. "She looks familiar."

"Yes, it's hard to mistake Clara Morrow for anyone else."

"Clara Morrow, the artist? The one who does portraits? She did the old and forgotten Virgin Mary. An incredible work. I could barely look at it and I could barely look away. Though I think my favorite is *The Three Graces*. I saw her solo show at the Musée d'art contemporain."

"She lives over there." Gamache pointed to a small house across the green.

They walked forward, meeting Clara halfway. After putting the puppy down, she was introduced to Paul Gélinas, who seemed more than a little starstruck.

"Have you met Leo?" Clara asked Armand.

"*Non. Bonjour*, Leo," said Armand, kneeling down.

Leo was, he had to admit, just about the most adorable puppy he'd ever seen. He had light brown fur, almost yellow, and rounded ears that seemed made of felt. They were perked forward. His tail wagged and he stood with his legs firm and straight. Eager and bright-eyed.

Like a very, very small lion.

Was it possible Clara got a lion and they got a weasel?

But no, Leo was definitely a dog. Of unknown breed, but a dog.

"How's Gracie?" Clara asked, and Armand searched her face for any hint of a smile.

It was not an exhaustive search. There was more than a little amusement.

He got to his feet as Gélinas squatted down and played with Leo.

"She's wonderful," said Armand.

"Really?"

"Well, she's peeing everywhere. But then, so did Daniel and Annie when we first brought them home. Granted, we were pretty sure they were human. It's not totally clear what Gracie is."

"Does it matter?" asked Clara.

"Obviously not to you," said Armand. "Are they really litter mates?"

He looked down at the very handsome Leo.

"Well, they were all found in the same bin. I guess it's possible a little raccoon cub crawled in there with them. Or maybe a skunk."

"Right," said Armand. "How did we end up with Gracie? Was she the only one left?"

"Not at all. Reine-Marie was given the pick of the litter. I think Billy Williams is a little sweet on her. She chose Gracie."

Of course she did, thought Armand. The runt. He'd have done the same thing.

"How's Henri adjusting?" Clara asked.

"He looks at her as though she's an hors d'oeuvre we dropped on the floor."

Clara grimaced, then turned to leave. "Well, good luck."

"Good luck to you."

Something in his voice made her turn around. "What have you done, Armand?"

"Oh, you'll see."

Clara scowled at him.

Behind her, in the bistro window, Gamache could see the four young people also scowling at him.

A litter of cadets. But who was the lion? Who was the runt?

Gamache drove back to the academy while Gélinas read the Commander's private file on Serge Leduc.

They'd discussed the broad strokes of the dead man's career, what was publicly known. What wasn't.

And his personal life, of which little was known.

"Both parents are dead. I spoke to his sister this morning," said Gamache. "She lives in Chicoutimi. They weren't close. She was shocked, of course, but I didn't get the feeling Leduc's death would leave a hole in her life."

"No friends among the other professors?"

"Not that I could see. Serge Leduc was hierarchical. He would never think of socializing with lower ranks. Not unusual in closed communities," said Gamache. "Where status is power and takes on an almost mystical quality."

"Which would make you . . . ?"

Gamache smiled thinly and chose not to step into that trap.

"Any special students?" Gélinas asked.

"By special, you mean did he have sex with any of the students? I hope not, but the truth is, I don't know. I tried to take opportunities away by, among other things, stopping the practice of freshmen cadets bringing professors their meals in their rooms. That reinforces the power professors have over students. It can lead to abuse."

"But you think he might have had affairs anyway?"

"He kept up the practice, despite my ban. And it wouldn't have been an affair," said Gamache. "That makes it sound consensual."

"Well, at least they'd both be over sixteen."

"Do you really think a freshman cadet is going to choose to have sex with Serge Leduc? If he was in any other position, they'd never give him another thought. Nor should they. No. If they had sex with him, or more accurately, he with them, they were forced. By their own fears and insecurities. Seduced by his promises and frightened by what would happen if they refused."

"Motive for murder," said Gélinas.

"It is a possibility."

"So you do think a student could have done this?"

"They're not children. And I'm sorry to say, even children kill. These are young men and women, more than capable of killing."

"Killing, perhaps," said Gélinas. "A police officer must be capable of it. But murder? We hope not."

Gamache said nothing and Gélinas went back to reading, finally looking up and letting the dossier drift closed on his lap. He thought for a moment before speaking.

"Why didn't you use this against him? There're all sorts of allegations. Hidden bank accounts, contract fixing. Intimidation."

"Allegations. But not enough proof," said Gamache. "I needed hard evidence before taking a run at Serge Leduc."

Gélinas looked down at the dossier. "I had no idea it was this bad. I was in Paris when the scandal in the Québec government and the Sûreté broke. I followed it, of course. And heard the rumors even there about the academy. But didn't know if they were true or the degree." He shook his head. "A second scandal."

"*Non.* Not a second. It's all part of the same one. Where did the corrupt agents come from? Why did Chief Superintendent Francoeur transfer Leduc to the academy? Francoeur was the head of the Sûreté, the architect of all that went wrong. He placed Leduc in the academy for a reason. What was happening in the school wasn't a separate scandal but the necessary first step for all that happened later."

"Did you know that when you took over?"

"I suspected. Ill-prepared, insolent young agents were showing up in the lowest ranks of the Sûreté, and being promoted. One or two could be considered normal in a population, but there were too many. The academy had become a nursery, a factory, a training ground and a conduit for brutality. It created and fostered an environment where that sort of behavior was normal, valued and rewarded."

"By Serge Leduc."

Gamache nodded. "He was their first role model for what a Sûreté agent should be. His nickname, you know, was the Duke."

"Not exactly original. Leduc. The Duke."

"But it was at least accurate," said Gamache. "A pretender to the throne. A tyrant."

"Then you show up, replace most of the professors with your own, make substantial changes. But you had to keep Leduc on, to get at the core of the problem. Did he know you were on to him?"

"*Oui.* I showed him the file."

"You did what? Why?"

"To rattle him."

Gélinas absorbed what he'd heard. "Did it work?"

Gamache opened his mouth, then closed it again. And finally he spoke. "How closely have you read that file?"

"Well, I've just skimmed it, but close enough to understand that Serge Leduc was on the take, at the very least."

"Read it more closely, and then we'll talk."

"Can't you just tell me?"

"No. I don't want to impose my thoughts on you. I want to see if you come to the same conclusion. I could be wrong."

While Gélinas reopened the file, Gamache drove, keeping his eyes on the road. Snow was drifting across the autoroute, leaving a thin layer beneath which there could be, he knew, ice.

Finally Gélinas looked up. There was silence for a moment as the RCMP officer thought.

"It doesn't say this anywhere," he said, choosing his words carefully. "But I don't think Leduc could have done all this himself, with lower-level accomplices. There must've been someone else. Someone smarter. Someone higher up. Maybe someone on the outside. And that's what you think too."

Far from being pleased that Deputy Commissioner Gélinas had come to the same conclusion, Gamache looked grim.

"Someone removed," Gélinas continued, "who could act without fear of being caught because no one would be looking in his direction."

Gamache was nodding. It was his thinking exactly, though there was no proof.

"Judging by this"—Gélinas looked down at the file—"Leduc was nothing if not shrewd. He must've known once the mess at the Sûreté was cleared up, the focus would turn to the academy. To him." He looked at Gamache. "If you showed this to him, isn't the wrong person dead?"

"You think it should have been me lying there?" asked Gamache.

"Don't you? If what you're describing is true, you were a threat. A man who'd already arrested or killed most of the others involved. From what I hear, those involved in the Sûreté scandal weren't just corrupt. They beat and murdered at will. You were a clear threat to Leduc and his accomplice. They were facing ruin. Prison."

He looked at Gamache's face in profile as he drove.

"If they've threatened and killed before, why stop at you?"

"They were weakened. Most of the agents they could count on for support and protection had been rooted out of the Sûreté. No, I was never in danger. Murdering me would bring the full weight of scrutiny crashing down on them."

"So you showed Leduc what you had," said Gélinas, tapping the file. "To spook him. Did it work?"

"Perhaps better than I thought," said Gamache.

"You think the accomplice killed Leduc? Because you were getting close?"

"It's possible. Whoever the accomplice is, he must've worried that Leduc, when cornered, would try to cut a deal."

"And so he shut him up. Then who is he? It would have to be someone in the academy now. One of the professors? Assuming for a moment it's not you—"

"For a moment?"

"There is someone who fits. Michel Brébeuf."

Gamache stared straight ahead. Then gave a curt nod.

Gélinas watched Gamache, the full implication dawning on him.

"You brought Brébeuf back. You put the two together, in the academy. Knowing that if Leduc was the Duke, Brébeuf was the king. You knew all this—"

"I suspected."

"—and you did it anyway. What were you thinking, man? That's lunacy."

"It could prove to be."

"What more proof do you need?" Gélinas all but shouted, then hauled himself back. "There's been a murder in the Sûreté Academy. Because you put two criminals together and gave them the run of the place—"

"That's not true."

"Near enough. You're just lucky one of the students wasn't hurt or killed."

They'd turned in to the parking lot, but when Gamache switched off the car Gélinas didn't move.

"Why did you leave the academy, Commander Gamache?"

"Last night? I didn't. I normally would have, but I stayed because I had late meetings."

"No, today. One of your professors is murdered and you suspect another professor. Instead of staying and making sure everyone is safe, you jump ship."

"You think I abandoned them?"

157

"I think it's strange in the extreme that a man who is responsible for hundreds of young lives would leave them locked in a building with a killer while he goes home and enjoys sandwiches in his kitchen. What's going on?"

CHAPTER 18

The body of Serge Leduc was removed, like a stain, from the Sûreté Academy. He'd arrived headstrong and left feet first.

On Commander Gamache's order, the cadets and professors lined the long, long marble hallway and stood at attention as the body was wheeled out. They were quiet, respectful. And not a single tear was shed.

"*True to his profit and his pride*," said Isabelle Lacoste, standing beside Gamache. "*He made them weep before he died.*"

"Jonathan Swift, again," said Gamache.

"A poem on the death of a duke," said Isabelle quietly as they watched Leduc's final progress down the hallway. "You quoted it earlier today. I looked it up. *Come hither, all ye empty things,/Ye bubbles raised by breath of kings;/Who float upon the tide of state,/Come hither, and behold your fate.*"

They saluted as the body was wheeled past.

"*Let pride be taught by this rebuke*," said Gamache quietly. "*How very mean a thing's a Duke.*"

"We need to talk," said Lacoste.

"*Oui.*"

Professor Leduc's body left the building, a dark spot in the bright sunshine that streamed in.

"But I have one more duty," said Gamache.

Down the long hallway he walked, toward the open door through which Leduc's body had exited and a fresh breeze entered. The students saluted the Commander. He knew better than to read any respect into the action. After all, they'd just saluted a dead man.

But he noticed that some looked at him with newfound deference. And Gamache knew why. He'd heard the rumors. They thought he was responsible for the body. There was a new tyrant in town.

Once outside, Gamache stood behind the morgue vehicle, watching them load the body.

"Making sure he really goes, Armand?"

Gamache turned to see Michel Brébeuf.

"I know it's a shock, but it must also be a bit of a relief," said Brébeuf.

"If you had anything to do with this, Michel, I'll find out. You know I will."

Brébeuf smiled. "And what will you do? Let me go again? Whoever did this cleaned up a mess, and you know it. Besides, if I had something to do with it, you were my accomplice. I wouldn't be here if it wasn't for you. This time you were the one who opened the gate. You knew who I was, and you let me in."

"Is that a confession?"

Brébeuf laughed and the morgue attendants looked over. It wasn't often that hilarity accompanied a corpse.

"A reminder, that's all. He was on his way out anyway, wasn't he?" Brébeuf turned and contemplated the body bag. "He held no real power anymore, though he didn't realize it. Strutting around like he was still in charge. I've known officers like that. Petty, officious, vicious. And not very bright. He was already gone. He just hadn't left. No, that's a waste of a good bullet."

Gamache turned and walked back to the large open doors of the academy.

"Be careful, Armand."

Gamache stopped and turned. Something in the voice had drawn his attention. It wasn't anger, it wasn't hatred. It was the gentleness with which those words were uttered that stopped him. So much more arresting than rage.

Michel Brébeuf stood there, the vast prairie behind him.

"You did me a good turn a few years ago—"

"Did I?"

"You let me resign. Didn't have me sent to prison, though on your evidence alone I would have been."

"Are you telling me you haven't been in prison all this time?" asked Armand, and saw Brébeuf blink. "If I did you a favor, Michel, it wasn't years ago, it was months ago. Don't stand here now and tell me I made a terrible mistake. Or if I did, at least admit it."

"I did not kill Serge Leduc."

The two men squared off, while the body was driven away.

Then Gamache turned and walked back through the doorway. Followed, a few paces behind, by his former best friend.

The cadets had moved from the bistro, which was getting too crowded to talk, over to the B and B. It was past four in the afternoon of a day that never seemed to end.

The sun was getting low on the horizon and a fire had been laid in the grate. Amelia lit it while Huifen made tea and Nathaniel found biscuits and cake in Gabri's kitchen. Something, he was pretty sure, that would be in short supply in the home of the crazy old woman who was putting him up.

The thought of what might be in that home made his skin crawl.

The cadets sat around the fireplace sipping tea, eating cake, and discussing the brutal murder of a man they all knew. Better than they cared to admit.

It seemed so far removed from this peaceful place that Nathaniel had to remind himself that what he'd discovered at the academy that morning wasn't a dream. This—he looked around at the comfortable faded furniture, the cheerful fire in the grate, the chocolate cake and biscuits—was the dream.

That other thing was real life.

The village had lulled him, however briefly, into forgetting that terrible things happened. He wondered if it was a gift, to forget however briefly, or a curse.

"Gamache brought us here to investigate the map," said Huifen, laying hers on the table. Nathaniel and Jacques did the same with theirs.

Then they looked at Amelia.

"I don't have mine," she said.

"Where is it? We were told to bring them," said Huifen.

"It's missing."

They stared at her.

"Missing?" asked Jacques. "Or found in the Duke's drawer?"

"Look, I don't know. I haven't thought about the map since we were here before. I put it away and now it's gone."

She looked at them defiantly.

"I believe you," said Nathaniel.

"You believe her?" demanded Jacques. "Why?"

"Why not?" he said. "We have no evidence either way. Might as well believe her."

"Some investigator you're going to make," said Jacques.

"He's a freshman," Huifen reminded him. "He'll learn."

"What?" asked Amelia. "What'll he learn? To judge without facts? To condemn without evidence? To be cynical and suspicious? Like you?"

"Not cynical, realistic," said Huifen. "The world's a dangerous place. We'll soon be up against organized crime. Drug dealers. Murderers. This isn't a tea party."

Despite the fact that it actually appeared to be.

"We have to assume the worst," said Jacques. "Every person, every situation, is a potential threat. Our lives depend on our ability to take charge."

"And how do you do that?" Amelia asked.

"Leduc told us," said Jacques. "Said it's not something we'd ever learn in a classroom or from a book. You find one person in a crowd and make an example of him. Everyone else falls into line."

"And by 'example,'" said Amelia, "you mean beat the shit out of him."

"If we have to, yes."

She looked at Jacques with disgust, then turned to Nathaniel.

"Thank you. And just so you know, I really didn't give my map to the Duke. I have no idea if the one they found was mine, or how it got there."

"Good enough," he said happily.

And looking at that open, trusting face, even Amelia had a sinking feeling that Nathaniel would not survive long in the force. At least, this Nathaniel wouldn't.

"Okay," said Huifen. "Let's assume you're telling the truth. That means someone took your map and gave it to the Duke. Why would they do that?"

"It could mean something else," said Nathaniel.

"What?" asked Jacques, exasperated with the freshman.

"Maybe someone discovered their own map was missing and stole Amelia's to replace it."

"By 'someone,' you mean one of us," said Huifen.

"Well, yes," said Nathaniel. "Who else could I mean? Or maybe the Duke wanted to see the map, and instead of giving him their own, they stole Amelia's."

"Again," said Huifen, "you mean one of us."

"I mean either you or Jacques, yes. I know it wasn't me. You had maps and were the closest to him, after all."

"Were we?" asked Jacques, staring hard at the younger man.

Amelia amended her opinion of Nathaniel. It was both comforting and disconcerting to see how cunning he actually was. And how clearly he saw things.

"I'm not accusing you," Nathaniel hurried on. "I'm just saying there're lots of ways to look at this."

"Okay, then, let's look at what we do know," said Huifen. "The facts. A copy of the map was found in the Duke's drawer. Why?"

Though the real question still seemed to be who.

Their eyes drifted from the three maps on the table to Amelia.

CHAPTER 19

⌐⌐

The photos of the crime scene were spread out on the long boardroom table in front of the investigators. Chief Inspector Lacoste was bringing Gamache and Gélinas up to speed.

"Most of the professors have been interviewed, along with the students."

"Did that produce anything?" asked Deputy Commissioner Gélinas.

"Not much so far. Leduc was very private, almost to the point of compulsion. Yesterday, from what we gather, was the same as every other day. Serge Leduc taught his classes, worked in his office without interruption in the afternoon, then dined last night at the professor's table. I believe you were there."

Gamache nodded.

"Professor Godbut is here, Chief Inspector," said an agent, popping her head in.

"Good." She turned to Gamache. "I thought you'd like to be here when we spoke with him."

"*Merci,*" said Gamache, with just a hint of sarcasm.

"Show him in, please," said Chief Inspector Lacoste.

A large man entered. He might have had muscle tone once, but now his middle jiggled and shifted as he walked.

"Marcel Godbut," he introduced himself, then took the chair offered. "This is terrible. I can't quite believe it."

"You've been at the academy for five and a half years, it says in your record," said Chief Inspector Lacoste.

"*Oui.*" He looked at Lacoste the way an uncle looked at a pretty young niece. "Before that I was a senior investigator in the Abitibi detachment."

"Of the Sûreté," said Deputy Commissioner Gélinas.

"Of course," said Godbut, regarding the RCMP officer with slight distaste.

"And you teach forensics?" said Gélinas, consulting his notes. "But not the DNA kind. You teach the cadets how to investigate records, finances. To look for fraud, racketeering. A paper trail, not a blood trail."

"*Oui*. Not very sexy, but effective. Not all of us get to chase murderers."

"Important work," agreed Gamache, but he was watching Godbut through narrowed eyes.

This was a man who, until Gamache arrived, had patrolled the hallways sniffing out cadets who were a little late for class, whose uniforms were slightly askew, whose hair a little long.

And he made them pay.

He humiliated and belittled students. While never actually beating them, he made them beat themselves up, giving them exercises in the quad, in their underwear, in winter. He made them run stairs and do near impossible numbers of push-ups and sit-ups. And when they failed, he doubled the numbers.

Marcel Godbut took them to the very edge of breakdown. Then brought them back.

It was an age-old form of torture. Some considered it training. Torment, relent. Torment. Relent.

They were made an example of. So that other students fell into line quickly. Eagerly. Some even, by third year, joined in the humiliation. Those were considered the successes and fast-tracked into good jobs in the Sûreté.

If Leduc was the architect, this man was the builder. Taking good material and making it rotten.

When he'd taken over as commander, Gamache had been sickened by what he'd found. The degree and depth of the abuse. And Marcel Godbut had not even been the worst. Those Gamache had summarily fired. One he'd had arrested. But he didn't quite have enough on Godbut. It was all anecdotal. Professor Godbut, the master of paper trails, would be careful not to leave one himself.

But Commander Gamache had watched him closely and made sure Godbut knew it. The abuse had stopped.

But when all that bile had to be contained, it created a volcano.

Had Professor Godbut erupted last night and attacked Leduc?

But motive was missing. It was not enough to simply say he blew. There had to be a reason. A push, however trivial it might appear from the outside.

And the crime scene didn't look like an explosion. It looked like an execution. Neat, orderly, bitterly cold.

"Tell us about the contract to build this school," said Gamache.

Godbut slowly turned in his chair and stared at the Commander.

"I know nothing about that."

"You taught fraud. You taught students how to spot it and yet you missed it when it was happening in your own house?"

"Was it? That's news to me. I'm just a professor. And as you've made clear since you arrived, Commander, I'm not a very good one."

"Did I ever say that? I think you are probably very good at what you do," said Gamache. "The question is, what do you do? What was your real job here?"

"Meaning?"

"Meaning Serge Leduc was on the take," said Paul Gélinas. "This whole structure was built on bribes and contract fixing. Someone organized it for him. Someone who not only knew how to do it, but how not to get caught."

"I hope you have proof, Commissioner. That's a serious charge."

"Not a charge, a theory." Gélinas smiled. "When was the last time you saw him?"

"Dinner last night. We discussed tactical exercises, as you know, Commander. And then Professor Leduc and I discussed the Montréal Canadiens."

It was a clear shot at Gamache. His opinions on the curriculum were no more important than a hockey game.

"And after dinner?" asked Gamache, as though unaware of the barb.

"I went back to my rooms and corrected papers and did coursework. Like any good professor."

"Did you see anyone? Any phone calls?" asked Isabelle Lacoste.

"No phone calls. No visitors. It was a quiet evening in. I awoke to that pathetic cadet screaming."

"You knew Professor Leduc as well as anyone," said Lacoste. "What do you think happened?"

"I think you're partly right," said Godbut. "I think his death did have something to do with this building. But not from the inside. I'd look outside, if I were you."

He gestured through the plate glass, past the quad, to the church spires beyond.

"The town?" asked Lacoste.

"Do you think Serge Leduc was killed by an ally? Or an enemy?" said Godbut. "That town is teeming with people who hated Serge Leduc."

Jean-Guy Beauvoir had slipped into the room. He and Godbut nodded to each other, the chill obvious.

Professor Godbut got up and paused for a moment to look out the window. The sun was just beginning to set and the huge sky was changing color, from blue to a soft rose.

And against it were the lights of Saint-Alphonse.

"One man's hatred stands above the rest," he said, turning away from the window. "That's where I'd start to look. But then, I'm not very good at my job, am I?"

If he expected Commander Gamache to mollify him, he was disappointed. Gamache sat silent and eventually Professor Godbut nodded and left.

"There's a piece of work," said Lacoste.

"A piece of shit," said Beauvoir, and beside him Gélinas gave a gruff laugh of agreement.

"But he might be right," said Lacoste. "It's not the first time today that's been mentioned. The hatred in the town toward the academy."

"But what's the story?" asked Gélinas, sitting forward and turning to Gamache. "What happened? The dossier you gave me refers to it, but only in terms of the subsequent contracts, not what led up to it."

"The town wanted this site for a recreation complex," Gamache explained. "Leduc promised to help them get it if they helped him find a site for the academy on the outskirts of town. They were thrilled to have the Sûreté Academy, knowing what it could mean to their economy. The mayor trusted him completely. Three months later, the site of the new academy was announced."

"The town's site," said Lacoste.

"The mayor and the townspeople had been lobbying and fund-raising for years to build a skating rink, a pool, an athletic center and community hall. It was more than a piece of land, more than a building. The people of Saint-Alphonse saw it as vital for their town's future. Especially the children. The mayor was apoplectic. Almost put him in the hospital."

There was silence in the room.

People had been murdered for far less.

"Could he have done this?" Lacoste asked.

The Commander thought for a moment. "I don't know."

Gélinas's brows rose. He couldn't remember the last time he'd heard a senior officer say, *I don't know.*

"I think it's possible," mused Gamache. "But if the mayor was going to

168

murder Leduc, I think it would've been a few years ago, when it first happened. I know him a little. I like him. He's a decent man, doing his best."

Gamache considered, then added, "But he does hold on to things. Lets them fester. Now, to be fair, it was a huge betrayal of his trust. It took a long time and a lot of effort to get him to agree to see me when I took over. Finally I convinced him to allow the community to share our facilities."

"You were doing that?" asked Gélinas.

"Seemed only fair, and didn't go nearly far enough to make amends. But it was a start. We were developing a program where the cadets would mentor and coach some of the children. And then this happened."

"Could your approaching the mayor have reopened old wounds?" Paul Gélinas asked. "Unintentionally, of course."

"It might have. On the one hand, the mayor is extremely upright, to the point of rigidity. A moralist. Almost fanatical in his defense of his town and his views of right and wrong."

"He'd consider murder wrong, I'm assuming," said Lacoste.

"True. On the other hand, he might see it as justice. Most killers manage to justify their actions. They don't see what they've done as wrong."

"The person getting what they deserve," said Gélinas.

"Often, yes."

"And in this case, Commander? Do you think the killer was after justice?"

Gamache looked at the photographs in front of them.

"Maybe."

"But?" said Lacoste.

"You've interviewed the professors and the students," said Gamache, and she nodded. "Each of the professors was a highly experienced Sûreté officer. All the students are being taught investigative skills."

"You're saying this is a school for murder," said Gélinas. "You might be teaching them how to catch a criminal, but in a roundabout way you're also teaching them how to be one, and not get caught."

Gamache was nodding. "The professors in particular. They'd know what we'd be looking for."

"And be able to stage a crime scene," said Lacoste. "Make it look like something it's not."

"A single shot to the temple," said Gamache. "Most murderers would at least try to make it look like suicide. Not a stretch. The narrative would be obvious. Serge Leduc knew I was closing in on him, and so he took his own life rather than go to prison."

"And all the killer had to do was drop the gun on the correct side of the body," said Lacoste.

"But he didn't," said Gélinas, looking at the photos. "Instead he does the opposite. Why?"

"He wants us to know it wasn't suicide," said Lacoste.

"But why?" asked Gélinas. "Why make sure we knew it was murder? So that we'd know that justice was done?"

They stared at the pictures. In certain ones, Serge Leduc looked like he was asleep. In others he was unrecognizable.

Perspective.

"You're being awfully quiet." Gamache turned to Beauvoir and saw a familiar expression on his face. "What do you know?"

"The alarm system was off last night."

As one, Chief Inspector Lacoste, Deputy Commissioner Gélinas, and Commander Gamache leaned toward him.

"But how's that possible?" asked Gamache. "It's integrated, computerized. The guards would have noticed. The board would have lit up."

"Well, guess where Leduc cut corners?" said Beauvoir. "Apparently, the guards knew the system was crap and had complained to the former commander, and gotten shit from Leduc for it. When you came, they said nothing."

"What do you mean by crap?" asked Lacoste.

"It's a cheap job—"

Gamache winced and shook his head. "They paid hundreds of thousands for the security system."

"Well, according to the guards, you could buy a better one at Canadian Tire."

Now Gamache groaned and massaged his head, trying to rid himself of a creeping headache. "There's an armory of weapons here. And almost no protection. This isn't just contract fixing, this is stupidity on a monumental scale."

"I've set up a meeting with the head guard for tomorrow morning," said Beauvoir, "to review security."

"Good," said Gamache.

"But whoever turned off the system would still have to know how," said Lacoste.

"True, but this system allows for more than one code," said Beauvoir, then turned to Gamache. "You have one—"

"I thought it was the only one."

"—and I suspect Leduc had his own code."

"And there may be others floating around?" said Gamache.

Beauvoir nodded, barely able to make eye contact with the Commander.

"You're thinking Leduc himself turned it off?" asked Gélinas. "But why?"

Beauvoir shrugged. "Beats me, and that's just one possibility. Someone could have easily hacked in and closed it down."

"And the guards wouldn't know?"

He shook his head. "And even if they saw some warning light, they tell me they're always going off. False alarms ten times a day."

"Could it be done remotely?" Gamache asked. "By someone outside the academy?"

"It would be more difficult," said Beauvoir, "but yes, it could be done. What're you thinking?"

"I'm thinking of a conversation I had with the mayor a few months back at his office. Being mayor of Saint-Alphonse isn't exactly a full-time job. He moonlights as a consultant in software design."

"I'll make an appointment with the mayor," said Lacoste. "Let's move on. We found the bullet from the gun. It was lodged in the wall across the room. We're having it analyzed, of course, but it looks like it came from the murder weapon."

"I've sent an email to the manufacturer," Beauvoir reported. "Some place in England. But Leduc could've picked the gun up secondhand on the black market."

"I haven't seen the weapon," said Gélinas. "Where is it?"

"Sent to the lab for tests, but we have pictures," said Lacoste.

As Gélinas studied them, his expression grew more and more perplexed.

"At what height was the bullet?" Gamache asked.

"Five feet eight inches."

"He was standing when killed. I wondered if he might've been kneeling."

"Begging for his life?" asked Beauvoir.

"Or killed execution-style," said Gamache.

"No," said Lacoste. "He seemed to be just standing there."

"Huh," was all Gamache said. "Huh." But it was what the others were thinking.

Huh. Why would someone just wait to be murdered, and not at least try to fight back? Especially someone like Serge Leduc.

Gélinas lowered the photographs and was staring at Isabelle Lacoste.

"It's a revolver. With a silencer?"

"*Oui*," said Beauvoir. "Custom. That's why no one heard the shot."

"Was he a gun collector?"

"*Non*," said Gamache.

"Then why would he have an old-fashioned revolver?" asked Gélinas, and got only blank stares in reply. He replaced the pictures and shook his head.

"Something very strange is going on in your school, monsieur."

CHAPTER 20

———

"Hello," Nathaniel Smythe called. *"Bonjour?"*

The front door was ajar. He took a deep breath and opened it enough to get his head in.

"Madame Zardo?"

He stepped inside, hitching his satchel up on his sloping shoulders.

It was past six. He was tired and hungry. Enough to finally seek out his billet.

The door opened straight into the living room, which was in darkness except for a single lamp.

He stood still.

There were no sounds. Not a creak. Or a quack. In the demi-darkness, all he saw were books. The walls were made of them. The tables were stacked with books. The one chair, illuminated, was covered in them, splayed open. Upholstered in stories.

He'd been holding his breath, pretty sure the place would stink. Of decay. Of dander and old lady. But now, no longer able to hold it, he breathed in. Deeply.

There was a familiar smell. Not a scent. Not an aroma. Nothing that exotic. It was more earthy. It certainly wasn't cooking.

It was books. Musky words filled the air.

"I'm in here."

Amelia dropped her bag in the kitchen and followed the voice.

At the door into the back room, she stopped.

Clara Morrow was sitting on a wooden stool with a wind-up seat, her back to the door. A paintbrush in her mouth. Staring at a canvas.

Amelia couldn't see that much of the painting. It was hidden behind a mass of Clara's hair.

"So what should I do?" asked Amelia. "Aren't you supposed to cook or something?"

Clara snorted, then turned. At her feet, a very tiny lion stirred.

She looked at her guest.

Jet-black hair. Luminous white skin, almost transparent. Piercings through her nose, her brows, her cheek. But the studs weren't black or blood-red. They were tiny faux diamonds. Gleaming where they caught the light. Like stars.

Her ears were encased in rings. Her fingers looked like they'd been dipped in metal.

It was as though this girl was encasing herself in armor.

And where skin was exposed, there were tattoos.

But the one thing this girl could not mark or pierce or hide were her eyes. The only original bit left. They were bright, like diamonds.

"What?" said Huifen when Gabri handed her an apron and pointed to the dishes in the bistro kitchen. "I'm—"

"Yes, I know. You're this close"—he brought his thumb and forefinger up—"to being a Sûreté officer. You've said. And I'm this close"—he brought the fingers even closer—"to kicking you out."

"You can't."

"Of course I can. This is a favor we're doing for Monsieur Gamache, not for you. I'm happy to put you up, but you have to work for your room and board. An hour a day here in the bistro or the B and B. Wherever we need you."

"That's slave labor."

"That's life in the real world. You sat here most of the afternoon ordering food. Then you went to the B and B and ate all the cake. Well, here's the bill."

He tossed her a tea towel.

"We didn't get off to a good start," said Myrna, putting a Coke down in front of Jacques. He was slumped on the sofa in her loft above the bookstore, hitting the screen of his iPhone with increasing force.

"Fucking thing doesn't work here."

"Language," said Myrna, sitting in a large chair in which her outline was permanently stamped.

"I heard that old woman say worse."

"And when you're an old woman, we'll tolerate it from you too. For now, you're a guest in my home, in this village, and you'll watch your language. And you're right. There's no wireless here, no satellite coverage."

Jacques shoved his iPhone into his pocket.

"Should we start again?" Myrna asked.

She'd calmed down since their confrontation in the bistro. Seeing Ruth as the reasonable one had been deeply humbling to her. She'd returned to her bookstore for the afternoon, then headed upstairs, made a bed for her guest, and began dinner.

"Do you want to talk about what happened at the academy?" she asked. "You were close to the professor?"

Jacques stood up. "You make me sick. A man's dead, murdered. And all you want is gossip."

Myrna also stood and stared at him. Her look steady, unwavering.

"I know what you're going through."

"Oh, really," he laughed. "You know about murder? In books, maybe. You have no idea what it's like out there." He waved out the window. "In the real world."

"Oh, I have some idea," she said quietly. "This isn't the peaceful village it appears."

"What? Has your car been scratched? Did someone steal your recycling bin?"

"Before I had a bookstore, I was a psychologist in Montréal. Among my clients were inmates at the SHU. You know it?"

Myrna could see some of the anger turn to surprise, then interest. But he was too invested in his opinion to change now.

"The Special Handling Unit," he said.

"The worst cases."

"And did you cure anyone?"

"Now, you know that's unlikely, perhaps even impossible."

"So you failed. And you came here. Like Gamache. A village filled with failures."

Myrna wasn't going to be goaded again by this kid. Though she felt anger crooking its finger at her. Instead, she nodded toward the laptop, plugged into a phone line. "You're welcome to use it. Look up some things. Change the facts and you'll change the feelings."

"Wow, thanks for that insight."

He grabbed his jacket and took the stairs two at a time, down to Myrna's New and Used Bookstore, then out the door.

Myrna stood at the large window in her loft and saw him on the road below, visible in the light thrown by the bistro.

He turned and looked up at her. Then he took long strides away from the bookstore and the bistro. Past Clara's home. Myrna watched him until he disappeared into the night.

And then the darkness was broken, by a small light.

After checking the house, including under the beds in case the demented old woman had died and rolled under one, Nathaniel went to the bistro.

She wasn't there. But the big guy, one of the owners, had suggested the house along the road. Clara Morrow's.

He headed there but met Amelia on her way out.

"Ruth Zardo? No, she's not there. I wish. Just that old painter woman. She keeps staring at me. Gives me the creeps. I had to leave."

"Why do you do that to yourself"—he indicated her piercings and tattoos—"if you don't want people to stare?"

"Why do you dress like that?" She waved her hand at him.

"What?" He looked down at his coat and jeans. "Everybody dresses like this."

"Exactly. Why do you want to be everyone?"

"Why do you want to be no one?"

The truth was, Amelia hadn't left because of Clara.

When her host had gotten off her stool, Amelia had seen the painting. A full-on portrait. A self-portrait. It had blasted off the canvas, getting right up to Amelia. Getting in her face. They'd locked eyes, the painting and the person.

The painted woman glared at her. Like she knew Amelia. And knew what she'd done.

And Amelia had fled.

The light was on and the door was open.

Amelia couldn't remember the last time she'd been in a church. Probably her christening, though now that she thought of it, Amelia didn't know if she had been christened.

It was a tiny church, the smallest she'd ever seen. It was actually too dark to see the building itself. All they could see was the light through a stained-glass window.

The image, though, wasn't of a crucifix, or a saint, or a martyr. What glowed in the night were boys. Barely men. Slogging through a glass battlefield.

"Come on," said Nathaniel, already up the stairs and at the door. "Gabri said if Madame Zardo wasn't at home or in the bistro or with the painter, she'd be here. Sleeping it off, probably."

"Why're you so anxious to find her?" asked Amelia, stomping up the steps after him.

"Because she's my home," he said. "Where else am I supposed to go?"

Ruth Zardo was indeed lying down, the duck nesting on her stomach. Her head propped on hymnals.

"Is she dead?" Nathaniel whispered.

"No, she's not fucking dead," said a voice.

Ruth sat up, but didn't look at them. She looked at the person who'd just spoken.

Cadet Jacques Laurin was sitting off to the side, his boots on the pew in front. Drinking a beer he'd taken from that black woman's fridge and shoved into the pocket of his jacket.

He'd given a near-perfect imitation of Ruth's voice. Right down to the cadence and tone. Both angry and wounded. Somehow catching the slight vulnerability.

Nathaniel laughed and was horrified when both Jacques and Ruth turned to look at him.

God help me, he thought.

"What're you doing here?" they all asked each other at once, just as Hui-fen arrived.

"I saw you guys come up here. Oh, wonderful." She sat down next to Jacques and, grabbing the bottle from him, she took a swig of beer. "Why're we here?"

"I'm here for some peace and quiet," said Ruth, glaring at them.

Jacques tilted his beer toward her, and after a moment's hesitation, she nodded. He got up and handed Ruth the bottle, sitting down beside her.

"I was watching you," he said. "Why're you staring at that?"

He lifted his chin toward the stained-glass window and the brittle boys.

"Where else am I supposed to look?" Ruth demanded, handing back the bottle.

The cadets scanned the chapel. There was a central aisle with wooden pews on either side that looked handmade, each slightly different. There were just a few rows of seats and then the altar, also handmade. Well made. Indeed, beautifully carved, with leaves and a huge spreading oak tree.

"I come here to write sometimes," Ruth admitted, and they saw the notebook wedged between her and the back of the pew. "It's quiet. No one comes into churches anymore. God has left the building, and is wandering. Or wondering."

"In the wilderness," said Amelia.

Ruth glared at her, but Amelia had the impression it was more habit than conviction. But she also had the impression it was more than peace and quiet the old poet was after.

Amelia sat across the aisle, on the hard pew, and looked past Ruth to the stained glass. From the outside it looked like the soldiers were arriving. In here, it looked like they were leaving. Going. Gone.

Below the window was writing, which she couldn't make out.

There were other windows in the chapel, including a nice rose window over the door. But this was the only one with a picture.

Though it wasn't simply an image. There was a feeling about it. Whoever had made this had done it with great care. Had cared.

It was detailed. Intricate. Their unraveling and mud-encrusted socks. The skinned knuckles and filthy hands that held the rifles. The revolver in the holster of one of the boys. The brass buttons.

Yes, great care had been taken. Down to the last detail.

And then Amelia saw it. She stood up and walked between the pews. Closer, closer.

"Shouldn't you be bursting into flames?" said Ruth as she passed.

Amelia walked right up to the stained glass and stared at the one boy. The one with the revolver. In his leather satchel, peeking out of one end where the buckle had broken, there was a piece of paper.

As she leaned closer, closer, she saw three pine trees. And a snowman.

CHAPTER 21

⁓

"Holy shit," said Myrna, taking a step back from the window.

"Language," said Jacques.

"She said, 'holy,'" said Ruth. "Weren't you listening?"

Myrna took another step back. Clara leaned in for a closer look.

Ruth had sent Amelia off to get Clara, Myrna, and Reine-Marie as soon as she'd seen what the boy soldier had in his satchel.

"The map," whispered Reine-Marie, who'd replaced Clara at the window.

And now they sat together, studying the copy of the map Nathaniel had pulled from his bag.

"Why would the soldier have it?" asked Reine-Marie, her words forming a mist on the glass boy. "A map of France, of Belgium, maybe. Of Vimy or Flanders. A battlefield map, I could see. But Three Pines isn't a battlefield."

"You obviously haven't been paying attention," said Clara.

She stood up and once again stepped closer to the stained glass. "I've always admired this, but never really looked at it close up."

"Who were they?" Huifen asked. "There're a bunch of names underneath. Are they there?"

She nodded toward the writing under the window.

They Were Our Children.

And then the list. No ranks. Just names. In death they were equal. *Etienne Adair. Teddy Adams. Marc Beaulieu.*

Ruth's rickety voice filled the tiny chapel. But when they looked over, they saw the old poet wasn't reading the names. She was staring straight ahead, toward the altar. Reciting them.

179

Fred Dagenais. Stuart Davis.

"You memorized them?" asked Myrna.

"I guess so," said Ruth.

She turned to look at the window, at the writing, at the boys she knew by heart.

"I'd assumed the window was a representation," said Myrna. "A composite of all those lost in the war, and not specific boys from the village. But now I wonder."

"Who they are," said Reine-Marie.

"Who he is," said Clara, pointing to the young man who was clearly the center of the work.

"He has a revolver, but the other boys only have rifles. Why is that?" asked Reine-Marie.

"I think officers had revolvers," said Myrna.

"But he can't be an officer," said Huifen. "He's a kid. He's our age. Maybe even younger. That's like saying he's"—she waved at Nathaniel—"a chief inspector. It's ridiculous."

"One day, maybe," said Nathaniel, though no one heard him.

"Not so ridiculous if everyone else is dead," said Myrna. "A battlefield promotion."

"But isn't the real question, why does he have that?" asked Clara, pointing to the map sticking out of his satchel.

They looked down at the map the cadets had brought. Even though theirs was a photocopy, they could still see all the tears and smears. They'd assumed it was dirty from being stuck in the walls for so long.

But maybe it wasn't just dirt.

"But that's incredible," said Armand into his cell phone, catching the eyes of the others in the conference room at the academy and making an expression of apology.

They'd had sandwiches and drinks brought in to the conference room. The sandwiches were on POM Bakery white bread and were curling up at the edges.

Only Jean-Guy was eating them. He would eat the utensils, Gamache knew, if no one was watching.

"You're sure it's the same map?" He listened for a moment. "The snowman. Yes."

All Beauvoir, Lacoste, and Gélinas could hear was Gamache's end of the conversation. His phone had rung as they were interviewing the last of the faculty.

Professor Charpentier sat with his hands in his lap. Completely contained. Except for the sweat pouring out of him. He was drenched. His face was so slick it glistened, and Jean-Guy was worried he'd pass out from dehydration.

"Water?"

He poured a glass from the pitcher and shoved it toward the professor, who shook his head.

Up to and including that moment, the professor had been monosyllabic. Not, it was felt, because he was trying to hide anything. In fact, the few damp syllables they'd squeezed out of him showed his acute willingness to help.

Had he seen anything?

A brisk shake of his head.

Had he heard anything?

Another shake.

Did he know Serge Leduc well?

A shake.

"What does he teach?" Deputy Commissioner Gélinas whispered to Beauvoir while Gamache was on the phone. "His file is empty."

He motioned toward the dossier, open in front of him.

"He's a tactician," said Beauvoir. "Commander Gamache hired him. He has the title of professor, but he only teaches one class. Advanced tactics to the graduating cadets."

"He could teach water sports."

Professor Charpentier sat absolutely still, like some wild animal startled. The only thing that moved was a large drip that was making its way to the end of his nose, and then hung there.

Lacoste, Beauvoir, and Gélinas stared at it, transfixed.

"Why's he here if he doesn't really teach?" Gélinas asked, once the drip dropped. In the background, they could hear Gamache still on the phone with his wife.

"He designs tactical exercises for the cadets," whispered Beauvoir. "A series of 'what ifs.' For the freshmen, it starts as written examples and tests, but then they progress to the role-playing and mock-ups. We've built scale models for the exercises, but it goes beyond that, to questions of how to handle different situations. It's new."

"Commander Gamache brought that in?"

"*Oui.* And the man with it. The idea is to teach the cadets other ways of handling situations besides force. But if they have to use force, they need to know the most effective way to do it."

Deputy Commissioner Gélinas nodded approval.

"Had the Commander ever met this Charpentier before hiring him?"

"Oh, yes, Hugo Charpentier was one of Monsieur Gamache's own recruits into the Sûreté, years ago."

"He's a Sûreté officer?" asked Gélinas.

"Was."

"One of Monsieur Gamache's protégés?"

"At first, but then someone else took him under his wing," said Beauvoir. "When Charpentier showed a knack for tactics."

"Really? Who?"

"Superintendent Brébeuf."

Gélinas nodded, tucking that information away. He looked at Charpentier's wheelchair. "Wounded?"

"No. He's got a condition like Parkinson's, I believe," said Beauvoir. "Some days he can walk with canes, but most of the time he gets around in the chair. Easier and faster."

"Did you work with him at the Sûreté?"

"*Non*, he didn't stay long. He left and set up his own company. Works as a consultant. He must be very good," said Beauvoir, "or Monsieur Gamache wouldn't have brought him here."

"He looks terrified."

"Yes, he always does."

"But how can a man who is permanently afraid teach attack techniques and strategies?"

"Who knows airplanes better than someone afraid to fly?" asked Beauvoir, and had the pleasure of seeing the Deputy Commissioner's brow rise.

"I'd like to see it for myself," said Gamache. "I'll be home later tonight and will bring the original map."

Gamache hung up and returned to the table.

"My apologies."

"Everything all right at home?" Lacoste asked.

"Oh, yes."

"They found a map?"

All eyes turned to Professor Charpentier. Sweat was now pooling at his collar, and as he spoke it overflowed down the sodden shirt.

The words seemed wrung out of him.

At that moment, Gélinas sat forward as though someone had punched the back of his chair.

"Wait a minute. You're H. E. Charpentier?"

Professor Charpentier ignored him and continued to look at Gamache, who nodded.

"Actually, the map was found a few months ago in the wall of an old building in a little village in the Eastern Townships," said Gamache. "My village, as it turns out. But now they've also found an image of it in a stained-glass window in the local chapel."

"Really?" said Lacoste, who was familiar with the church and the memorial window. "That's strange. The same map we found—"

"In the wall, yes," said Gamache, cutting her off.

Another plump drip was making its way down Charpentier's cheek. And into the crevice of his smile.

"That Charpentier?" Gélinas whispered to Beauvoir, who nodded. "But he's a recluse. Good God, I've hired him as a consultant in tactics, but he won't even talk on the phone. Only by email. I thought he was older. And bigger."

Charpentier rolled his chair a millimeter closer to the conference table. Either not hearing what Gélinas said, or not caring.

"That's interesting. Important maps are sometimes found in attics or the back of an old desk, but you say this one was in a wall?"

"I don't think it has any historic value, or even monetary," said Gamache. "It's just a curiosity."

"It is that," agreed Charpentier, glancing from Gamache to Lacoste.

"*Oui*. Now," Gamache turned to the others, "can we get back to the matter at hand?"

"Where is it now?" asked Charpentier.

"What?"

"The map."

"I have the original," said Gamache, clearly trying to be patient while redirecting the conversation. "I can show it to you later, if you like."

"You say 'original.' That means there're copies?"

"I'm sorry, professor," said Gamache, "but how can any of this possibly matter?"

"That's what I'm wondering." He was studying Gamache in a disconcerting manner. Talk of maps had opened the verbal floodgates. "You seem to think it is, or you wouldn't have spent such a long time on the phone discussing it."

"Perhaps we can talk about this later," said Gamache.

"I'd like that."

Charpentier pushed away from the table.

"But we're not finished," said Gélinas. "We have more questions."

"No you don't," said the young man. "All the pertinent ones have been asked. And I have nothing to add to this investigation. If I did, I'd tell you. Anything beyond this is a waste of time."

Beauvoir, who'd had respect for this strange man, now found himself developing a slight affection for him.

Charpentier sat there, drenched in his own fluids. Skinny. Sallow. Out of his depth among these highly functioning officers. And completely unaware of it.

As far as Charpentier was concerned, he was the normal one.

Beauvoir admired that, though he did not agree with it.

"There is one last question," said Gamache. "And then I'll show you the original map."

There was now a very slight smile on the tactician's face, as though he approved of Gamache's use of the age-old quid pro quo.

"What did you think of Serge Leduc?"

"I thought he was a stupid man. I thought he was better suited to be a shoe salesman."

Deputy Commissioner Gélinas laughed and then stopped when Charpentier looked at him.

"You don't agree?"

"*Non, non*, it's not that. What you said was funny."

"Really? Professor Leduc would have been good at selling footwear. High end. Convincing people to buy something that would eventually hurt them. And to pay good money to do it. He was a sadist."

"Could he have run a corruption ring?" Gélinas asked.

"Never. He'd have been caught immediately. He didn't think two or three steps ahead. A shoe salesman doesn't need to."

"Ironic really," said Lacoste, though only Gamache caught what she meant and smiled.

"But the head of the Sûreté Academy should," said Charpentier, looking at Gamache.

"Where would you look for his killer?" asked Isabelle Lacoste.

"Matthew 10:36," said Charpentier, after thinking for a moment. "Yes. That's where I'd start. Now, can we go?"

"I'll meet you in my rooms in fifteen minutes," said Gamache.

"Strange man," said Lacoste as the door closed.

"A genius," said the RCMP officer. "And yes, a strange man." He thought for a moment. "A person like that could do a lot of damage, *non*?"

"You think he was involved in Leduc's death?" asked Chief Inspector Lacoste.

"Or the corruption. Or both. Don't you?" He'd looked at Gamache as he spoke. "Isn't that why you brought him here? A professor who doesn't really teach? A brilliant tactician? So you could observe him? You brought all the suspects together. Leduc, Brébeuf, Charpentier. And then watched what would happen. But you made a mistake. One I've heard assigned to you in the past. You thought you were smarter than them. Than him. You thought you could control the situation. But you couldn't. It's spun out of control, Commander. And he knows it. That wasn't an observation, about needing to think a few steps ahead, it was a joke. He was mocking you."

Gamache got up.

"You might be right," he said as he made for the door. "Time will tell."

"Time has spoken. Did you not hear it? And in case you missed it, it dropped a body into your great experiment, Monsieur Gamache. And if you don't get control soon, there will be more."

When the Commander had left, Paul Gélinas turned to the others.

"Was that a biblical reference Charpentier made?"

"Matthew 10:36," said Lacoste. "When he was head of homicide, it was one of the first lessons Gamache taught his agents."

"*And a man's foes shall be they of his own household,*" said Beauvoir.

Gélinas nodded. "And H. E. Charpentier would start in this household, to find the killer."

"I'd have thought that was obvious," said Lacoste, getting up to go.

"A household isn't just a house," said Gélinas. "There's an intimacy implied in that quote. It speaks of someone close. Very close."

CHAPTER 22

⌐◡⌐

"Huh," said Charpentier as he looked at the framed map.

Gamache had taken it off the wall and handed it to the professor.

"Huh?" said Armand. "Could you be more specific? Is it an important map?"

"Not in the least." Though Charpentier continued to study it.

"I'm afraid I have to leave." Gamache looked at his watch. It was almost seven in the evening. "But I'll be back in the morning. Chief Inspector Lacoste and some of her team will stay, as will Inspector Beauvoir. They'll have the forensics report by morning."

Gamache reached over to take the map from the professor, but Charpentier seemed reluctant to give it up.

"I'm coming with you," he said.

"Why?" asked Gamache. "Not to be rude, but I'm not sure why you'd want to."

"I collect maps. This one is curious. The image was also found in a stained-glass window in your village, you said?"

"*Oui.*"

"I'd like to see it."

"But you said it's not an important map."

"It's not. And yet it's important to you," said Charpentier. "As a map, or as something else?"

Gamache weighed his options while looking at the drenched young man, then finally said, "Pack an overnight case and meet me at the main doors in fifteen minutes."

When Charpentier left, Gamache picked up the map. The glass was slick with perspiration. He turned it over, and carefully, carefully, removed it from the frame.

They arrived in Three Pines just after eight thirty, going directly to St. Thomas's Church, which was still bright with lights.

Eight people turned their heads as they entered. Four villagers and the four cadets. A crowd any minister would envy.

"Armand," said Reine-Marie, going forward to greet him. Then she turned to the slender man leaning on canes beside him. Armand had warned her they'd have an overnight guest, but he hadn't told her everything.

If people were mostly water, then this young man was more human than most.

"This is Hugo Charpentier," said Gamache. "He's on the faculty."

"You're one of our professors," said Jacques. "You teach advanced tactics."

"And you need to pay closer attention in class, Cadet Laurin," said Charpentier. "As I remember, you've been shot dead in the last two tactical exercises, and taken hostage in a third. The factory test. You failed."

Huifen tried to suppress a smile, while Amelia and Nathaniel looked at Jacques with interest. The golden boy not just tarnished, but dead.

Hugo Charpentier turned to the Commander.

Gamache held his gaze, knowing exactly what the tactician was thinking.

Four cadets. Not in the academy, but in this small chapel, miles away. It would not be an exaggeration to say they were hidden away, though they themselves might not realize it.

"Professor Charpentier collects maps," Armand explained. "I thought he could help. Well, he thought he could help."

So far, on the drive down, Hugo Charpentier had said nothing about the map, or anything else. They'd driven in silence, which was fine with Armand. He had things to think about.

"It's over here," said Reine-Marie, walking to the stained-glass window. "How could we not have seen it before?"

"You weren't meant to," said Charpentier. "Look at his face."

Two of the soldiers were in profile, heading forward. But the one young man was staring straight out. At them.

"That's what you're meant to see." Charpentier waved one of his sticks at the boy. "His expression is so striking, it wipes everything else off, well, the map."

"You think the map was hidden on purpose?" asked Myrna.

"Misdirection," said Huifen, who'd been reading about just that in her tactics textbook. By one H. E. Charpentier.

"There was a purpose," said Charpentier. "But was it to hide the map? I don't see why anyone would put it there, then direct everyone's attention away from it."

"Why not just leave it out, you mean?" asked Reine-Marie.

"Or make it obvious," said Myrna.

"Maybe it's not important. A detail," said Clara. "Like the buttons and the mud and the gun in the holster. There just to add accuracy."

"Accuracy? A map with a snowman?" asked Ruth. "Who do you think the Canadian Expeditionary Force was fighting? Frosty the Hun?"

Gamache brought out the original, and Charpentier took it from him without asking. Comparing it to the glass one.

It was the same map.

Other copies were scattered on the pews, as were plates with the remains of roast beef, arugula and Camembert on baguette. Chicken, pesto and sliced apple on Sarah's fresh-baked, soft multigrain. And various beers and soft drinks.

When they'd first moved to Three Pines and noticed that villagers sometimes took picnics into the chapel, both Armand and Reine-Marie had been surprised. Perhaps even, he admitted, disapproving.

But after a couple of months, Reine-Marie had asked, "Who made the rule that people shouldn't eat or drink in a church?"

So they'd tried it. At first it felt awkward, wrong. As though God would be offended if people took a meal in his house. Until they realized that the sacrilege wasn't eating and talking and laughing in the chapel. It was leaving it empty.

"How did you come to see it?" Commander Gamache asked Amelia.

"How did you miss it?" she asked.

Clara was about to snap at her when she stopped, realizing it was actually a fair question. How had they missed it? Were they really so riveted on the soldier's face that everything else faded into the background, as the young professor suggested?

And, more perplexing, was it intentional misdirection?

"I was looking at her." Amelia waved toward Ruth. "She was going on and on about something—"

"The true nature of man and his place in the universe," said Ruth to Charpentier. She seemed to admire his two canes to her one. "Basically, the meaning of life."

"Of course," said the young man.

"—so my attention drifted," explained Amelia, "to the window behind her. That's when I saw it."

"Can we go somewhere else?" Jacques asked, getting up from the pew. "My ass hurts."

"I have a pain in my ass too," said Myrna, looking at her houseguest.

"Let's go," said Clara. "I'm tired, and Leo here will need to go out."

The little lion was asleep on her lap, while Henri and Gracie slept on the floor beneath Reine-Marie's pew.

Once outside, Amelia heard the two women pleading in the darkness, "Pee. Poop."

She stood on the road, waiting. Her back to the chapel. To the window.

"Pee. Poop."

When asked how she came to see the map, she hadn't been completely truthful. While everyone else was drawn to the soldier boy's face, she'd been repelled by it.

His terror.

But mostly what gave her the creeps, and made her turn away, was the look of forgiveness on his young face.

And so, unlike the others, she'd been free to, forced to, stare at other parts of the window.

That's when she'd seen the map.

Finally, his business done, Leo was picked up by Clara, who handed a small, warm bag to Amelia.

"Let's go home."

Once home, Armand showed Hugo Charpentier to his room on the main floor, and the shower, while he himself changed and Reine-Marie put the kettle on and rustled up some dinner.

Twenty minutes later, Charpentier came out in his dressing gown, smelling of fresh soap and rubbing his dull brown hair.

Gamache was in the living room, in front of the fire. Their dinner of poached salmon and asparagus on foldout tables in front of them.

"Waiting for me?" Charpentier asked. "Where's Madame Gamache?"

"I asked her to join us, but she's taken a tray to the bedroom. She wanted to leave us alone to talk."

"We have that much to talk about?"

"I think we do. Don't you? Wine?"

"Please, *patron*."

There weren't many whom Hugo Charpentier called *patron*, but Monsieur Gamache was one.

He poured them each a glass of white.

"Why are those students here?" Charpentier asked.

Armand Gamache had been waiting for just that question.

"They were the four who were closest to Professor Leduc. Cadets Cloutier and Laurin are in their final year and have been his protégés for almost three years now."

"You think they've been infected," said Charpentier. "Too close, for too long, to the plague that was Leduc."

Gamache didn't disagree.

"The other two are freshmen. Leduc's newest protégés."

"Why did he choose them?"

"I don't know. We might never know."

"Oh, I think we suspect, don't you? Cadet Smythe is Anglo and gay and too eager to please. A disastrous combination in the hands of someone like Leduc. And the other? The Goth? Cadet Choquet? You only have to look at her to see the wounds. A man like Leduc crawls in through hurts like that."

The tactician studied Gamache.

"Now the question, Commander, is whether you brought them here for their own good or to protect the rest of the student body? Did you bring possible victims to your village, or the killer?"

"Recently, at one of the soirées, I gave them the exercise of investigating that map," said Gamache, choosing not to answer the question directly. "To hone their investigative skills. This morning, I told them that a copy of it was found in Leduc's bedside table, and that what had started as a simple assignment was now part of the murder investigation."

"Clever. It gave you an excuse to bring them here, and gave them something apparently important to do."

"Well, it wasn't completely without value."

"What do you mean?"

"A copy *was* found in Leduc's bedside table."

Hugo Charpentier stared. It was difficult to surprise a man who specialized in seeing all possibilities at once, but this did.

"How did it get there?"

Gamache shook his head.

"Whose was it?" Charpentier asked. "One of the students'? Had to have been. But which one?"

"Amelia Choquet's map is missing."

Charpentier nodded, his head bobbing up and down like a toy on a dashboard.

"The bedside table," he finally said.

"*Oui*," agreed Gamache. "That struck me too. The map was put away, but not hidden."

"The killer wasn't looking for it," said Charpentier. "So it was of no consequence to him, only to Leduc."

"But why would Leduc care about this?"

They both looked down at the map. It had taken on a slight rose hue in the fading firelight.

"There is another possibility," said Gamache.

"That it was placed there by the killer to implicate one of the cadets," said Charpentier. "Choquet's is missing? Then she's the next victim. He'd make it look like suicide. A troubled, vulnerable freshman who killed a professor, then took her own life once the investigation closed in."

Gamache showed no surprise at this scenario. It had occurred to him too.

That's what he'd had to think about, in those few minutes alone in Leduc's room with the body.

What the map meant. And where it might lead them. And what to do about it.

The only answer was to spirit the four cadets away to someplace safe. Quickly. Quietly. Before the murderer could implement the next phase of his plan.

"Of course, maybe her map was a random choice by the killer," said Charpentier, thinking out loud. "It's possible hers was the most easily taken. He just needed someone's. It wouldn't matter to the killer. He wanted a scapegoat. A cadet tethered to the body. Her suicide would close the case. Unless, of course—"

"Yes, I know."

The other thing Gamache had thought about, in those long minutes with the dead man.

"Unless she killed him."

"Or one of the other three did," said Charpentier. "After all, they'd know she had the map. Who better to place it there, to implicate her, than one of the others? And you brought them all down here. Together."

"I have at least placed them in separate billets," said Gamache.

Charpentier nodded. "A wise precaution. Makes a pillow over the face in the middle of the night more difficult."

The professor picked up the map. "We can surmise why it was in the bed-side table of a dead man. To point suspicion at one of the cadets." He looked at it closely. "But why are you in a stained-glass window?"

Charpentier waited, as though the snowman, or cow, or one of the pines might tell him.

And then Charpentier smiled and handed it to Gamache. "I think I know."

"It told you?"

"In a way. May I have some tisane? It helps me sleep."

As Gamache walked to the kitchen to put on the kettle, Charpentier called after him. "Chamomile, if you have it."

"We do."

There was the sound of water running into the kettle, then quiet. Into the silence Charpentier placed a question.

"You say you gave them the assignment at one of your soirées? But I thought you said the senior cadets were Leduc's people."

"They are," came the answer from the kitchen. "He had them appear to attach themselves to me so they could report back." Gamache leaned out of the kitchen door and his face broke into a smile. "I'm smarter than I look."

"Thank God for that," said Charpentier.

Gamache walked back in with their tisanes and a jar of local lavender honey.

Charpentier placed the spoon in the tea and looked up into the intelligent eyes.

"You were going to tell me why the map was in the boy's satchel," said Gamache.

"*Oui*. It's because maps are magic."

If he didn't have the Commander's full attention before, he did now. Gamache lowered his tea to the table and stared.

"Magic?"

"Yes. They've become so mundane we've forgotten that. They transport us from one place to another. They illuminate our universe. The first maps were of the heavens, you know. What the ancients could see. Where their gods lived. All cultures mapped the stars. But then they lowered their sights. To the world around them."

"Why?"

"Ahhh, monsieur," nodded Charpentier with approval and growing excitement. "Exactly. Why. And how? It seems easy, now, but can you imagine the first person who figured out how to represent something three-dimensional

193

in two dimensions? How do you draw distance and time? And why go through the trouble? It's not like they didn't have enough to do. So why did they create maps?"

"Necessity," said Gamache.

"Yes, but what drove that necessity?"

Gamache thought about it.

"Survival?"

"Exactly. Maps gave them control over their surroundings, for the first time ever. It showed how to get from one place to another. It sounds simple now, but thousands of years ago it would have been an incredible feat of imagination and imagery. All maps are drawn as though looking down. From a bird's point of view. From their god's point of view. Imagine being the first person to think of that. To be able to wrap their minds around a perspective they'd never seen. And then draw it. Incredible. And think of the advantage."

Gamache had never in his life thought of these things, but now he understood how a master tactician would revere maps. As a tactical tool, they were revolutionary and second to none. They would give whoever possessed them an insurmountable advantage.

They would be magic.

"It meant they could plan, they could strategize," said Charpentier. "They could see into the future. Where they were going. And what they'd find. The tribe, the nation, the enterprise with the most accurate maps won."

"Is that how you became a tactician?"

"It started with maps, yes. I was an awkward child," he said, as though that might be in doubt. "I found the world chaotic. Unsettling. But there was order in maps. And beauty. I love maps."

It did not seem an exaggeration. He looked down at the paper on the coffee table with affection. A newfound friend.

"Even the word is interesting. Map. It comes from *mappa mundi*. *Mappa* is Latin for napkin. *Mundi* is world, of course. Isn't that wonderful? A napkin, with their world on it. The mundane and the magnificent. Map."

He said the word as though it was indeed magic. And in the young man's drenched face, Gamache saw the world opening up for an unhappy boy.

Map.

"Monks did some of the first European maps," said Charpentier. "Gathering information from mariners and merchants. They're sometimes called Beatine maps because some of the earliest were done by a monk called Beatus in the eighth century. They were for his work on the Apocalypse."

"Not that again," muttered Gamache.

Charpentier glanced at him, but returned to the paper on the table.

"Every map has a purpose," he whispered. "What's yours?"

"Can you guess?"

"I can give you my educated and informed opinion from years of studying maps and tactics," offered Charpentier.

"Fine," said Gamache. "I'll take that instead."

"This was done by a cartographer. A mapmaker. It's not the work of a hobbyist. Whoever drew this was probably a professional."

"Is it the cow that gave it away, or the pyramid?" asked Gamache.

"Neither," said Charpentier, missing the humor. "You can tell by the contours." He pointed to the thin lines denoting elevation. Hills and valleys. "I suspect if we investigate, we'll find this is extremely accurate."

"Not completely. The cow was rescued and the snowman would've melted a hundred years ago, and I can guarantee you there's no pyramid nearby."

He pointed to the triangle in the upper-right quadrant.

"That's what makes this map especially interesting," said Charpentier. "Old maps show history. Of settlement, of commerce, of conquest. This one seems to show a very personal history. It's a map meant for one person. One purpose."

"And what is that purpose?" asked Gamache again, not expecting an answer. But this time he got one.

"I think it's an early orienteering map."

"Orienteering? The sport?"

"But it didn't start out as that," said Charpentier. "The soldier in the window is from the First World War, right? Orienteering was developed as a training tool to help soldiers find their way around battlefields."

"So it is a battlefield map?" asked Gamache, losing his way.

"Of course not. There's a snowman in it with a hockey stick. This isn't Ypres. This is here. You wanted to know why this map was made?"

In the background, the fire sputtered as the last of the embers died. Henri snored on the floor at Gamache's feet, and little Gracie had stopped whimpering.

Gamache nodded.

"It was made for that young soldier as an *aide-mémoire*," said Charpentier. "To remind him of home."

Armand looked at the three young, playful pines.

"To bring him home," said Charpentier.

But it hadn't worked. Not all maps, Gamache thought, were magic.

CHAPTER 23

⁓

Myrna sat up straight in bed. Awoken by what sounded like a gunshot. Still groggy from sleep, she listened, expecting it was just a dream.

But then there was another shot. And not a single one, but rapid fire. Unmistakable. Automatic weapons fire.

And then shouting. Screaming.

Tossing the duvet aside, she ran to the door of her bedroom and opened it. But even as she did, her dream state fell away and she knew what she'd find.

Jacques Laurin sat at the laptop, his face lit only by the flickering images on the screen.

It was two in the morning and Jacques had finally followed her advice and googled "Armand Gamache."

And the link to this video had come up.

More shouts, commands. Controlled, forceful. The voice cut through any panic, cut through the gunfire, as the Sûreté agents moved deeper and deeper into the abandoned factory. Pushing the gunmen ahead of them. Engaging them.

But the gunmen were everywhere, swarming the agents.

It looked to be an ambush, a slaughter.

But still, on the man's urging, by voice and swift, decisive hand signals, they moved forward.

Huifen Cloutier sat up in bed.

This was the first quiet time she'd had since the death of Professor Leduc. The murder of the Duke.

197

That's what he'd be remembered for, she knew. The man would be erased by the murder. Serge Leduc no longer existed. He'd never lived. All he'd done was died.

She pulled the map onto her lap, and stared at it.

Cadet Laurin's face grew paler and paler.

He recognized this. It was their tactical exercise, in their mocked-up factory. The one where he'd been killed twice and taken hostage once. The one they never won.

But this was no exercise. It was real.

The video had been edited from the cameras the agents wore. The point of view changed from one agent to another. It was jerky, shaky. As they ran. And crouched behind concrete pillars that exploded as bullets hit.

But it was clear. As were the looks on the agents' faces. Determined. Resolute. As they moved forward. Even as they fell.

Amelia lay in bed, staring at the ceiling.

The duvet was warm around her as the cold, fresh air came in through the open window. The sheets smelled faintly of lavender. Not enough to be off-putting. Just enough to be calming.

And slowly, slowly, her mind slowed. Stopped its whirring. Stopped its worrying. She breathed in the lavender, and breathed out her anxiety.

The Duke was dead. Resting in peace, and now, finally, so could she.

The sounds were even more jarring than the images. Jacques flinched as the bullets struck all around. The walls, the floors. The agents. It was so much louder than in the exercise at the academy. His mind had gone numb, overwhelmed by the din, the chaos, the shouts and explosions, the screams of pain. His hands gripped the arms of the chair, holding tight.

All his senses were shutting down.

On the screen, an officer in tactical gear was moving forward. Then he suddenly stopped. And stood straight up. And in a grotesque parody of a ballet move, he spun gracefully. And fell.

A voice called, "Jean-Guy."

Jacques watched as Professor Beauvoir was dragged to safety. Then the camera switched and he saw Commander Gamache, completely focused.

Quickly assessing the wounded man, as gunfire sounded, pounded, around them.

Beauvoir stared up at Gamache as he tried to stanch the bleeding. Beauvoir was silent but his eyes were wide with terror. Pleading.

"I have to go," said Gamache, putting a pressure bandage in the younger man's hands and holding it to the wound. Gamache paused for a moment. Then leaning forward, he kissed him gently on the forehead.

Ruth Zardo stood at the threshold and stared at the boy in the bed.

He slept soundly, deeply. She listened to the rhythm of his breathing. Then she closed the door and went downstairs.

The old poet didn't sleep much anymore. Didn't seem to need it. What she needed was time. She could see the shore ahead. A distance away still, she thought. But visible now.

The boy had left his copy of the map in the kitchen. Ruth made a cup of chamomile and sat in her usual seat next to Rosa, who was asleep in her rag bed beside the oven.

Rosa muttered in her sleep, exhaling, "Fuck, fuck, fuck."

Ruth stared at the map. She'd thought maybe she'd be moved to write a poem. To purge her feelings onto paper. As the person who'd made this map had so obviously done.

But now she felt there was no need. The map said it all.

In the fine contours. The roads and rivers. The stranded cow, the elated snowman.

The three small but vibrant pines.

And the smears. Of mud. Or blood.

Yes, the map said it all.

She looked up. Heavenward, but not all the way to the heavens. Her thoughts stopped at the second floor of her home. Where a young man, who just that morning had found one of his professors murdered, lay dead to the world.

A thing like that would scar a person. Invade his waking and sleeping mind.

And yet young Nathaniel slept, apparently undisturbed by what had happened.

Jacques Laurin's heart pounded in his chest, his temples, his throat.

The gunmen were dead. And Sûreté agents were also dead or wounded.

199

But, incredibly, a few had escaped unhurt. Because of the calm and the tactics, on the fly, of their commander. Who'd led them through the factory and beaten the unbeatable scenario and now lay unconscious on the concrete floor. Paramedics working on him. Blood seeping from his head.

An agent, a woman, knelt beside him, holding his bloody hand.

Cadet Laurin turned off the laptop and pushed away from the desk.

CHAPTER 24

"Café?"

Mayor Florent tipped the carafe toward the two investigators.

Paul Gélinas, out of his RCMP uniform and into civilian clothing, shook his head but Isabelle Lacoste nodded.

The mayor's office in the town hall was infused with the scent of stale and slightly burnt coffee. She suspected the glass pot, stained with decades of caffeine, sat on the hotplate all day. If nothing else, this man could give his constituents a coffee.

At seven thirty on a cold March morning, it was no mean offering.

He added milk and sugar, at her request, and handed Lacoste the mug.

This was not an office made to impress. Once, perhaps, but not anymore. The laminate wood paneling on the walls was coming loose in spots and there was more than one dark mark on the acoustic tiles of the ceiling. The carpet had seen better days, and God only knew what else it had seen.

And yet, for all that, the room was cheerful, with mismatched fabric on the chairs and a desk recycled from some old convent school, Lacoste suspected. The walls were crammed with photographs of local sports teams, smiling and holding up pennants proclaiming they'd come in third, or second, or fifth in some tournament.

Among the young athletes was the mayor. Beaming proudly from each picture.

Some of the photos were quite faded, and as they progressed around the office walls, the mayor had grown more and more rotund, as his hair had thinned. And grayed.

Many of these girls and boys would have children of their own now.

On Mayor Florent's desk were smaller framed pictures of his own family. Children, grandchildren. Hugging dogs and cats and a horse.

The mayor took his seat and leaned toward them, a look of concern on his face.

He was not at all what Chief Inspector Lacoste had expected. Given Monsieur Gamache's description, she was prepared to meet some wiry whip of a man, worn thin by disappointment and worry and the north wind.

But as she looked into those mild, expectant eyes, the eyes of her grandfather, she realized that Monsieur Gamache had never described him physically, but had only said the mayor had a keen sense of right and wrong. And held on to resentments.

She had filled in the rest.

He'd also said he liked the man. And Lacoste could see why. She liked him too. Beside her, the RCMP officer had relaxed and crossed his legs.

Mayor Florent might very well have murdered Serge Leduc, but he did not seem a threat to anyone else.

Isabelle Lacoste decided to take a tack she rarely used.

"Did you kill Serge Leduc, Your Honor?"

Mostly because it was almost never successful.

His bushy gray eyebrows rose in surprise, and Deputy Commissioner Gélinas turned in his seat to stare at her.

Then the mayor laughed. Not long, not loud, but with what seemed genuine amusement.

"Oh my dear, I can understand why you'd think that."

Not many could get away with calling Chief Inspector Lacoste "my dear," but she felt absolutely no annoyance with him. It was so obviously said without wanting to belittle her.

"I'd think that too," he went on. "If I was you. I'm sorry, I shouldn't laugh. You weren't joking. A man's been killed, and I should be sad. Upset. But I'm not."

The mayor interlocked his fingers. His jovial eyes grew sharp.

"I despised Serge Leduc. If I was ever going to commit murder, it would be him. If anyone deserved to be killed, it was him. I go to church every Sunday. Sometimes I go there on weekdays, to pray for a citizen in trouble or distress. And I always pray for Serge Leduc."

"For his soul," said Gélinas.

"For his death."

"You hated him that much?" Lacoste asked.

Mayor Florent leaned back in his chair and was quiet for a moment, and in the silence Isabelle Lacoste thought she heard the distant shouts and happy screams of children at play.

"You're here because you know the story. Because Commander Gamache has told you what happened with your academy."

Lacoste was about to say it wasn't her academy, but decided to let it pass. She understood what he meant.

"I won't repeat the details then, but I will tell you that this is a small community. We don't have much. Our wealth is our children. We worked for years to raise money to build them a proper place to play. Where they could have social clubs and do sports all year round. So that they could grow up strong and healthy. And then they'd almost certainly move away. There isn't much here anymore for young people. But we could give them their childhoods. And send them into the world sturdy and happy. Serge Leduc stole all that. Could I have killed him? Yes. Did I? No."

But as he spoke, he throbbed. With rage suppressed.

Here was a bomb, Lacoste knew. Wrapped in flesh. Human, certainly. But that only made him more likely to explode.

"I understand Commander Gamache and you have worked out a plan where the local children can use the academy's facilities," said Lacoste. "Surely that helps."

"You think?"

The mayor stared at her with shrewd eyes, and she stared back with an equally penetrating gaze.

"Where were you two nights ago, sir?"

He pulled his agenda toward him and turned back a page.

"I had a Lion's Club dinner that night. It ended at about nine." He looked up at them and smiled again. "We're all getting quite old. Nine is about as late as we can manage."

Lacoste smiled back, and hoped and prayed she wouldn't have to arrest this man.

God, she knew, sometimes answered prayers. He had, after all, answered the mayor's.

"I went home after that. My wife was there with her bridge club. They broke up at the end of that rubber, and we were asleep by ten."

"How old's your wife?" Paul Gélinas asked.

The mayor looked at him, surprised by the question but not upset.

"A year younger than me. She's seventy-two."

"Does she wear a hearing aid?" Gélinas asked.

"Two. And yes, she takes them out at night." He looked from one to the other of the agents. "And yes, I suppose it might be possible for me to leave and she'd never know it. I sometimes have trouble sleeping. I go downstairs

203

to the kitchen and do some work. As far as I know, Marie doesn't notice. I try not to disturb her."

He was, Chief Inspector Lacoste realized, behaving like a man with nothing to hide. Or nothing to lose.

"You design software," said Lacoste, and the mayor nodded. "What sort?"

"Programs for insurance companies mostly. Actuarial tables. You'd be surprised how many variables need to be taken into account."

"Do you do security software?" asked Lacoste.

"No, that's a specialty."

"The information you work on for insurance companies would be confidential," said Gélinas. "Private."

"Extremely," agreed Mayor Florent.

"So you create it in such a way that it can't be stolen?"

"No, I just do the programming. Someone else worries about security. Why? Wait. Let me guess." He studied the two officers in front of him, no longer amused. "You're wondering about the academy's security system and if I could break in. Perhaps, but I doubt it. I'm sure their system is very sophisticated. You're welcome to take my computer and see what I've been up to. Any porn you find is my wife's."

Even Deputy Commissioner Gélinas smiled at that.

"You must be quite good at what you do," said Chief Inspector Lacoste.

The mayor looked around. "Does this look like the office of a successful man? If I was that good, don't you think I'd be in Montréal or Toronto?"

"I think this looks like the office of a very successful man," said Lacoste.

Mayor Florent held her gaze. "*Merci.*"

The investigators got up and shook hands with the mayor, who told them they were always welcome back. As they walked down the scuffed hall toward the door and the bright March morning, Lacoste said to Gélinas, "Actuarial tables. They try to predict—"

"When a person will die."

Classes were back in session at the academy. Jean-Guy Beauvoir saw to that on Commander Gamache's orders.

Not simply to maintain structure and discipline, but also to try to keep the cadets from doing their own investigations. Beauvoir had found them snooping in the halls outside the Duke's rooms. He found them hanging around the dead man's office, taking fingerprints from the door handle as though the homicide investigators might have failed to do that.

He found them in the weight room, where Leduc worked out, searching the lockers. For clues. Though, of course, they didn't have a clue what they were looking for.

It was natural and would have been endearing even, if it wasn't so extremely annoying. This was the problem with having a building crammed full of partly trained investigators. And a murder.

Once the eight a.m. classes had started, Inspector Beauvoir picked up the phone. He'd been hoping for a reply to his email, but there was none.

He punched in a long line of numbers and listened to the unusual ring tone. The two throbs instead of the one long one he was used to.

"McDermot and Ryan," came the cheerful voice, as though she were selling teddy bears or flowers, and not guns.

"Yes," said Jean-Guy, struggling to keep his Québécois accent under control. "I'm calling from Canada. I'm with the Sûreté du Québec and we're investigating a homicide."

"One moment, please."

Hold? he thought. She put me on hold? Could there possibly be a lineup of calls from police around the world, investigating murders?

Maybe they had a department dedicated to it.

Jean-Guy sighed and listened to the classical music, but it didn't take long for a less cheerful voice to pick up the phone.

"Inspector Beauvoir?" she said.

"*Oui.*"

"My name is Elizabeth Coldbrook. I'm the vice president in charge of public affairs here at McDermot. I received your email and was just writing a response. I'm sorry it's taken so long, but I wanted to be sure of my facts."

Her voice was brusque, and somehow Beauvoir had the feeling he'd done something wrong. He often had that feeling when speaking with people in Paris or London.

"Can you send me the email anyway," he asked, "so I have a written record? But I'd like to speak to you now, if you don't mind."

"Not at all. It's a terrible thing that's happened. Your email said a death. An accident?"

"*Non.* Deliberate. A single shot to the temple."

"Ahhh," she said, with some sadness but without surprise.

When you make handguns, thought Beauvoir, what exactly do you think will happen?

Instead he asked, "Have you found anything?"

"Yes. We have an order here for a .45 McDermot MR VI. It was picked up by Serge Leduc on September 21, 2011."

"Picked up? In England?"

"No, at our distributer in Vermont. I can send you the order number and information."

She was sounding less brusque. Or he was getting used to it.

She was certainly being helpful, but then, he suspected, she had a lot of experience speaking with the police about handguns.

"*S'il vous plaît.* Is this a popular gun?"

"Not much anymore. A few police forces still use it, though they're turning more and more to automatic pistols, of course."

"You make those too?"

"We do. The one you're interested in, the McDermot .45, is a very old design. A six-shooter."

"Like the Wild West?"

She laughed in a semiautomatic manner. "I guess so. Colt based their design on ours. At least, we like to think that. The height of the McDermot's popularity was during the Great War. We also supplied quite a few in the Second World War, but then demand fell off."

"So why would someone order one today?"

"Collectors like them. Was your man a collector?"

"*Non.* He was a professor at an academy that trains police officers here in Québec."

"Then he was interested in weapons."

"Yes, but modern ones. Not antiques."

"It might be antique, but it does the job."

"The job being to kill?"

There was a pause. "Not necessarily."

Beauvoir let that sit there, the pause elongating.

"Well, yes. Sometimes. Or to prevent bloodshed. We don't sell handguns into Canada. They're banned, of course. Which is why Mr. Leduc ordered from the United States. I'm not sure how he got it across the border."

"It's not that hard."

The border was more porous than anyone cared to admit.

"If he wasn't a collector, can you think why else he'd want this particular make?" asked Beauvoir.

"Well, it's sturdy, and there's not as much kickback as with other revolvers. And it's very accurate."

"Accuracy was not an issue," said Beauvoir. "And it's not like he was heading for the trenches. Why would anyone want a six-shooter when they could have an automatic weapon?"

He could almost hear her shrug. Not out of disinterest, but because she didn't have the answer any more than he did.

Beauvoir decided to take another tack.

"Why would he order from you, all the way from England, and not get a Colt, if they were so similar?"

"History. And quality. Gun people know our make."

"But a Colt or a Smith and Wesson are still good and would be cheaper, *non*? They're made right in the States."

"Yes, they would be less expensive."

"But maybe they don't make silencers," said Beauvoir.

"We don't either."

"You must. The revolver had one. I mentioned that in the email."

"I thought that was a typo, or a mistake on your part."

"You thought I didn't know what a silencer was?" he asked.

"Well, it didn't make sense to me," she said. "Revolvers don't have silencers. They don't work."

"This one did."

It seemed one had attached itself to Madame Coldbrook. The quiet became uncomfortable.

"Who made the silencer?" Beauvoir finally asked.

"I don't know."

"If not McDermot, then who?" he pushed. "If someone asks for one, where do you send them?"

"To the automatic weapons department. Revolvers do not have silencers." The imperious voice had surfaced yet again. Like Jaws. And then the voice softened. "It's tragic when someone commits suicide, and this company takes it very much to heart. I take it to heart."

And for some reason, he believed her. How many calls in a month, a week, a day did this woman receive from police around the world, a body behind the conversation?

"It wasn't a suicide," said Beauvoir. He didn't know if that made it better or worse.

"You said accuracy wasn't an issue. I assumed . . ." There was a pause. "It was murder?"

"Yes. A single shot to the temple," he repeated.

And now the pause elongated. Stretched. On and on. But it wasn't empty.

207

Even down the phone line, across the miles, across the ocean, he could hear her thinking. Considering.

"What's going through your mind, Madame Coldbrook?"

"I was thinking about the specific design of the gun and its uses. And why someone would want one. Especially someone who didn't collect guns. Why a revolver?"

She seemed to be telling, rather than asking.

"Why do you think?" he asked. In the background, he heard a knock and a voice.

"How should I know?" she demanded. "We simply make them. As your National Rifle Association is fond of saying, guns don't kill people. People kill people."

"I'm Québécois, madame. Canadian. The NRA has nothing to do with me."

"And McDermot and Ryan had nothing to do with this death. I'm sorry it has happened. Very sorry. A single shot to the temple using a revolver. Poor man. But I'm sure you'll figure it out. I'll send you the email with all the information I have, and attach the sales slip."

He was about to thank her, but the line was already dead.

Elizabeth Coldbrook's email arrived a few minutes later with a brief boilerplate description of the .45 McDermot MR VI, and then specifics about Leduc's order.

At the bottom of her covering letter was her name. Elizabeth Coldbrook-Clairton. Something seemed slightly off, and when he studied it more closely he noticed that "Clairton" was typed in a different font. Not far off—she might not have noticed. But he did.

Then there was a ding. The forensics report had just arrived in his inbox.

"You're welcome to stay in the village, if you'd like," said Gamache as he put his winter coat on. "You don't have to come back to the academy with me."

"You'd like me to stay?" asked Charpentier, as he pulled on his boots. "Or you want me to stay? You're not trying to get rid of me, are you?"

It was said with a smile, but there was an edge to the question.

"*Moi?*" asked Gamache, also with a smile. But then his voice changed and grew serious. "It's your choice, Hugo. And if I want something, you'll know it."

"Who else knows they're here, *patron*?"

"The cadets? Now that's a difficult question."

The two men said good-bye to Madame Gamache and walked slowly through the snow and mud over to the bed and breakfast, where the Commander had told the cadets to meet them.

Charpentier was swinging his canes ahead of him and hauling his weak legs after them in a kind of lurch he'd perfected.

"Their classmates needed to know they were gone, as did their professors," said Gamache. "I told them they'd gone home."

"Without specifying whose home."

Gamache stopped at the steps up to the B and B and turned. "No one must know those cadets are here, do you understand?"

Charpentier nodded. But Gamache could see he considered this a game. For the tactician, it was a puzzle in which the cadets were pieces, not people.

"But you let me come down," said Charpentier, his nose turning red in the brisk March air. "You let me know they're here. Why?"

If he starts perspiring, thought Gamache, he'll turn into an ice sculpture.

"Because I think you can help."

Charpentier nodded. "I can. I already have."

The men climbed the stairs, Gamache behind Charpentier in case he should slip and lose his balance. Charpentier stopped at the top. Walking was exhausting for him, and climbing stairs was even worse.

"Are you playing me, Commander?" His words puffed into the late winter air.

"How?"

"Is it that you want me here? Or you don't want me at the academy?"

"You know maps. The one we found could prove important."

"True. But last night at the academy, you didn't think I could be a big help. You didn't even know I collected maps. But you let me come down here. You let me see the cadets you have hidden away."

Gamache smiled broadly. His face breaking into deep lines. He leaned so close to Charpentier that the younger man could smell the mint toothpaste and the cologne of sandalwood. With a slight hint of rosewater.

"Do you think, when I was speaking to Madame Gamache on the phone during our meeting at the academy, that I had to mention the map out loud?"

Charpentier's eyes widened.

"You did it to lure me?"

"I know more about you than you realize."

The comforting scents of the man were tugged away by the cold breeze that now blew between them.

And Hugo Charpentier started to perspire.

"I think we should get inside," said Gamache. "Don't you? They'll be waiting for us."

CHAPTER 25

⟨⟩

The cadets were indeed waiting in the dining room of the B and B for Commander Gamache and Professor Charpentier.

Clara and Myrna had decided to join their houseguests, though not at the same table. They sat by the fireplace, and were finishing their French toast with bacon and maple syrup when Gamache paused to say hello. And to ask, "How did it go?"

"Last night?" asked Myrna. "Fine. I got under the sheets as soon as we got home. I think he got into his. I'm going to check for eyeholes. And a pointy hat."

Armand grinned and grimaced at the same time. "I'm sorry about that."

"Amelia's a sweet girl," said Clara. "Up at the crack of dawn this morning. Made her bed and even did some light housework before I got up. When I came down, she had the coffee already on."

"Really?" both Armand and Myrna asked.

"No, of course not," snapped Clara. "She told me to fuck off when I knocked on the door to wake her up, half an hour ago. Then she demanded coffee. It's like living with a wolverine. Which reminds me, how's Gracie?"

Armand gave her a thin smile.

"She's fine."

He left to join the cadets and Charpentier. The students were just finishing off their breakfasts and Gabri brought each of the men a *café au lait*.

"Do you want breakfast? I have blueberry crêpes, French toast, and Eggs Gabri."

"Eggs Gabri?" asked Gamache. "That's new."

"I add a bit of lemon zest to the hollandaise."

Armand thought about that, then smiled. "A little tart."

"A little tart." Gabri bowed with great dignity.

"I'll have an Eggs Gabri, *s'il vous plaît*," said Armand.

"And you, monsieur?" Gabri asked Charpentier, who ordered blueberry crêpes with sausages and syrup.

"Professor Charpentier and I are returning to the academy," Gamache said to the cadets. Across from him, Charpentier's brows rose very slightly. "But when I come back tonight, I'd like a report on what you find out about the map."

"Come on," said Jacques. "It doesn't matter, and you know it. I want to return to the academy. You can't keep us here."

He was glaring at the Commander, and the other three cadets turned to look, first at Jacques, then over to Gamache. Jacques had clearly never been a fan of the new commander, but now his scorn seemed to have reached new heights. Or depths.

Even Gabri, bringing Myrna and Clara a small cheese plate, paused and looked over, as did the women.

Myrna cocked her head slightly, puzzled.

"You could be right," said Gamache as he put down his large mug. "The map might mean nothing. But then again, you could be wrong."

"Don't believe everything you think," said Amelia.

"So now you're on his side?" asked Jacques.

"Side?" said Amelia. "There aren't sides."

"Oh, don't kid yourself," said Jacques. "There're always sides."

"Enough," said Gamache. It was the first time he'd raised his voice at them, and they immediately turned to look at him. "I'm tired of this child-ish behavior. You need to stop this sniping. You're not in a schoolyard. You're cadets in the Sûreté Academy. You've been conscripted to help in a homi-cide investigation. Do you know how many cadets would love to be included? And you sneer at it? And want to leave? To pick up your marbles and go home? Because you haven't been handed a piece of evidence dripping in blood? How do you know what's important and what isn't? If I don't know, you certainly don't."

He stared at them, and one by one they lowered their eyes.

Even Jacques.

Over by the fireplace, Myrna and Clara exchanged glances.

There was unmistakable, and rare, anger in Armand's voice. But below that they recognized something else. Gamache was afraid that these stu-dents weren't taking this seriously enough. And in that error lay not just a failing grade, but a grave. Someone had killed, and they'd kill again.

"You don't have the luxury of choosing when you'll work, where you'll work, and who you'll work with. I'm your commander and I've assigned you to work together on the map. There is no debate, no argument. A murderer thrives on chaos, on creating divisions and diversions. Infighting is all those things. It divides the focus and saps the energy. You have to learn to get along. With everyone. Everyone." He looked from one to the other to the other. "Everyone. Your lives will depend on it. Do you think those boys in those trenches fought each other?"

"A house divided cannot stand," said Charpentier. "You don't need to be a brilliant tactician to figure that one out."

"No, just a master of clichés," mumbled Jacques.

"And you wonder why I'm a recluse," said Charpentier to Gamache.

"Oh, there are days I don't wonder at all," said Gamache.

"The house fell anyway, didn't it?" said Jacques. "They all died, those soldiers. Together, maybe. But they all died. That's not mud on the goddamned map. It's blood."

A copy was sitting on the table, and he shoved it at the Commander with such force a glass fell over. Water flooded the table, making its way toward the Commander.

But while the others moved away from it, Gamache stayed where he was, staring at the boy.

Jacques was so upset he was almost in tears. He stared at the Commander's face. Taking in the deep scar by his temple. And meeting his eyes. Holding them.

"They died," he whispered.

"Yes, many did," said Gamache, studying the cadet. And then he reached out and slowly pushed the map back across the table. Away from the water. To safety, and the young man.

Gabri arrived at that moment with their breakfasts and wiped up the water, giving Gamache a quizzical look before he left.

Gamache turned to Charpentier. "Tell them what you told me."

"I believe that," the professor pointed to the paper, "is an early orienteering map."

"A what?" asked Amelia.

"Orienteering," said Nathaniel. "It's a sport."

"Like curling's a sport?" asked Amelia.

"Curling's a great sport," said Huifen. "Have you ever tried it?"

"I don't have to—"

"Oh, for God's sake," said Gamache. "Just listen to the professor."

"Orienteering's a training tool, disguised as a sport," said Charpentier.

213

"Training for what?" asked Huifen.

"War. It was used in the Boer War and the First World War to teach officers how to find their way around a battlefield. That's why it shows things other maps never would. A rock, a fence, an odd-shaped tree, an abandoned house. But it also has contours, like a topographical map."

He tapped the map on the table.

"Whoever made this knew how to make maps and was also an orienteer, when it was in its infancy."

"And they must've lived around here," said Nathaniel.

"Do you think the soldier made it himself?" asked Amelia.

"It's possible," said Charpentier.

"But?" asked Huifen, picking up on the hesitation.

"But this was done by an experienced mapmaker. The soldier was just a boy. He wouldn't have had time to learn. Not to this degree."

"It was done by his father," said Jacques, who'd been staring at the map while they talked. "To take with him."

"To remind him of home," said Nathaniel.

"To bring him home," said Jacques.

Charpentier looked at Gamache, who nodded. "We think so."

"Where should we start?" asked Huifen.

"We can figure it out," said Jacques. "We don't need their help."

"But—"

"You'll ask for help, cadet," said Gamache. "And you'll take it."

"Why?" asked Jacques. "I've seen what happens when people follow your orders."

Armand Gamache put down his knife and fork slowly, with studied care, and stared at the cadet with such intensity, Jacques started to tremble. Even the others at the table, including Charpentier, leaned away.

"The town hall in Saint-Rémy will have records of sales and purchases," said Gamache quietly, coldly. "Going back a hundred years or more. They'll know who owned the bistro, when it was a private home. That's the place to start."

Nathaniel wrote that down, but Jacques continued to stare into the cross-hairs.

Commander Gamache got up, as did they, rising quickly to their feet. Jacques got up too, but slowly.

"I'll be back by seven tonight. I want your reports then."

"Yes, sir," said three cadets.

Gamache turned to Jacques, who said, "Yes, sir."

"*Bon*," said the Commander, and walked over to Myrna. "May I have a word?"

Myrna, feeling called to the principal's office, followed him into the living room.

"Yes, he found the video," she admitted before Armand could say anything. But still he was quiet, and she nodded. "I might have suggested he google you."

"Why?"

"Why? Because he so clearly believed what that Leduc man was saying about you. He needed to know the truth if he was ever going to learn. There's a murderer. The boy has to start paying attention."

"No one needs to see that video."

"Look, Armand, I know you hate that it's out there, but the fact is, it is. It might as well have a purpose. If it teaches that young man the reality of the situation, then maybe some little good will come of it."

"Does he look like he's changed his mind?" asked Armand, and Myrna glanced in the direction of the dining room. And shook her head.

"I think there's something else at work here," she said. "I saw his face as he watched the video of that raid. He was shocked. But not in the usual way. He seemed to have walked right into the screen. To experience it, as it was happening. It's a rare ability, to empathize that intensely. It's almost as though he was there."

On seeing Gamache's face, she repeated, "Almost."

Gamache looked toward the dining room, then back at Myrna.

"He saw all of them," said Armand. "Réal and Etienne and Sarah."

He recited the names of the dead, as Ruth had done the day before.

Myrna nodded. "And Jean-Guy. And you. I think for the first time he realized what being a Sûreté agent would mean. The Duke, that's what they called him?"

Gamache nodded.

"The Duke probably filled them with stories of power and glory, and any violence was heroic and cartoonish, like the old war movies or westerns. Death was clean, and mostly us doing it to them. And they loved him for it. But the video shows how horrific it really is. I think it's terrified him. And he hates you for it."

Gamache realized he'd been wrong. He'd been afraid Cadet Laurin wasn't taking this seriously enough, when in fact he was near paralyzed with fear.

Jacques was asking himself the question they all did, eventually. When faced with it, would he move forward or would he run away?

215

"It's time he learned what might be expected of him," said Gamache. "It's time they all learned."

Then he smiled. Quickly, briefly. Sincerely.

"That's a nice thought, Myrna. That good might come out of what happened. Their deaths might save lives. Might save his life, especially if it convinces him to quit."

"Do you think he will?"

"I think perhaps he should."

"But will he die at the appointed hour anyway?" she asked. "In his bed, in his car, or in a gun battle?"

"Fate? Don't start on that again," said Gamache. It was a conversation they often had, but not that day.

The two men left, as did Myrna and Clara, but the cadets stayed behind.

Huifen, after all, had dishes to do. Amelia grudgingly got up to help her. Then Nathaniel joined in. And finally Jacques came into the kitchen. Grabbing the dish towel from Nathaniel, he snapped it at him before picking up a wet dish.

Nathaniel laughed, knowing it was done in jest. And yet, there had been something vicious about that snap, and the sting it left behind.

CHAPTER 26

"He could have done it," said Isabelle Lacoste.

They'd gathered in the conference room at the Sûreté Academy. Gamache, Professor Charpentier, Beauvoir, and Gélinas listened as Lacoste reported on their early morning meeting with the mayor.

Light poured in through the picture window, and outside the snow was melting in the brilliant sunshine.

"He had the motive and the opportunity. Even, perhaps, the expertise to override the security system here."

"Though we don't know if it was done intentionally, or the system just failed on its own," said Beauvoir.

"What did you make of Mayor Florent?" Gamache asked.

"I liked him. An interesting man. He put up a sort of mist of bonhomie. Of good cheer. But he readily, almost cheerfully, admitted he could've left his home, driven over here, killed Leduc and got back home without anyone knowing he was gone."

"But when you asked if he killed Leduc, he said no," Gélinas pointed out. "So I guess he didn't do it."

"You tried that again?" asked Gamache.

"Still hasn't worked, eh?" said Beauvoir.

She shook her head and smiled. "One day it will and we can all go home early."

"But the mayor did admit he despised the man," said Gélinas, watching with interest and some envy the easy familiarity of these people. He had to remind himself that his job was to judge them, not join them. "That was the word he used. 'Despised.' And that he prayed him dead."

"If everyone we prayed dead died, the streets would be littered with corpses," said Beauvoir.

"*Non*," said Gélinas. "We might wish someone dead, but for a religious man to sit in a church, before God, and pray that someone dies? Not a loved one who's sick and in pain, whose suffering we want to see ended, but a vigorous man who could live, should live, another forty years? To pray that man dead is something else entirely. It's a hatred that overwhelms his morals and ethics and beliefs. It's a hatred that's hooked in the soul."

Gamache listened to Gélinas and wondered if he was himself a religious man.

"So you think Mayor Florent is a religious fanatic and God was his accomplice?" asked Beauvoir.

"Now you just make it sound silly," said Gélinas with a rueful smile, then he shook his head. "He might be a religious man, but I think if he killed Leduc, it was driven by hatred of the man and not love of God. I've learned never to underestimate hatred. There's a madness that goes with it."

"We have the forensics report," said Beauvoir, tapping the screen of his tablet.

It was a relief to be investigating a murder in a place with high-speed Internet. The report flashed up on all their screens.

It was also a relief to now be dealing with facts rather than speculation.

"The bullet we dug out of the wall was the one that killed him. And it came from the gun we found. The McDermot .45. No surprise there."

"There is one surprise," said Gélinas. "I'm not a homicide investigator, but I'd have thought most murderers take the weapon with them. To dispose of it. Less for the investigators to work with, if there's no weapon."

"Amateurs," said Charpentier. He'd been bone-dry and silent so far, but as he spoke, sweat began pouring from his pores.

"Professionals know that as soon as murder is committed, the weapon stops being a gun or a knife or a club and becomes a noose," he said. "It attaches itself to the killer. He might think he's being clever, taking the weapon, but murder weapons are harder to get rid of than people think. The longer he holds on to it, the tighter the rope gets, the bigger the drop."

Charpentier mimicked a length of rope, and then jerked it with such sudden violence, and such relish, it gave those watching pause. A kind of ecstasy had come over the quiet man as he glistened in the morning sun and talked of execution.

Gamache leaned forward slightly, toward Charpentier, his thoughtful eyes sharpening. And he knew then what his former pupil reminded him of. His thin, tense body was that rope, and his outsized head the noose.

If Gamache was an explorer and Beauvoir a hunter, Charpentier seemed a born executioner.

And Gélinas? Gamache shifted his gaze to the senior RCMP officer. What was he?

"Amateurs panic and take it with them," confirmed Beauvoir. "Leduc was killed by someone who knew what he was doing, or at the very least had thought it through."

"But why a revolver?" asked Gélinas. "Why did Leduc have one, and why did the murderer use it instead of an automatic?"

"Well, the revolver had the advantage of already being there," said Gamache. "And couldn't be traced back to the murderer. And it has another advantage."

"What's that?" asked Lacoste.

But now Beauvoir smiled and leaned forward. "That we're talking about it. And spending time wondering about it and investigating it. The revolver's an oddity. And oddities eat up time and energy in an investigation."

"You're thinking the revolver is both the murder weapon and a red herring," said Lacoste.

"Not a red herring, a red whale," said Beauvoir. "Something so obviously strange we have no option but to focus on it, and maybe miss something else."

"It bears considering," said Gamache.

"Too much speculation," said Lacoste. "Let's move on. I see there's a preliminary report on the DNA at the crime scene."

"A lot of different DNA was found," said Beauvoir, returning to his screen. "It'll take a while to process."

"Quite a few fingerprints too." Gélinas scanned ahead. "And not just in the living room."

"True," said Beauvoir, and tapped the tablet again.

A schematic of Leduc's rooms came up on everyone's screen. It was a floor plan showing the layout of furniture and the body. Then another tap, and the image was overlaid with dots. So many they obliterated almost everything else.

"The red dots are Leduc's own prints," said Beauvoir, and hit a key. They disappeared, leaving black dots. There were far fewer of those.

"As you can see, the other prints are mostly in the living room, but some were found in the bathroom and a few in the bedroom."

"Have you identified them?" asked Lacoste.

"Not all, but most. The majority belong to one person. Michel Brébeuf."

"Huh," said Gamache, and leaned closer to his screen, bringing his hand up to his face. "Can you show us just his prints?"

Beauvoir tapped again, and again the screen changed. The dots were in the living room, in the bathroom. In the bedroom.

Gamache studied them.

Gélinas hit an icon on his own screen and the forensics report replaced the floor plan. He found computer imaging of limited use. It helped to visualize, but it could also confuse. It was both too much information and too narrow.

Instead, he preferred to read the report.

"There're other professors' fingerprints, I see, besides Brébeuf's," he said. "Professor Godbut, for example. It looks like the three of them, Leduc, Godbut, and Brébeuf, spent some time together."

"It does," said Beauvoir. "But of course we can't tell if the prints were made at the same time or separately."

"How often were the rooms cleaned?" the RCMP officer asked.

"Once a week," said Beauvoir. "Leduc's was cleaned three days before the murder."

"But it wouldn't be thorough enough to wipe out all the prints," said Gamache. "Some of these might be quite old."

"I can see Leduc and Godbut getting together," said Gélinas. "But how does Michel Brébeuf fit in? I honestly can't imagine him having a few beers with Leduc and watching the game."

Gamache smiled at that image. The refined Brébeuf and the pug that was Leduc, kicking back. Then he remembered that evening in his rooms early in the semester. Reine-Marie, the students. The fire lit and drinks handed around. The snowstorm pounding the windows, just feet from where they sat.

The first informal gathering with the cadets. It seemed ages ago now, but was only a couple of months.

Michel Brébeuf had arrived late and Serge Leduc went over to him, all but genuflecting. Clearly recognizing the man, and admiring him despite, or probably because of, Brébeuf's disgrace.

Jean-Guy Beauvoir had also noticed, and been afraid that that was the beginning of some unholy alliance. And he might have been right.

"They seemed friendly," said Gamache, "though I doubt you'd call them friends. I'll talk to him about this."

"Perhaps it would be better if I did," said Gélinas.

The implication was obvious, and Gamache raised his brow but could hardly object. This was, after all, the reason the outsider was there. To assure a fair investigation. And it was well known that Gamache and Brébeuf had a history, as great friends and colleagues, and as near deadly adversaries.

"With your permission, I'd like to be there," said Gamache, and when Gélinas hesitated he went on. "There's an advantage to knowing him well."

Gélinas gave a curt nod.

Beauvoir and Lacoste exchanged glances before Lacoste said, "What about the mayor? Any of his prints?"

"No, none."

"Then who do these other prints belong to?" she asked, pointing to the unclaimed dots in the bathroom and bedroom.

"Some aren't identified yet," said Beauvoir. "But most belong to cadets."

"In a professor's bathroom and bedroom?" asked Gélinas. "That would be unusual, wouldn't it?"

"I encouraged the professors to meet with students casually," said Gamache.

"Just how casual did they get?"

"That, unfortunately, is a good question," said Gamache. "My instructions were to meet in groups."

"You were afraid of something happening?"

"It seemed wise," said the Commander. "For everyone's protection."

"And did they?"

"*Oui*," said Beauvoir. "Most met once a week with students. My group came over on Wednesday evenings. We had sandwiches and beer and talked."

"A sort of mentorship?" asked Gélinas.

"That was the idea," said Gamache.

"Were they assigned or did they choose the professors?"

"They chose."

"And a few went with Serge Leduc?" asked Gélinas, looking down at the black spots on Lacoste's screen, then back up again. Incredulous.

"I expected that," Commander Gamache admitted. "For the seniors especially, he was their leader."

"He wasn't a leader, he was a bully," said Gélinas. "Surely they'd welcome the chance to get out from under his thumb."

"When police first started intervening in child abuse cases," said Lacoste, "they developed a simple test. It was often clear the child was being abused, but it wasn't clear which parent was doing it. So they put the child at one end of a room and the parents at the other. And they watched to see who the kid ran to. The other was obviously the abuser."

"Can we get back on topic?" asked Gélinas.

"It took a while before they realized they were wrong," Lacoste continued quietly. "The child ran to the abuser."

That sat like a specter in the room, the revelation nesting comfortably among the photographs of a murdered man.

"How could that be?" asked Gélinas. "Wouldn't they run as far as possible from the parent who hurt them?"

"You'd think. But abused children become desperate to please the abuser, to appease them. They learn early and quickly that if they don't, they pay a price. No child would risk upsetting the parent who beat them."

Gélinas turned to Gamache. "Is that what happened with Leduc?"

"I think so. Some cadets no doubt gravitated to him because they're cut from the same cloth. He offered a free pass to cruelty. But some went to him because they were afraid."

"But they're adults, not children," said Gélinas.

"Young adults," said Gamache. "And age isn't a factor. We see it in adults all the time. Those desperate to please a powerful, even abusive, personality. At home. At work. On sports teams. The armed forces, and certainly in police forces. A strong, often brutal, personality, takes over. He's followed out of fear, not respect or loyalty."

"And in a closed school environment, he becomes a role model," said Lacoste.

"But that stopped when you showed up," said Gélinas to Gamache. "And deposed the Duke. And tried to teach them Service, Integrity, Justice."

He tried not to make it sound as though in quoting the Sûreté motto he was mocking it, or the Commander.

"*Oui*," said Gamache. "*Exactement*."

The RCMP officer had rarely met anyone who actually knew the motto, never mind believed it. Though he was also familiar with Gamache's history, and knew that he sometimes had his own definitions of those three things.

The Royal Canadian Mounted Police motto was more prosaic.

Maintiens le droit. Defend the Law.

Paul Gélinas had never been completely comfortable with that. He knew that law wasn't always the same as justice. But it had the advantage of being fairly clear. Whereas justice could be fluid, situational. A matter of interpretation. And perception.

He looked down at Serge Leduc.

His murder broke the law, but did it uphold justice? Maybe.

"When you took over, Commander, Leduc went from being the teacher to being the lesson," said Charpentier. "The students learned a tyrant always falls, eventually."

"But some still chose Leduc as their mentor," Gélinas pointed out. "That doesn't show much of a learning curve."

"These things take time," said Gamache. "Their world had been turned upside down. Some might not have believed it was permanent. They might've thought that I'd last a semester and Leduc would rise again. I was honestly surprised that more students didn't go with him."

"Most went with you?"

Gamache smiled. "The new sheriff in town? *Non*. Hardly any. I think I might've been a step too far, a clear sign of disloyalty. But more and more cadets were coming to the gatherings in my rooms. Mostly freshmen. And some I especially invited."

"And who were those?" asked Gélinas. "The most promising?"

Gamache smiled. "The pick of the litter?"

Gélinas tilted his head slightly at that phrase.

"Can we get back to the forensics report?" asked Lacoste, looking at her watch.

"Of course," said Gélinas. "*Désolé*."

They dropped their eyes to their screens once again as Beauvoir walked them through it.

"As you see, the fingerprints of a number of students were in Leduc's bathroom," said Beauvoir. "Including the cadets in the village. No surprise there, I think. We knew they were among his protégées. But one was also on the chest of drawers and the gun case."

He hit a key and only a single dot remained.

"The cadets in the village?" asked Gélinas, looking from Beauvoir to Lacoste. "Saint-Alphonse? Are some of the cadets local?"

Beauvoir glanced at Gamache in slight apology.

"Whose was on the gun case?" asked Gamache.

"Cadet Choquet's."

Gamache drew his brows together.

"And the weapon?" asked Lacoste.

"The prints on the revolver were smudged, unfortunately, but there were partials of a number of people. The coroner's report came in too. Nothing unusual about Leduc. He was a healthy forty-six-year-old male. No evidence of recent sexual activity. He'd had a meal and some Scotch."

"Intoxicated?" asked Gélinas.

"No. And no bruising or cuts to indicate a fight."

"So he just stood there while someone put a gun to his temple and pulled the trigger?" asked Lacoste.

She looked around the conference table, all of them also trying to imagine how that could happen. Especially to someone like Leduc who was, by all accounts, combative at the best of times.

The RCMP officer leaned forward and shook his head. "No. It makes no sense. We're obviously missing something. The partials on the gun. Could Leduc have handed it around? And eventually handed it to his killer?"

"Who shot him in front of a crowd?" asked Lacoste.

"So what're you thinking?" asked Gélinas.

"I'll tell you what I think," said Beauvoir. "I think Leduc was proud of that revolver for some reason and wanted to show it off. So when people visited, he brought it out and handed it to them. Maybe made up some story about a long-lost relative's heroics in the war. That's where all the prints came from."

"Did you read the footnote from the forensics team?" Gélinas asked.

Gamache had, as had, he could see, Beauvoir and Lacoste. Though they'd chosen not to say anything.

"It's the extrapolation on the partial prints on the gun," continued the RCMP officer. "Not admissible, but suggestive. Who the various prints might belong to. I see that this Cadet Choquet's prints are there too."

"As partials. Too smudged to clearly identify. We don't take that seriously," said Lacoste. "It's more guess than science. This is complex enough. We need to stick to facts."

"I agree," said Gélinas, letting it drop. But not before he looked over at Gamache, who held his gaze.

The footnote gave percentage likelihood of the partials belonging to certain people. Not surprisingly, the largest percentage match was Leduc himself. More surprising was another name that showed up, besides Amelia Choquet. There was a forty percent chance that at least one of the prints belonged to Michel Brébeuf.

A number of other names showed up in the report. There was, according to the computer extrapolation, a very small chance Richard Nixon, the former American president, had handled the gun. Which was why the investigators tended not to take these results seriously. They also ignored the possibility, admittedly remote, that Julia Child was the murderer.

But there was one other name that stood out.

The analysis found a forty-five percent probability that at least one of the prints belonged to Armand Gamache.

Gélinas looked from the report to the Commander, while Lacoste and Beauvoir looked away. Only Charpentier spoke, in a sputter of sweat.

"Now, how did your prints get on the murder weapon?"

Armand Gamache gave him a tight, cold smile.

"Partials," Beauvoir reminded Charpentier, and anyone else in the room who harbored doubt.

"Did you handle the weapon?" Lacoste asked Gamache.

"I did not."

"Good. Then can we move on, please?"

"I spoke to the head of public affairs at the gun manufacturer," said Beauvoir, changing the subject. "McDermot and Ryan. A woman named Elizabeth Coldbrook in," he checked his notes, "Dartmouth, England."

He forwarded copies of her email and the attachments.

The second page was the receipt, which they all scanned.

"I see that Madame Coldbrook-Clairton insists they didn't make the silencer," said Lacoste.

"I believe her," said Beauvoir. "She had no reason to lie, and it would be easy enough to disprove. We're trying to trace it now. She'd assumed by my email that it was a suicide. She was upset to find out it was murder."

"You'd think she'd be used to it by now," said Gélinas. "Why else have a handgun?"

"Did she say why he might have ordered a revolver instead of, say, an automatic weapon?" Gamache asked.

"She said collectors like them, but when I pointed out that Leduc wasn't a collector, she had no answers."

Lacoste nodded, then looked up as Gamache cleared his throat.

The Commander was still studying the first page, then he looked over his reading glasses to her. Taking them off he used them to point to a paragraph.

"This is interesting."

They consulted their screens again.

"How?" asked Chief Inspector Lacoste. "It's a boilerplate sales pitch giving the history of this model."

"Yes. The McDermot .45 came into its own in the First World War," said Gamache. "In the trenches."

"*Oui*," said Lacoste. "Soooo?"

"It's probably nothing," admitted Gamache. "But you know that a copy of the map that was in Leduc's bedside table was found in the stained-glass window in Three Pines. The one of the soldiers from the Great War. The soldier had the map, but he also wore a revolver. I'm guessing a McDermot."

"*Pardon?*" said Gélinas. "I'm not following."

"Are you saying the two are connected?" Beauvoir asked.

"Wait a minute," said Gélinas, holding up his hand. "A map?"

"Yes. A few months ago, an old map was found in a wall of the bistro in Three Pines," said Gamache. "We were talking about it yesterday in the meeting."

"I remember, but you didn't say a copy was found in Leduc's bedside table."

"It's in the report," said Lacoste.

Gélinas turned to her. "There's a lot in the report. Not all of equal weight. That's why context is important, don't you think?"

He spoke as though lecturing a failing cadet. Then he returned to Gamache.

"You kept this from me."

"We're telling you now," said Gamache. "A couple of weeks ago, before any of this happened, I decided to use the map as a training tool. A few of the cadets were invited to investigate it. I gave them copies of the map."

"And one of them was found in the dead man's bedroom?" Gélinas asked. "How did it get there?"

"Well, that's the question, isn't it?" said Lacoste.

"Whose fingerprints are on it?" Gélinas scanned the report.

"There're three sets," said Beauvoir, not needing to consult his iPad. He'd read the report when it had arrived in his inbox that morning. And while not everything was memorable, a few things leapt out. Including this.

"Leduc's, Cadet Choquet's, and Commander Gamache's."

"Monsieur Gamache made the copies and handed them out," said Lacoste. "So his prints would naturally be there. Cadet Choquet's copy of the map is missing."

"Then it's his," said Gélinas. "Who is this Cadet Choquet? He seems very involved."

"She," said Gamache. "Amelia Choquet. A freshman."

Gélinas went back a page in the report. "I see her name in the list of people whose prints were on the revolver case and might be on the revolver itself."

"Right next to Nelson Mandela's," Lacoste pointed out.

"Still, we need to speak to her," said Gélinas. "Can you have her brought here now?"

"She's not in the building," said Chief Inspector Lacoste.

"Where is she?"

Lacoste looked at Gamache, who said, "Three Pines. I had her and three other cadets taken there the day of the murder."

Gélinas stared at Gamache, his mouth open. Unable to process what he'd heard.

"You what?" he rasped. "Is that what was meant by the four cadets in the village? Not Saint-Alphonse, but your own village? Who are they?"

"The students closest to Professor Leduc," said Gamache. "Amelia Choquet and Nathaniel Smythe are freshmen—"

"—Smythe? The one who found the body?" demanded Gélinas.

"*Oui.* As well as two seniors. Cadets Laurin and Cloutier."

"And you knew?" Gélinas looked at the others.

When even Professor Charpentier nodded, the Deputy Commissioner exploded.

"Everyone knew, except me? Why? What are you playing at?" Now he was staring directly at Gamache. "Do you know how serious this is? You're withholding evidence, you're hiding witnesses. My God, man, what're you doing?"

"I took them there to protect them, not to hide them. And the chief investigating officer knows exactly where they are. But it's vital that no one outside of this room knows."

"Well at least one person in this room didn't know," said Gélinas, his anger only mounting. "You had no right, no authority, to do that. You're actively interfering with an investigation."

"I had every right, and all authority," said Gamache. "I'm the Commander here. These students are my responsibility. Their training is entrusted to me, and so is their safety."

"Do you hear yourself?" Gélinas leaned close to him. "You're as bad as Leduc. Treating the Sûreté Academy as your personal city-state. This isn't the Vatican and you're not the pope. You're behaving as though you're all-powerful. Infallible. Well, you've made a terrible mistake."

"Not necessarily," said Charpentier. "Tactically it makes sense if—"

"The fewer who know where the students are the better," said Gamache, cutting off the tactician.

"Better for who?" asked Gélinas. "Not me. Not the investigation. Better for you, perhaps."

"What's that supposed to mean?" asked Beauvoir.

"Whose prints were on the murder weapon?" Gélinas demanded.

"Partials," said Beauvoir.

"Whose prints were on the map? Who stayed with the body, refusing company, until others arrived?" said Gélinas. "How many minutes? Ten? Twenty? Plenty of time to set the scene, to manipulate it. And then almost the first thing you do, sir, is scoop up important suspects, including the one who actually found the body, and take them away. That's why you left right after the murder, isn't it? To take the cadets down to the village."

"To make sure they were safe, yes," said Gamache.

"Safe? What danger could they be in here, any more than any of the other cadets? Why them?"

"As I said, they were closest to Leduc," said Gamache, the throb underneath the words warning that he was straining to keep his temper. "Don't the prints alone tell you that? They had extraordinary access to the man. And he to them. They're the most likely to know something. They had to be protected."

"The only thing that will protect them is telling us everything they know," said Gélinas. "And it's possible, probable, that if they do know something it's because one of them did it. One of them killed Leduc. Have you thought of that, your holiness?"

"Don't call me that, and of course I have," said Gamache. "Even more reason to isolate them, don't you think?"

"Or to hide them," said Gélinas. "So they can't tell me and others who mentored them into murder."

Gélinas glared at Gamache.

"Are you suggesting Commander Gamache did this?" asked Lacoste, trying to control her own anger. "That he convinced one or all of the cadets to murder a professor?"

"The evidence is suggesting it," said Gélinas. "His own actions are screaming it. It's as though you're just begging me to suspect you."

"I didn't kill Serge Leduc," said Gamache. "You know it."

"You asked for me specifically, monsieur, apparently to make sure it's a fair and thorough investigation—"

"You asked for him?" Lacoste looked at Gamache, confused, while Charpentier leaned back in his chair and watched. No longer perspiring.

"Now I'm beginning to wonder if you chose me because you thought after years away, I'd be out of practice," Gélinas continued. "I might be easily misdirected. Might even fall under your influence, like the cadets? Be flattered by the great man's attentions? Was that it?"

"I asked for you, Deputy Commissioner, because I admire you and knew you'd be rigorous and fair," said Gamache. "And would not be taken in by attempts to confuse. You would defend the law."

"Oh, is that what this is?" Gélinas pointed to the tablet and the forensics report. "Not an indictment of your own actions, but an attempt to confuse? Are you saying someone is setting you up?"

"Why are there prints on the revolver?" asked Gamache. "Don't you think it's strange in the extreme that the killer knew enough to drop the weapon, but not enough to wipe it or wear gloves? If I killed Leduc, don't you think I'd at least do both?"

"So you think all this is staged?"

"I think we have to consider that."

"Who better to stage it than the former head of homicide for the Sûreté? The man most learnèd in murder? I want you to consider something."

Deputy Commissioner Gélinas turned away from Gamache and spoke to the others.

"Is it possible he killed Serge Leduc," he held up his hand to stop Beauvoir's protest, "to protect the students? He came to suspect abuse. Not simply inappropriate punishments of cadets, but something systematic and targeted and shattering. The emotional, psychological, physical and perhaps sexual abuse of certain cadets. He had no proof. He invited those students he suspected were most at risk to join his informal gatherings, in the hopes they'd grow to trust him. He invited them to research the map, as a way of bonding with them. But they kept running back to Leduc. To their abuser. There was only one way to save them. And others."

Beauvoir and Lacoste sat silent. Imagining the scenario.

"Could you see Monsieur Gamache murdering, to save young lives?"

It was clear both Lacoste and Beauvoir wanted to deny it. To defend Gamache. But it was also clear that they could, in fact, see it. If Armand Gamache was ever to commit murder, if would be to save others.

"He's also the only person here who didn't have to kill him," said Charpentier, calmly, and all eyes swung to him.

"Explain," said Gélinas.

"He's the Commander. He alone could get rid of Leduc by just firing him."

Beauvoir nodded approval and turned to the RCMP officer. Waiting for his reply.

"And pass the problem on to someone else?" asked Gélinas. "The Commander himself has admitted he would not do that."

"You know he didn't do it," said Beauvoir. "You're just playing into the murderer's hands. Chasing the whale."

"All that most maddens and torments," said Gélinas, glaring at Gamache. "All truth with malice in it, all evil were visibly personified, and made practically assailable—"

"—in Moby Dick," said Charpentier, finishing the quote. "You got it mostly right. I have the students read it as an insight into obsession. Into what can drive a man mad. I see you know it too."

"—but not a whale," said Gélinas, his eyes never leaving Gamache. "A man. For you, sir, it was personified by Serge Leduc. And like Ahab, you had to stop him."

Gamache sat immobile. Neither agreeing nor disagreeing.

In the face of his silence, Gélinas continued. "The pick of the litter. You used that phrase just now. Your wife had the pick of the litter and she chose the runt. You did the same thing. You picked the runts and invited them to your soirées. Invited them into your home. Like she did with Gracie. You want to save them. Sometimes that means removing them from danger. And sometimes it means removing the danger."

Armand Gamache took a deep breath and looked at the photograph of a man he'd grown to despise. A man now dead. Then he looked up at Gélinas.

"I'm not Ahab. And Leduc was not my whale. Yes, I know a lot about murder. Enough not to commit it." He tapped his glasses a couple of times on his hand, considering Paul Gélinas. "I just finished telling the cadets that it's in the murderer's best interest to create chaos. To make us turn on each other. Suspect each other even."

"Maybe, but last night when you, Professor Charpentier, were asked where you'd start to look for the killer, do you remember what you said?"

Charpentier hesitated, perspiration now pouring off him. He glanced at Gamache, who gave the slightest of nods.

"I said Matthew 10:36."

"*Oui*." Gélinas turned to Gamache. "You know the reference."

"I taught it to all the new Sûreté agents," said Gamache. "I've asked Michel Brébeuf to use it as the core of his course."

"And a man's foes shall be they of his own household," said Gélinas. "Powerful advice. You were right, professor. That's where I'd start too, to look for the killer. In our own household."

"He didn't do it," said Lacoste. "You know that. Why are you even pursuing it?"

"Because you won't."

And for a moment he looked like a man with a whale in his sights.

CHAPTER 27

⁓

"Yup, that's what it is," said the young woman as she wiped her hand on her white apron. "An orienteering map. But it's old, eh? Where'd you get it?"

She looked from the slender, simply dressed Chinese Girl to the Goth Girl. An odd couple if there ever was one.

"It was found in a wall when they were doing renovations," said Amelia. "What can you tell us about it?"

The girl looked surprised. "Nothing, except what I've already said. I've seen maps sorta like this, in history books on orienteering, but never actually seen one in person. It's sorta cool, isn't it?"

Amelia wondered if she knew what "cool" meant.

The girl kept looking over her shoulder at the long line of customers waiting for coffee and doughnuts. And at her frantic supervisor, who was shooting her vile looks.

I'm on break, she mouthed to her boss, then turned her back on the pimply young man, her eyes drawn to the map again. There was something compelling about it. Perhaps the simplicity. Perhaps the unbridled joy. Perhaps the cow.

"Any idea who would've made this?" Huifen asked.

"Nope. None. This was made by hand. No surprise. There weren't many people doing orienteering back then."

As opposed to here now, thought Amelia, and asked, "What is orienteering, anyway?"

Like Huifen, she'd looked it up online, but this girl was the head of the local club, which consisted of her, her brother and two cousins, and might be able to tell them something not found on Wikipedia.

"It's like a scavenger hunt," the girl said. "But instead of written clues and puzzles to solve, we have a compass and a map. Certain spots are marked and we have to get to them as fast as we can. We call them controls."

"So it's a race?" asked Huifen.

"Yes. What makes it fun is that the fastest way between the controls isn't always the shortest. We have to figure out the best route. And then we run."

Amelia wondered if she knew what "fun" meant.

"You must be in good shape," said Huifen.

"We are. We're running flat out, and not always on roads or even paths. It's cross-country. Through fields and forests and up and down hills and over rivers. It's crazy. You get pumped."

She seemed to have a good grasp on "crazy," thought Amelia.

"What happens when you get to a, did you call it a control?" asked Huifen.

"There's a little flag and a stamp to show we've been there. And then we run to the next one. I don't know why it isn't more popular."

Amelia had an idea. There was, though, a virtual game of orienteering that was apparently gaining popularity.

"Do you know anything about the history of orienteering in the area?" Huifen asked. "Who started it? Who first did it?"

"Not really," she shook her head. "It started before the First World War, I know that, and had something to do with military training. The guys like hearing about that. They pretend they're on a battlefield. But I don't know anything about how it started locally. It sorta dies out, then comes back."

She looked down at the map, wistfully.

"It's beautiful, isn't it? Whoever did this must've loved orienteering. But you know, it's also sorta strange. I mean, there're landmarks from different seasons. And what's with the pyramid?"

She pointed to the upper-right quadrant of the map.

Amelia looked at it again herself. Of all the strange things about the map, that was the weirdest. The rest could be explained, but that could not.

"Is it an orienteering symbol?" she asked.

The girl shook her head. "Not that I know of. What's there? Anything?"

Huifen brought up a map of the area on her iPhone. They crowded around as she made it larger, then smaller.

There was, not surprisingly, no pyramid. In fact, there was no nothing. Just forest.

"Maybe it's a tent," said Amelia.

"Or a hill. A mountain," said the girl, getting into the spirit.

But Huifen shook her head as she examined her iPhone. "*Non*. Ahh, well, maybe it's an in-joke, like the snowman and the cow."

"Must be," said Amelia.

She took a sip from the thick white mug. A Tim Hortons double double. It tasted not at all like coffee, but it did taste of treats from childhood. Sweet and rich. She looked across the table and could almost see her dad sitting there. He'd brought her to Timmy's, as he called it, after her figure skating class. He all gruff and she in her pink sequined costume. Sitting primly.

He'd give her one sip of his double double. *Don't tell your mother*, he'd say. She hadn't. Never did. It was a secret she kept even now.

The girl had nothing else to offer and her break was up. She went back behind the counter and Amelia watched her running from customer to coffee machine to doughnut counter.

Huifen pointed to her mouth and Amelia quickly picked up a thin napkin and wiped away some strawberry jam and icing sugar.

They sat in the sun streaming through the window and looked at the parking lot of the Tim Hortons in Cowansville. Sun bounced and magnified off the ice and snow and the puddles where it had melted. Outside, the world was brilliant silver and gold and diamonds, and inside the doughnut joint it smelled of yeast and sugar and coffee and tasted of an as yet unmarred childhood.

"What now?" Amelia asked.

"Professor Charpentier said this was made by someone who knew how to do maps," said Huifen.

"A cartographer," said Amelia. "I wonder who was mapping the area back then. Around 1900."

"I guess someone must've been," said Huifen.

The two young women looked at each other.

Maps were just something they took for granted, never thinking someone had had to actually walk the land and survey every hill and river.

"Is there a government office of cartography?" Huifen asked, picking up her iPhone once again, as did Amelia. It was her generation's compass, how they navigated through life.

They silently clicked away, in an unofficial race for the answer.

"There's the Geological Survey," said Amelia. "They do maps."

"That's federal," said Huifen. "Go further."

Amelia did and looked up a minute later. "The Commission de toponymie du Québec?"

Huifen nodded. "I think that should be our next stop. There's a government building here in Cowansville."

"But it says here the toponymie department only started in the 1970s."

"Read further."

Amelia did. "Oh."

"Oh," said Huifen. "Let's go."

They folded up the map and left, waving to the young woman behind the counter, who was gracefully and rapidly moving from station to station.

Huifen drove while Amelia punched the coordinates of the government office into the GPS, asking it to choose the quickest route.

Their research, albeit superficial, had uncovered that while the Commission de toponymie had only existed since 1977, it had been the job of successive government employees to map Québec towns, villages, mountains, lakes and rivers and to give them their official names since 1912.

"You wanna know who owned a building in the early 1900s?" asked the town clerk in Saint-Rémy.

The two young men nodded.

"Why?"

Nathaniel could see Jacques bristling at the question and jumped in.

"A school project," he said. "History of the area. They're public record, aren't they?"

The clerk admitted they were. "But good luck finding the information."

"Why?"

"Our property records go back two hundred years or more," he said. "But they're not all on computer."

"Then where are they?" asked Nathaniel.

"On cards. In the basement."

"Of course they are," said Jacques.

The clerk opened the wooden door and turned on the light. A single dirty bulb hung by a suspiciously old cord from the ceiling, lighting the stairs down.

"Keep your coats on," he advised.

"It's cold?" asked Nathaniel.

"Among other things. You might want gloves too." He made a face and all but crossed himself as the two young men descended the wooden steps.

They stood on the dirt floor, wiping real or imagined cobwebs from their faces. Rows of gunmetal gray filing cabinets lined the cinder-block walls, containing the records of ownership. Somewhere in there was a card telling them who'd owned the bistro when it had been a private home.

And that would tell them who'd made the map, and sealed it in the wall.

"Shit," said Jacques, surveying the banks of records.

"You've got the wrong department," said the receptionist.

She was middle-aged and tired. The only members of the public who ever came into her office were there to complain. And seemed to blame her personally for their tax bills, the potholes in their roads, blackouts, and one mother screamed at her for twenty minutes because her child had measles.

"We want to find out who made this map," said Huifen, pushing it across the worn counter toward the weary woman.

"And I want you to understand," she said, slowly pushing it back. "I. Don't. Care."

"But the Commission de toponymie has an office here, doesn't it?" asked Amelia.

The clerk looked at her with distaste, then turned back to the least objectionable of the two. The Chinese Girl.

"The commission puts names on places," she explained. "It doesn't map them."

"But it used to, didn't it?" asked Amelia, but now the receptionist refused to even look in her direction.

"Can we speak to the person anyway?" asked Huifen, and beamed at the receptionist, who was impervious to good humor.

"Fine."

"Yeah," said Amelia. "I bet you are."

The clerk picked up the phone and jabbed her finger at a button.

"Someone here to speak to you. No, I'm not kidding. Some Chinese Girl. Stop laughing, it's true."

Hanging up, she waved at the waiting area, then turned back to her desk.

"I've become the Invisible Woman," said Amelia, as they took their seats.

"That must be a new experience for you," said Huifen, and Amelia smiled.

After a few minutes of waiting, Huifen turned to Amelia. "Why did you apply to the academy? You don't exactly fit in."

"And you do? Chinese Girl."

Huifen smiled. "Ahh, but Chinese Girl with Gun fits in everywhere."

Amelia laughed, and the receptionist looked over, disapproving.

"I can't actually remember why I applied," said Amelia. "I must've been drunk or stoned."

The landlady, fat legs splayed, cigarette hanging loosely between her yellowed fingers. And on the TV, a smartly dressed woman, feminine and poised.

Amelia saw her two futures, right there.

"I didn't think I'd be accepted," she admitted. "And you're right, I don't fit in. Anywhere. Might as well not fit in there."

"With the academy, that's not exactly a bad thing," said Huifen. "Why didn't you listen to me?"

"What? When? I am listening to you."

"I don't mean now, I mean at that first party, in the Commander's rooms. I told you to stay away from him."

"I didn't know who you meant, the Commander or Leduc."

"Well, now you know."

Amelia nodded. She wished with all her heart she'd known then what she knew now.

"Do you have any idea who killed him?" she asked Huifen.

"The Duke? No."

"But you must've known him well."

"Why d'you say that?"

"You seemed chummy."

"Chummy? With the Duke?" said Huifen. "No one was chummy with him. Like you, we did as we were told. Were you ever alone with him?"

"No."

But the Goth Girl colored, and Huifen knew that was a lie. She hesitated, then touched Amelia's hand. Lightly. As though a moth had landed, then taken off.

Just then the receptionist stood up and looked over. Seeing the gesture, she shook her head. It was worse than she'd thought.

"He'll see you now. Down the hall, first door on the right."

"*Merde*," said Jacques.

He leaned over the open drawer and looked down the long line of file cabinets marching into the darkness.

"How're we ever going to find the records on that property? These aren't even in chronological order. They're alphabetical. It's fucking crazy."

Nathaniel didn't disagree.

To make matters worse, the township didn't recognize the village of Three Pines as a separate entity. There were absolutely no references to it.

And to make matters even worse, Jacques was getting antsy. Bored. Impatient. And Nathaniel knew what that meant. Once he stopped berating the filing system, Jacques would go looking for another target.

"You're right," said Nathaniel. "Since they're alphabetical, we could look up the names of the boys until we find one that fits."

Nathaniel brought out his iPhone and tapped it a few times until he came to the photographs he'd taken of the memorial window in the chapel and the names below it.

"The stained-glass boy is probably one of them. If we look up the family names, we might find someone who lived in that building in 1914. Good idea."

Jacques nodded, either not realizing, or not admitting, that the idea hadn't been his. He had, in fact, been thinking about how dark and cold it was. And wondering what was in the corners. And what was dangling overhead. And how to get out if there was a fire. Or an earthquake. Or a huge spider that had lived down here, undisturbed, for years . . .

Something brushed against his face and he jerked away, flailing his arms and wiping wildly at his head. Putting his tuque and gloves back on, he grudgingly got to work.

Down the wall, Nathaniel's bare head was leaning over the files while his fingers worked nimbly, almost frantically, through the cards.

Monsieur Bergeron, the manager of toponymie for the region, was a balding, precise, desiccated man. His office was also bald and precise, with no personal items at all, except for a dusty Plexiglas plaque congratulating him on thirty years of service to Québec. The entire wall behind him was taken up by a detailed map of the area.

The dry little man hooked his fingers on the edge of his desk like a little bird and sat forward.

He gave an audible sigh, then looked from the map to the Chinese Girl and the Goth Girl.

"A Turcotte." He sighed again. "Where did you find this?"

"In a wall, in Three Pines," said Huifen.

"Where?"

"The village," said Amelia.

He looked momentarily lost, then dropped his eyes to the map.

"Turcotte," said Huifen. "Is that the person who made it?"

"*Oui, oui*," said Monsieur Bergeron dreamily.

"How do you know?" asked Amelia.

She was both amused and annoyed by the reaction of this man. He seemed to be not only absorbed in the map, but absorbed by it. As though he'd fallen between the thin topographical lines and gotten trapped there. Happily.

"It's unmistakable, isn't it?" he said, with all the confidence of an expert who was surprised that everyone couldn't see what was so obvious to him. "May I touch it?"

The young women nodded, not mentioning that just a few minutes earlier a jelly doughnut had touched it.

He reached out, letting his thin finger hover over the paper, as though it might bring the map to life, like Michelangelo's Adam in the Sistine Chapel.

When his finger did finally descend, it was an act so delicate, so intimate, Amelia felt she should look away.

She was about to tell him it was just a photocopy, not the original, but decided not to. This man knew that perfectly well. And he was still smitten.

"Turcotte was a mapmaker?" asked Huifen.

"Not just a mapmaker. Antony Turcotte was the father of all of Québec's modern maps. He created a department dedicated to mapping and naming the province. That was back in the early 1900s. He was a giant. He recognized the connection a people have to where they live. That it isn't just land. Our history, our cuisine, our stories and songs spring from where we live. He wanted to capture that. He gave *les habitants* their *patrimoine*."

Monsieur Bergeron had used the old word, the slang word, for the inhabitants of Québec. *Les habitants*. Over the years it had become almost an insult, conjuring images of lumbering rustics.

But this man, and Antony Turcotte before him, used the word correctly. *Les habitants* had tended the land. They'd cleared it, farmed it, built homes and businesses. They'd lived on it and loved it. They were born on it and buried in it.

Without *les habitants* there would be no Québec.

But he'd also used another word, a word charged with meaning for the Québécois. Their *patrimoine*. Their heritage. Their language, their culture, their inheritance. Their land.

"He lived in Montréal but decided to move down here, to the Townships," said Bergeron. "He set up cartography offices around the province, but chose to map this area himself. I think he must've fallen in love with the Townships and its history."

"Don't you mean geography?" asked Amelia.

"They're the same thing." The middle-aged bureaucrat looked across his desk at her. "Antony Turcotte knew that you can't separate history and geography."

"I can," muttered Amelia. "So could my teachers."

"Then they were fools." The bald statement was made all the more forceful by its simplicity. "A place's history is decided by its geography. Is the terrain mountainous? If so, it's harder to invade. The people are more independent, but also isolated. Is it surrounded by water? If so, it's probably more cosmopolitan—"

"But easier to conquer, like Venice," said Amelia, picking up on what he meant.

"*Oui*," said Monsieur Bergeron, turning an approving eye on the Goth Girl. "Venice gave up trying to defend herself and decided to open her doors to all comers. As a result, it became a hub of commerce, of knowledge and art and music. Because of its position, geographically, it became a gateway. Geography decides if you're the invaded or the invader."

"Look at the Romans," said Amelia. "And later the British."

"*Oui, c'est ca*," said Monsieur Bergeron, looking slightly manic now. "Britain was invaded over and over, until it realized its weakness was also its strength. Britannia turned her efforts to ruling the waves and so, in turn, ruled the world. That wouldn't have happened had it not been an island nation."

"Geography is history," said Amelia, taken with the idea. She loved history, but had given absolutely no thought to geography.

"But what does that mean for Québec?" Huifen asked.

"Stuck between two powerful forces?" asked Monsieur Bergeron. "The Americans to the south and the British to the west and east? There was no defense militarily. But one way to defend the *patrimoine* was to map it and name it."

"And claim it," said Huifen.

"There're earlier maps, of course. Most famously, Champlain's maps of New France and David Thompson's maps. Antony Turcotte is less well known, but more beloved, because he didn't make maps for governments or conquest or commerce. He made them for the people."

He looked at the paper, as though the map was the man.

"This"—his hand hovered over the map—"isn't one of his official maps, of course. It looks like one he made for fun. It actually looks like an orienteering map."

"We think so too," said Huifen. "You know about orienteering?"

"Of course. But this is different from even those old maps."

"How so?"

"Well, the snowman, for one thing." Monsieur Bergeron smiled as he looked at it. "This looks like a sort of hybrid. A real map showing all the topography though without place names, and an orienteering map, showing the man-made structures like stone walls and mills. But then there're those whimsical touches, like the three little pine trees that appear to be playing. It must have been a map made for his own amusement."

Monsieur Bergeron leaned in even closer, as though the paper might whisper to him.

"Or maybe it was made for his son." Huifen laid her iPhone on the desk. "We think this is him."

The stained-glass boy appeared to be walking into the map.

Monsieur Bergeron shifted his gaze to the iPhone. "A remarkable expression. Where was this taken?"

"It's part of a stained-glass window, a memorial window, for those killed in the First World War," said Amelia.

Monsieur Bergeron grunted. "Poor boy." Then he looked up. "What makes you think this is Turcotte's son?"

Huifen enlarged the image and Bergeron's eyes widened when he saw the map just sticking out from the soldier's knapsack.

"*Mais, c'est extraordinaire*," said Monsieur Bergeron, then he shook his head. "When you think of the lives lost for inches of soil."

He tsked three times, disapproving of war and the slaughter of youth.

Amelia got up and walked to the huge map behind him. Her finger followed the roads and rivers, and stopped in a valley.

She turned. "There's no Three Pines."

"There must be," said Huifen, going over. "I can see it being forgotten by the GPS and commercial maps, but this's the official map, right?"

Monsieur Bergeron got up and turned to face it. "If it's not here, it doesn't exist."

"But of course it does, we're staying there," said Huifen, staring. "This map is incorrect."

"Can't be. Turcotte drew it himself," said Bergeron. "His work was the foundation. We add new roads and towns, but it's all built on Antony Turcotte's original surveys. Maybe he just missed it. It must be pretty small. I've never even heard of it."

"But Turcotte lived there himself," said Amelia. "Why would he leave his own village off the official map?"

"Maybe we got it wrong and he didn't live there," said Huifen. "Maybe he made the orienteering map and gave it to someone else. Someone who did live there."

"Then how did it get into the stained-glass window in Three Pines?" asked Amelia. "*Non.* That map was made by someone who not only lived in the village, but loved it."

"So why did he disappear it?" asked Huifen. She turned to Bergeron. "What do you know about him?"

"Not a lot, really. I don't think many people actually even met him."

"Was that unusual?" asked Amelia.

Monsieur Bergeron smiled. "Not many meet me. The Société des carte-logues du Québec tried to do a biography of Turcotte for the Canadian Encyclopedia. Here, let me find it."

He pulled a thick book from his shelf. Wiping off the dust, he found a page, then handed the book to Huifen.

"Antony Turcotte, cartographer," she read. "Born in LaSalle, in 1862. Died in 1919."

"But not in Three Pines," said Amelia, reading over her shoulder. "It says here he's buried in a place called Roof Trusses. Roof Trusses?"

She looked at Monsieur Bergeron, who smiled. "I'm afraid so. Turcotte's one great error. It's become legendary in the toponymie world."

"He named a village Roof Trusses?"

"We can't explain it. Well, actually we can, sort of. At the entrance to the village, there used to be a small business that made—"

"Roof trusses?"

"*Oui.* Those wooden things that hold up roofs. We think, because he didn't speak much English, that he mistook the sign for the name of the village."

"He never explained?"

"He was never asked. He sent in his map, with the place names, but this was a tiny village and no one noticed until years later."

"So how do you know he didn't make other mistakes?" asked Huifen.

Monsieur Bergeron looked affronted and even slightly confused, as though the idea of Antony Turcotte making another error was incomprehensible.

"He was human, after all," she prompted, despite the mythologizing that had apparently happened over the years.

243

"Antony Turcotte did not make another mistake, and the one he made he owned for eternity, by choosing to be buried there," said Bergeron, his voice clipped.

Amelia was about to point out that Turcotte had left the village of Three Pines off the map, but stopped herself. She suspected that had not been a mistake.

"This biography doesn't mention a wife or children," said Huifen.

"No, there was no record of either. It doesn't mean he didn't have them, just that the records were lost. As you can see, we couldn't find out much about him."

The entry was indeed sparse.

"Can you show us Roof Trusses on the map?" asked Huifen.

Monsieur Bergeron looked a little sheepish. "I'm afraid not."

"Don't tell me—" started Huifen.

"It doesn't exist anymore," said Bergeron. "When the error was discovered, it was renamed, something the villagers themselves chose. But then it disappeared too."

"Disappeared?" asked Amelia.

"It happens," said Bergeron. "Villages spring up around a single industry and when it dies, the village dies."

And now Roof Trusses, like Three Pines, was not even a tiny dot on a large map, thought Amelia.

Jacques rammed the drawer of the filing cabinet shut with such force the sound knocked Nathaniel out of his skin.

Hands trembling, breath short and shallow, his pupils dilated, Nathaniel dropped his head, but not before he saw Jacques turn and look down the long, long line of files. And focus. On him.

The younger cadet went back to the cards, desperately going through them, trying to find the one with the answer. But Jacques was bearing down on him with purpose. He'd reached the end of his patience with the search, and had found something more interesting to do.

Please, oh please, thought Nathaniel as his fingers fumbled. But his eyes no longer took in the words on the cards, and he waited, numb, for the shove, the punch, the slap. The harsh word. Or worse.

Instead, a few feet away, Jacques stopped. A familiar buzzing had halted him. And, like Pavlov's dog, he couldn't help but react to it, bringing his iPhone out.

His face lit up from the screen.

"Where're the Ts?"

"Over here," said Nathaniel, scuttling over a few cabinets. "Why?"

But Jacques didn't answer. He found the drawer and flipped through the records mumbling, "Turcotte. Turcotte. Here's one. No, not him."

After a few minutes, Jacques stepped back, too puzzled to be annoyed, yet.

Huifen's phone beeped.

"Jacques just texted from the registry office. There's no record of an Antony Turcotte."

Amelia tapped her phone a few times, once again bringing up the photograph of the memorial window. Scrolling down, she read the names.

"No Turcotte here either."

"Are you sure our map was drawn by Antony Turcotte?" Huifen asked.

"Positive," said Monsieur Bergeron.

"Then why can't we find him?" asked Huifen.

And why, thought Amelia, is everything to do with Antony Turcotte disappearing?

CHAPTER 28

"*Salut*, Armand." Michel Brébeuf rose from behind the desk in his office. "I'm sorry. Commander."

There was a slight nip in the air.

He put out his hand with exaggerated courtesy and Gamache shook it, then introduced Deputy Commissioner Gélinas.

"Of the RCMP." Brébeuf pointed to the small pin Gélinas wore on his lapel. "I've noticed you in the halls. Here to assure fairness in the investigation?"

When Gélinas nodded, Brébeuf turned to Gamache.

"Still doing the right thing, I see."

The nip became a bite.

"And we're hoping you will too," said Gamache, and saw the smile drift off Brébeuf's face. "May we?"

But before Brébeuf could answer, the two men had taken seats. Gamache crossed his legs and made himself comfortable.

"Now, Michel, we have a few questions."

"I've already been questioned, but always happy to help further. Are you any closer to finding out who killed Leduc?"

"We're plodding along," said Gamache. He turned to Gélinas, who'd been watching with interest.

To say there was animosity between the men would be a gross understatement. The air was almost unbreathable for the sulfur. Most of it emanating from Brébeuf, but Gamache was giving off his fair share. It was hidden beneath a razor-thin, and crackling, sheen of civility. But the stink of a long-rotted relationship was squeezing through the cracks.

Any thought the RCMP officer had that these two had colluded in the murder of Serge Leduc disappeared immediately. He doubted these men could bake a cake together, never mind plan and execute a killing.

"How well did you know Serge Leduc?" Gélinas asked.

"I'd heard of him, of course. I was still with the Sûreté when he was transferred here. Second-in-command under that old fool, though Leduc actually ran the place."

"You were a senior officer at the time," said Gélinas. "A superintendent."

Michel Brébeuf gave a shallow nod of assent.

"You won't remember, but we met once," said Gélinas. "Years ago, at a consular function."

"Did we?"

It was said politely, but it was clear Brébeuf did not remember and didn't care to put in the effort to try. Paul Gélinas would have been just another guest. But Michel Brébeuf was always memorable. A small man who took up a lot of space, not because he demanded it but because he radiated authority.

Unintentionally, or perhaps not, he became the center of attention in any room.

The only other person Gélinas had met who could immediately and naturally command a room was the man sitting beside him. But Armand Gamache had another skill that Brébeuf didn't seem to possess.

He could disappear, when he chose. And it appeared he chose to disappear at that moment.

Armand Gamache sat quietly. Almost a hole in the room.

It was in some ways more disconcerting than the energy throbbing off the man across the desk.

"So you knew him," said Gélinas.

"Serge Leduc? We were introduced a few times, at formal occasions. When I came here to speak to the graduating class, and at parades. But he was generally on the field with the cadets while I was on the podium."

A not-so-subtle reminder of their relative positions.

"And when you accepted to teach here, did you rekindle the relationship?"

"Now you're being deliberately misleading," said Brébeuf with amusement that did not extend to his gray winter eyes. Eyes, Gélinas thought, that looked like the slush in the street. Not water, not snow. Some in-between state. March eyes.

"There was nothing to rekindle. We were barely acquainted, but yes, we came to know each other slightly better after we were thrown together here."

"You make it sound like you were trapped."

"Do I? I don't mean to."

"How well did you get to know him over these past few months?"

Brébeuf looked at him, and Gélinas could almost see his thoughts. *He's wondering how much we've found out. He knows by now the DNA and fingerprint results are in.*

He knows exactly what steps we're taking, and in what order. And how to be a step ahead.

"I'd visited him a few times in his rooms."

"And did he go to yours?"

The question surprised Brébeuf and he raised his brows slightly. "No."

"What did you talk about, when you were together?"

"We exchanged war stories."

"And did he tell you about fraud and contract fixing and the numbered accounts he holds in Luxembourg?" asked Gélinas.

There was a slight movement off to his left, from Gamache.

He doesn't approve of my telling Brébeuf about Leduc's criminal activities, thought Gélinas. *But it was too late, and the RCMP officer had done it deliberately, to see Brébeuf's reaction.*

"He alluded to some less than legal activity on his part," said Brébeuf. "I think in an attempt to flatten the playing field. He was aware, of course, of my history."

"He wanted to let you know that he didn't judge you?" asked Gélinas, and saw Brébeuf bristle.

"Believe me, Deputy Commissioner, Serge Leduc's judgment was of no importance to me."

"And yet, it appears you had a great deal in common. You were both senior Sûreté officers. Both misused your positions and were eventually caught and expelled from the Sûreté for criminal activity. Both of you were saved from prosecution by friends in high places. In your case, Monsieur Gamache. In his case, the Chief Superintendent. And you both found yourselves here, at the academy."

"Have you come here to insult me, or ask for my help?"

"I'm pointing out the commonalities in your CVs," said Gélinas. "That's all."

"There might be commonalities, as you put it, but I had nothing in common with him," said Brébeuf. "He was just that. Common. A lump of coal that thought it was a diamond. He was a moron with a big office."

"Then what were you doing in his living room? His bathroom? His bedroom?" asked Gélinas, his voice no longer quite so cordial. He shoved a hard copy of the forensics report across the desk. "What were you doing handling the murder weapon?"

Beside him, Gamache stirred again, and then subsided.

Brébeuf picked up the paper and scanned it with the practiced eye of a seasoned investigator. Going straight to the pertinent information.

His face, at first grim, relaxed a fraction. Gélinas realized, in that moment, why Gamache had reacted, albeit subtly, when the report was given to Brébeuf.

Yes, it showed that Michel Brébeuf might have held the murder weapon. But it also showed it was even more likely that Gamache had.

"You know as well as I do," said Brébeuf, sliding the page back to Gélinas, "that this is supposition. Inadmissible."

"Then you deny it?"

"Of course I do. I had no idea he had a gun, though I should've guessed. Only a fool would keep one in his rooms at a school. Though I'd never have expected this type of gun. A revolver? Does this make sense to you?"

He'd asked the question of Gamache.

"I would've expected a missile launcher," said Gamache, and Brébeuf laughed.

And in a flash, in that easy laugh, Gélinas saw something else.

How these two could have once been friends. They'd have made a formidable team, too, had one not stepped back and the other stepped up.

The mood in the room seemed to have changed, with that moment between the two men.

Michel Brébeuf grew quiet, contemplative.

"Do you want to know why we sometimes had dinner and drinks together?" Brébeuf asked. His voice deepening, softening.

Paul Gélinas nodded and glanced over at Gamache, who hadn't moved. He was still watching Brébeuf with keen, attentive eyes.

"I went there because I was lonely," said Brébeuf. "I was surrounded by people here, but no one wanted anything to do with me. I don't blame them. I did this to myself, and I came here to try to make amends. I knew it would be difficult to talk to the senior cadets, every day, about corruption and my own temptation. About all the things that can go wrong, when you're given authority and a gun and no boundary but your own. It's one thing to be told that power corrupts," he turned to Gamache, "but you were right. It's far more effective to see an example. I told them about what I'd done, how it started small, insignificant even. And grew. I told them about the dangers of falling in with the wrong people. I taught an entire class on the theme of one bad apple. And admitted that had been me. And on the very first day of class, I wrote Matthew 10:36 across the top of the blackboard, and left it there. It was humiliating, but necessary."

He'd spoken quietly, and directly to Armand.

"I thought the worst would be the classroom, but it wasn't. The worst was the evenings, when I could hear laughter and music. When I knew you were just down the corridor, talking to your cadets. And I sat there, alone, waiting for someone to perhaps show up."

Paul Gélinas felt he had vanished, been overwhelmed, buried. A climber caught up in the avalanche that was the relationship between these two men.

"I visited Serge Leduc every now and then because he was the only one who smiled when he saw me."

"Did you kill him, Michel?" asked Armand quietly.

"Would you put a bullet in your life raft?" asked Brébeuf. "No, I didn't kill him. I didn't like or respect him. But then, I don't like or respect myself. But I didn't shoot the man."

"Do you have any idea who did?" asked Gélinas, clawing his way back into the interview.

"I wish I could tell you I think it was a professor and not a student, but I can't," said Brébeuf. "The cadets these days aren't like we were. They're rough, coarse. Look at that freshman, the one with all the tattoos and piercings. And the language I've heard out of her. To professors. Shocking. What's she doing here? One of Leduc's recruits, no doubt."

"Actually, she's one of mine," said Gamache. "Amelia Choquet is top of her class. She reads Ancient Greek and Latin. And she swears like the criminals she'll one day arrest. While you, Michel, are gentility itself. And have broken most of the laws you promised to uphold."

Brébeuf took a deep breath, either steadying himself, or readying the attack. The thin ice they'd been on had given way. Gamache himself had shattered it.

There was a moment when the world seemed to stop entirely.

And then Michel Brébeuf smiled. "I was the more senior officer, Armand, but you were always the better man, weren't you? How comforting for you to know that. And to always remind me." He leaned his lean body across the desk. "Well, fuck you."

It was said with a strange mixture of humor and anger. Was he joking, Gélinas wondered, or was the insult real?

He looked over at Gamache, who'd raised his brows but was also smiling.

And Gélinas understood then how well these two men knew each other. And while there was malice, there was also a closeness. An intimacy.

It was a bond that could only have been formed over many years. But hate bonds as surely, and closely, as love.

Paul Gélinas made a mental note to look into their pasts. He knew them professionally, but now it was time to dig into their personal lives.

"The murder of Serge Leduc didn't happen out of the blue," said Brébeuf. "If it had, you'd have caught the person by now. No. It was considered. He enjoyed tormenting people. Especially people who couldn't fight back. But he obviously chose the wrong target."

"You think Leduc hurt and humiliated someone so badly that they got their revenge?" asked Gamache.

"I do, and I can see you do too. And you, Deputy Commissioner?"

"I reserve judgment. You're both more experienced in murder than I am."

"Do you think he means murder, or investigating murder, Armand?" asked Michel as they got to their feet.

"I think Monsieur Gélinas says exactly what he means," said Gamache.

"Then I think you're in a bit of trouble," said Brébeuf. He laughed. With genuine pleasure.

Paul Gélinas felt nauseous as he walked down the hall. Made seasick by Brébeuf's wildly corkscrewing emotions.

Neither man looked behind him, but they could feel Brébeuf's eyes on their backs. And then they heard the office door quietly click shut.

"You two were friends?" asked Gélinas.

"Best friends," said Gamache. "He was a good man, once."

"What happened?"

"I don't know."

"Do you think he still is?" Gélinas asked when they reached the stairs.

Gamache paused at the top step. The stairwell was flooded with light from the three-story window that framed the vast thawing prairie.

The echo of cadets calling to each other to hurry bounced off the walls, and urgent steps were heard on the marble stairs below.

And Armand remembered how he and Michel would race up an old, scuffed mahogany staircase, taking them two at a time. Late for class. Again. Because of some sudden discovery the young men had made. A trap door. The way into the attic. A bone that might be human. Or from a chicken.

The poor pathology professor. Dr. Nadeau. Armand smiled slightly at the memory of the harried man, bothered yet again by the two cadets and another bone, or a piece of hair, that might be human. Or mouse.

And each time the verdict. Not human.

But Michel and Armand developed a pet theory. Their finds were in fact some poor victim, and Dr. Nadeau the killer. Covering up. They didn't believe it, of course, but it became a running joke. As was their search for more and more ludicrous things to take to the poor man for analysis.

"Gamache?" said the RCMP officer. "Do you think Brébeuf is still a good man, underneath?"

"I wouldn't have brought him here if I didn't think there was good still in him," said Gamache, the distant laughter echoing off the glass and concrete.

"But do you regret the decision? Do you think he killed Leduc?" asked Gélinas.

"Not long ago you were accusing me, now you're accusing him," said Gamache, taking the steps down, his hand on the rail. He stopped on the landing as cadets raced by, late for class. They paused to salute, then ran on, taking the stairs two at a time.

"I've found in homicide it's natural and even necessary to suspect everyone," said Gamache, when the stairwell was clear, "but best not to say it out loud. Undermines your credibility."

"Thanks for the advice. Fortunately, in the field of homicide, I have no credibility."

Gamache grinned at that.

"I actually thought you might've done it together," said Gélinas, as they continued down the steps.

"Killed him together? Why in the world would we do that?"

"To get rid of a problem. You wanted Leduc dead, to protect the cadets. But you couldn't quite bring yourself to do it. But you knew someone who could. Someone who owed you. That would also explain Brébeuf's presence at the academy. As an object lesson for the students, perhaps, but mostly as a tool for you. To get rid of someone you couldn't just fire. So while it was your idea and planning, Brébeuf was the one who actually did it. It was one last spectacular amend for what he did to you."

"And now?"

"I no longer think that."

"And yet you just asked if I thought he'd killed Leduc."

"I asked if you thought he did it, I didn't say I thought so."

"You mean you wanted to see if I'd throw him under a bus, to save myself?"

Gélinas was silent. That was exactly what he'd done. He'd handed Gamache an opportunity to condemn Michel Brébeuf. And he hadn't taken it.

253

"Brébeuf is the only person in this whole place who actually needed the dead man alive," said Gélinas. "While I said I'd learned never to underestimate hatred, I've learned something else since the death of my wife."

Gamache stopped at the next landing and gave his full attention to Paul Gélinas.

"Never underestimate loneliness," said the Mountie. "Brébeuf wouldn't kill the only person not just willing but happy to keep him company. What did he call Leduc?"

"His life raft. And now? Are you still lonely?"

"I was talking about Brébeuf."

"*Oui.*"

He paused to let Gélinas know he was listening, if he wanted to talk. The RCMP officer said nothing more, but his lips compressed, and Gamache turned away to give the man at least the semblance of privacy.

He looked out the window, across a snowy field gleaming in the sun, to an outdoor rink where the village children were playing a pickup game of hockey. One of the last of the season. Even from a distance, Gamache could see the puddles where the ice was melting. Before long the rink would be gone, would be grass, and another game would begin.

It seemed not so much a window as an opening into another place and time. A million miles from where they stood.

"I remember doing that on the lake at our chalet in the Laurentians," said Gélinas, so quietly it was almost a whisper. "When I was a kid."

When I was a kid, thought Gamache. Now there was a sentence. *When I was a kid . . .*

The two men stood in silence, watching the game.

"They could be using the indoor rink of the academy," Gélinas gestured toward the arena. "But maybe they prefer to be outside."

"Would you have?" asked Gamache, and Gélinas smiled and shook his head.

"*Non.* Give me a warm arena and scalding hot chocolate from the vending machine after the game," he said. "Heaven."

"The mayor has stopped them coming to the academy," said Gamache.

He watched as one of the players had a breakaway and another plowed him into the snowbank surrounding the rink. There was a great poof of flakes and then they emerged, covered in snow, red-faced, laughing.

"They'll be back," said Gélinas. "Give it time."

The kids skated up and down, up and down the rink, chasing the puck. All of them wore blue and red tuques with bobbing pompoms and Montréal Canadiens hockey sweaters. It was impossible to tell one team from another. But they seemed to know. By instinct.

They knew who was on their side.

When did it get so difficult to tell? Gamache wondered.

CHAPTER 29

⁓

"I'm sorry, but there's no Mrs. Clairton here," said the pleasant young woman on the phone.

"I said, 'Clairton,'" repeated Isabelle Lacoste.

"Yes. No. Exactly. Clairton."

Lacoste stared at the phone. She hadn't been looking forward to this call, knowing it would probably end up like this. The woman with the thick British accent trying to understand the woman with the Québécois accent.

Both speaking apparently unintelligible English.

It was doubly annoying that Beauvoir, whose rough English had been picked up on the streets of east-end Montréal, had absolutely no trouble making himself understood. And understanding. While she, who'd actually studied English, was constantly misunderstood.

Lacoste looked down at the email from the woman at the gun manufacturer, McDermot and Ryan, in the UK.

She'd clearly signed it Elizabeth Coldbrook-Clairton.

"This is McDermot and Ryan?" asked Lacoste.

"No, you've reached McDermot and Ryan."

Lacoste sighed at the completely predicable response.

"Well, good-bye then," said the cheerful young woman.

"Wait," said Lacoste. "How about Coldbrook? Do you have an Elizabeth Coldbrook?"

There was a long pause, during which Lacoste wondered if the receptionist had hung up. But finally the voice came down the line.

"No, but we do have an Elizabeth Coldbrook."

"Yes, yes," said Lacoste, hearing the desperation in her own voice.

"One moment, please."

A few seconds later another voice, this one more efficient but less cheerful, said, "Hello, how may I help you?"

"Elizabeth Coldbrook-Clairton?"

There was a very slight hesitation. "Elizabeth Coldbrook, yes. Who's this?"

"My name is Isabelle Lacoste. I'm investigating the murder of a professor here in Québec. Canada."

"Oh yes, I spoke to your supervisor this morning."

"Actually, I'm the supervisor. Chief Inspector Lacoste, of the Sûreté du Québec. You were speaking with Inspector Beauvoir."

There was laughter down the line. "Oh, I am sorry. You'd think I'd know better than to assume, especially after all these years in public affairs and being the head of a department myself. *Désolé.*"

"You speak French?" asked Lacoste, still in English.

"I do. Your English is better than my French, but we can switch if you like."

Oddly, Lacoste could understand this woman's English perfectly. Perhaps her clipped tones made it closer to the mid-Atlantic accent she was used to in Canada.

"English is fine," said Lacoste. "I'd like to send you a photograph. It's a revolver."

She hit send.

"I've already seen it. Your colleague emailed it to me this morning," said Elizabeth Coldbrook. "Oh, wait a minute. This isn't the same picture. What is it?"

"It's a detail of a stained-glass window."

Lacoste hit send on another picture and she heard the click as Madame Coldbrook opened it as well.

"I see. A memorial window. Striking image."

"*Oui.* The sidearm the soldier is carrying, can you tell the make?"

"I can. It's definitely one of ours. The styling is distinctive. A McDermot .45. They were issued to most of the British Expeditionary Force in the First World War."

"This was a Canadian soldier."

"I believe many of them were also issued that revolver. At least, the officers were. He looks so young."

Both women, both mothers, looked at the boy, with the rifle and the revolver and the frightened, determined, forgiving expression.

"This is the same make but not the same gun used in your crime," said Madame Coldbrook. "That revolver was new. Sold to the man just a few years ago."

"Yes, I understand."

"You think there's a connection between a man who died and a soldier of the Great War?"

"We're really just tying up details."

"I see. Well, if there's nothing more I can do . . ."

"*Merci*. Oh, there is one other little thing. Just curious, but do you go by the name Elizabeth Coldbrook, or Clairton, or Coldbrook-Clairton? For our report."

"Elizabeth Coldbrook is fine."

"But you signed your email Coldbrook-Clairton. And I notice the Clairton is in a slightly different font. Is there a reason for that?"

"It's a mistake."

Chief Inspector Lacoste let that statement sit there. How, she wondered, did someone mistake their own name? Misspell, perhaps. Her best friend had, out of nerves, signed her first driver's license Lousie instead of Louise. That had haunted her well beyond the expiry date, as her friends resurrected the error every time they had a few drinks.

But perhaps Madame Coldbrook had been married and was recently divorced. And reverted to her maiden name. That would explain the disappearing hyphen and the mistake, on all sorts of levels. And her guarded tone when asked about it.

"Thank you for your time," said Lacoste.

"I hope you find out what happened," said Madame Coldbrook, before hanging up.

Isabelle put the receiver down but remained unsettled by the conversation. Madame Coldbrook has been polite and helpful, readily volunteering information. But something didn't fit.

It wasn't until she and Beauvoir were driving down to Three Pines later in the afternoon that it struck her.

If Madame Coldbrook had once used her husband's name, hyphenated, then surely the receptionist would have recognized it.

"Unless the receptionist was new," said Jean-Guy, when she brought up the issue. "The one I spoke to sounded young."

"True."

It was just past six in the evening, but the sun was already touching the horizon. After turning off the autoroute onto the secondary road, Beauvoir spoke again.

"You're still not sure?"

"If her separation or divorce was so new that she still mistakenly signed her name that way, then the receptionist must have only just started. She sounded young, but experienced."

"How do you know? Did you understand a word she said?"

"I understood the tone," said Lacoste in a mock-defensive voice.

"I don't see how it matters," said Beauvoir. "What name she uses, or even the gun and the map and the stained-glass window."

"I'm not sure either," admitted Lacoste. "And it wouldn't, except for one thing."

"Serge Leduc had a copy of the map in his drawer."

"And the soldier boy had the map in his knapsack."

"And both died violent deaths," said Beauvoir. "But not because of the map."

"At least not the boy," agreed Lacoste. "But why in the world would Leduc have the map and keep it so close to him? Not in his desk, not in his office, but in his bedside table. What do you keep there?"

"Now that's a little personal."

"Let me guess." Lacoste thought for a moment. "A package of mints. Some very old condoms, because you can't be bothered to throw them out. No, wait. You keep them because they remind you of your wild yout."

"What's a yout?" he asked, and she laughed at their running joke, quoting the famous line from *My Cousin Vinny*.

"Okay, so what else would be in your bedside table? Some AA reading and a photograph of you and Annie. Noooo. The sonogram showing the baby. So that when you wake up in the middle of the night and can't get back to sleep, you can look at it."

Jean-Guy stared straight ahead. It seemed Isabelle had made it well past his drawers and right into his private parts.

"My turn," he said. "You haaavvvve . . ."

He thought for a kilometer. The road was getting rougher and rougher as it changed from asphalt to dirt, and the heaves and holes of the spring thaw grew more obvious and devious.

"Used Kleenexes from wiping your kids' noses when they came to you crying in the night. You have scraps of paper with scribbles on them you can't make out but are afraid to throw away in case they turn out to be important. Probably a mix of thoughts on a case and random fears about the kids. Oh, and you have the note Robert left you the first time he signed, 'Love, Robert.' Oh, and a cigar."

"A cigar?"

"That was a guess. You seem the sort."

"Asshole."

"But I see what you mean," said Jean-Guy as he turned onto the almost invisible side road. "There's some junk, but mostly we keep things that are precious in our bedside tables."

"Or at least intimate things," said Isabelle. "The map wasn't like your condoms, shoved there and forgotten. The Duke didn't just keep it, he kept it close. But not visible. Why?"

Beauvoir tried to imagine Serge Leduc, sleepless, turning on the lamp and opening the bedside drawer and pulling out the old map. As he did the sonogram. Jean-Guy had to admit he was still trying to make out the limbs, the head, the light heart of their baby.

Did Leduc stare at the map, trying to figure it out? Did it give him comfort on long winter nights?

Beauvoir could not imagine Leduc needing comfort, never mind finding it in the odd little map.

"Maybe it wasn't important to him in a personal way," he suggested. "People also keep things there they don't want others to see."

"But the map wasn't secret or something to be ashamed of," said Lacoste. "Monsieur Gamache has the original framed on his wall at the academy. He gave copies to the cadets."

"Yes, but Serge Leduc didn't want anyone to know he'd gotten his hands on a copy."

"But again"—she raised her hands and let them drop into her lap in exasperation—"why did he have a copy?"

She could see his face harden.

"What's wrong? What've you just thought?"

"Leduc probably got the map from Amelia Choquet."

"Right."

"Okay, let's say she gave it to him. And he put it in his bedside drawer. What's the natural conclusion? What did you really think, Isabelle, when you heard that?"

"I wondered if Professor Leduc hadn't just gotten his hands on the map, he'd also gotten his hands on the cadet. Had it been found in his office, I probably wouldn't have thought that, but a bedside table's different."

"Yes," said Beauvoir. "I thought the same thing. I think that's what everyone would suspect. That Leduc and Cadet Choquet had a relationship. An intimate, sexual one. And the map was a kind of prize, a talisman. Proof of his conquest."

"A notch in the bedpost," said Lacoste with distaste.

"And it might be true," said Beauvoir. "Or it might not."

"Cadet Choquet is the unusual one, right?"

"That's one way of putting it. Spiky black hair. Unnaturally pale skin. Nose, eyebrows, ears, lips and tongue pierced."

"Tattoos," nodded Lacoste. "I've seen her. This isn't your parents' academy. What do you think of her? Could she have done it?"

It was the most serious of questions, and needed reflection.

"Absolutely," he said immediately. "She's smart and angry."

"But is she clever?"

Now Jean-Guy reflected. That really was the ingredient necessary to get away with murder. To commit murder, all you needed was rage and a weapon. Any fool could kill. It took cleverness to baffle the best minds in homicide in the nation.

Was she clever? It went beyond smart. Beyond cunning. Clever was a combination of all those things, with an added twist of guile.

"I don't know if she's clever. There's a sort of innocence about her."

He surprised himself with that, but he knew it was true.

"Probably explains the anger," said Lacoste. "The innocent are often upset when the world doesn't live up to their expectations. Doesn't mean she's innocent of the crime."

Jean-Guy nodded. "I spoke to her professors this afternoon. She shows up to class, sits at the back, rarely contributes, but when called upon is almost always unconventional but insightful. She frankly intimidates most of her profs, who don't much like her."

"She intimidates with her looks, her demeanor, or because she's so obviously smarter than they are?"

"Probably all three. She certainly doesn't conform."

"And her uniform?"

It was a good question. Many of the freshmen, unused to uniforms, adjusted them to make them more personal and stylish. In the past, Leduc had meted out punishments for that, but Commander Gamache had chosen a different route. Much to the surprise of the seasoned professors, the new commander allowed the adjustments.

"But it's disrespectful," Professor Godbut had protested at a staff meeting.

"How so?" asked Gamache.

That had flummoxed the professor, until Leduc had said, in a drawl, "Because it's not just a uniform. It's a symbol of the institution. Would you have allowed your Sûreté agents to dye their uniforms, or wear smiley-face buttons, or do up their slacks with their ties?"

"Never," admitted Gamache. "But if the agents wanted to do that, they were clearly in the wrong job. You're right, the uniform is a symbol of the institution. And if they have so little respect for the institution, then they need to leave. Here, at the academy, is where we earn their respect. We don't teach it. We don't impose it. We model it, we work for it. We're asking these young men and women to be willing to die in that uniform. The least we can do is earn that sacrifice. Let them wear the uniform inside out if they want to, now. If at the end of the year they still are, then we know we haven't done our jobs."

"Bet that shut them up," said Lacoste, when Beauvoir related the story.

"It did, though I don't think it convinced them of anything other than that Commander Gamache was soft."

"And Cadet Choquet's uniform?"

"Spotless. Absolutely perfect."

"Where's she from? Her background?"

"Montréal. She lived in a rooming house in Hochelaga-Maisonneuve before coming here. According to notes Monsieur Gamache attached to her application, it seemed there was some question of prostitution and drug use. He doesn't say it outright, but if you know him, you know the shorthand."

"A drugged-up whore?" said Lacoste. "Excellent."

And yet, it wasn't a complete surprise. She suspected if they looked in Gamache's bedside table, they'd find all sorts of lost souls he put there for safekeeping. And maybe a baguette.

"Her high school marks were mixed. She barely scraped by, though she did well, but erratically, in history, languages and literature."

"She only did what interested her," said Lacoste. "Lazy?"

"Looks like it. Or at least, not motivated."

"Now, why would someone like that apply to the Sûreté Academy?" asked Lacoste.

"A dare, maybe? A joke. And then when she was accepted, she decided to try it out."

"Does she strike you as the joking kind?"

"No." He drove in silence, thinking of the dark girl with the pale face. The contradictory girl.

"She sounds like she can take care of herself," said Lacoste. "Doesn't sound like the sort Leduc could take advantage of."

Beauvoir opened his mouth to say something, taking in a breath, but then changed his mind.

"Go on. Say it," said Isabelle.

Their headlights picked up the snowbanks on either side of the road, and the leafless, lifeless, trees.

"Imagine being nineteen or twenty and on the streets," he said. "Prostituting yourself. Numbing yourself with drugs. And ahead all you see is more of the same. And you know, at nineteen, that life is not going to get better. What would you do?"

The two agents stared at the distorted, grotesque shadows of the bare trees, thrown onto the snow by the harsh headlights.

"Put a bullet in your brain?" he asked quietly. "OD? Or would you make one last mighty leap for the lifeboat?"

"You think the academy is her lifeboat?" asked Lacoste.

"I don't know, I'm just guessing. But I do think Monsieur Gamache thought so, and he rowed out to get her. She'd been turned down, you know, by Leduc."

"I'd have thought Leduc would want someone so broken."

"No. I think he preferred to do the breaking."

"Goddamned Leduc," said Lacoste. "He'd know her background, and he'd know she'd have no choice but to submit and be quiet about it. You think she killed him? You think she couldn't take it anymore and shot him with his own gun?"

"It's possible," said Beauvoir.

"But?"

"I think Leduc had more on his mind than sexual gratification. I think he was even more devious."

"Go on," said Lacoste.

"Who was the biggest threat to Serge Leduc?"

"That's easy. Monsieur Gamache."

"Exactly. He knew Monsieur Gamache was coming after him. He must've felt him getting closer and closer. And he wasn't facing just losing his job. If that's all it was, Gamache would've fired him months ago. No, once Gamache had the proof of his criminal activities, Leduc would be arrested. And this time there'd be no one there to save him. He must've grown more and more desperate."

"Yes," said Lacoste, getting a better idea of where this might be heading and not liking it at all.

"There're two ways Leduc could stop Monsieur Gamache," said Beauvoir. "Kill him, or completely undermine his credibility."

Lacoste's mind raced ahead, seeing the scenario unfold.

"The map," she said. "Leduc didn't take it for himself. He took it to plant in Gamache's bedside table as proof the Commander was having an affair with one of the students. Amelia Choquet."

"Or if not proof, then enough to raise suspicions, gossip. And we know how potent that is."

"No one would believe her when she denied it," said Lacoste. "Her history of prostitution would come out. A history Monsieur Gamache was aware of."

"A student originally turned down, that Gamache accepted," said Beauvoir. "A young woman no one thought should be in the academy. It would look suspicious."

"It already does," said Lacoste. "But anyone who knows Monsieur Gamache would never believe it."

"True, but who knows him at the academy? The cadets? Their parents? The other professors? He was already distrusted because of all the changes he'd made. Rumors are hard to prove, but they're even harder to disprove. We both know that character assassination is easy. All it takes is a suggestion. A well-placed word in someone's ear."

"Like a bullet to the brain," said Lacoste quietly, imagining the whispering campaign. Murdering a man's reputation.

"And once it got out to the media and the public . . ." said Jean-Guy.

"But Monsieur Gamache wouldn't care," said Lacoste. "He's had worse leveled at him. He and his friends and family would know the truth."

"That's not the issue. All Leduc needed was to undermine his credibility," said Beauvoir. "Accusing Leduc of criminal activity would then seem like the desperate act of a cornered man."

"There is one other way Leduc could stop Monsieur Gamache's investigation," said Lacoste slowly. "Something more sure to work than blackmail or character assassination. After all, if Monsieur Gamache had proof of Leduc's crimes, charges would still be laid. It wouldn't matter what people thought of Gamache. The evidence against Leduc would speak for itself. No, Leduc would have to stop his investigation completely. And what could possibly get Monsieur Gamache to stop?"

Beauvoir was quiet. He too had thought of it, but had chosen not to say anything. He should have known Isabelle Lacoste would see it too. Though maybe she didn't have the same thing in mind.

"Earlier this month, Monsieur Gamache said he thought a car followed him home to Three Pines," said Lacoste, and Beauvoir wilted a little.

"Suppose it was Leduc?" she said. "Suppose he followed Gamache, and the map?"

"And it led him to the village," said Beauvoir.

"It led him to the solution to his problem."

They sat in strained silence, both following dark thoughts.

"You don't think . . ." began Lacoste.

"That Gélinas is right?" asked Beauvoir. "That Monsieur Gamache killed Serge Leduc? *Non.*" Jean-Guy gave one firm shake of his head. "He would never kill an unarmed man, and he sure as hell would never do it in the school. *Non.* It's ridiculous."

"But suppose Leduc found out where Gamache lived, and had the map to retrace his route," insisted Lacoste. "So he could find his way back to Three Pines."

Beauvoir stared straight ahead, blinkered.

But Isabelle Lacoste pushed forward, into territory Beauvoir was refusing to enter. Deeper into the darkness.

"Suppose he knew that Gamache was about to expose him. Suppose the two men met later in Leduc's rooms, and Leduc threatened Madame Gamache. Or . . ."

"Annie."

The very suggestion of anyone even thinking of harming his pregnant wife made Jean-Guy white with rage.

And he knew then that the scenario Lacoste was putting forward was possible. Not probable. But possible. Just.

Because he could see himself doing the same thing.

"I don't think Monsieur Gamache killed Leduc," said Beauvoir. "But if he did, in a moment of madness, to protect his family, he'd admit it."

Isabelle Lacoste nodded. She tended to agree. But then, who knew what people would really do in that situation? Gélinas was right about one thing. If anyone could stage a murder scene to misdirect, it would be Armand Gamache.

"Something else is strange, Jean-Guy."

When she used his first name, he knew it was serious. And off the record.

"*Oui?*"

"Deputy Commissioner Gélinas said in the meeting this morning that Monsieur Gamache had asked for him specifically."

Beauvoir had forgotten about that, in the press of other issues raised in the meeting.

"But I thought you put in the request," he said.

"Yes, I thought so too. But Monsieur Gamache admitted it. He even said he'd asked for Gélinas because he admired him."

"So Monsieur Gamache went behind your back?" asked Beauvoir. "And arranged for the RCMP Deputy Commissioner to come down and be the independent observer?"

"Yes."

"But why?"

So much of what his father-in-law was doing seemed out of character. Could murder possibly be one of those things?

"I have a bad feeling about this, Jean-Guy."

Beauvoir remained mute. Unwilling to agree, but unable to disagree.

The world ahead of them disappeared. The distorted shadows, the snowbanks, even the road. There were just stars and the night sky. And for one giddy moment it felt as though they'd floated off the end of the world.

And then the nose of the car dipped down, and out of nothing there appeared the cheerful little village of Three Pines.

CHAPTER 30

⌒

"What would you call a group of Sûreté cadets?" asked Myrna, nodding across the crowded bistro to the four students drinking Cokes and hungrily grabbing fries from the mounded platter in the center of their table.

"What do you mean?" asked Ruth, speaking into her glass so that the words came out muffled in a Scotch mist.

"Well, there's a cackle of hyenas," said Myrna, watching the cadets feed.

"A litter of puppies," said Olivier, delivering two more bulbous glasses of red wine to their table by the fireplace. "These are for Clara and Reine-Marie. Don't touch them." He gave Ruth the stink eye, and got one in return. "They just finished walking the dogs. I expect them any moment."

"Dogs?" said Gabri. "Aren't you the optimistic one, *mon beau*."

The Gamaches had had Gracie for a couple of days and she was not looking any more like a puppy. Nor, truth be told, was she looking like anything else. Except Gracie.

Gabri reached for a piece of baguette with aged Stilton and a dab of red pepper jelly on top, narrowly avoiding Rosa, who'd decided to peck him every time he went for food or drink.

"A flight of butterflies," said Myrna.

"A *confit de canard*." Gabri glared at Rosa.

"I see," said Ruth, putting down her glass and picking up a red wine. "You've finally said something that interests me."

"I can die happy now," said Myrna.

Ruth looked at her expectantly and seemed disappointed when Myrna didn't keel over.

"So what would you call a gathering of students?" asked Myrna.

"A disappointment?" asked Ruth. "No, wait. That's children. Now, students? What would you call a group of them?"

269

"Hello," said Reine-Marie, as she and Clara joined them. "A group of what?"

Myrna explained, then excused herself, returning a few minutes later with a thick reference book from her shop. She sat down heavily on her side of the sofa, almost catapulting Ruth into the air.

"I always suspected Ruth would end up a stain on the wall," Gabri said to Clara. "But I never thought the ceiling." He turned to Myrna. "I'll give you five dollars to do that again. Maybe we can make this a game at the next fair. You win a stuffed duck."

"Fag," muttered Ruth, wiping red wine off Rosa. Not, they suspected, for the first time.

"Hag," said Gabri.

"Do you know these people?" Clara asked Reine-Marie.

"Never met them before in my life," she said, settling into the armchair and handing Clara the remaining glass of red wine.

"And to think," said Clara, "we could've been having a quiet drink in my studio."

That had in fact been the plan. Henri and Gracie and Leo would play together, while Reine-Marie went through a box of archival material from the historical society and Clara painted.

Until Reine-Marie had arrived and seen what Clara had done to her portrait.

It was, apparently, a self-portrait. But something had happened. It had shifted, evolved. And not in a Darwinian direction. This was not, Reine-Marie had to admit to herself, an improvement on the species.

For the first time since knowing Clara and seeing her astonishing portraits, Reine-Marie had the sinking feeling that Clara had lost her touch.

For a few minutes they sat in silence in the studio. Clara painted while Henri crawled onto the sofa, exhausted by the puppies, and laid his head on Reine-Marie's lap. She kneaded his extravagant ears as they watched Gracie and Leo play.

Clara's self-portrait looked not at all like Clara anymore. What had been brilliant was now distorted. The nose was off, the mouth was set in a strange expression, and there was something wrong with the eyes.

There was cruelty in them. A desire to hurt. They looked out at Reine-Marie as though searching for a victim. She looked at the mirror leaning against the armchair and wondered what Clara had seen there, to produce that.

"What do you think?" Clara asked, before putting the brush between her teeth like a bit and staring at her work.

Clara had said her portraits began as a lump in the throat, but it was Reine-Marie who felt like gagging.

"Brilliant," she said. "Is it for a show, or for yourself?"

"For myself," said Clara, getting off the stool.

Thank God for that, thought Reine-Marie, and had to remind herself that art is a process. Art is a process.

Art is a process.

"Let's go over to the bistro," she said, lugging herself off the sofa, unable to watch what Clara was doing anymore. "Armand's on his way back and he'll probably be looking for me there."

"Does he even know he has a home here?" asked Clara, putting her brush down and wiping her hands.

Reine-Marie laughed and picked up the small box of old photographs she'd planned to go through. "He thinks our place is just another wing of the bistro."

"He's not far off," said Clara.

While Clara washed up, Reine-Marie took Henri and Gracie back home, then met her friend just outside the bistro.

Through the window, they could see the four students gobbling fries and gesturing, arguing, the map on the table between them. They looked like generals arguing over a battle plan.

Very young generals, and a very strange plan.

"Has Armand told you why he has the cadets chasing down that map?" asked Clara.

"No. I think it started as a kind of lark. An exercise. But after the murder, it became something else."

"But what?" asked Clara. "I don't see what the map could possibly have to do with the killing of that professor."

"Neither do I," admitted Reine-Marie. "And I'm not sure Armand knows. Maybe nothing."

"It's funny how often nothing becomes something when Armand is around. But it's at least kept the students busy. They were off all day."

The two women had continued to watch the cadets through the windows. But Reine-Marie realized that Clara wasn't watching the cadets. She was looking at just one. Closely.

"Is it much of an imposition, Clara? Putting her up?"

"Amelia?" Clara was quiet for a moment. Studying the girl. "I wonder how old she is."

"Armand would know. Nineteen, twenty, I'd guess."

"In certain light she looks very young. Maybe it's her skin. But then she'll turn and her expression will change. She's like a prism."

Feeling chilled standing in the damp March evening, the two women had gone inside to join the others around the fireplace.

"A clowder of cats?" said Gabri, reading the huge reference book open on Myrna's lap.

"A misery," said Ruth.

"*Pardon?*" asked Reine-Marie.

"The students," said Ruth, cocking her wineglass in the direction of the cadets, who were talking animatedly among themselves. "A misery of cadets."

"I think that's a misery of poets," said Gabri.

"Oh, right."

"What're we going to tell him?" asked Huifen, reaching for another fry, even though she was now feeling overstuffed and a little nauseous. One fry over the line, sweet Jesus. "It's almost seven. He's going to be here any minute. Oh, shit."

Headlights flashed through the window.

"He's here."

The light caught their faces, and Reine-Marie, a few tables over, saw what Clara meant. There was anxiety in Huifen's face. Nathaniel was clearly afraid. Jacques looked defensive, marshaling his excuses.

And Amelia looked resigned. Like she knew what was about to happen. Had been waiting a long time, a lifetime, for it. Perhaps even longer.

She looked old. And very, very young.

She looked a bit like the boy in the stained-glass window.

And she looked a bit like the portrait Clara was painting. Reine-Marie turned to her friend in astonishment.

Jean-Guy and Isabelle got out of the car. The snow, which had been melting during the day, was now freezing again as the sun and the temperature dropped.

"The sap'll be running," said Jean-Guy, knocking his gloves together in the chill. He turned to look back up the hill, where a car's headlights had appeared, shining like eyes.

"A good year for maple syrup," said Isabelle. "We're taking the kids to a *cabane à sucre* this weekend."

Jean-Guy felt a moment of utter joy, like a breath on his face. Next year, he and Annie would be taking their child to a maple sugar shack for the annual sugaring-off celebration. They'd get in a horse-drawn sleigh and go deep into the woods, to a log cabin. There they'd listen to fiddle music and watch people dance, and eat eggs and bacon and baked beans and sweet, sticky *tire d'érable*, the boiled maple sap poured over spring snow and turned into toffee. Then rolled onto a twig, like a lollipop.

Just as he'd done as a child. It was a tradition, part of their *patrimoine*. And one they would pass on to their child. His and Annie's son or daughter.

He glanced toward the bistro and saw the cadets, someone else's sons and daughters, staring at them.

And he felt an overwhelming need to protect them.

"He's here," said Isabelle, and Jean-Guy turned to see that the car had pulled up right behind theirs.

Deputy Commissioner Gélinas and Armand Gamache got out. Gélinas was walking toward them, his feet crunching on the refrozen ice and snow, but Gamache had paused to tilt his head back and look into the night sky.

And then he lowered his eyes and looked straight at Jean-Guy.

And in an instant, Jean-Guy understood how Chief Inspector Gamache must have felt for all those years when he was head of homicide. Commanding young agents.

And losing some of those agents, until the loss had become too great. Until his heart had finally broken into too many pieces to be cobbled together again. When that had happened, he'd come here. To find peace.

But Monsieur Gamache had traded in his peace for the cadets' safety. He'd left here to go clean up the academy, so that the next generation of young agents might survive long enough to brush gray hair from their faces. And to one day retire, to find their own peace and enjoy their own grandchildren.

Jean-Guy Beauvoir watched Armand Gamache approach, and had the overwhelming need to protect him.

He immediately dropped his eyes, staring at his feet until he could control his emotions.

Hormones, he thought. Damned pregnancy.

Gamache and Gélinas had made small talk in the car on the drive down, until it had petered out and both men had been left to the company of their own thoughts.

Paul Gélinas had no idea what was going through Gamache's head, but he himself was preoccupied with what he'd found. And what it meant. And how it could be pertinent, and useful.

Gélinas had spent the afternoon researching the backgrounds of Michel Brébeuf and Armand Gamache. It was like archeology. There was digging and there was dirt. And there were broken things.

He'd thought Brébeuf and Gamache had first met in the academy, as roommates, but he soon found out he was wrong. Their friendship went back to the streets of Montréal as children. They'd been neighbors. Attended the same kindergarten, played on the same teams, double-dated and went to dances together. Bummed around Europe for six months before joining the academy. Together.

The only time they were really apart was when Armand Gamache went to Cambridge to read history. That's where he'd picked up his English. While Brébeuf stayed behind and went to Laval University in Quebec City.

They'd been each other's best man at their weddings, and stood up for each other at christenings.

Michel Brébeuf had excelled in the Sûreté, rising quickly through the ranks to the position of Superintendent. Poised to become the next Chief Superintendent.

Armand Gamache had quickly achieved Chief Inspector in homicide, and built that department into one of the finest in the nation.

And then he'd stalled. And seen his best friend's rise continue.

There had been no hint, though, of envy. They'd remained close friends outside of work, and collaborative colleagues at work.

Their lives had been lived side by side. Until the two roads, the personal and the professional, collided. And went downhill. Fast.

Armand Gamache had gotten whiffs of something wrong within the Sûreté. There were always scandals, of course. Misuses of power. But they'd been swiftly dealt with in the past by the senior officers, including Brébeuf.

But this was different. So huge as to be almost invisible, the scale impossible to comprehend.

At first Gamache gave little credence to the rumors. They'd come through back channels. People who had reason to smear the Sûreté.

But something stuck, and he started to quietly investigate.

It started in the northern territories. Among the Cree and the Inuit. Remote areas that were almost impossible to penetrate. And for good reason, Gamache knew.

Try as he might, he couldn't get purchase on the rumors.

Until one day he'd met a Cree elder on a bench outside the Château Frontenac in Quebec City. Her community had spent months raising enough money to send her down south, to speak to the leaders. To tell them about the beatings and murders. The missing. So desperate was their need, they'd finally risked trusting the white authorities.

But no one would listen. No one would even let her past the front door.

And so she'd sat down. Exhausted, hungry, out of money and hope.

Until she was joined on the bench by the large man with the kind eyes. Who asked if she needed help.

She told him everything. Everything. Not knowing who he was, but having no choice. He was the last house, the last ear, the final hope.

He'd listened. And he'd believed her.

And so began a battle that lasted years and that landed at the door of the very person Gamache trusted the most.

Michel Brébeuf.

The rot went even deeper than that and ended in catastrophe. But not the great scale of disaster it would have been had Armand Gamache not stopped it.

Brébeuf had been banished and Gamache had resigned, losing his job and almost losing his life.

And it wasn't over yet, Gélinas knew.

The Sûreté had been cleaned out, but there remained the academy. The training ground for cruelty and corruption.

The corrosion within the Sûreté and subsequent events were well known to the general public. The media had covered it to the point of their own brutality.

What interested Gélinas now was what was unknown. The men's personal lives.

He'd dug and he'd dug that afternoon. Until he struck dirt.

For all his professional venality, Michel Brébeuf's personal life appeared conventional. He'd married. Had three children. Joined service clubs.

Brébeuf was a model husband and father and grandfather. But his home life had shattered when the degree of his professional deceit became known. His wife had left him, and there was a rift with his children that had yet to be healed.

But the dirt the RCMP officer sought and found came from a different source.

Not Brébeuf. But Gamache.

Gélinas had found it when he'd dug deep enough into Armand Gamache's personal life and found a few lines in a long-dormant document. The words had uncurled and re-formed. And walked off the page. Into the present.

Into the waiting hands of the man charged with ensuring a fair investigation.

"A shrewdness of apes," Myrna read from the reference book, smiling and shaking her head in amusement, before looking up to see Armand and the others arrive.

Reine-Marie got up to greet her husband.

"We're playing a game," she explained. "Naming groups of animals."

"We started off trying to come up with a collective name for a group of Sûreté cadets," said Myrna, gesturing toward the students.

"I'm thinking it's a gloom of cadets," said Ruth.

Paul Gélinas rubbed his forehead and grinned. It was his first time in the bistro and he seemed a little stunned as he took in the beams and stone hearths and wide plank floors. And the old woman with the duck.

Then his eyes fell on the cadets.

Amelia Choquet was unmissable, unmistakable.

And while Gélinas stared at her, she was also staring. Past him. Her mouth open wide enough for him to see the stud through her tongue.

He turned to see who had so enthralled the Goth Girl.

It was Isabelle Lacoste. Amelia Choquet's polar opposite.

"But then it evolved into animal groups," Myrna was saying.

"A sleuth of bears," said Gélinas, returning to the conversation. "That sort of thing?"

"Exactly," said Clara. "Good for you. You're on my team."

"There're teams?" asked Gabri, leaning away from Ruth.

"Who are you?" Ruth squinted at Gélinas.

Gamache introduced Deputy Commissioner Gélinas, of the RCMP.

"*Bonjour*," he said, offering his hand to Ruth.

She gave him the finger, turning it sideways. "And one for the horse you rode in on, Renfrew."

"Don't get too close," Gabri whispered to him. "If she bites you, you'll go mad."

Gélinas withdrew his hand.

"The only one I know is a murder of crows," said Lacoste.

"You made that up," said Beauvoir. "Why would crows be called that?"

"Funny you should ask," said Myrna.

She flipped through the reference book and read out loud, "A murder of crows is believed to come from a folk tale, where crows will gather to decide the capital fate of another crow."

"*C'est ridicule*," said Beauvoir.

But his eyes slid across the crowded bistro to the gathering of cadets.

"A crowd of faults," Ruth said with certainty. "That's what they are."

Gamache made a guttural sound, somewhere between amusement and astonishment.

CHAPTER 31

———

"*Bonjour,*" said Lacoste, when she arrived at the cadets' table.

All four stood up. She introduced herself to those who hadn't yet met her.

"I'm Chief Inspector Lacoste. I'm leading the investigation into the murder of Serge Leduc."

For Amelia, it was like watching a play. A replay.

There was the head of homicide, petite, contained, in slacks and sweater and silk scarf, with three large men standing respectfully behind her.

"This is Deputy Commissioner Gélinas, of the RCMP," said Lacoste, and Gélinas nodded to the cadets. "And you know Commander Gamache and Inspector Beauvoir."

Four senior officers. Four cadets. Like before-and-after shots.

Olivier had dragged another table over, and they sat, the investigators fanned at one end and the cadets at the other. Regarding each other.

"What did you find out about the map?" Commander Gamache asked.

"Nothing," said Jacques.

"That's not true," said Nathaniel. "We found out a lot."

"Just none of it very useful." This time no one contradicted him.

They described what they'd found out about the mapmaker, Antony Turcotte. As they spoke, they looked down at a copy of the map he'd made, sitting not far from the wall where it had been hidden for almost a hundred years.

It still had the red stain from the strawberry jelly. And a dusting of icing sugar. So that it looked like a drop of blood on snow.

"You've done well," said Lacoste, and meant it. "You found out who made it and confirmed it was probably an early orienteering map."

"Maybe to train his son, knowing the war was coming," said Beauvoir, and wondered how a father could do that. How would a father feel, seeing the war on the horizon?

What would I do? Jean-Guy wondered.

And he knew what he'd do. He'd either hide his child, or prepare him.

Jean-Guy looked down at the map and realized it wasn't a map at all. At least, not of land. It mapped a man's love of his child.

"But there's a problem," said Huifen.

"There always is," said Commander Gamache.

"There's no record of him ever owning this place. Or any place."

"Maybe he rented," said Beauvoir.

"Maybe," said Jacques. "But we couldn't find Antony Turcotte anywhere. In any of the records."

"There's a mention in *The Canadian Encyclopedia*," said Amelia, her voice eager for the first time since Gamache had known her. She handed the photocopied sheet to Lacoste.

"*Merci*," said Lacoste, and examined it before passing it along to the others. "According to this, Monsieur Turcotte eventually moved to a village called Roof Trusses and was buried there."

"Roof Trusses?" the other officers said together.

"What did they say?" demanded Ruth.

"I must've misheard," said Gabri. "It sounded like Roof Trusses."

"Oh yes, I know it," said Ruth. "Just down the road a few kilometers."

"Of course," said Gabri. "Not far from Asphalt Shingles."

"Ignore him," said Olivier. "He just likes saying asphalt."

"I've never heard of it." Clara turned to Myrna and Reine-Marie, both of whom shook their heads.

"That's because only old Anglos still call it Roof Trusses," said Ruth. "The Commission de toponymie changed its name a long time ago to Notre-Dame-de-Doleur."

"Our Lady of Pain?" asked Myrna. "Are you kidding? Who calls a village that?"

"Pain," said Reine-Marie. "Or maybe grief."

Our Lady of Grief.

It was not much better.

"Jesus," said Gabri. "Can you imagine the tourist posters?"

"Roof Trusses?" asked Beauvoir. "Who calls a village that?"

"Apparently Antony Turcotte," said Huifen. "His one big mistake when mapping and naming the area."

She explained.

"Have you been there?" Gamache asked.

There was silence, none of the cadets wanting to be the one to speak.

"The toponymie man said the village died out," said Huifen.

"Might still be worth a visit," said Lacoste. "Just to see."

"See what?" asked Jacques, and was treated to one of her withering looks.

"We don't know, do we? Isn't that the point of an investigation? To investigate."

Amelia was nodding as though hearing the wisdom of ages.

"If Turcotte made this for his son"—Gamache touched the edges of the map—"that would mean the soldier's name was also Turcotte."

"That's another problem," admitted Huifen. "None of the names on the memorial list is Turcotte."

"Maybe he survived," said Nathaniel. After all this time staring at the young soldier, Nathaniel had grown to care. The boy would be dead now, of course. But maybe of old age, and in his bed.

"Do you think so?" asked Amelia, speaking to Chief Inspector Lacoste.

"Do you?" Lacoste asked her.

Amelia shook her head, slowly. "Whoever he was, he didn't come home."

"What makes you say that?"

"His face," said Amelia. "No one with that expression would have survived."

"Maybe he never existed. He might be a composite of all the young men who were killed," said Beauvoir.

"The stained-glass version of the Unknown Soldier," said Gamache, and considered. "Made to represent all the suffering. Perhaps. But he seems so real. So alive. I think he did exist. Briefly."

"What're they saying now?" demanded Ruth.

"The stained-glass soldier," said Reine-Maire. "They think his name might've been Turcotte."

Ruth shook her head. "Saint-Cyr, Soucy, Turner. No Turcotte on the wall."

"He's there somewhere," said Gamache. "One of the names matches that boy."

Once again, Huifen pulled out her phone and displayed the photograph they'd taken of the list of names.

They all leaned forward, reading. As though the lost boy might make himself known.

"He's there somewhere," said Ruth. "Maybe not Turcotte, but one of them. Etienne Adair, Teddy Adams, Marc Beaulieu . . ."

They Were Our Children, Jean-Guy thought.

"Bert Marshall, Denis Perron, Giddy Poirier . . ."

"We're going to need to speak with each of you," said Gélinas. "Alone. Beginning, I think, with you."

He turned to Amelia.

"Joe Valois, Norm Valois, Pierre Valois."

They listened to Ruth. It was one thing to read the names etched into the wood, and another to hear them out loud. The old poet's voice like the tolling of a bell. As they searched for the one boy, among the dead.

"There's a private room just through there," said Gamache, getting to his feet with the others.

"*Merci*," said Gélinas. "But I don't think we need you, Commander."

"I'm sorry?" said Gamache.

"We can take it from here."

"I'm sure you can, but I'd like to be present when you interview the cadets."

The students, as well as Lacoste and Beauvoir, looked from Gamache to Gélinas as the two men faced each other. Each with a pleasant look hardening to his face.

"I insist," said Gamache.

"On what grounds?"

"*In loco parentis*," said Gamache.

"What did he say?" asked Ruth.

Around them the murmur of conversation continued, interrupted by the occasional burst of laughter.

"I think he said he was crazy," said Clara. "Loco."

"In parentheses," said Gabri.

"Why parentheses?" asked Ruth.

"*In loco parentis*," said Reine-Marie. "Standing in place of the parent."

"You're standing in for her parents?" asked Gélinas, half amused, half disbelieving. "Standing in for her father?"

"For all their parents," said Gamache. "The students have been entrusted to my care."

"I'm not a child," snapped Amelia.

"I don't mean to be patronizing—"

"That's exactly what you mean to be," said Amelia. "That's what *in loco parentis* means."

"We can contact her father, if you like, Commander," said Gélinas. "If that would make you happy. We can probably have him here within the hour."

"No," said Amelia, and while Gamache didn't speak he looked startled. For an instant. As though slapped.

Reine-Marie, across the room, noticed and wondered if anyone else had.

"Don't be angry at Monsieur Gamache," Gélinas said to Amelia. "He can't help it. I suspect he has an overdeveloped sense of protection because of his own experience. He doesn't want anyone to suffer as he did."

"What do you mean?" asked Huifen.

"That's enough, Commissioner," warned Gamache.

"His parents were killed by a drunk driver when he was a child. The driver would've been just a little younger than you at the time," he said to the students. "How old were you?" he asked Gamache, who was staring at him, barely containing his outrage. "Eight, nine?"

"Why would you bring that up?" demanded Beauvoir. "It has nothing to do with this."

"Really?" asked Gélinas, and stared, in heavy silence, at Gamache before going on. "At the very least, the cadets need to understand that we all have burdens, don't you agree, Commander? Some so weighty we carry them our whole lives. They can blight our very existence, or they can make us stronger. They can make us bitter or teach us compassion. They can drive us to do things we never thought ourselves capable of. Wonderful achievements, like becoming Chief Inspector and Commander. Or horrific things. Terrible dark deeds. Maybe Michel Brébeuf isn't the only object lesson. Maybe they can learn from you too, Monsieur Gamache."

Now the entire bistro was watching and listening.

"A discomfort of cadets," said Ruth.

And she was right. But the students weren't the only ones squirming. The whole bistro twisted in their seats while Gamache himself stood perfectly still.

"You see," Paul Gélinas turned to the cadets, "you aren't the only ones with unhappy childhoods. Some are beaten. Some are bullied. Some are ignored. And some wait at home for a mother and father who will never return."

He considered Gamache, like a specimen.

"Imagine what that does to a child. And yet he rose above it." He returned his attention to the students. "And you can too."

Reine-Marie stood up and went to her husband, taking his hand.

"That is enough, monsieur," she said to Gélinas.

"Madame," the RCMP officer bowed slightly. "I meant no harm. But it's important that these students understand that their burden is shared by everyone and can't be used as an excuse for their own brutality."

"He's right," said Armand, his voice bitterly cold. "We all make choices."

He spoke directly to Gélinas, who shifted his shoulders, as though some tiny, sharp object had just been inserted between his blades.

"*Bon*," said Gélinas, decisively. "This is an active police investigation. Chief Inspector Lacoste has been very kind to include you so far—"

"And I see no reason to exclude Commander Gamache now," said Lacoste.

"Well, I do. Speaking as the independent observer, I think it's now time for him to step aside. Had he been anyone else, he would never have been this involved. We must treat Monsieur Gamache as we would any other suspect."

"Suspect?" asked Reine-Marie, and there was a murmur of surprise in the bistro.

"Well, yes, of course," said Gélinas. "Your husband isn't above the law or above suspicion."

"It's all right," said Armand, squeezing her hand. "Once again, Deputy Commissioner Gélinas is correct."

He took a small step back, away from Gélinas. Away from the cadets. Away from Lacoste and Beauvoir.

At the door to the private room, Beauvoir turned to see Gamache staring after them. No, not them, Jean-Guy realized.

He was staring at Amelia Choquet.

Beauvoir glanced at Reine-Marie, who was also watching her husband. Perplexed.

Beauvoir followed Amelia with his eyes as she walked past him into the room. And wondered just what her relationship was with the Commander, that Gamache would look at her in such a way.

He had an idea. An unwanted one. An unworthy one.

Beauvoir closed the door, shutting out the man and the thought.

But the gate had been opened and the traitor thought had slipped in.

In loco parentis. But was it really in place of?

CHAPTER 32

⌒

"How well did you know Professor Leduc?" asked Isabelle Lacoste.

She'd placed Amelia to her right and the two men further down the table, on the cadet's right, so that Amelia's head was turned to her, and only her.

It was a technique Lacoste had picked up early in her career in homicide. While many of the male investigators preferred to intimidate by having two or three agents looming over suspects, shooting questions to try to push them off balance, Lacoste went in the other direction.

She created an atmosphere of extreme intimacy. A semblance of conspiracy even. Isabelle Lacoste wasn't surprised that it worked very well with the women she interviewed. What had come as a surprise was how well it worked with the men.

They were steeled against an onslaught. But had no defenses against gentle, even friendly, conversation.

"Not well," said Amelia. "Professor Leduc taught us crime prevention."

"Oh, I hated that course. I wanted to learn about weapons and tactics," said Lacoste with a laugh. "Was he a good teacher?"

"Not really. I think it wasn't his favorite course either. He used to run the academy, didn't he?"

"Not officially, but in every other way, yes. Until Monsieur Gamache took over."

Amelia nodded.

Isabelle Lacoste watched her closely. She could see what Beauvoir had meant. Cadet Choquet would be striking anywhere, but especially so in the Sûreté Academy. She'd stand out. But she'd also stand apart.

Lacoste took in the piercings. The rings and studs, like bullets. A girl pierced and pieced together. Like the Tin Man in *The Wizard of Oz*. Looking for a heart.

287

Hints of tattoos flicked out of her clothing.

The eyes that watched her were bright, inquiring. Smoldering, but not burning. But where there was smoke . . .

This was a young woman of unusual intelligence and intensity, thought Lacoste. A girl not afraid to be different. But that didn't mean she wasn't afraid of something.

Everyone was, Isabelle knew. Maybe this young cadet was afraid of being the same.

How isolating that must be, she thought. But we all seek solace somewhere. Some in friendships and family and beliefs. Some in drugs, in a bottle, in food or gambling or good deeds. And some in casual sex. It masqueraded as human contact, but was closer to loathing than liking. And certainly wasn't love.

On the far side of Amelia, Gélinas opened his mouth, but shut it quickly at one eviscerating glance from Lacoste.

Jean-Guy Beauvoir's mouth compressed, squashing the smile. He'd received more than a few of those looks in the past. He was happy to see it worked on someone else besides him.

"Did you like the Duke?" Lacoste asked.

"I didn't know him."

"I don't know you, but I like you. I like your bravery."

And it was true. Isabelle Lacoste knew how much courage it must take Amelia Choquet to face each day. Alone.

Amelia's eyes widened, and her small fists tightened. But she said nothing.

And Isabelle wondered when the last time was that someone, anyone, had told Amelia they liked her.

She also wondered how she was going to get this guarded girl to open up.

"Come hither, all ye empty things, / Ye bubbles raised by breath of kings," she found herself saying, and saw Amelia cock her head to one side. *"Who float upon the tide of state, / Come hither, and behold your fate."*

Beyond Amelia, Lacoste could see the faces of the two men, their expressions ranging from despair to incredulity.

"What is that?" Amelia asked.

"A satirical poem. By Jonathan Swift," said Lacoste.

Beauvoir's eyes rolled to the back of his head.

"On the death of a duke. I understand you like poetry."

Amelia nodded and repeated, *"Come hither, and behold your fate."*

"If ever there was an empty thing, it was Serge Leduc. The Duke," said Lacoste. "What was his fate?"

"I guess it was to die, at the hands of another."

"But who?"

"Do you think it was me?" Amelia asked.

"Your fingerprints were on the map in his bedside table. It was your map, wasn't it?"

"I don't know," Amelia admitted. "It must have been, I guess. No one else's is missing. But I didn't give it to him."

"What was your relationship with Serge Leduc?" Lacoste repeated.

"He wanted to screw me."

"And did he?"

"No. I told him I'd cut off his dick and shove it down his throat."

Now the men's eyes widened.

"What did he say to that?" asked Lacoste.

"He threatened to expel me."

"And what would that mean?" Isabelle asked. Her voice steady. No hint of the outrage she felt.

"I would die," said Amelia.

Isabelle Lacoste forced herself to be quiet. To give no easy comfort. To not dismiss the gravity of those words by saying she was sure it wasn't true.

Because she knew it was true.

Amelia Choquet would leave the academy and go back to the streets. This time without hope. And she would die.

"Did you kill him, Amelia? To stop him from expelling you? To save yourself?"

The young woman looked at Isabelle Lacoste. Here was the woman she longed to be, hoped to be. Could be. But it wasn't to be. Amelia knew that now.

She shook her head, and when she spoke her voice was clear, certain.

"I did not."

"Your fingerprints were also on the case where the murder weapon was kept," said Lacoste. "And on the gun itself."

Amelia just stared at her. "If I killed him, I'd have wiped the gun. I'm smart enough to do that."

"Probably true," said Lacoste. "But I don't think we're looking for an exceptionally stupid person, do you?"

Amelia was quiet now.

"You don't seem surprised that your prints were on the gun. Are you?"

She just shook her head, but was silent.

"What was your relationship with Commander Gamache?"

So she had noticed, thought Jean-Guy. That look on Monsieur Gamache's face as they'd led Amelia away.

"I have no relationship with him."

"Then why is he so protective of you?" asked Lacoste.

Down the table, Paul Gélinas shifted in his chair, preparing to interrupt, and once again Lacoste flicked a warning glance at him.

"He isn't," said Amelia. "Not more than any of the others."

"But he is," said Gélinas, finally ignoring Chief Inspector Lacoste. "He's the one who got you into the academy. You'd been turned down, you know. He changed that."

"He did?" asked Amelia, turning to look at the RCMP officer. Breaking the carefully woven connection with Lacoste. "The Duke told me Commander Gamache had rejected my application, but that he'd reversed it. And he could reverse it again."

"Well, he was lying," said Gélinas. "It was Monsieur Gamache. Why would the Commander do it? Especially when, forgive me, you're so clearly unsuited to the place."

Isabelle Lacoste stared at Gélinas. Amazed by his casual brutality.

Gélinas had ignored her wishes and destroyed an atmosphere between the two women that was clearly working. Was that his intention? Was he afraid Amelia was about to say something, reveal something?

But for all that, Lacoste had to admit the RCMP officer wasn't wrong. It was a good question. Why had Commander Gamache reversed his predecessor's decision and admitted the Goth Girl to the Sûreté Academy?

Isabelle Lacoste was growing more and more concerned about the answer.

CHAPTER 33

"What're you thinking?" asked Reine-Marie.

They'd left the bistro and gone to St. Thomas's Church, drawn by the quiet there, and the peace.

She sat next to Armand in the pew. He was staring straight ahead, and though his eyes were open, she had the impression he'd been praying.

Her question, she knew, wasn't accurate. What she really wanted to know was what he was feeling.

Armand took a deep breath and exhaled, forcefully. As though he'd been holding it in for a long time.

"I was remembering waiting for my mother and father. Kneeling on the sofa with my arms on the back of it. Looking out the window. *Batman* was on the television. I can still hear the theme song."

As he softly hummed it—*dah-dah, dah-dah, dah-dah, dah-dah*—Reine-Marie imagined the little boy. Who always waited when his mother and father left, for their return.

Who roused from sleep when they tiptoed into his bedroom and kissed him good night.

Who always found a treat in the fridge in some elaborate tinfoil sculpture. He'd thought his mother had made them for him. And even when, later, all evidence pointed to some stranger at the restaurant making the swans and baskets and boats that contained the treats, Armand still clung to the certainty that his mother had created them. For him.

As far as Reine-Marie knew, he still believed it.

"*Batman*," Armand sang beneath his breath. "I saw the headlights from the car, but I knew it wasn't them. It was too early. And there was something different about the lights. And then I saw the two men walking up the path. But I wasn't afraid. I thought they were just visitors."

Reine-Marie took his hand. She'd heard this before. Once. And only once. Early in their courtship, when he knew he loved her, and he knew she loved him. And he'd wanted her to know.

He talked about his parents quite often, relating anecdotes of vacations and celebrations. But this was only the second time in their lives together that he'd talked to her about their deaths.

Lines appeared at his eyes and mouth.

"I was excited to meet these strangers. The doorbell rang and my grandmother came out of the kitchen and opened the door."

Now the lines disappeared. And for an instant Reine-Marie saw the smooth face of a nine-year-old boy. In pajamas. Standing by the sofa.

"She turned to me and when I saw her face, I knew. They were gone."

They sat in silence for a moment, not even the ticking of a clock to mark the passage of time. It could've been a few seconds, a minute. An hour. Decades.

"My grandmother tried to comfort me, but she had her own grief. It was Michel who stayed with me. He never left my side. He took me outside after their funeral to play king of the castle." Armand smiled. "It was our favorite game. He always won. *I'm the king of the castle, and you're a dirty rascal,*" Armand sang under his breath. "I could barely walk and talk. For weeks. I just plodded along. And Michel never left me. Never went to find more fun friends. Though he could have. I miss him. And I miss them."

Reine-Marie squeezed his hand. "Paul Gélinas shouldn't have brought it up. It was cruel."

"It was almost fifty years ago."

"It wasn't necessary," she said, and wondered about the real reason Gélinas had told the cadets about the death of Armand's parents.

"I've been sitting here thinking of my mother and father, but not really how much I miss them. I was wondering what it must've been like for the parents of those boys. It's one thing to lose a mother or father, but can you imagine?" He paused to gather himself, to say the unthinkable. "Losing Daniel. Or Annie?"

He looked over to the stained-glass boys.

"Have you noticed their names? Not Robert, but Rob. Not Albert, but Bert. There's even a fellow named Giddy. Their real names, the ones their parents shouted when it was dinnertime. The names their friends screamed while playing hockey. Some would've been lost. Missing. They'd have gone over the top and disappeared. Forever. And their parents would never have known what happened to them. They'd have waited, forever."

He took another deep breath.

"Losing Maman and Papa was devastating, but I've been sitting here thinking how lucky I am that I at least knew what happened, and I could stop waiting. But some of these parents never did."

Reine-Marie dropped her eyes to his large hand and gathered her courage to ask the question.

"Armand?"

"*Oui?*"

"Who's the cadet? Who's Amelia? There's something special about her, isn't there?"

Reine-Marie's heart began to pound. But having gone this far, there was no going back. She knew she had to move forward.

Armand looked at her with such sadness that she wished she hadn't asked. Not for his sake now, but for her own.

Armand would never . . . Amelia couldn't possibly be—

"*Patron?*"

She felt like a woman saved from the gallows, but not grateful. Having finally found the courage to get there, who knew if she'd find it again?

Reine-Marie felt a flash of rage that was incandescent.

"I'm sorry to interrupt," said Olivier.

He could see the backs of their heads, but neither turned to him, and he hesitated in the aisle.

Reine-Marie dropped her eyes from her husband's face and counted.

Un, deux, trois . . .

Until she felt she could look at Olivier without screaming at him to go away.

. . . quatre, cinq . . .

Olivier stopped a few pews away. Uncertain what to do. Neither of them had turned. Neither had acknowledged him.

"Are you all right?" he asked, leaning forward. They were so still, like wax figures.

"Yes, we're fine," said Reine-Marie, and for the first time truly understood that the title of Ruth's poetry book, *I'm FINE*, wasn't purely a joke.

"Are you sure?" he asked, edging forward.

Armand turned around and smiled. "We were just talking about the soldiers."

Olivier glanced at the window, then took a seat across the aisle.

"I wasn't sure if I should follow you, but, well, that was strange. In the bistro. How the RCMP officer treated you. What he said."

Armand raised his brow and smiled. "I've been treated worse. It's nothing. Just part of the cop culture."

"It's more than that," said Olivier. "And I think you know it. You're a suspect. He said it himself."

"It's his job to suspect everyone, but I'm not worried."

"You should be," said Olivier. "He means to prove you killed that man. I could see it in his face."

Gamache shook his head. "Whether he thinks it or not, there's no proof. And besides, I didn't do it."

"So innocent people are never arrested?" demanded Olivier. "Never tried and convicted? For a crime they didn't commit? That never happens, right?" He glared at Gamache. "You should be afraid, monsieur. Only a fool wouldn't be."

"Armand?" asked Reine-Marie. "Could that happen? Could Gélinas arrest you?"

"I doubt it."

"Doubt?" asked Reine-Marie. "Doubt? Then there is a possibility? He can't seriously believe you murdered a man."

"He does," said Olivier. "I've seen that look before. On your husband's face, just before the arrest."

"We have to do something," said Reine-Marie, looking around as though proof of her husband's innocence could be found in the chapel.

"Here you are," came the familiar voice of Jean-Guy from the door. "We've interviewed the cadets—"

"Do you think Armand killed that professor?" Reine-Marie stood, turned and faced her son-in-law, who stopped in his tracks.

"No, of course not."

Lacoste had entered behind him, and Reine-Marie saw her look away, unwilling to meet Reine-Marie's eyes.

"Isabelle, do you?"

Reine-Marie was in full flight now. Pounding at the gates. Demanding the truth. Demanding to know who were allies and who were enemies.

This was another world war. Her world. Her war.

"I don't think Monsieur Gamache killed Serge Leduc," said Isabelle.

"Reine-Marie," said Armand, getting up and putting an arm around his wife's waist.

She stepped away.

"But you're not sure, are you, Isabelle?"

The two women stared at each other.

"You need to know something, madame. I held your husband's hand as he lay dying. On that factory floor. I've never told you this. You didn't need to know. He knew he was dying. I knew it. He could barely breathe, but he managed to say one last thing."

"Isabelle—" said Gamache.

"I had to lean over to hear it," said Lacoste. "He whispered, '*Reine-Marie*.' And I knew he wanted me to tell you how much he loves you. Forever. Eternally. I never had to tell you that. Until now. Armand Gamache would never murder anyone, for all sorts of reasons. One of them is that he would never, ever do anything to hurt you, Reine-Marie."

Reine-Marie brought her hand to her mouth, and screwed her eyes shut. She stood there for a second, a minute. Years.

And then she dropped the hand and reached for the harbor of her husband, even as she noticed the look that passed between Lacoste and Beauvoir.

Armand kissed her, and whispered in her ear. Something that made her smile. Then he motioned to the pew at the front of the chapel, and while the investigators took seats there, Olivier and Reine-Marie sat at the very back.

"Did anything come out of your interviews?" asked Gamache.

"Not much," said Lacoste. "But Cadet Choquet didn't seem surprised when I told her her prints were on the murder weapon."

"It was an extrapolation," Gamache reminded her.

"I didn't tell her that."

"Did she explain it?"

"No. She did say that Leduc threatened to expel her if she didn't have sex with him."

"And did she?" asked Gamache.

"She says not, but she's used to trading sex for what she wants."

Gamache gave a curt nod.

"I haven't had a chance to tell you," said Lacoste, "but I called the UK and spoke to the woman at the gun manufacturer that Jean-Guy interviewed."

"Madame Coldbrook-Clairton?" asked Gamache.

Lacoste laughed. "I had this conversation with Jean-Guy on the drive down. There's no Clairton, just Coldbrook."

"Then why—" Gamache began.

"Did she sign her name with Clairton?" asked Lacoste. "Good question. She says it was a mistake."

"Odd," said Gamache, frowning. "But she confirmed the revolver that killed Leduc and the one in the window are both McDermot .45s?"

"Did he say Clairton?" asked Olivier, sitting in the back with Reine-Marie. "There's a town in Pennsylvania called that."

"Now how would you know that, *mon beau*?" asked Reine-Marie.

"I don't know how I know about Clairton," said Olivier, drawing his brows together in concentration. "I just do."

"Maybe you were born with the knowledge," suggested Reine-Marie with a smile.

"That would be a shame. So many more useful things I could innately know. Like how to convert Fahrenheit into Celsius, or the meaning of life, or how much to charge for a croissant."

"You charge?" asked Reine-Marie with exaggerated surprise. "Ruth says they're free."

"*Oui*. Like the Scotch is free."

"She confirmed the guns are the same," said Jean-Guy. "But I can't see how it could matter."

"Neither can I," admitted Gamache.

He turned to look at the stained-glass window. He'd seen it so often over the years that he felt he knew each pane. And yet, he always seemed to discover something new. As though the person who made it stole into the chapel at night and added a detail.

He still marveled that over the years he'd never noticed the map poking out from the boy's rucksack.

Gamache realized he'd spent so much time staring at the one boy, he'd all but ignored the other two.

He looked at them now. Unlike the soldier who was looking straight at the observer, the others were in profile. Moving forward. One boy's hand was just touching the arm of the soldier in front. Not to pull him back. But for comfort.

Less effort had been put into them. Their faces looked exactly the same, like they were the same boy, with exactly the same expression.

There was no forgiveness there, only fear.

And yet they moved forward.

Gamache's eyes dropped to the third boy's hands. One grasped a rifle.

But with the other he seemed to be casually pointing. Not ahead, though, but behind.

"Do you know something strange?" asked Reine-Marie.

"I know someone strange," offered Olivier.

"I've been sorting through the papers from the archives of the historical society in Saint-Rémy. The letters and documents and photographs go back a few hundred years. Not the pictures, of course. Though some of them are very old. Fascinating."

"That is strange," said Olivier.

"No, not that," she laughed, and gave him a little elbow. "I didn't realize until this very moment that I haven't found anything from the First World War. The Second, yes. All sorts of letters home, and pictures. But none from the Great War. If there were, I might be able to find that boy. Find all three of them, in fact, by comparing the faces in the window with photographs in the local archives."

"How could all the documents be missing?" asked Olivier. "There must've been something, wouldn't you think?"

"There might be some boxes still in the basement of the historical society, but I thought we cleaned it out pretty thoroughly. I'll take a closer look tomorrow."

"You could ask Ruth. I'm pretty sure she was a drunk old poet in the Great War."

"But on whose side?" asked Reine-Marie.

She got up, just as Armand and the others rose.

"I don't know about you, but I'm hungry," she said. "You're welcome to come home. We have plenty of leftovers. Might even throw on a movie. I feel the need for distraction."

As they left, Armand paused to look back at the stained-glass window and the boy. Pointing. He followed where he was indicating, but there was nothing there. Just a bird in the stained sky.

"Armand?" Reine-Marie called from the porch of the chapel.

"Coming," he said, and turned off the lights.

CHAPTER 34

There was no denying, it was awkward.

Jean-Guy and Isabelle had headed back to the academy, but Paul Gélinas asked to spend the night with the Gamaches. Reine-Marie was on the verge of telling him where he could go, but Armand jumped in and said they'd be delighted.

"Did you actually say 'delighted'?" asked Reine-Marie, when they were alone in the kitchen.

"*Oui*. It'll be de-wonderful, don't you think?"

"I think you're demented."

He smiled, then bent down and whispered, "He didn't expect us to agree. Did you notice his discomfort?"

"I was too busy noticing my own," she whispered back.

In an effort to put if not distance then people between herself and Gélinas, Reine-Marie had gone to the bistro and invited their friends over for dinner.

"What're we going to feed them?" Armand asked.

Reine-Marie glanced toward the bin of kibble.

"Oh, don't tell me—" he began.

Reine-Marie laughed. "No. Ruth wouldn't notice, but the others might."

"And that's the only reason you wouldn't feed our guests dog food?"

"I wouldn't criticize if I were you, monsieur, given why we have guests in the first place. Delightful." She shook her head. "But I was actually looking at Gracie and thinking she needs to go out."

"Let me," volunteered Armand. At the door, he gave her a stern look of warning.

"I promise, no kibble," she said, then mumbled, "probably," loud enough for him to hear.

Smiling, Armand took Gracie out of her crate, put her on a leash, and tried not to step on her as she got underfoot. Henri went with them.

The shepherd and Armand flanked the little creature as they walked around the back garden, Henri digging through the patches of snow to find grass and Gracie copying him.

"I hope you weren't upset by what I said in the bistro," came Paul Gélinas's voice.

Armand looked around and saw the man standing on the back terrace.

"Surprised, definitely." Armand paused before going on. "Why did you bring up my mother and father?"

It was pitch-dark except for the light from the house. Gélinas was a black cutout against the light from the living room. Through the French doors, Armand could see Clara and Myrna talking, Clara gesturing to make some point. Gabri was listening or, more likely, waiting to talk. Ruth was invisible, having slumped down in the sofa. Rosa and Olivier were staring out the window.

"I think you know why." Gélinas stepped off the terrace and joined his host.

Gamache's face was clearly visible in the light from his home. The RCMP officer could see every contour.

There was a small tug on the leash as Gracie strained to join Henri.

Gélinas fell into step beside Gamache. "Are you leading me up the garden path, monsieur?"

Gamache grunted in mild amusement. "Leading you astray? You don't need me for that. You're doing quite a good job on your own."

"I've gone off the path? Probably true, but isn't that where you normally find criminals?"

Gamache stopped and turned to his guest. "And you think I'm a criminal?"

"I doubt you see it that way. To be a criminal, you have to have committed a crime. I suspect you think the murder of Serge Leduc was not a crime."

"Then what was it?"

"A consequence. A happy opportunity."

"Happy?"

"Well, perhaps not happy. But a fortunate opportunity. You saw a chance and you took it."

"And why would I do that?" said Gamache.

"We all reach a sort of crossroads, don't we?" said Gélinas, his voice grave now. "Some sooner than others. Driven there by some dreadful event. In your case, the death of your parents. In my case, the death of my wife. When faced with an event of that magnitude, some go in one direction and become embittered. They want others to suffer, as they have. Some, though, choose the more difficult route. They become compassionate and kind and patient with the imperfections of others. They want to save others the pain they themselves have felt."

"*Oui*," said Gamache, curious where this was going.

"The difficulty is telling them apart," said Gélinas. "A person can look one way, but behave in another. They can say one thing, but be thinking something else entirely. Most of the real monsters I've encountered look like saints. They have to. Otherwise someone would've stopped them years ago."

"Is this a confession?" asked Gamache, and heard laughter in the darkness.

"I was hoping you'd confess, sir. It would make my job easier. It would make your family's life easier. Stop this charade. We both know what happened, and why."

Gamache glared at Gélinas.

"If you're going to arrest me, do it now. But don't you dare bring my family into it."

"It's too late. Your family is all over this case, isn't it? I know who Amelia Choquet is."

"You know nothing."

"I know everything."

Gamache took a small step toward him, but stopped.

Gélinas did not recoil. He stood erect, almost daring the man.

"Another happy opportunity?" Gélinas whispered. "Will I be, what's that English expression, pushing up daisies in your pretty garden, monsieur? Does it get easier to kill?"

"I think dinner must be ready," said Gamache, saying one thing but thinking something else entirely. He stepped away from the RCMP officer. "We should go inside. Come along, Gracie. Henri!"

He scooped up the puppy, turned and walked back to his home, the shepherd bounding after them. Through the kitchen window, Armand could see Reine-Marie moving about the kitchen. Pushing her hair back from her face. Muttering to herself as she always did when figuring out a large meal.

And he longed to tell her something he should have admitted years ago, certainly months ago. When he first saw the name Amelia Choquet.

"How long have I been asleep?" asked Ruth, looking down at her plate.

"Victoria is no longer on the throne, if that's what you're wondering," said Myrna.

"The good news is, we do have another queen," said Olivier, glancing at Gabri.

"I heard that," said Gabri. "A nasty stereotype. Oooh, crumpets."

"What time is it?" Ruth persisted.

Each had an omelette in front of them, with fresh tarragon and oozing melted Camembert.

A platter of back bacon sat on the pine table, along with a basket of golden toasted crumpets, butter melting into the crannies.

"Breakfast?" asked Ruth, looking more confused than normal.

"Dinner," said Reine-Marie. "I'm sorry, it's all we had."

"It's delicious," said Myrna, taking three pieces of maple-smoked bacon.

"Some might even call it delightful," said Reine-Marie, catching Armand's eye and smiling.

They all knew why they were there, except perhaps Ruth. They were human shields between the Gamaches and the RCMP officer.

And yet they noticed that Armand had placed himself right across from Gélinas.

Perhaps, Clara thought, to show he wasn't intimidated.

Perhaps, Myrna thought, to act as a shield himself, for Reine-Marie, who was shooting unpleasant glances his way.

Perhaps, Olivier thought, to keep an eye on his accuser.

Perhaps, Ruth thought, because evil really was, in the words of Auden, *unspectacular and always human.*

"*And shares our bed,*" she murmured. "*And eats at our own table.*"

Gamache, who was beside her, turned slightly to the old poet.

"*And we are introduced to Goodness every day,*" he whispered back. "*Even in drawing-rooms among a crowd of faults.*"

She held his steady gaze while conversation flowed around and past them.

"Do you know how it ends?" she asked quietly

"This?" he whispered, nodding toward Gélinas.

"No, the poem, you moron."

He grimaced and thought for a moment.

"*It is the Evil that is helpless like a lover,*" he said haltingly, struggling to remember. "*And has to pick a quarrel and succeeds—*"

"*And both are openly destroyed before our eyes.*" Ruth finished the poem. "That's how it ends."

There was a long pause while they locked eyes.

"I know what I'm doing," said Armand.

"And I know an epitaph when I hear it."

"You said that the cadets are a crowd of faults. You think so?"

"Don't know about them," said Ruth. "But I know for sure you are. Bacon?"

Gamache took the platter, which was empty. She was demanding, not offering.

"I have a question for you, Ruth," said Reine-Marie from down the table. "I can't find anything in the archives from the First World War. Any idea what happened to all that material? There must have been a lot."

"Why does everyone think I know everything?"

"We don't," said Gabri.

"Well, I knew about Roof Trusses. No one else here did."

"What do you know about it?" asked Paul Gélinas.

But Ruth was ignoring him, except to mumble something that sounded like "shithead." So Myrna jumped into the cavernous silence that had opened up.

"The reason you can't find it is that it isn't called Roof Trusses anymore. The name was changed some time ago."

"To what?"

"Notre-Dame-de-Doleur," said Gabri.

"Our Lady of Pain?" asked Gélinas.

Armand sat back in his chair. "Or it could be Our Lady of Grief."

"It's not there anymore," said Ruth. "It died."

"Can't think the name helped," said Gabri.

"Can you show us on a map?" asked Gamache.

"Have you not been listening, Miss Marple?" asked Ruth. "It's not on a map. It's gone."

"Thank you for clarifying that," said Armand, with exaggerated courtesy. "I did just manage to grasp it. But can you show us where the village once was?"

"I suppose."

"Can we get back to the archives?" asked Reine-Marie. "Any idea where all the material on the Great War might've gone?"

"Do you know," said Myrna slowly, "I do have an idea. Didn't the historical society put on a special retrospective at the Legion in Saint-Rémy a few years back?"

"That's right," said Clara. "In 2014, to mark the hundredth anniversary of the start of the war."

"So where's all that material now?" asked Olivier.

"*Damnatio memoriae*," said Reine-Marie.

Like Three Pines. Like Roof Trusses and Notre-Dame-de-Doleur, the war to end all wars had been banished from memory.

Armand and Reine-Marie walked Ruth home after dinner. Olivier and Gabri offered, but the Gamaches felt the need for fresh air, and distance from Paul Gélinas. They both hoped he'd be asleep by the time they returned.

The cadet Nathaniel was sitting on the sofa in Ruth's living room, reading. He sprang up as though kicked in the derriere when he heard them come in.

"Sir," he said.

"No need to call me sir," said Ruth. "Sit."

Nathaniel sat.

"No, I meant them." She pointed to Armand and Reine-Marie, who also sat smartly.

Reine-Marie turned to Nathaniel. "What're you reading?"

"A book I found on the table."

He showed it to them.

"We have that same book," said Armand.

"Exactly the same book," said Reine-Marie. "That's ours."

"Oh."

"Come here," commanded Ruth from the kitchen.

And they did.

She'd found a worn old map of the area and spread it out on her white plastic table. A notebook with her crablike scribbling was open, as it always was, beside a curdling cup of tea.

Armand recognized the cup. It was theirs.

Ruth believed in precycling. An evolution on recycling. She made use of things before people threw them out.

"We're looking up Roof Trusses," Armand said to Nathaniel, who was studying the map with excruciating earnestness.

"But we already tried," said the cadet, looking up. "It's not there, remember?"

"Why didn't you ask me?" demanded Ruth.

"Wh— ah— um."

"The future of the Sûreté?" Ruth asked Armand.

"He didn't ask you, Ruth," said Reine-Marie kindly, with patience, "because he thinks you're a crazy old woman."

"I do not," said Nathaniel, turning very red, then very white.

Ruth stood there, duck feathers on her pilled sweater, with Rosa muttering obscenities in her flannel nest beside the stove.

And Ruth laughed. Reaching out her hand to Reine-Marie to steady herself.

Nathaniel took a small step behind the Commander. Now she looked like a crazy old woman.

"Well, I suppose you're right," Ruth said, finally getting some control over herself. "But I'm happy. Are you?"

The young man, practically peeking out from behind Gamache, colored.

"Are you happy, Ruth?" asked Reine-Marie, touching her thin arm.

"I am."

"Oh, I'm so pleased to hear it. I was—"

"Roof Trusses?" asked Armand. He could see the two women were settling in to discuss the human condition and the nature of happiness. Normally a conversation he'd love to hear, but not that evening.

"There." Ruth's gnarly finger landed on the map, squishing a spot about ten kilometers from Three Pines. "That's where Roof Trusses used to be. But the name was changed to Notre-Dame-de-Doleur a while back."

Nathaniel wrote that down, then took a closer look at the map.

"But there's nothing there. You're just pointing to a field."

He stared at Ruth. Ruth glared at him.

"And now, Cadet Smythe, comes another lesson in police work," said the Commander. "Who to believe. Is Madame Zardo telling you the truth, or messing with you?"

"Could be a mind-fuck," agreed Ruth.

"How can you tell?" Nathaniel asked Gamache.

"You can't, with certainty. You can be taught to gather facts, evidence, but the very best investigators learn to trust something we're told early in our lives is useless. Even dangerous. Instinct. You use your head and your heart and your gut. The whole animal, like a good hunter. What does your instinct tell you about Madame Zardo? Is she telling the truth?"

Nathaniel turned back to Ruth, who was watching him with some interest.

"I think she is. At least, I think she believes it. I'll go tomorrow and find out."

Gamache nodded approval at the distinction between truth and fact.

"May I?" The cadet pointed to the map and Ruth grunted.

Armand watched the boy carefully fold up the worn paper. His red hair just touching his pale forehead as he bent over. There was the ready blush, the smooth, perfect skin. The bashful personality.

And Armand reflected on his conversation with Gélinas in the garden.

Gamache knew Gélinas was wrong. The real criminals, the worst criminals, weren't found off the beaten path. They were found in our kitchens, at our tables.

Unspectacular and always human.

CHAPTER 35

—⁀—

"I'm telling you, it should be here."

Nathaniel Smythe looked around, almost frantic now, barely wincing as sleet slapped his face. The map he'd borrowed from Madame Zardo was just a sodden mess in his hands.

The other three had turned so that the combination of rain and snow and ice pelted against the backs of their coats and hoods. The relentless noise almost drowned out Nathaniel's protests, which were rapidly descending into whining.

"There's nothing here," called Jacques. "Gamache fucked with you."

His shoulders were hunched and his chin was bent into his chest, so that from behind he could have been a crooked old man. The winter coat he wore came to his hips. More a ski jacket than something appropriate for standing on the side of a muddy half-frozen road, in a sleet storm, staring at flat gray fields and forest.

Jacques's slacks were soaked through, he could barely feel his legs, and he was beginning to shiver uncontrollably.

Nathaniel looked from him to the other two, but they also had their backs turned against the rain and snow and the cadet who'd brought them there with the claim of having found Roof Trusses.

Nathaniel turned full circle, blinking against the sleet that slid off his face. He squinted at the fields, scanning the horizon. Desolate.

No sign of the village. No sign of life.

"Come on," shouted Jacques, trudging back to the car.

Huifen and Amelia followed. Nathaniel stood rooted in place, obstinate, until he heard the car start up. Then he ran back to it, more than a little afraid they'd leave him there. He got into the backseat beside Amelia, who had her arms wrapped tightly around her chest and her nose tucked into her sodden jacket.

Notre-Dame-de-Pissed-Off.

The heater was on full blast and the tight car smelt of wet wool.

"This was a waste of time," said Jacques from the driver's seat, holding his trembling hands to the heat vent.

"But she said it would be here," said Nathaniel.

"She? I thought it was Gamache."

"He suggested we investigate, but the information came from the woman I'm staying with."

"I must've missed that class at the academy where they told us to believe old drunks," said Jacques.

Huifen snorted. In amusement or because she'd caught pneumonia.

Back in Three Pines, they went to change, but when Nathaniel came down the stairs at Ruth's place in warm, dry clothes, he found Amelia in the living room with the poet.

When they both looked at him with sharp, assessing eyes, he felt he'd descended into a Grimms' tale. Those stories rarely ended well for fey boys with bright red hair and a smile he hoped was ingratiating but knew just made him look like dinner.

"I lost your map."

"That's okay," said Ruth, getting to her feet. "I don't need a map anymore."

"There was nothing there," said Nathaniel.

He realized he'd failed the Commander's test. Or, at least, his instinct had. This woman wasn't reliable. She was exactly as she appeared, after all. A crazy old drunk.

"Well, nothing you could see, anyway," said Ruth.

"What else is there?" he asked.

"Come on," said Amelia, getting to her feet.

He followed her out, but instead of taking refuge with the others in the bistro, Amelia got in the car.

A few minutes later, they were back at exactly the same place they'd been an hour before.

Nothing had changed, except it seemed even more desolate.

"I asked Madame Zardo to repeat what she told you, and she said the village was here," said Amelia.

"That's what I told you," he said.

"I also called the toponymie man. He gave me the map coordinates. Here."

The sleet hit the windshield and slid slowly down the glass, to pile up as slush on the wipers at the bottom. "He looked it up and confirmed that the name Roof Trusses had been officially changed in the 1920s. To Notre-Dame-de-Doleur."

"Why?"

"Well, Roof Trusses was obviously a mistake," she said. "He told us that. It should never have been the name to begin with."

"I know, but why Notre-Dame-de-Doleur?"

"I asked, but he didn't know. Probably the name of the church."

"I've heard of Notre-Dame-de-Grace," said Nathaniel. "And Notre-Dame-de-Paris, and Notre-Dame-de-la-Merci. And—"

"Okay, I get it. Notre-Dame-de-Doleur is unusual—"

"Unique."

"Maybe. But there's nothing wrong with unique, is there?"

They looked at each other. The girl who was trying so hard to be different, and the boy who was trying so hard to be the same.

"I guess not," he conceded, without conviction.

"Monsieur Toponymie was surprised by the name," Amelia admitted. "But there're other weird ones around. Saint-Louis-du-Ha! Ha!, for instance."

"There's really a town called that?"

"*Oui.* Complete with an exclamation mark after each 'Ha.'"

"You're kidding."

"Do I look like I'm kidding?"

"No, but you sound like you are. Ha ha."

He caught the faintest upturn at the corners of her mouth. It looked like victory.

"Makes the people in Notre-Dame-de-Doleur seem pretty lucky, doesn't it?" she said. "It could've been worse."

"It was worse. Roof Trusses."

But he was impressed that she'd pursued it. Not giving up, where the others had. Where he had.

But did it matter? Even if this was where the village once stood, it wasn't there anymore.

They sat side by side and looked through the slowly fogging windows.

"It's gone," he said.

"You're missing the point. It might be gone, but it was here once. And I bet some people stayed behind. They always do. Let's go."

She got out of the car before he could point out that no one had stayed behind. At least, no one living.

And then he understood what Amelia meant. And what Madame Zardo had meant.

They were six feet under. The remaining villagers were remains.

Notre-Dame-de-Doleur, née Roof Trusses, had become a ghost town.

It took them almost an hour, and they were soaked through and chilled to the bone, but finally they found the cemetery. It had been overcome by the forest, especially lush in that area. The gravestones had sunk and toppled over, but most could still be read. Whoever had made them had etched the names deep into the local granite.

Amelia and Nathaniel barely noticed that the sleet had turned to full-on snow until after they'd examined every gravestone they could find.

Then they turned to each other, the huge spring flakes falling between them.

There was near silence, except for the familiar tapping as the snow landed. On them. On the trees. On the ground.

And they noticed another sound now. A plopping. Plunking. Plinking.

A timpani.

The forest was playing music for them.

An hour later, they walked into the bistro and handed two metal buckets to Olivier.

He looked into them warily, then smiled. "Sap buckets. Where'd you get these?" He placed them on the floor and admired them. "You don't see originals like this much anymore. And they're full."

"We emptied most of the other buckets into these two," Nathaniel explained.

"Seemed a shame to waste the sap," said Amelia. "They were in the woods by Roof Trusses."

"You found it?"

They nodded.

Behind Olivier, over by the fire, Ruth lifted her hand, and when the cadets waved at her, she extended her finger in greeting.

"Does she know what that means?" Nathaniel whispered to Olivier.

He laughed. "She sure does. Do you?"

"Well, it means—"

"It means she likes you," said Olivier.

Jacques and Huifen were also there. They sat at what they now considered their table in the bistro, with hot chocolates and the map, and nodded to the younger cadets.

But Amelia and Nathaniel walked right by them with just a friendly *"Bon-jour."* And joined Ruth.

"I'd ask you to sit," said Ruth, "but I don't want you to."

Nathaniel lifted his hand and slowly unfolded his finger. He'd never given anyone the finger. Had wanted to, many, many times. But never had. And the first time he flipped someone off, it was an old woman.

It didn't seem a good reason to be proud of himself, and yet he was. Between the waves of terror.

Rosa, nesting in Ruth's lap, muttered, "Fuck, fuck, fuck."

And Ruth laughed.

"Oh, what the hell. Sit down, but don't order anything."

They took off their wet jackets and hung them on nails by the fire, then moved their chairs a bit closer to the warmth. Ruth leaned toward the cadets and examined them. Soaked through, chilled to the marrow. But happy.

"You found Roof Trusses," she said, and they nodded. "But did you find the grave?"

Clara and Myrna followed Reine-Marie into the historical society in Saint-Rémy. The secretary there confirmed that there'd been a very successful retrospective on the region's involvement in the Great War.

"Then perhaps you can tell me where all the material is?" asked Reine-Marie.

"We gave it to you, didn't we?" said the elderly Québécoise volunteer.

"You gave me a lot of boxes," Reine-Marie confirmed. "And I've been through most of them, but I can't find a single item relating to the First World War."

"Are you sure?"

The woman clearly suspected Reine-Marie had either lost or stolen the items. Reine-Marie was feeling slightly defensive when she realized she'd almost certainly given that very same look to researchers who claimed not to have something she believed was in the material they'd been given.

She looked at the courteous, suspicious face. And smiled.

"I know it sounds unbelievable, but I really did look and it really isn't there."

"Hmmm." The woman sat back in her plastic chair. "Now where could it be?"

While she pondered, and Reine-Marie waited, Clara and Myrna passed the time by wandering the permanent exhibit in the large room that opened up behind the volunteer desk. It was filled with clothing, and photographs, and maps.

"Look, this one's signed," said Clara. "Turcotte."

"And dated. 1919."

It clearly showed Saint-Rémy, a bustling lumber town, and Williamsburg, and it even had Roof Trusses. Not yet rebaptized Notre-Dame-de-Doleur.

But it did not have Three Pines.

"Why?" asked Clara.

But Myrna had no answers. Instead she'd wandered over to a mannequin wearing a lace wedding dress. The mannequin's waist was about the size of Myrna's forearm.

"People were smaller then," she explained to Clara. "Lack of nutrition."

"Lack of croissants."

"How did they survive?" asked Myrna, shaking her head.

"The pioneer spirit," said Clara.

"Got it," Reine-Marie called from the front desk. "We're off."

"Where to?" asked Clara and Myrna, hurrying to catch up.

"The Legion. The show was there, and the secretary thinks the things might've been boxed up and put in the basement, and they forgot about them."

"Ironic," said Myrna.

Commander Gamache spent most of the day in his office at the academy. The door closed, if not actually locked.

But the message was clear.

Stay away.

Beauvoir could not.

For the umpteenth time that day, Jean-Guy Beauvoir stood outside the closed door and stared at it.

"He's inside?" he asked the Commander's assistant, sitting at her desk, for the umpteenth time.

"*Oui.* Has been all day," said Madame Marcoux.

"What's he doing?"

She looked at Beauvoir, incredulous and amused. He knew she wouldn't tell him, even if she could. But he had to ask.

He leaned closer to the door, but couldn't hear anything.

Now the amusement disappeared from Madame Marcoux's eyes, to be replaced by disapproval.

"He asked not to be disturbed. Have you found out who killed Professor Leduc?" she asked.

"Not yet, but—"

"Then maybe you should be doing that, don't you think?"

It wasn't a question.

Finally, at the end of the day, Jean-Guy returned, hoping to find the assistant gone, but she was still there.

Beauvoir smiled at her, walked right by, tapped. And entered. As she stood and called, "Stop."

Armand Gamache looked up sharply, his hand instinctively going to the lid of his laptop.

And as he looked at Jean-Guy Beauvoir, he slowly closed it. In a gesture that felt more like a slap to the face than any hand ever could.

The two men stared, then Jean-Guy's eyes dropped to the slender computer, closed.

"I'm sorry, sir," said the assistant, standing at the door and glaring at the intruder.

"It's not a problem, Madame Marcoux," said Gamache, rising behind his desk. "You can leave us. I'm finished for the day anyway. Thank you for staying."

Madame Marcoux hesitated at the door.

"It's all right, Chantal."

With a severe look at Beauvoir, she left, closing the door softly behind her while the two men stared at each other.

"We found out about the silencer," said Beauvoir. "Made by a company in Tennessee. It specializes in customized weapons. They have a record of Leduc's order. He must have smuggled it across the border."

Gamache made a sound of disapproval but not of surprise, and waved toward the sitting area of his office. Away, Beauvoir noticed, from his desk. And the closed laptop.

"Is that what you came here to tell me?" asked Gamache, sitting down and taking off his reading glasses.

Beauvoir took the chair across from him and leaned forward. "The joke's over, *patron*. What's this about? What're you doing in here?"

"Beyond the fact it's my office?" There was an edge of annoyance in Gamache's normally composed voice. "What do you want, Jean-Guy?"

Beauvoir, faced with such a simple question, felt overwhelmed.

He wanted to know why Monsieur Gamache had hidden away all day.

He wanted to know why he'd just closed his laptop. What was on it?

He wanted to know why he'd really taken those students down to Three Pines.

He wanted to know why Gamache's fingerprints were on the murder weapon.

He wanted to know why he'd specifically asked for Paul Gélinas to join the investigation, and lied to Chief Inspector Lacoste, and himself, in the process.

He wanted to know who Amelia Choquet really was.

And he wanted to know who killed Serge Leduc, because in the early dusk it was slowly dawning on Beauvoir that Monsieur Gamache might know.

But Jean-Guy Beauvoir sat there, mute. Staring at the familiar face, the familiar man. Who was becoming a stranger.

"I want you to let me in."

Jean-Guy's eyes left Gamache's, and he slowly turned his head to the desk and the closed computer.

"Why does Paul Gélinas suspect that I killed Serge Leduc?" asked Gamache.

"I think it started with the fingerprints."

Gamache nodded. "And how did my prints get on the murder weapon?"

Beauvoir sat there, a lump forming in his stomach.

"I don't know," he said quietly, almost in a whisper. "But they're only partials. They're obviously not your prints."

"Oh, they're mine."

And now there was complete silence. Except for the thrumming in Beauvoir's ears, as the blood abandoned his extremities and ran to his core. Retreating. Running away. And leaving him light-headed.

"What're you telling me?"

"You and I both know that partials aren't admissible," said Gamache. "We tell people we don't take them seriously. But the fact is we do. And we should. How often have they led us to the murderer?"

"Often," admitted Jean-Guy.

"And they do this time too."

"You're not—"

"Confessing? *Non*. I have never touched that gun. I didn't even know he had it, and would never have tolerated it had I known."

"Brébeuf's partials are on the gun. Are you saying it was him? But he'd have wiped the gun. As would you. Amelia Choquet? Her prints were on the revolver, and the gun case, and it was her map. Is she the one who killed him?"

Into the silence he placed another question.

"Who is she?" Jean-Guy asked.

"I can't tell you that."

"Who is she?" Beauvoir asked again, more firmly this time. "There's a personal connection, isn't there? That's why you reversed the earlier decision and admitted her to the academy. Paul Gélinas was right."

"Yes, he was. But I need to speak to Madame Gamache first."

"Is she—"

"I won't tell you any more, Jean-Guy. And the only reason I've gone this far is because I trust you."

"But not enough to tell me the truth."

"I have told you the truth. I just can't tell you more right now. You need to trust me." Gamache got up, and Jean-Guy rose with him. They walked to the door.

"Do you know who killed the Duke?" asked Beauvoir.

"I think I do, but I have no proof."

"Then tell me."

"I can't. But I will tell you that the key is in the fingerprints on the revolver."

Beauvoir stopped at the door, his foot against it so that Gamache couldn't open it. "Deputy Commissioner Gélinas is planning to arrest you for murder, isn't he?"

"I think so."

"But you don't seem worried."

"Just because I'm not screaming up and down the hallways doesn't mean I'm not worried. But I'm not panicked. He has his plans and I have mine."

"You must regret bringing him in," said Jean-Guy. "Why did you? You went behind Isabelle's back to do it. You'd never have tolerated that when you were chief inspector, and yet you did it to her."

Now Gamache did look tired. He met Beauvoir's gaze. At first Jean-Guy thought Monsieur Gamache was trying to make up his mind whether to confide in him, but then it became something else.

Monsieur Gamache was holding on to Jean-Guy's eyes like a mariner clings on to a bit of flotsam in a gale.

He was a man overboard.

"It seemed too good an opportunity to pass up," said Gamache. "The Deputy Commissioner of the RCMP actually visiting Montréal. I had to ask."

"But you could've gone through Lacoste."

315

"Yes, but I doubt he'd have come down for her. He doesn't know her."

"He doesn't know you, if he suspects you of murder."

"You suspect me too, don't you?"

"I do not," snapped Beauvoir, though they both knew that was a deception, if not a lie. "Is Gélinas going down to Three Pines with you again tonight?"

"He is. I invited him down again."

"Why?" asked Beauvoir.

"So he can keep an eye on me," said Gamache, then smiled. "And I can keep an eye on him."

"Do you want me to come down with you? I can stay over."

"No, you need to be with Annie. I spoke with her this afternoon. She sounds happy."

Armand Gamache offered his hand to the younger man in a gesture that was oddly formal.

Jean-Guy took it.

"Don't believe everything you think," said Gamache, before releasing the hand and opening the door. "Pema Chödrön. A Buddhist nun."

"Of course," said Beauvoir and gave a heavy sigh as the door closed behind him. He turned to go, only to come face-to-face with Chantal Marcoux, who was standing by her desk in a long cloth coat. She was just putting a knitted hat on her head.

She opened the door to the corridor and ushered him out.

As he walked one way down the hallway, and she walked the other, Beauvoir wondered how much Madame Marcoux had heard. And he wondered if she'd been Serge Leduc's assistant, before the putsch and the arrival of Commander Gamache.

CHAPTER 36

"So that was Roof Trusses after all," said Jacques, when Nathaniel and Amelia finally joined them at their table in the bistro. "You can't tell the little shithole was ever there."

"True," agreed Amelia. "It wasn't obvious. We had to actually work at it."

She glared at Jacques before taking the rich hot chocolate, topped with fresh whipped cream, from Olivier. *"Merci."*

Slightly startled by the pleasantry, Olivier smiled. *"De rien."*

"And after all that, all you found were a couple of buckets of maple syrup." Jacques shoved his empty mug toward Olivier, who took it and left. "Well done."

"Sap," said Nathaniel.

Huifen had been watching the younger cadets' earlier conversation with the old poet, and while she couldn't hear what was being said, she could see that it had held the crazy old woman's attention.

It was more than sap they'd found.

"What did you find?" she asked.

"What's it to you?" asked Amelia.

"What's it to us?" asked Huifen. "We might not have been there, but we're all working together."

"No, we're not," said Nathaniel. "You left me on the side of the road. You got in the car and were about to drive away."

"No, I wasn't," said Jacques. "I just turned it on to get heat and to hurry you up."

"I wasn't slow, I was still looking for Roof Trusses and you gave up, you lazy shit."

"You little piece of crap—" Jacques leaned toward Nathaniel, who jerked away. But Huifen stopped Jacques with a hand to his arm.

317

Amelia noticed the subtle gesture and not for the first time wondered at the power this small woman held over the large man. And, not for the first time, wondered just how much influence she did have over Jacques.

Huifen could stop him from doing something, but could she also get him to act?

"You're just afraid to admit you were wrong," said Amelia.

"I'm not afraid. Of anything." Jacques glared at Amelia. "How many times do I have to prove it?"

"Oh, you're afraid now," Huifen said quietly. "And you were afraid then. We all were."

The laughter, the warmth of the bistro disappeared as the four young people stared at each other.

And then with a bang they were brought back to the bistro, as the front door slammed shut.

Commander Gamache and Deputy Commissioner Gélinas had just arrived, the door blowing closed behind them.

They stomped their feet, brushed wet snow off their coats, and slapped their hats against their legs. It was a singular Québec jig learned in the womb.

The snow had turned back to sleet as night fell and now it was pelting against the bistro windows and piling up on the mullions.

Gamache took off his wet coat and, after hanging it on a peg by the door, he looked around, rubbing his hands together for warmth and taking in the fires crackling away in stone hearths at either end of the beamed room. The bistro was surprisingly full for such a dreadful night. But some of the regulars were missing.

He'd left Reine-Marie, Clara, Myrna, Ruth, and Gabri at his home in front of the roaring fire in the living room, sipping red wine and going through the boxes and boxes of items found in the basement of the Royal Canadian Legion.

"Look." Clara had picked up a picture. "There's my place in the background."

She showed them the photo of two young men in puttees tied from their knees to their ankles. Their uniforms were too tight and their grins, Clara knew, way too big.

They stood on the village green and between them was a farm woman in her Sunday best, awkward and bashful and full of pride, her robust sons on either side of her, their arms around her soft shoulders.

"Look at the pines," said Gabri. "They're the same size as the boys."

They'd walked right by those same trees on their way to the Gamaches' home. They now towered over the village, strong and straight and still growing.

"I thought the trees had been here for centuries," said Myrna. "Like Ruth."

"They have," said Ruth. "Three pines of some sort have always been on the village green."

She spoke with such authority that Myrna began to wonder if Ruth really was a few centuries old. Rooted and pickled. Like an old turnip.

"Maybe the originals died," said Clara. "Is either of the boys in this photograph also in the stained-glass window?"

Clara passed the picture around.

"Hard to tell," said Myrna. "They aren't the main boy, but the other two are in profile."

"Is there a name?" Gabri asked.

Ruth turned the picture over.

"Joe and Norm Valois," she read.

The friends looked at her, their encyclopedia of loss.

Ruth nodded. "And there was a third Valois on the wall. Pierre. Probably another brother."

"Oh, dear God," sighed Reine-Marie, and looked away from the picture, unable to meet the eyes of Madame Valois.

"I wonder if Pierre was taking the picture," said Gabri. "Or maybe it was their father."

Clara took the photograph back. Was Pierre the younger son, or the oldest? Had he joined up later, to be with his brothers? Or was he already there? Did they find each other before they died? Most of the boys joined the same regiment, often the same unit. And ended up in the same battles.

Ypres, Vimy, Flanders, the Somme, Passchendaele. All familiar names now, but unknown to the three in the photo.

Clara stared and stared at the picture, with the young men and the young trees and her house, unchanged, in the background.

Had they grown up in her home? Had the telegram been delivered there? Had they fluttered out of their mother's hand, to the flagstone floor, one after the other? Piling up. A storm of grief.

We regret to inform you . . .

Is that why her cottage always felt so soothing? It was used to offering comfort to the inconsolable.

Clara put the photograph on the sofa beside her and went back to the job at hand, searching through the boxes, looking for the boys in the window.

Photograph after photograph showed fields of mud where French and Belgian villages had been bombed to oblivion. Disappeared, until they were a divot in the landscape.

"Can we help?" Armand had asked when they'd changed out of their office clothes before heading to the bistro.

He'd spoken to Reine-Marie, but she was silent, staring into a shoe box on her lap. He leaned over and saw what was in there.

Telegrams.

"Look at this," said Gabri, breaking the silence. He held a compass and was turning it this way and that. "I never did learn how to read one of these things."

"A lost boy if there ever was one," said Myrna, and Ruth snorted in amusement, or because she had an olive lodged in her nostril again.

"You should take up orienteering," said Gamache as Gabri handed him the compass.

"I'm quite happy with my orientation, thank you," said Gabri.

The glass was shattered, but as Armand turned it, the needle still found true north.

"When you stop playing with that, Clouseau, go see to your young people," said Ruth. "They're over at the bistro. They want to speak to you."

"Shall we?" Gamache asked Gélinas, who nodded.

"A quiet Scotch by the fire sounds good."

After arriving at the bistro, Gamache gestured to Olivier for two Scotches, then he and Gélinas wound their way through the tables toward the cadets. Once at the table, the cadets rose and Commander Gamache waved them to sit back down.

"Ruth said you'd like to speak to me," Gamache said, smoothing his hair, disheveled from his tuque, and sitting down. "Is something wrong?"

The four young people looked upset. Two of them pale, two of them flushed.

"We were just arguing," said Huifen. "Nothing new."

"About what?" asked Gélinas, taking a seat.

"These two found Roof Trusses, or Notre-Dame-de-Doleur, or whatever it's called," said Huifen. "We gave up."

"Hardly matters," said Jacques. "There's nothing there but snow. And maple syrup."

"Sap," said Nathaniel. "And there was something there."

"What did you find?" asked Gamache, after thanking Olivier for the Scotches.

"The cemetery." Nathaniel's voice was eager now and his eyes bright.

"It was overgrown," said Amelia. "But still there."

"And?" asked Gamache.

Nathaniel shook his head. "No Antony Turcotte."

"No Turcotte at all," said Amelia.

Gamache sat back, surprised. Considering.

"Didn't the toponymie man say Turcotte had been buried there?"

"Yes. It was even in the Canadian Encyclopedia."

Gamache leaned forward again and, putting his elbows on the table, he folded his hands together and rested his chin on them. And stared out at the darkness, the snowflakes furious in the bistro light.

"Could the gravestone have fallen over or been buried?" he asked.

"It's possible," Amelia admitted. "But it's not a big cemetery and most of the stones were fairly easy to find. We can go back tomorrow and take a closer look."

"But why bother?" asked Jacques. "He's just trying to keep us busy. Can't you see that? How can it possibly matter? Besides, he's not part of the investigation anymore."

"And you're not Sûreté officers," snapped Gamache. "You're cadets and I'm your commander. And you'll do as I say. I'm losing patience with you, young man. The only reason I tolerate your insubordination is because I think someone messed with your head. Told you all sorts of things that aren't true."

"So you're here to reeducate me, is that it?" demanded Jacques.

"Yes, as a matter of fact. You're very close to graduation, and then what?"

"I'll be a Sûreté officer."

"Will you? Things have changed at the academy and you're not changing with them. You're stuck. Frozen. Perhaps even petrified." Gamache lowered his voice, though the rest of the table could still hear. "The time has come, Jacques, to decide if you are going to move forward, or not."

"You have no idea who I am, and what I've done," Jacques hissed back.

"What have you done?" Gamache demanded, holding the young man's eyes. "Tell me now."

Huifen reached out. The warning touch. Again. Subtle, but Gamache saw it.

And the moment passed when Jacques might have said something.

Gamache glared at Huifen, then turned to Nathaniel and Amelia. "You've done well."

"What should we do now?" Nathaniel asked.

"Now you join us for dinner," said Gamache, getting up. "You must be hungry."

"Us too?" asked Huifen, also rising along with Jacques.

The Commander looked at them and gave a brusque nod before going to the long wooden bar and paying for the cadets' food and drinks for that day, and inviting Olivier to join them.

"You okay?" asked Annie.

Jean-Guy was rubbing her swollen feet and both were on the sofa, watching the news. Though Jean-Guy was clearly distracted.

"Just thinking."

"About what?"

He hesitated, not wanting to upset Annie with ideas that seemed at one moment crazy and the next perfectly plausible.

"Do you think your father could have ever . . ."

"*Oui?*"

She took a huge bite of the éclair she'd been having as an hors d'oeuvre.

Now, looking into his wife's unsuspecting gaze, it seemed crazy to Jean-Guy. Armand Gamache would never—

"Nothing."

"What is it?" She lowered the éclair to a plate. "Tell me. Is Dad in trouble? Is something wrong?"

There, he'd upset her after all, and he knew she wouldn't let it go until he told her.

"There's a senior officer from the RCMP who's joined us as an independent observer and he seems to think your father might've—"

"Had something to do with the murder?" asked Annie.

"Well, no, not really, it's just, well—"

She swung her legs off his lap and sat up. Annie the lawyer was in the building.

"Is there any evidence?" she asked.

Jean-Guy sighed. "Circumstantial, at best."

"And what's the worst?"

"Fingerprints."

Annie's brows shot up. She hadn't expected that.

"Where?"

"On the murder weapon."

"Jesus. Which was a revolver, right?"

322

"Your father said he never touched it, never even knew Leduc had it."

"He wouldn't allow it," said Annie, her eyes narrowing in thought.

"That's what he said. The prints are partials. His and one of the cadets and Michel Brébeuf's."

"Partials?" The tension left her face. "Then they're not admissible. And they're obviously not his."

"He told me this afternoon that they were."

"Wait a minute." She leaned toward her husband. "He says he never touched it, but also says the prints are his. That doesn't make sense."

"I know. He said he thinks the solution to the murder lies in those prints."

"The other ones, then. Uncle Michel and the cadet," said Annie. "That's what he must mean. Who is he?"

"The cadet? She. Amelia Choquet."

He watched his wife, but there was no reaction to the name. Jean-Guy struggled with what to say next and Annie homed in on that.

"There's more. What is it?"

"There seems a kind of connection between them."

"Between Dad and Michel Brébeuf, yes, of course. You know that."

"No, between Amelia Choquet and your father."

"What do you mean?" she asked, her voice guarded.

"I don't know. I just wondered if the name meant anything."

"Should it? Come on, Jean-Guy, tell me what you're thinking."

He heaved a sigh and wondered how much damage he was about to do.

"Do you think your father could've had an affair?"

The question landed on Annie like an anvil on a cartoon cat. She looked dazed and he could almost see stars and little birds flying around her head.

Annie stared at him, incapable of speech. Finally blurting out, "Of course not."

"Many men do," said Jean-Guy gently. "Away from home. Tempted. A moment of weakness."

"My father is as human as the next man, and he has his weaknesses," said Annie. "But not that. Never that. He would never, ever betray my mother. He loves her."

"I agree. But I had to ask." He took her hand and absently turned her wedding ring around and around. "Have I hurt you?"

"You've made me angry that you'd even ask. And if you have to ask, then what must others think? Like that RCMP person. He doesn't know Dad, does he?"

"No, but he's staying with your folks in Three Pines."

"You have to go down there, Jean-Guy. You have to be with Dad. Make sure he doesn't do anything stupid."

"Like kill someone or have an affair?"

"Well, seems you've already messed that up," she said with a wan smile.

"I offered to go down, but he wanted me to be with you."

"I'll be fine. Baby isn't due for a few weeks."

He got up and hauled her off the sofa.

"You want me gone so you can finish off that box of éclairs, don't you?"

"Actually, the pizza boy's arriving in a few minutes. I need you gone by then. He's very jealous."

"Replaced by a pepperoni. My mother said it would come to that."

"So did Gloria Steinem."

CHAPTER 37

"*Mary Poppins*," said Clara. "Oh, perfect."

She sighed with relief as she fell into the sofa and Armand opened the armoire to reveal the television.

They'd had dinner. Shepherd's pie made by Myrna. Fragrant crispy garlic bread brought by Clara. And a massive chocolate cake that Gabri had baked that afternoon, knowing they'd be working through dinner.

It had been rougher slogging than any of them realized. They'd been so focused on the mystery of the boys in the window, none of them had really thought about what those boxes, forgotten in the basement of the Legion, actually contained.

The remains of so many young men. The Great War had destroyed the flower of Europe and had taken with it the wildflowers of Canada. A generation of young men, gone. And all that was left of them sat forgotten in dusty old boxes in a basement.

One of the letters home contained a poppy. Pressed flat. Frail but still a vibrant red. Picked fresh one morning, just before a battle in a corner of Belgium called Flanders Fields.

The friends had given up then. Unable to go on.

Reine-Marie, Clara, Myrna, Ruth, and Gabri had put down the boxes and filed into the kitchen, where the others had prepared dinner. It was a somber meal until they noticed the young people, gobbling food as though they'd never seen it before. Huge forkfuls of shepherd's pie disappeared into the four bottomless pits.

They all went back for more. Since the villagers' appetites were gone, there was plenty for the cadets.

Even Ruth smiled at the sight. Though it might have been gas.

"Chocolate cake?" asked Gabri.

The magic words restored the villagers' appetites, and they all took their tall wedges of moist cake into the living room, along with coffees.

"*Mary Poppins?*" asked Reine-Marie.

"*Mary Poppins*," said Clara. "Oh, perfect."

"The girls watch it every time they visit," said Reine-Marie, handing the disk to her husband.

"Girls?" asked Huifen.

"Our granddaughters," said Reine-Marie. "Florence and Zora."

"Zorro?" asked Jacques, an earnest expression on his face.

But a stern look from Gamache wiped it away.

"Zora," he corrected. "She's named after my grandmother."

"Not really your grandmother, though," said Gélinas. "Wasn't she one of the DPs after the Second World War?"

Gamache looked at him. The message, once again, was clear. Paul Gélinas had done his homework. And the home he'd worked on belonged to Gamache.

"DPs?" asked Nathaniel.

"Displaced persons," said Myrna. "Those without a home or family. Many of them from the concentration camps. Liberated but with no place to go."

"My father sponsored Zora to come to Canada," Armand explained.

He knew he might as well tell them. After all, it wasn't a secret. And it wasn't going to remain private for long. Gélinas would see to that.

"She came to live with us," said Gamache, turning on the receiver and the DVD. "We became her family."

"And she became yours," said Gélinas. "After your parents died."

Gamache turned around and faced Gélinas. "*Oui.*"

"Zora," said Reine-Marie with fondness. "The name means 'the dawn.' The beginning of light."

"And she was," said Armand. "Now, are we sure we want to watch *Mary Poppins*? We also have *Cinderella* and *The Little Mermaid*."

"I've never seen *Mary Poppins*," said Amelia. "Have you?"

The other cadets shook their heads.

"Supercalifragilisticexpialidocious?" said Myrna. "You've never seen *Mary Poppins*?"

"That's something quite atrocious," said Clara. "Okay, Armand. Turn it on."

"Count me out," said Olivier, getting up. "That nanny gives me the creeps."

As the establishing shot of 1910 London appeared, Olivier disappeared into the kitchen. A few minutes later, Armand arrived to make more coffee. He found Olivier in one of the armchairs by the fireplace. The small television was on and he wore headphones.

"What're you watching?"

Olivier almost leapt out of his skin.

He shoved the headphones off his ears. "Jeez, Armand. You almost killed me."

"Sorry. What's on?"

He stood behind Olivier's chair and watched a very young Robert De Niro and Christopher Walken in a bar.

"The Deer Hunter."

"You're kidding," said Armand. *"Mary Poppins* scares you, but *The Deer Hunter* is okay?"

Olivier smiled. "Talking about Clairton reminded me how great this movie is."

"Why?"

"Well, I think it's the bond—"

"No, I mean, why Clairton?"

"It's the town the main characters come from. There, that's it."

He waved at the screen as a shot of a steel town in Pennsylvania came on. "I'll leave you to it."

Olivier watched Armand walk back into the living room and the world of Mary Poppins, where the father was singing "The Life I Lead."

On his screen, Robert De Niro was threatening a barroom brawl with a Green Beret.

Jean-Guy's wipers were taking the sleet off the windshield as fast as they could.

He liked driving. It was a chance to listen to music and think. And at the moment he was thinking about those fingerprints, and the blatant contradiction in what his father-in-law had said.

The prints were his. But he had never touched the gun.

The key to the crime was in the prints.

Did he mean Amelia Choquet?

Despite Annie's protests, and his own gut feeling, Jean-Guy retained a fragment of doubt. Could the Goth Girl be Gamache's daughter? She didn't look at all like either Annie or her brother, Daniel. But maybe she did, and he was simply distracted by all the accoutrements. The tattoos and piercings disguising who and what she really was.

Could Amelia, who perhaps not coincidently shared a name with Gamache's mother, be the result of a momentary lapse twenty years earlier?

But if he knew who she was, why did Gamache admit her to the academy?

Maybe he didn't know Amelia existed until he saw the application, saw the birth mother, saw the birth date. Saw the name. And put it all together.

And then he'd want to see the girl.

And after the crime, he'd want to protect her. The daughter he never knew he had.

Did Gamache think she killed Serge Leduc? And was he shielding her, intentionally muddying the investigation by admitting the prints were his, when they weren't?

Misdirection. Another whale.

All truth with malice in it.

The wipers swished the slush, clearing the windshield. And despite the mess, Jean-Guy felt he was seeing clearer. Getting closer.

Suppose he took a different tack? Suppose Gamache was telling the truth. The prints were his, even though he'd never touched the gun.

How could that be?

Swish, swish, swish.

Jean-Guy was almost there, he could feel the answer just ahead, in the darkness.

Swish, swish— He slowed the car and pulled off into a service station. And there he sat in the idling vehicle, the sleet slapping the roof and steamy windows.

If Monsieur Gamache hadn't touched the revolver, but the prints were his, then someone must've placed them there. Someone with such skill and expertise that even the Sûreté's own lab didn't detect the fake.

While the Sûreté Academy was stuffed with professors, top in their field, and soon-to-be agents and visiting experts, few people had the ability to do that.

It demanded not just skill, but someone especially gifted in forensics and manipulation. This was a plan that didn't just happen. It must've been months in the making.

It needed patience, and timing, and nerve. To plant evidence like that needed a great tactician. And the academy had one of those. Someone recruited by Gamache himself.

Hugo Charpentier.
Swish, swish, swish.

Armand placed his hand over Reine-Marie's, which was gripping the shoe box even as she watched the movie.

Just as Mary Poppins slid up the banister, to the astonishment of the Banks children, Armand leaned over and whispered, "I'll do this."

"I should."

"No, I should."

Her grip loosened and her hands slid off the old cardboard box.

Armand took it and stepped between the cadets sprawled on the floor, their eyes glued to the screen. Walking into the kitchen, he poured himself another coffee and sat at the harvest table.

At the far end of the room, Olivier had his feet up watching his movie.

Taking a deep breath, Armand looked down at the box filled with telegrams and remembered the number of times he'd been the one to deliver the news.

To see the door open and the expectant, then perplexed, then frightened faces of parents, or spouses, or siblings, or children.

And then to tell them what had happened.

He remembered each and every time over the past thirty years. He closed his eyes and could see all those faces, those eyes, pleading with him. To tell them it wasn't true. And he could feel their hands gripping his arm, as they fell. Mothers, fathers, husbands and wives crumpled to the floor. While he held them, and gently lowered them. To the ground.

And stayed with them until they could get up again. A strange resurrection. Changed forever.

To the accompaniment of Mary Poppins singing about a spoonful of sugar and medicine, he opened the box. And started reading the telegrams. Looking for one name. Turcotte.

He thought he could just hurry through, scanning for the name. But he could not. He found himself reading each and every one. There was a devastating sameness about them. The commanding officers clearly overwhelmed by the number that had to be written. After a while, the telegrams were written in a sort of shorthand, a scrawl, that made sense a hundred years later when the place names were familiar, but that must have, at the moment of delivery, been meaningless. Their child gone, forever. In some unintelligible foreign field.

The worst, perhaps, were the number of missing, presumed dead. The ones lost and never, ever found.

There were plenty of those. Lots of those.

But none of them bore the name Turcotte.

Had he survived?

In his gut Gamache knew the young soldier in the window, with the map, had not come home.

He replaced the lid and sat there, his hand resting on top of the box. He looked over at Olivier and the mute television.

In the background, the Banks children were being warned by Bert, the chimney sweep, that what Uncle Albert suffered from was serious and contagious.

Uncle Albert was giggling, then, unable to contain it any longer, he burst out laughing.

"*I love to laugh,*" Uncle Albert sang, long and loud and clear.

While on Olivier's screen, Robert De Niro, filthy and emaciated, spun the barrel of the revolver, then held the gun to his head. His eyes crazed, his mouth open in what must have been a scream, but all Armand heard was Uncle Albert's laughter, bubbling in from the other room.

De Niro pulled the trigger.

Armand fell back in his chair, his eyes wide, his mouth open, his breathing shallow.

Staring at the gun in Robert De Niro's hand.

A revolver. A revolver.

Gripping the chair for support, Armand slowly rose. And looked from Olivier's movie through the door and into the living room. At Jacques, and Huifen, and Nathaniel. And Amelia. Laughing along with Uncle Albert.

And he knew.

CHAPTER 38

When the movies ended, their guests left. Gélinas stayed up for a final drink by the fireplace, then went to bed while Reine-Marie and Armand cleaned up.

"It was pretty bad?" she asked. Thinking his pallor must have come from the shoe box, still sitting on the kitchen table. She was wrong.

"Young lives wasted," he said. *"The Hell where youth and laughter go."*

"Armand?" she asked, having rarely seen him so upset.

"Désolé. I was just thinking about what they were made to do."

She thought he was talking about the boys in the box. She was wrong.

"Did you find the young Turcottes?" she asked.

He took a deep breath and brought himself out of it. *"Non.* Those telegrams might've been lost. It's surprising so many were kept."

He looked at her and forced a smile. "Did you enjoy the movie?"

"I must've seen it a hundred times, and I still love it."

She hummed "Let's Go Fly a Kite" while handing him warm, wet dishes.

"Coming?" she asked, when the kitchen was clean and in order.

"No, I think I'll stay up for a bit."

She kissed him. "You okay?" When he nodded, she said, "Don't be late."

Reine-Marie climbed the stairs to bed while he sat by the fireplace in the living room, Henri's head on his lap.

Their home creaked and then was quiet again, except for the sleet scratching the windows. He just needed a few quiet minutes to himself. To think.

Then Armand got up and began turning off lights. As he approached the front door to lock up, the handle began to turn. It was midnight. Everyone had gone home. Everyone else was in bed.

Gamache gestured Henri to his side, then the two moved swiftly to stand behind the slowly opening door. Henri's ears were pointed forward, his hackles up, a snarl coming from him.

331

But he stood slightly behind Gamache. In case.

Armand motioned with his hand, and Henri's growling stopped. But he remained alert. Ready to run away at any moment.

Gamache watched the door push open. And his racing mind remembered the car at the top of the hill, looking down into the village. And then withdrawing. Backing up. Waiting, perhaps, for a better time.

And this, he thought, was it.

The intruder was almost certainly armed, and Gamache was not. But he had the great advantage of surprise. And surprised he was, when he saw who appeared.

"What're you doing here?"

"Holy shit, Armand, you scared me to death."

Henri gave a little yelp of pleasure, and relief. His tail wagging furiously, he looked from Jean-Guy Beauvoir to the bowl of treats by the door, then back again. A dog with an agenda. A big one, with only one entry.

As Jean-Guy gave Henri a biscuit, Armand hung up his coat and reflected that it was the first time, ever, that Jean-Guy had called him Armand. He'd asked his son-in-law many times, since the marriage, to do that in private, but the younger man had never quite managed it. Settling on *patron* as a compromise.

But the shock had jarred loose an "Armand."

"Why are you here? Annie's all right, isn't she?"

"If she wasn't, I'd call," Jean-Guy pointed out. "Not drive all this way through a fucking awful night. Pardon my English."

He took off his boots and put on the slippers he kept by the door.

"Then what is it? Not that I'm unhappy to see you."

"Annie told me to come."

"Why?"

"Because I told her about Gélinas's suspicions and she's worried."

Armand was on the verge of asking why Beauvoir would do such a thing when he remembered that he told Reine-Marie everything. Or nearly everything.

And now Jean-Guy had found a confidante in his own wife. Gamache could hardly protest, though he wanted to.

Looking at the familiar face, at a man he trusted with his life, Armand felt a surge of relief, and was grateful to Annie for sending him down.

"Where's Gélinas now?" asked Beauvoir.

"In bed, asleep. Come with me," he said. "Are you hungry?"

"Starving," said Jean-Guy.

In the kitchen, Beauvoir went over to the cage in the corner. "How's Gracie settling in?"

He bent down, then straightened up and stepped back on seeing what was sleeping in there.

"Are dragons a real thing?" he asked.

"Puppy," said Gamache with conviction, putting a heaping helping of shepherd's pie in the microwave.

"Monkey?" asked Jean-Guy.

Armand refused to reply. The microwave beeped, the dinner was put out, a Coke was poured, and the two men sat at the pine table.

Jean-Guy took a long sip of his drink and a huge forkful of shepherd's pie, and looked at his father-in-law.

"Something's happened, *patron*. What is it?"

"I think I've found the motive for the murder, Jean-Guy."

Beauvoir lowered his fork.

"What is it?"

"First I need you to call the woman at McDermot and Ryan, and ask her about her name."

"Coldbrook?"

"Clairton. Find out why she really used that name in her correspondence with you. Why it was in a slightly different font. Push her, Jean-Guy. And if she won't tell you, say, *Deer Hunter*."

"Come on. You have to give me more."

"I can't. She has to come up with it on her own. I don't want you to lead her more than that. And even that you need to keep in your pocket unless it's absolutely necessary."

"*D'accord*." Beauvoir looked at his watch. "Five in the morning in the UK. Too early to call."

He looked at his father-in-law. At the drawn expression.

"But I'll call and leave a message asking her to get back to me as soon as she gets in."

Armand Gamache nodded. "*Merci*."

Beauvoir finished off his dinner while Gamache cut him a huge slice of Gabri's chocolate cake.

But didn't give it to him. Instead Gamache took the cake to the table and placed it in front of himself.

"Your turn."

"What do you mean?"

"You have something too, don't you?"

Beauvoir had been staring at the cake, and now he raised his eyes.

"Are you holding that hostage?"

"I am."

"You're a mean, mean man."

"And you have information I want."

"It's not so much information as a thought. You said the key to the crime lies in the fingerprints. You also said the prints on the gun are yours, but that you never touched it. That leaves two possibilities. You're lying. Or you're telling the truth, in which case someone else placed your prints there. Not many could do that. And do it so subtly. Not place a great goddamned print on the gun, but to blur it just enough. So that it's identifiable, but not obvious. I don't have the skill to do that, I doubt you do."

His father-in-law shook his head.

"But one man does," Jean-Guy continued. "A former Sûreté officer you yourself recruited, and then invited to the academy as a visiting professor. To teach tactics. A man who uses Machiavelli as a textbook. Manipulation. Hugo Charpentier."

"Yes," said Gamache, sliding the cake across the old pine table. "Hugo Charpentier could certainly do it."

"But why would he kill Leduc?"

"Now there's a good question."

"And he's hardly Leduc's match, physically. Leduc could knock him down with a look. Unless Charpentier's condition isn't as bad as it looks."

"It is," said Gamache. "I've seen his medical records. It is, in fact, worse than it looks."

Jean-Guy ate the chocolate cake and thought. "Then he might be a man with nothing to lose. And we know how dangerous they can be. Will Madame Coldbrook really be able to tell me why Leduc was killed?"

"I think she knows more, or suspects more, than she's willing to volunteer."

When the phone rang three hours later, Armand was still up. Sitting in the kitchen by the woodstove. A single light on. Staring ahead of him.

On his lap was a box. But not the one from the basement of the Royal Canadian Legion.

This one came from his own basement.

The phone did not ring a second time. Jean-Guy had obviously grabbed it.

A few minutes later, Armand heard footfalls on the stairs, soft and rapid. Slippered feet hurrying down.

It took Jean-Guy a moment to find Armand, looking first in the bedroom, then coming downstairs and checking the study. And finally, seeing the glow from the kitchen, he hurried in.

Gamache had placed the box on the floor and was just shoving it between the armchair and the wall when Jean-Guy arrived. He took in the furtive action but was too overwhelmed by what he'd heard from the UK to question it.

He stood in the doorway, his eyes wide.

Armand stood up and turned, and the two men faced each other.

"She confirmed it?"

Jean-Guy nodded, barely able to breathe, never mind speak.

Armand also nodded, a single, curt movement. It was confirmed.

Then he sank into the chair and he stared ahead. Out the windows, into the night.

"How did you know?" Jean-Guy asked quietly, taking the armchair across from him.

"The revolver," said Gamache. "There was no reason someone like Leduc would have one. Except there must have been a reason. A purpose. Last night, while everyone else watched *Mary Poppins*, Olivier came in here and watched *The Deer Hunter*."

Armand refocused on Jean-Guy. "Did you ever see the movie?"

"*Non.*"

"Neither had I. That's why we missed it when she added Clairton to her name. It meant nothing to us. Only to someone who knew *The Deer Hunter* well and had seen that scene. Did you have to say the name of the film to Madame Coldbrook?"

"*Oui.* I asked her about Clairton, but she just repeated that it was a mistake. It was only when I said *Deer Hunter* that it all came out."

Their conversation was seared into his brain.

"What did you say?" Madame Coldbrook had asked.

"*The Deer Hunter*," Beauvoir repeated. "The movie."

He prayed she wouldn't ask him why, because he had absolutely no idea.

"Then you know the scene, with the revolver. What they make Robert De Niro do."

"Yes," Beauvoir had lied.

There was a long pause.

"When did you know?" he asked.

"Not at first. Not from your email or even the beginning of our conversation. And I still don't know, for sure."

"But you suspect. Enough to send us that hint. You wanted me to ask, and I'm asking."

"Let me ask you a question, Inspector. Was there a special case made for the revolver?"

Now it was Beauvoir's turn to be silent, for a moment.

"Yes," he finally said.

"Then it's almost certainly true." He heard the long sigh all the way from England. "We get a lot of calls from police forces saying our handguns had been used in a crime. Most are street violence, gangs. Revolvers aren't common these days, but neither are they uncommon. It was only when you said that it was uncharacteristic for the victim to have a revolver and he was killed by a single shot to the temple—"

"You knew then," said Beauvoir.

"I wondered. I thought it was something you should consider."

"Then why didn't you tell me during our call?" he asked. "Why that vague hint?"

"It's against company policy to admit our revolvers are used for something that cruel. I could be fired. But I needed you to know. I realize it wasn't the most obvious of hints, but it was the best I could do. I was hoping you'd know that scene from the film."

"I didn't, but a colleague saw it last night and put it together. Why did you ask about the special case for the revolver?"

"From what I gather, a ritual is often created. A special case is made. It becomes a sort of ceremony."

He could hear the disgust in her voice.

"I could be wrong," she said.

"But you don't think you are, do you?"

Beauvoir was still lost, but one answer had appeared on the very edges of his mind. An outlier. A terrible monster of an idea. Lurking, pacing, just beyond his reason.

And with the next thing Madame Coldbrook said, it raced across the border, clawing its way to the very front of his mind.

"Only a revolver can be used. The barrel has to spin for the game to work. Was he killed playing it, do you think?"

The game.

The blood raced from Beauvoir's extremities so quickly he almost dropped the phone.

The game.

They now knew why Leduc had a revolver.

In the single light of the kitchen, Jean-Guy looked at his father-in-law.

Gamache was staring at the floor and shaking his head slightly.

"You can't have known, *patron*. It must've been going on for years."

Jean-Guy immediately regretted that last statement, as Gamache winced.

Then he looked up and met Jean-Guy's gaze.

"Can you imagine?" he said quietly. "Their terror? And no one did anything to stop it. I did nothing to stop it."

"You didn't know."

"I could have fired him. I should've fired him. I kept him on to keep an eye on him while I gathered more information on his corruption. I was looking in that direction and completely missed the worst thing Leduc was doing."

"No one saw it."

"Oh, someone saw it," said Gamache, his rage bursting out.

He managed to rein it in, but it roiled just below his skin. Turning it red.

"You're right," said Jean-Guy. "Someone knew what was happening. They put a gun to Leduc's head and pulled the trigger."

He saw a look on the older man's face. A primitive, primal, savage moment. Of satisfaction. And then it was gone.

"Was that the motive?"

"*Oui*," said Gamache. "I think so."

Madame Coldbrook had asked if Leduc had died playing the game. He hadn't. Never did. But still, it killed him. He'd been murdered. Executed. Not in the game, but because of it.

"Whoever killed him tried to implicate you," Beauvoir said. "By placing your fingerprints on the revolver. Making it look like you'd murdered Leduc. It was Charpentier, wasn't it?"

Gamache looked at the kitchen clock. Three thirty in the morning.

"We need to get some sleep," he said. "We have a big day ahead of us."

But sleep eluded Jean-Guy. He lay staring at the ceiling. Gamache had asked if he could imagine. He lay there and tried to imagine what it was like for those cadets, who were not just cadets. They were someone's sons and daughters. Someone's children.

And he imagined his own child, in that situation. With no one doing anything to stop it. To help them. And Jean-Guy began to understand that look of savagery on his father-in-law's face.

But he also, then, remembered something else. The subtle movement of Gamache's foot as he shoved something between the chair and the wall.

Unable to sleep, Jean-Guy got up and tiptoed down the stairs, into the kitchen. Turning on the lamp, he found the box and picked it up. And held it, staring at the lid. There were fingerprints on it. One set, and one set only, he knew.

Gamache's.

He stared at the shoe box. It wasn't one of the ones from the historical society. He knew that. This one was private and personal.

And in it sat the answer to so many questions.

Then he slowly bent down and replaced it.

Turning around, he almost fainted. There in the doorway stood Gamache.

"Did no one tell you, Jean-Guy, if you're going to do a clandestine search, never turn the light on?"

"I missed that class."

Gamache smiled and, walking forward, he stopped in front of Jean-Guy and looked from the man to the box on the floor, then back to the man. "*Merci*."

"I shouldn't have even considered looking," said Jean-Guy. "I'm sorry."

"*Non*, not at all. It's human to be curious. It was superhuman to put it back down. Thank you for respecting my privacy."

Then Armand Gamache walked past Jean-Guy, picked up the old box, and handed it to his son-in-law.

Without a word, he returned upstairs, while Jean-Guy returned to the armchair and opened the box.

CHAPTER 39

———

Armand Gamache looked at the cadets, one at a time.

First Nathaniel, then Huifen, then Jacques, and finally his eyes rested on Amelia.

"I know," he said quietly.

Jacques turned his head slightly, eyes narrowing. "Know what?"

"I know what happened in Leduc's rooms."

There was silence then. The cadets looked at each other, and then all, naturally, turned to Huifen.

"What?" she asked. There was defiance in her voice.

Jean-Guy Beauvoir was sitting a few benches back. He and Armand had brought the young people up to the chapel first thing in the morning. They needed to speak to them, and they needed someplace private. And neutral. And peaceful.

"I've long known that Serge Leduc was corrupt," said Gamache. "I came out of retirement to clean up the academy. And not just of corruption. It was clear by the quality of new agents entering the Sûreté that something was very wrong at the school. They were competent in the techniques, but they were also cruel. Not all, of course, but enough. More than enough. There was something wrong either with the recruitment process, or with the training. Or both."

As he spoke, Commander Gamache watched them. And they watched him.

If Gamache and Beauvoir thought the four would break down and tell them everything, they were wrong. The conspiracy of silence was so ingrained as to be almost unbreakable.

"The first thing I did was fire most of your professors, and I brought in my own. Officers with real-life experience of investigations. Men and

women with integrity. But who also know that with power comes temptation. Those are the real threats to Sûreté agents. The self-inflicted wounds."

Jean-Guy could hear their breathing now. At least one, perhaps more, of
the cadets was on the verge of hyperventilating.

And still they were still. And silent.

"But I kept Serge Leduc, the Duke, on."

"Why?" asked Nathaniel.

Looking at the pale young man, Gamache tried to catch his own breath.
He looked down at his hands, clasped together. Holding on tight.

Serge Leduc might have done great damage. But so had he.

If he expected the students to tell him the truth, he had to be willing to
do the same.

"I didn't know," he said, looking back up and into the young man's cold
eyes. "I thought he was a brute, a sadist. I thought he was corrupt. I thought
I could gather enough evidence against him to put him in prison, so he
couldn't do the same damage someplace else. I thought I could control him
so that while I was there, his abuses would stop."

"Don't believe everything you think," mumbled Amelia.

Gamache nodded. "They did not stop. It never occurred to me he could
be that sick."

"When did you find out?" asked Huifen.

"Last night, while watching the movie."

"*Mary Poppins?*" she asked. She must've missed that scene.

"*The Deer Hunter.* The one Olivier was watching." He leaned toward
them. "I'm going to get you help."

"We don't need your help," snapped Jacques. "There's nothing wrong
with us."

Gamache thought before he spoke again. "Do you know where this comes
from?"

He smoothed his fingers over the deep scar by his temple. Three of the
cadets shook their heads, but Jacques just glared.

"There was a raid I led, on a factory. A young agent, not much older than
you, was being held hostage and time was running out. We gathered as much
intelligence as possible on the terrain and the hostage takers. Their number,
their weapons, where they were likely to be positioned. And then we went in.
Inspector Beauvoir here was critically injured, shot in the abdomen."

The cadets turned in their seats to look back at Inspector Beauvoir.

"Three agents lost their lives," Gamache continued. "I went to their
funerals. Walked behind the caskets. Spent time with their mothers and

fathers and husbands and wives and children. And then I went into therapy. Because I was broken. I still see a counselor when I feel overwhelmed. It's human. It's our humanity that allows us to find criminals. But it also means we care, and get hurt in places that don't bleed. Every day, when I see this scar in the mirror," this time he didn't touch it, "it reminds me of the pain. Mine. But mostly theirs. But it also reminds me, every day, of the healing. Of the kindness that exists. *We are introduced to Goodness every day. Even in drawing-rooms among a crowd of faults.* It's so easy to get mired in the all too obvious cruelty of the world. It's natural. But to really heal, we need to recognize the goodness too."

"It wasn't our fault," said Jacques.

"That's not what I mean. I think you know that."

"Why should we trust you?" demanded Jacques. "Three agents lost their lives because of you. I saw the recording. I saw what happened. And I also saw that somehow you came out of it a hero."

Gamache's jaw clamped shut, the muscles working.

Beauvoir stirred but said nothing.

"It's a trick," said Jacques, turning to the others. "He's just trying to get us to say things that will look bad. We have to stick together. Don't tell him anything."

"You don't have to tell me anything," agreed Gamache. "Only if you want to."

He paused, to let them think, before going on.

"When did it start?"

He asked Jacques and Huifen. Who said nothing.

Then he turned to the other two.

Nathaniel opened his mouth, but a sound from Huifen made him close it. It was Amelia who finally spoke.

"When I refused to have sex with him, he decided to fuck with me in every other way," she said, hurrying on before she changed her mind. "I had to do it, he said, or be expelled. He said you never wanted me there, and he was the one fighting to keep me. But if I refused, he'd let you throw me out."

Gamache listened and nodded.

"You believed him, of course. Why wouldn't you?"

"I didn't believe him," said Amelia. "I knew he was a shit. And you seemed so," she searched for the word, "kind."

They looked at each other, in a moment of intimacy that was almost painful. Jean-Guy felt he should look away, but did not.

He knew what was in that box. And he knew what was in Gamache's stare. And he also knew that Amelia Choquet almost certainly had no idea who she was.

And who Armand Gamache was.

"But I didn't think you could stand up to him," she admitted. "I couldn't take that chance. You'd let him stay, after all."

It wasn't meant as a mortal blow, just as an explanation. But Jean-Guy could see the internal bleeding those words produced. Gamache was reduced to silence.

"We trusted you, sir," said Huifen. "We thought when you arrived it would end, but it only got worse."

Jean-Guy thought he could hear Gamache's heart pounding in his chest, and expected it to explode at any moment.

"I made a terrible mistake," he said. "And you all paid for it. I'll do all I can to make it up to you."

And then there was another sound. Completely unexpected.

Laughter.

"The Duke was right," said Jacques. "You are weak."

His laughter was replaced by a sneer.

"Leduc made me stronger. I arrived a kid. Spoiled, soft. But he toughened me up. Got me ready for my job as a Sûreté agent. He said nothing would scare me again, and he was right. He chose the most promising agents and made them even tougher."

"You're wrong," said Huifen. "He chose the biggest threats to him. The independent-minded. Those who'd one day have the backbone to stand up to what he was teaching. Do you remember what you were like that first day at the academy? I do. You weren't soft and spoiled. Leduc told you you were, but you weren't. You were funny, and smart, and eager. And you wanted to help, to do good."

"I was a kid."

"You were kind," said Huifen. "Now look at you. Look at me. He chose us. And he broke us."

"I'm not broken," said Jacques. "I'm stronger than ever."

"Things are strongest where they're broken," said Amelia. "Isn't that right, sir? You put that on the blackboard that first week."

"As long as they're allowed to mend," said Gamache. "Yes."

"Three years."

They looked at Huifen. She spoke matter-of-factly. Just giving a report to the commanding officer.

342

"It began the first month we arrived. We'd never know when the call would come, and we'd have to go to his rooms. Sometimes it would be on our own, but mostly it was with others."

"What would happen?" asked Gamache. So clearly not wanting to hear, but needing to know.

"He'd bring out his revolver," she said. "He made a whole ritual of it, putting it on a tray engraved with the Sûreté motto. He'd choose one of us to carry it into the living room."

"It was an honor," muttered Nathaniel.

"But the biggest honor was reserved for the cadet chosen to carry the next tray," said Huifen. "The one with the bullet."

"We'd draw lots," said Nathaniel. "The long straw won."

He started to giggle, and when he couldn't stop and was on the verge of hysteria, Amelia touched his arm. And steadied him.

"I won," Nathaniel said, his voice barely audible now. "Three times."

He sat up straight then and looked right at Gamache. His eyes defiant.

"Three times I had to put that single bullet in the chamber. And spin the barrel . . ."

When Nathaniel couldn't go on, Huifen stepped in.

"And bring the gun up." She placed her finger to her temple, mimicking a handgun.

When she couldn't go on, Amelia stepped in.

"And pull the trigger," she said softly.

"Three times," whispered Nathaniel.

"Twice," said Amelia. She raised her chin and compressed her lips.

Neither Huifen nor Jacques said anything, and with horror Gamache realized they'd lost count.

"You are very brave," said Gamache, holding their eyes that held a touch of madness.

"If I was brave," said Nathaniel, "I'd have refused to do it."

Gamache shook his head vehemently. "*Non.* You had no choice. Sitting here now, safe in this chapel, it seems you did. But you didn't. It was Serge Leduc who was the coward."

"That last time," whispered Nathaniel, staring at Gamache, his eyes wide and tears rolling slowly down his face, "I prayed it would go off. I wet myself."

His voice was barely audible.

Armand Gamache stood up and drew the young man to him, and held him tight as he sobbed.

Broken. But now, perhaps, healing.

There was a slight sound behind Beauvoir and he turned to see Paul Gélinas closing the chapel door.

And then the RCMP officer joined Beauvoir.

"He made them play Russian roulette?" said Gélinas.

"The man was a monster," said Beauvoir.

Gélinas nodded. "Yes. But someone finally stopped him. And now we know why. We have the missing piece. Motive. Serge Leduc was killed with a single bullet to his brain. And we know the killer is in this room. No matter how well deserved, it's still murder."

Paul Gélinas at least had the decency to look saddened by the fact that they'd have to arrest a person who had dispatched a monster.

"It could have been self-defense," said Jean-Guy. "Or even an accident. Maybe Leduc did it to himself."

"Did he seem the sort to take that chance? To put the revolver to his own temple and pull the trigger, the way he made the cadets do? To play Russian roulette?"

"No," Beauvoir admitted.

"No. And there was no residue on his hands. Someone did that to him. Someone who knew about the revolver and the game. Someone who wanted to end it."

"Commander Gamache didn't know."

"Maybe he found out just that night," said Gélinas. "And went there to confront Leduc. And killed him."

Gélinas got up, crossed himself, then bent down to whisper in Beauvoir's ear.

"Out of respect for Monsieur Gamache, I won't arrest him here, now. We can consider this sanctuary. But we're going back to the academy this morning. You need to be prepared. I'll get a warrant first. Then I'll be coming for him."

"You're making a mistake," said Beauvoir. "He didn't kill Leduc."

"Does that look like a man who doesn't have murder on his mind?"

Gélinas gestured toward Commander Gamache, at the front of the chapel, surrounded by the cadets.

The RCMP officer straightened up.

"Your father-in-law likes poetry. The death of the Duke was almost poetic, don't you think? Knowing what we now know. A bullet through his brain. *Come hither, and behold your fate.*"

Jean-Guy heard the door click shut as he watched the cadets and Armand at the front of the chapel.

There was nothing at all poetic about what had happened. Or what was about to happen.

CHAPTER 40

———

Commander Gamache stood at the back of the classroom, listening as Professor Charpentier finished his lecture.

His students were third-year cadets, those who already had the basics and were into the next, critical level.

Advanced tactics.

Gamache watched as Hugo Charpentier, perspiring freely, explained that tactics wasn't about the best position to get in to shoot someone.

"If you have to do that, then you've already failed," he said. "A successful tactician rarely gets to that stage. It's about manipulation, about anticipation. About outmaneuvering your opponent intellectually. Seeing his moves even before he does. And limiting them. Guiding him, forcing him to do what you want, without him even realizing it. Whether that opponent is a mob boss, a banker, or a serial killer."

Charpentier turned to the large blackboard and wrote, "Your brain is your weapon."

He turned back to them.

"Any idiot can use a gun. But it takes real skill, real patience and control to use your mind."

A hand went up and Charpentier pointed. "Yes, Cadet Montreaux."

"Was it an idiot, then, who killed the Duke?"

"Now there's an interesting question. What do you think?"

"I think since the investigators haven't yet made an arrest, the killer can't be that stupid."

"Good point," said Charpentier. "I've been trying to teach you about being a Sûreté officer, not a killer. Murderers, of course, need to use a weapon of some sort. But again, the most successful start off using their brains."

"And in your opinion, Professor, did the murderer of Serge Leduc use his brain?"

The students turned around, surprised by the voice from the back of the room.

Hugo Charpentier smiled.

"*Oui*, Commander. In my opinion, it started with a thought, that became a plan, that ripened into an action. A good one."

"Good?"

"Not, perhaps, in the legal or moral sense," said Charpentier. "But it meets the criteria."

"Of what? A good tactician?" Gamache asked across the field of cadets.

"A great tactician," said Charpentier.

"Based on what?"

"On the simplicity of the crime. On the apparent simplicity of the scene."

"Apparent?"

"Well, yes. Once looked at closely, the depth of evidence becomes clear. Layer after layer, carefully placed."

"Put there to misdirect?"

"To direct. Like a sheepdog, nipping at your heels, Chief Inspector."

"Commander now," Gamache reminded him.

"Once a homicide investigator . . ." Charpentier left that hanging.

"And once a great tactician . . ." replied Gamache. "We need to talk. May we?"

Charpentier looked at the clock above the doorway.

"Tomorrow you have a field test," he reminded the students as he wheeled between the desks. "Back in the factory. If you need to resort to violence, it must be controlled. You use tactical thinking, with an emphasis on thinking, even as the bullets fly. As soon as it devolves into chaos, into panic, you're doomed. You die. You control yourself, you control the situation. So far, I'm dumbfounded to report, you've failed every time. Been killed every time. We've been over the flaws in your last attempt. You have one more day to come up with a plan that will work. Now, go away."

"Yessir," came the chorus, as chairs scraped loudly on the floor.

But the cadets didn't want to go away. They milled about as Charpentier arrived before Commander Gamache, and waited to hear what these two men were about to say to each other.

"Go," Charpentier demanded, and they went.

And Armand Gamache and Hugo Charpentier were left alone.

"Where's Commander Gamache?" Gélinas asked, as he entered the conference room at the academy.

"He had some work to do," said Isabelle Lacoste. "He'll be back soon."

"Please tell me where he went."

Paul Gélinas stood erect, his attitude and speech formal. Behind him, on either side, were two tall young Sûreté agents. Recent academy graduates. Their smug faces, if not their youth, told her that.

Getting up from her seat at the conference table, she walked over to the RCMP officer.

"Is there something I can help you with?"

"You know why I'm here," he said, not unkindly. "I didn't want to humiliate Monsieur Gamache in front of his friends and family."

"He's not easily humiliated," said Lacoste, though her face had grown pale and her hands were tingling. As they always did when entering dangerous territory.

"I waited to do this until after we'd left Three Pines," said Gélinas. "Out of professional respect, and awareness that he did us all a favor."

"By killing Serge Leduc?" she asked.

"*Oui*."

"You're here to arrest Monsieur Gamache?"

"*Oui*." He spoke softly, so that the agents behind him wouldn't hear what he said next. "And if you don't tell me where he is, Chief Inspector, I will have to arrest you too."

Isabelle Lacoste nodded slowly and thrust out her lower lip in thought. Then she walked back to her seat, picked up her laptop, hit a few keys, and carried it to Gélinas.

"Before going to his meeting this morning, Monsieur Gamache came by to apologize for going over my head and inviting you into the investigation."

"You didn't know he'd done that?"

"No. He went directly to Chief Superintendent Brunel. She made the arrangements. Monsieur Gamache explained that when he heard you were in Montréal, visiting the RCMP headquarters there, it seemed too good an opportunity to pass up."

"To have me as the independent observer."

"To watch, yes. But mostly to be watched."

"*Pardon?*"

Lacoste turned the laptop around, and Gélinas's eyes widened a little and his lips compressed, just a little. Tiny changes that did not escape Lacoste.

He took a small step away from her and the laptop. "When Commander Gamache returns, have him come see me. I'll be in my rooms. He has a great deal of explaining to do."

"As do you, sir."

She slowly lowered the lid of the laptop.

"When did you know?" Gamache asked Charpentier.

He'd taken a seat and the two men were eye to eye.

"Not for a long time. In fact, I don't really know anything even now, except what I was able to deduce."

"And by that you mean guess?" said Gamache, and saw the sweaty younger man smile.

"Your actions, sir, made no sense," Charpentier said. "Especially your actions toward Deputy Commissioner Gélinas. Until I factored in one possibility. And that became a probability. And that eventually became a certainty. It explained everything."

"Go on," said Gamache.

"Serge Leduc was rotten, corrupt. He was more than that, obviously, but let's just focus on what you knew when you first arrived."

Gamache nodded.

"Leduc had stolen millions in the building of the academy. Taking kickbacks and bribes from contractors," said Charpentier. "Perhaps even allowing substandard construction."

"We're having the buildings inspected, yes," said Gamache.

"A very good idea. But you had a problem. While there was a ton of suggestive material, there was no smoking gun, so to speak. You had to find hard evidence. You had to find the money."

"It would help."

"It would nail him. And he knew it. He might have initially thought you'd taken the job as commander to get control of the academy—"

"And to be fair, that was the main reason."

"*Oui*, but it went hand in hand with gathering enough evidence on Leduc to arrest him. To get him out of circulation. It didn't take Leduc long to realize that was on your agenda."

"I told him as much."

"And so began a game of cat and mouse," said Charpentier. "But while intelligent, Leduc wasn't very bright. He was no match for you, and he knew it. He must've felt your breath on his neck. He became desperate. And so he did something he should never have done."

"He contacted his partner," said Gamache, watching Charpentier closely. "His very silent partner. The one who'd really planned most of this. The one who knew how and where to hide the money."

Now it was Charpentier's turn to watch Gamache closely.

"So I asked myself," Gamache went on, "where was this partner? Where had he been all this time? In the academy? Not likely. In the Sûreté? Again, possible but not likely. That rot had been removed. So where was he? And there was only one answer. Far away. Beyond suspicion."

"*Oui*." Charpentier smiled and moved his wheelchair back and forth, by inches. Agitated. Or excited.

"But when Leduc broke the cardinal rule and contacted him a few months ago, Leduc himself became the target," said Gamache. "And needed to be taken care of. The partner returned, accepting a job that surprised everyone."

Charpentier stopped rocking his chair and went very still.

"Where's Jacques?" asked Huifen.

"I don't know," said Nathaniel, and looked at Amelia, who frowned and shrugged.

"Wasn't he in class with you?" she said.

The four cadets had been driven back to the academy that morning, after their conversation in the chapel with Gamache.

"Commander Gamache showed up to speak to Charpentier, and we were dismissed early. I was supposed to meet Jacques here. He hasn't been in?"

Huifen looked around the study hall. A few cadets were sitting at the long tables, reading or tapping on their tablets. But there was no Jacques.

"He'll be here soon," said Amelia. "Don't worry."

"Why is Gamache speaking to Charpentier?" asked Huifen. "What's he telling him? Is he telling him about us?"

"Why would he?" asked Amelia.

Huifen sat down, but immediately got up.

"What's the matter?" asked Amelia.

But on seeing Huifen's face, she also rose. As did Nathaniel.

"What's wrong?" he asked.

"You know more than you're saying," said Gamache.

"Better than knowing less, don't you think?" said Charpentier.

"The time has come, Hugo, to tell me everything."

The young professor nodded. "I agree. I began to wonder how much you really knew when you didn't tell Deputy Commissioner Gélinas about the four cadets. You told Inspector Beauvoir and Chief Inspector Lacoste that they'd been taken to Three Pines, but you kept it from him. I thought there could be only one explanation. You didn't trust him. And yet you were the one who'd invited him here. To do that, you didn't just go over Lacoste's head, you went behind her back. An uncharacteristic thing for you to do. I knew there had to be a very good reason. You thought Deputy Commissioner Gélinas was Leduc's partner. His very silent, very senior partner."

"You've done well," said Gamache. "You know a surprising amount."

"Not surprising, really. You should know me by now, sir. You recruited me."

"And Michel Brébeuf trained you."

"At your suggestion."

"Yes. We all have strengths and weaknesses. Michel's greatest strength is that he's a masterful tactician. It's how he was able to get away with so much for so long. And he trained you. Well."

Now Charpentier grew wary.

"There is, of course, another possibility," said Gamache. "Why I specifically invited Deputy Commissioner Gélinas to be the independent observer. Yes, I might have suspected him—"

"Or maybe you didn't, at all," said Charpentier, guessing where Gamache was going. "Maybe Gélinas wasn't the one you had your eye on. He was another whale. A great lumpen redirection. If anyone grew suspicious, you wanted that suspicion to fall on the senior RCMP officer. Who'd been away in Europe. Who had access to private Swiss banks. Your real target would think you were focused on Gélinas, and that would leave him unguarded."

"You think I'm that calculating?"

"I know you are, *patron*. I've seen it. How you've maneuvered through the rat's nest of the Sûreté. You don't survive as long as you have without being cunning."

"You, of course, would know," said Gamache, and Charpentier colored a bit, unsure if that was a compliment or an accusation.

"But I quit, remember?" Gamache continued. "Burned out."

"And now you're back. Risen from the ashes. With a vengeance."

"*Non*." Gamache shook his head. "Not a vengeance. Never that."

"Service, Integrity, Justice," said Charpentier. "Despite all that's happened to you?"

"Because of it. A belief of convenience isn't much use, is it?"

"Why are you here?" Charpentier asked.

"In this room? Just to talk."

Hugo Charpentier looked toward the closed door and struggled to get up from the chair.

"What's happening out there?"

"Nothing that concerns you, Hugo. Please, sit down."

Charpentier glanced once more at the door, then sat.

"More misdirection, monsieur?" he asked warily, wearily.

"Depends where you were heading," said Gamache. "But I'm not here to talk to you about Serge Leduc's corruption. I'm here to talk about his murder."

"The two are connected, *non*?"

"Serge Leduc's corruption went far beyond simply his ethics. Far beyond money. His very being had become corrupt, twisted. Perverted." Gamache leaned forward, into Charpentier's personal space. And whispered, "*He made them weep before he died*. Someone knew. And someone killed him for it."

"Do you think the Commander's going to tell everyone?" Huifen asked. "What we did?"

"Would it matter?" asked Amelia.

"Maybe not to you," said Huifen. "You're already an outsider, but it would to Jacques."

"Why?"

"You don't understand," said Huifen. "You can't. Jacques's whole thing is about being admired. The strong leader. The hero."

"Head cadet," said Nathaniel.

"*Oui*. But if it came out, what we allowed Leduc to do, he'd be humiliated. No one would understand. They'd think we were weak, stupid. They'd look at us like we were freaks. He'd rather die than have that happen."

"You're kidding, right?" said Nathaniel. "That's just a figure of speech, right?"

"Fucking Leduc knew that about him," said Huifen, walking rapidly out of the study hall as she spoke. "He used it against him. Feeding that need in Jacques. Until Jacques would do anything to stay on the pedestal. Contort into anything Leduc wanted."

"You hated him," said Amelia, almost running to keep up with Huifen. "Leduc."

"Of course I did. And so did you. But Jacques's feelings were more complicated."

Nathaniel reached out and grabbed her arm, forcing her to stop. The corridors, now teeming with cadets getting from class to class, surged around them.

"What? Tell us."

"You could see it, couldn't you?" said Huifen. "Jacques and the Duke were close."

"Yes, we know that."

"No, very close. Like father and son. He believed everything the Duke told him. He accepted everything he said and did, believing Leduc when he said it was for his own good. Jacques trusted him completely."

"What father does that to his son?" asked Nathaniel.

"Have him put a gun to his head and pull the trigger?" asked Huifen. "For Leduc, it was never about love. It was about control. You've had it for a few months, Jacques had it for three years."

"So did you," Amelia pointed out.

"Believe me, I'm fucked up, but nothing compared to Jacques. I never saw the Duke as anything other than crazy. I was trapped. But Jacques was there by choice. Not at first, but by second year Leduc could make him do anything. If he'd told Jacques to murder another cadet, he probably would've done it."

"Do you really believe that?" asked Amelia.

Huifen compressed her lips and nodded.

"And now that Leduc is gone?" asked Amelia.

But she knew the answer.

Jacques was directionless, rudderless. The grip on the tiller was gone. And Jacques was lost.

"I wish you'd known him before. He was . . ." Huifen searched for the word. "Glorious. Smart and funny. Sweet. A natural leader. The Duke saw that, and ruined it. Because he could."

Huifen spoke with such venom the other two exchanged glances.

CHAPTER 41

—

"Come in." Brébeuf stepped back from the threshold.

"You don't seem surprised, Michel," said Gamache.

He'd come directly there after speaking with Charpentier, Michel Brébeuf's protégé and perhaps his greatest success.

"I wasn't exactly expecting you, but I'm not altogether surprised either," said Brébeuf, waving toward the sitting area.

Armand Gamache glanced around the little room, swiftly taking in the details. In the months since Michel had arrived at the academy, Armand had never once been in his private quarters.

He was surprised by how many things he recognized. The framed photographs of family. A couple of paintings that had once hung in the Brébeuf home.

Michel had brought his favorite chair too. Which he was now offering to Armand. Gamache sat, and Brébeuf took the chair across from him.

"What can I do for you, Armand?"

"You must have known I'd figure it out."

"Ah." Brébeuf sighed. "So that's it."

He managed a small, almost wistful, smile and studied his guest.

"It's possible I've always underestimated you, Armand. I've loved you and admired you, but maybe part of me has always seen you as a boy. Funny, isn't it? All that we've been through. I saw you go off to Cambridge, saw you get married, have children, become a senior officer in the Sûreté, and yet part of me will always think of you as the boy who lost his parents. The boy I needed to protect."

"You betrayed me, Michel, years ago. I was almost killed because of you."

"I never meant that to happen."

"Really? The master tactician never saw that coming?"

"It was a mistake," admitted Brébeuf.

"And was killing Leduc also a mistake?"

Brébeuf slowly shook his head, holding Armand's eyes the whole time. "*Non.* That was intended. I knew that would happen almost from the day I arrived. When I discovered two things."

"*Oui?*"

Gamache knew he was being played, was being led. Guided or misguided, as Charpentier would have it. But he needed to know.

"Serge Leduc was a stupid man," said Brébeuf. "A man driven by an infected ego. But he was also a powerful man, I'll give him that. A charismatic personality. Stupidity and power. A dangerous combination, as we've found out many times, eh, Armand? Especially for anyone young and vulnerable. He'd have made a good cult leader, if he hadn't joined the Sûreté and ended up here. In fact, he'd turned the academy into a sort of cult, hadn't he?"

Gamache listened, but didn't nod. Didn't agree or disagree. He was bending much of his will to disengaging from Brébeuf, while still listening closely.

"After that party in your rooms the first night, Serge Leduc decided to make me his best friend. Bound by a shared loathing of you. He assumed we had that in common. He had no idea of my depth of feeling for you."

Michel Brébeuf looked at Gamache with undisguised tenderness.

But what, Armand asked himself, did that tenderness itself disguise? What was lurking, swishing its tail, in those depths?

"And yet you spent quite a lot of time with Leduc. You said it was because you were lonely."

"That was part of it," Brébeuf admitted. "And perhaps I was attracted by his obvious respect for me. Something I hadn't felt from anyone for a long time."

Brébeuf smiled in the impish way Gamache knew well. Here was a man he'd known longer than anyone else on earth. A person he had loved, man and boy, for decades.

And despite all that had happened, he still felt that tug. As though Michel had coiled himself around Armand's DNA. What happened in childhood had fused itself to Gamache. The losses, but also the laughter and hilarity, the roaring freedom, the friendship. The friendship. The friendship. They were brothers-in-arms. Storming the castle.

And now he looked at that smile and could have wept.

"What happened, Michel?"

"That first night, he invited me back to his rooms. After too many drinks, Leduc brought out his revolver."

Armand had actually been asking about their friendship. About where and when and how Michel had veered away. And fallen off a rampart in the darkness.

But the answer he got was far different.

"He told me what he did with the gun," said Michel. "I've done many things I'm ashamed of. Many things that cannot and should not be forgiven. But what Leduc told me that night shocked and sickened even me."

Brébeuf's gaze drifted beyond Gamache and above him, toward the door. His eye caught something and Michel suddenly smiled, as though surprised by something pleasant. He gestured toward it.

Armand tried to stop himself, but his head turned and his eyes followed.

There, above the door, was a small frame. And in it was what looked like a stylized red rose. But wasn't.

Gamache recognized it immediately. He himself had given it to Michel years, decades, ago.

It had once been Armand's most precious possession.

It was a handkerchief. A Christmas gift from Armand's mother to his father.

He remembered watching her embroider his father's initials, HG, in the corner of each one. Zora had offered to help. His mother thanked her, but refused. She wanted to do them herself. Not because it was easy, but because it was difficult. Embroidery did not come naturally to her. And so the HGs were slightly bizarre, and only really intelligible to someone who knew what they were meant to be.

Some looked like H6. Some looked like #Q. Some had tiny dots of blood, where she'd pricked herself.

But all said the same thing, if you knew how to read them.

HG, Honoré Gamache, was loved. By Amelia.

His father had carried one in his pocket every day of his life.

The morning after their deaths, Armand had gone into their room. The scent of them, the sense of them, almost too much to bear. The clothing. The book. The bookmark. The bedside clock, still ticking. He'd thought that strange. Surely it should have stopped.

And there, on the chest of drawers, a clean handkerchief for a day that would never come.

He'd shoved it in his pocket. And kept it with him always.

Until one day, while playing king of the castle, Michel had fallen and gashed his knee. Armand had taken the handkerchief out of his pocket and pressed it to the wound. And when the bleeding had stopped, he'd looked at it, then at Michel, who was wiping away tears with the sleeve of his sweater.

Armand brought out his penknife and made a very small cut in his own finger. Michel took a stuttering breath, tears stopping as he watched Armand dab his finger on the blood-soaked handkerchief.

On that day they had become more than brothers-in-arms.

"Blood brothers," Armand had said, offering the handkerchief to Michel. Who took it. And kept it. All these years.

And now, a lifetime later, it had returned. Armand's *mappa mundi*. The map of his world. The mundane and the magnificent, fused.

The blood had made a sort of rose pattern, just touching the HG in the corner.

Armand looked away and met Michel's eyes.

"I'm many things," said Michel. "But I am not a murderer."

"Then who killed Serge Leduc?"

Paul Gélinas stood at the window, looking out across the fields. A few months ago, he'd been in Paris, looking out over the Jardin des Tuileries. He'd been in Luxembourg, admiring the medieval ruins. He'd stood on the Bridge of Sighs in Venice.

Now he surveyed this endless, lifeless prairie.

"*Let's go fly a kite*," he sang under his breath.

In showing him the laptop, Lacoste had shown him his fate. His barren future.

And now he waited for the knock on the door.

"I've done nothing," said Huifen, hurrying along the corridor. "I should have, but I didn't. It's Jacques I'm worried about."

"What did he do?" asked Nathaniel, running beside her.

"It's what he's about to do that worries me."

"Where're we going?" asked Amelia. "Wait. We have to have a plan. We can't just run around looking for him."

"I do have a plan," said Huifen, staring straight ahead of her as she half walked, half ran. "I think I know where he is."

"Where?"

"The factory. The mock-up."

"Shit," whispered Amelia. But she knew Huifen was probably right.

Where else would the Golden Boy, disgraced, go but to the place that had defeated him? That had exposed his flaws, his faults.

Where he had been killed. Over and over again.

What was one more death?

"*Merde*," Amelia heard Nathaniel mutter.

And they picked up their pace.

"Tell me," said Armand.

Like the ghost stories they'd once told on sleepovers, hoping to scare the *merde* out of each other, now Michel told his final story.

But was the boogeyman real this time? Was he in the room with them? Not hiding under the bed or in a closet, but sitting in plain sight? Unspectacular and always human.

"That first night, when he invited me back to his rooms, Leduc was talking about the new cadets, and not in glowing terms. But he said he knew how to fix them. After a few more drinks, he went into his bedroom and returned carrying a tray. There was something formal, ceremonial, about the way he held it in front of him. As a person might when handing out medals."

Gamache could see Leduc, short and powerful, walking across the room, his stubby arms out, holding the tray. Making his offering to his hero. Thinking Michel Brébeuf, of all people, would appreciate what he had done. What he was doing.

"It was the last thing I expected to see," said Michel. "An old revolver. But then I realized it wasn't really old. The design was. Classic. But the gun itself was fairly new. I picked it up."

He mimicked weighing the weapon in his hand.

"I'd never held one. Have you?"

"Now, yes. But not before."

Before a bullet was put in Leduc's brain.

"Makes our service pistols seem puny. Though I know they're actually far more effective."

"Depends on the effect you're going for," said Armand.

"True. And the revolver was perfect for Leduc's needs. He told me about the first time he'd handed it to a cadet. He'd had the revolver for a year but couldn't bring himself to do it. Not because he felt it was wrong, he was quick to assure me, but because he was worried the cadet would tell someone. But then he realized he had to work up to it. To choose the right student. Not a weak one, as you might expect. Those he could already control. No. He went for the strongest. The ones who might not bend to his will."

Brébeuf thought for a moment, throwing his mind back to that night.

"I didn't know what he was talking about, and he could see that. Finally he came right out and told me. He had cadets play Russian roulette with that revolver."

He looked down at his hand, as though he still held the gun. And then he raised his eyes.

"I came to your rooms that night, after I left Leduc. I wanted to tell you."

"Why didn't you?"

"I thought by our conversation that you already knew. When I asked what you were going to do about Leduc, you told me to worry about my side of the street, and you'd worry about yours. I took that as a sign that you knew what Leduc was doing. And intended to act."

Armand shook his head. "I only found out last night. I should've known earlier, but it honestly never, ever occurred to me someone could do that to the cadets. Not even a sadist like Leduc. But it does explain the revolver, and the special silencer he had made. In case."

"One bullet, placed in one chamber, and spun," said Michel. "Only a revolver does that. When that wretched little man told me what he was doing, smiling all the time, I understood why you were here."

"Me?" asked Armand, surprised by the turn the conversation had taken.

"I knew what you were planning to do. You came to the academy to get rid of Serge Leduc. You'd fired all the other corrupt professors, but kept him. Why? I asked myself. Because you had other plans for him. Something more permanent. So that he could never torture anyone else."

"But I told you, I didn't know about the Russian roulette," said Armand. "I wish I had. I wish they hadn't gone through months of that, while I did nothing."

"You'd have found out eventually. You were digging. Trying to get something on him. And when you dug past the corruption to the real horror, then what? What would you have done?"

Armand was silent.

"You'd have confronted him, and then I think you'd have killed him. You'd have had to, to save the cadets."

"I could have arrested him."

"For what? He'd never admit it, and he had those poor cadets so confused, so disoriented, they don't know up from down. They'd never admit to playing Russian roulette. Not while the Duke lived."

He watched Armand and could see the struggle. Brébeuf spoke softly now. Quietly. Almost in a whisper.

"He had to die. He had to be killed. You'd have tried to find other options, as I did. But finally there would be no choice. You'd have visited him one night, asking to see the revolver. You'd have taken it and put bullets in the chamber, as he watched, mystified, trying to explain that you should only use one bullet. And then you'd have put it to his temple. And when it dawned on him what was about to happen, and he began pleading for his life, you'd have pulled the trigger."

The two men held each other's eyes. The story had done the trick. It had horrified them both.

"But the worst would be yet to come, Armand. Pulling that trigger on an unarmed man, executing him, would have killed you too. You'd have done the unthinkable, you'd have damned yourself to save the cadets. I couldn't let that happen. So I did it for you. I owed you that."

Deputy Commissioner Gélinas heard the footsteps before he heard the knock.

Picking up his pistol, he stood in the middle of the bedroom he'd been assigned in the academy. A junior professor's room, Gamache had explained. Apologizing. Bed, living room, kitchenette, all in one small space.

But Gélinas's needs, as it turned out, were simple. He enjoyed the fine dining and luxury hotels in Europe, but without the companionship of his wife, the pleasure was shallow and fleeting.

He found all he really needed was a bed, a small bookcase, and a place to put the photo of Hélène, which now lay facedown on the table.

She'd inspired him to be a better man than he actually was, and he wondered if she knew it. Knew what he was really like, beneath the layer of integrity, worn like a uniform.

On Hélène's death, there seemed no reason to keep it up. All the constraints fell away, and he was free. And he was lost.

And now he stood there, in the little room, and raised the gun.

"Deputy Commissioner Gélinas?" came Isabelle Lacoste's voice.

"Come in."

Isabelle Lacoste opened the door, and stopped. She thought for just a moment before turning and speaking to the agents behind her.

Then she entered alone, closing the door behind her.

"Give me the gun," she said, holding out her hand.

"I think he might have a gun," Huifen told Nathaniel and Amelia just as they reached the factory mock-up.

"What?"

"How?"

"The Duke gave him one for his birthday."

The freshmen stared at Huifen.

"And you knew?" Amelia demanded.

"I guessed. It didn't seem strange. At the time."

Amelia understood. What seemed incredible now seemed normal then. Leduc had the ability to create an entire world, with its own rules and gravity. Nothing he did could be strange, because he decided what was normal.

"Why didn't you tell Gamache?" Amelia asked. "After Leduc was killed."

"I didn't want to get Jacques into trouble. After the Duke died, I asked him if he had a gun and he denied it. I wanted to believe him."

"We have to assume he does," said Amelia.

They'd arrived at the tactical training area and looked at the closed door to the factory.

"Shouldn't we get a professor?" asked Nathaniel, glancing up and down the empty hallway.

"While Jacques uses the gun?" asked Huifen. "You can go if you want to."

"Will he use it on us, do you think? Will he shoot at us?" asked Nathaniel.

"Does it matter?" asked Huifen.

"A little," said Nathaniel.

"No, I mean, will that stop you from going in?" She nodded to the door. He considered, then shook his head.

Huifen looked at Amelia, who also shook her head and stared at the door.

Four months ago, she was giving blow jobs in exchange for dope.

Four months ago, Nathaniel was waiting tables in Old Montréal, for tips.

Four months ago, Huifen held a gun to her own head.

She reached out for the handle, while the other two stood side by side.

Then she opened the door, and they moved forward.

"Give me the gun."

Brébeuf had gone to his liquor cabinet and poured them both large

Scotches, but when he turned around, he held a glass in one hand and a pistol in the other. It was hanging lazily at his side, as though it was a napkin or stir stick.

On seeing it, Armand slowly stood up.

"Is it my turn now? Are you going to shoot me?"

"Like when we played soldier, running all over Mont Royal?"

"I thought we were on the same side," said Gamache. "Back then. Give me the gun."

"I'll give you the drink. You might need it."

Gélinas stood in the middle of the room, his gun aimed at Isabelle Lacoste.

"You were Serge Leduc's partner, weren't you?" she said, not asking but telling. Her voice was steady, calm, almost conversational. But the blush in her cheeks betrayed high emotion.

"He was a moron," he said. No use denying anything now. "But perfectly placed."

"To fix contracts. You must've made millions."

He gave one jerk of his head, in agreement. "It's sitting in an account in Luxembourg. I made a mistake when I was talking to Gamache, didn't I? I mentioned Luxembourg. I knew as soon as I'd said it that I'd said something stupid. It was too specific. And too true. I wasn't sure if he caught it."

"He heard. But it just confirmed what he already suspected."

"When Leduc contacted me to say that Gamache was here and investigating the contract fixing, he panicked. But so did I. I knew Leduc wasn't clever enough to outwit him. So I came back."

"To kill Leduc."

"Maybe. I don't know."

The gun was by his side now, still clutched in his hand.

"But I didn't have to kill him. Gamache got there first."

"*Non*, not Monsieur Gamache," said Lacoste.

"Then who?" asked Gélinas.

Once again, Lacoste put out her hand. As steady as her gaze.

"There're two armed Sûreté officers outside this room, as you know. It's over. You're guilty of theft, but not of murder. Give me your weapon, please."

And he did.

CHAPTER 42

The cadets raced through the factory silently. Taking stairs two at a time. Glancing into empty rooms before moving deeper and deeper.

Huifen had the map of the factory memorized by now, after many failed attempts to end the mock hostage taking and capture the gunmen.

She'd never been the officer in charge. That had always been Jacques. And it had always ended in disaster for the Sûreté. Hostage dead. Agents slain. Gunmen escaped. It was an impossible scenario, they knew. But Leduc had always told them, told Jacques, that he could do anything.

And every time Jacques failed and had to report that to the Duke, the revolver would come out. Not as punishment, Leduc explained. But as a consequence. A teaching tool. For their own good.

Now Huifen led her little team. The freshmen were baffled by her hand signals, so she kept it simple. And clear. And they moved carefully and swiftly forward.

Finally she stopped and they regrouped.

"I don't think he's here," she said, looking around.

"But if not here," said Amelia, "where?"

"You shouldn't be here," said Jean-Guy, walking slowly into the room.

He'd been going to Commander Gamache's quarters, hoping to find him there, when he'd noticed that the Scene of Crime seal on Leduc's door was broken.

With his foot, he'd gingerly pushed the door open. His pistol was still on his belt, not yet drawn.

There, in the middle of the room, stood Cadet Jacques Laurin. Holding a gun.

"The hours I spent here," Jacques said, looking around almost casually, as though he didn't see the Scene of Crime tape and evidence markers. And blood spray. "I sat there." He gestured with the pistol. "And the Duke would sit there. Just the two of us. He gave me this, you know. For my birthday."

Beauvoir looked at the automatic weapon. The same as the one on his belt. Police issue.

"He said I'd be great one day. He said I'd be running the whole Sûreté. And he'd help me. Be my mentor, my patron. He said all great men need a patron."

"But you didn't, did you?" said Jean-Guy, closing the door behind him. "You needed something else. Someone who genuinely cared. About you. And you thought you'd found it in Professor Leduc."

"I did find it," snapped Jacques. "He cared."

"But then Commander Gamache arrived, and the world began to tilt," said Jean-Guy. Not venturing forward, but staying where he was. "I understand."

"No you don't."

"I do. The same thing happened to me, when I first met Monsieur Gamache. I thought I had the world figured out. Then everything I knew to be true, I started to question. And I hated him for it."

Beauvoir kept his eyes on Jacques. The young man had moved his gaze out the window.

"But then the hate shifted," said Beauvoir, speaking as though telling him a fable, a bedtime story. "I began to hate the very people I'd trusted. The ones who told me the world was filled with terrible people and that brutality was the same as strength. I'd learned to hit first, and hard, and fast."

"He did care," said Jacques quietly.

"On Professor Leduc's orders, you joined Commander Gamache's evening groups. To report back to the Duke. But there you learned something unexpected. People weren't so bad after all."

Jacques stood defiant.

"The world turned upside down," Beauvoir continued. "It was at once more beautiful and more frightening than you'd been led to believe. And suddenly you didn't know what to do. Who to trust. Where to turn. It's terrifying. Being lost is so much worse than being on the wrong road. That's why people stay on it so long. We're too far gone, or so we think. We're tired and we're confused and we're scared. And we think there's no way back. I know."

Jacques didn't move, didn't acknowledge the words.

Beauvoir searched his mind for something, anything, to say, to bring the boy back.

"You saw the video?" said Beauvoir.

There was a slight movement from Jacques, but still silence.

"Commander Gamache never, ever talks about that day with anyone, except trusted family and friends. And even then, it's rare. But he talked about it with you. He opened that wound, for you."

Jean-Guy Beauvoir watched the young man, who had suffered for years at the hands of a madman and could no longer recognize goodness. Could no longer even see it. What Jacques saw in front of him, all day, every day, was a wasteland.

"When someone shoots at us, we return fire," said Jean-Guy.

Now Jacques did nod.

"But it's equally important that when someone is kind to us, we return that as well," he said quietly. Careful. Careful not to scare the young man off.

"It took me a very long time to come to that. The hatred I felt for Monsieur Gamache, and then for the others, shifted again, and I began to loathe myself."

"Do you still?" Jacques asked, finally turning from the window, from the wasteland. "Hate yourself?"

"*Non.* It took a long time, and a lot of help. Jacques, the world is a cruel place, but it's also filled with more goodness than we ever realized. And you know what? Kindness beats cruelty. In the long run. It really does. Believe me."

He held out his hand to the young man. Jacques stared at it.

"Believe me," Jean-Guy whispered.

And Jacques did.

"How did you know it was me?"

"The fingerprints," said Gamache.

"Huh," grunted Brébeuf.

"I knew they weren't mine, and yet there they were. Which meant they'd been placed there. Not many could reproduce prints well enough to fool even the forensics team. Hugo Charpentier was one. And his mentor was another. You. You had to smudge every other fingerprint, including Leduc's own, and leave just partials. Including yours. A nice touch. You had to make the investigators work for it. That's what a great tactician does. He suggests. He doesn't lead, he herds. From behind."

Michel Brébeuf didn't disagree. Now it was his turn to be silent.

They'd returned to their seats, the pistol lying on the chair beside Brébeuf. A large Scotch in front of each of them, untouched.

"You say you killed Serge Leduc so that I didn't have to. As a favor."

"An amend," said Brébeuf.

"And yet, you put my partial prints on the weapon. You implicated me."

"No. Never. I used yours because I knew you were beyond suspicion."

"And yet I was, I am, suspected."

For the first time, Brébeuf looked baffled. "Yes. I could see that. The RCMP officer, Gélinas. Your own people wouldn't, of course."

"Don't be so sure," said Gamache. "It's a little humbling to realize the pedestal isn't quite so high after all."

Brébeuf chuckled. "Welcome to earth, Armand. It's a little dirty down here."

"And the map, Michel? The one in Leduc's drawer? It also had my prints, and showed my village. You placed it there, didn't you? More herding."

"But not toward you."

Gamache studied Brébeuf, searching the nooks, the crannies, the crevices of his face. The geography and history created by time and worry and loneliness. By too much drink and not enough peace.

And there, finally, he found the truth.

"You said that the first night here you made two discoveries. One was the game of Russian roulette. What was the other?"

Brébeuf stared back at Armand. Studying the roads radiating from his eyes and mouth. Some made by stress and sorrow, but most created by laughter. By contentment. By sitting beside a fireplace, watching his family and friends, and smiling.

That could have been his face. Had he turned left instead of right. Had he stepped forward instead of stepping aside. Had he locked the gate, instead of opening it.

Michel Brébeuf had long hated Armand. But he had loved him even longer.

"I think you know what it was," said Michel.

"Tell me."

"Amelia Choquet."

And there it was. There she was.

"When Leduc was talking about the pathetic new crop of cadets, he mentioned her specifically. The name was familiar, but I couldn't quite place her. But when Leduc told me that he'd rejected her application, and that you'd reversed the decision and accepted her, it fell into place. I knew who she was and I knew why she was here."

"Why?"

"Service. Integrity. Justice. You were handed the means, finally, for justice."

"You think I meant to hurt her?"

"Didn't you? Why else bring her here? Why else admit a girl so clearly unsuited to police work?"

"Unsuited? Why? Because she's different? *Non*, Michel. The purpose wasn't revenge or even justice. It wasn't to hurt her. It was to save her."

Michel Brébeuf stared. Blank. Uncomprehending.

"And to save myself," admitted Armand. "The only way I could really be free wasn't to add hurt to hurt, but to do something decent. I won't say it was easy. You have no idea how many times I returned her dossier to the rejected pile. Knowing what it would mean for her. A life of despair. And finally Amelia Choquet would be found in an alley or gutter or rooming house. Dead."

Armand looked down at his hands, at the tiny scar on the one finger.

"You did it to save her?" asked Michel, dumbfounded. "Her?"

"*Oui*. And you know what, Michel? She's the brightest, the most remarkable young woman. She'll be running the Sûreté one day."

And still Michel stared.

Gamache leaned in. "You put her partial prints on the gun, knowing she'd be suspected. You stole her copy of the map and placed it in Leduc's bedside table. And that was the other reason I knew it was you. The scene was so beautifully set. Everything subtle, suggestive. No glaring finger pointing her way. Just tiny crumbs through a forest of evidence. Leading to Amelia Choquet. With me as a temporary way station. But they'd have gotten to her eventually."

Michel Brébeuf moved his hand to the gun, slowly closing it around the grip.

"And that was your plan. You wanted her charged and found guilty of the murder of Serge Leduc."

"I did it so that you didn't have to."

He stood up and raised the gun.

Armand got to his feet and held out his hand.

"The gun, please, Michel."

Brébeuf stepped back and, tightening his grip on the weapon, he put it to his temple.

"*Non*," said Gamache, trying to keep the panic out of his voice, trying to bring reason into a situation that was spinning out of control.

The look on Michel's face was the same one he'd had when Armand had pressed the handkerchief to his bleeding knee. Such pain.

And once again, Armand was desperate to stanch the wound.

His hand, still held out, had begun to tremble, and he forced himself to steady it. "Do you remember at my parents' funeral, the gathering in my home after? With the finger food and the silence. All the adults moving about like zombies. Avoiding me because they had nothing to say." He spoke quickly, urgently, trying to form a bridge with his words, to bring Michel back. "I just sat there. You came over and sat beside me, and then you whispered so that no one else heard. Do you remember what you said?"

The gun lowered just a little.

"You're a dirty rascal," Michel whispered.

Armand nodded. "You made me smile. I didn't think I'd ever do that again, but you showed me I could. You gave me hope that it would get better."

The gun lowered a little more.

"It seems hopeless now, I know," said Armand. "It feels like there's no way out. I understand. You know I do."

Michel nodded.

"But it will get better. Even this. I promise."

"I followed you home, you know, one night," said Michel. "To your village."

"That was you?"

"I wanted to see where you lived." He paused. "It was so peaceful. I sat in the car and longed to drive down and join you. To maybe buy a little cottage and have drinks every evening in that brasserie. Maybe join a book club."

This was the worst ghost story yet. The phantom life that might have been.

"I'll die in prison. You know that. Of old age. Or someone, one night, will beat me to death. Someone who knows who I used to be. How is it better to die there than here?"

The gun was raised again, and now Armand brought up both hands. Not reaching for the gun, but for the man, just out of reach.

"Give me your hand," he pleaded. "It's okay. It'll be okay. Come with me. Please, Michel."

Michel dropped his eyes to the outstretched hands, then raised his gaze to Armand's eyes as he pressed the gun to his temple.

"For God's sake," Armand whispered. "Don't. I'm begging you. Please." He searched his mind for something, anything, to say. To stop this. "Would you condemn me to seeing this for the rest of my life?"

"Then turn your back, Armand."

At the sound of the shot, Jean-Guy Beauvoir leapt up.

He and Jacques had gone to Commander Gamache's rooms, where Jacques splashed water on his face while Beauvoir secured the gun and poured them each a Coke. They'd just sat down when the shot rang out.

"Stay here."

Jean-Guy was out the door and into the corridor, where the sound was still reverberating. He skidded to a stop in front of Brébeuf's rooms and yanked the door open.

Armand Gamache stood in the middle of the little room. Specks of blood on his face. A figure crumpled at his feet. Gamache squeezed his eyes shut then. But it was too late.

He had not turned his back on Michel.

CHAPTER 43

A wail filled the air, followed quickly by an expletive and a familiar voice. "Oh, for God's sake. Does the crying ever stop?"

"Probably just thirsty," said Clara. "Sounds like you when you want a drink."

"Jeez." Myrna turned around from the pew in front of them. "I thought that was Ruth."

There was another piercing wail.

"Nope," Myrna said. "Not loud enough."

Ruth cackled. "I could use a shot of Liebfraumilch."

Shhhh, said the rest of the congregation.

"Me?" said Ruth. "You're telling me to shush? Tell that to the kid."

She thrust Rosa, her appendage, toward the altar.

It was a warm morning in late spring, and Three Pines was gathered in St. Thomas's Church.

Armand stood at the front and looked out at the congregation.

Daniel and Roslyn were there from Paris, with their daughters Florence and Zora.

Jean-Guy's family were elbowing each other in the front pew.

And beyond them, friends, sitting and standing. At the very back stood the four cadets.

Jacques, Huifen, Nathaniel, and Amelia.

The graduation ceremony had been held at the academy the day before. It was more solemn than most, given the events of that term.

The cadets had stood as one, somber, erect, silent, when Commander Gamache entered the auditorium and walked alone across the stage.

He gripped the podium and stared out at them, in their dress blues. Those about to graduate and enter service, and those returning the following year.

The uniforms were perfectly pressed, the creases sharp, the buttons polished, the young faces shiny and clean.

He stared in silence, and they stared back. The specter of the tragedies filling the space between them. Filling the room. Darkening the past, dimming the present, and eclipsing their bright futures.

And then he smiled.

Armand Gamache's face broke into a radiant smile.

He smiled. And he smiled.

First one, then a few, then they all smiled back. They beamed at each other, Commander and cadets. Until the darkness was banished. And finally he spoke.

"Things are strongest where they're broken," said Commander Gamache, his voice deep and calm and certain. The words entered each of the cadets. And their families. And their friends. And filled the void.

And then he talked about what had happened. The shattering events. And the healing.

He ended his address by saying, "We are all of us marred and scarred and imperfect. We make mistakes. We do things we deeply regret. We are tempted and sometimes we give in to that temptation. Not because we're bad or weak, but because we're human. We are a crowd of faults. But know this."

He stood in complete silence for a moment, the huge auditorium motionless.

"There is always a road back. If we have the courage to look for it, and take it. I'm sorry. I was wrong. I don't know." He paused again. "I need help. Those are the signposts. The cardinal directions."

And then he smiled again, the creases deep, his eyes bright.

"You are extraordinary and I'm very proud of each and every one of you. It will be an honor to serve together."

There was a pause, and then the cheering began. Lusty, robust, joyful. They threw their caps in the air and hugged each other, while Armand Gamache stood at the podium. And smiled.

Under each of their seats, the graduates found a package, wrapped in simple brown paper. In it were two books. Marcus Aurelius's *Meditations* and Ruth Zardo's *I'm FINE*. Gifts from the Commander and his wife.

After the ceremony, cadets came up, eager to introduce Commander Gamache to their parents.

Jean-Guy stood beside him, never leaving Gamache's side, scanning the crowd. And finally, he spotted them. Working their way toward them.

Beauvoir stepped forward, but a hand was laid on his arm.

"Are you sure?" Jean-Guy asked.

"I'm sure."

Though Gamache did not look certain. He was pale, but his cheeks were flushed, as though his very body was conflicted. Engaged in a not entirely civil war.

The two men watched as Amelia Choquet wove through the crowd.

"I can stop them," whispered Jean-Guy urgently. "Just say the word."

But Gamache was silent, his eyes wide. Beauvoir could see the tremble in his right hand.

"Commander Gamache," said Amelia. "I'd like to introduce you to my father."

The man was slight and older than Gamache by about ten years.

Monsieur Choquet studied him for just a moment, then held out his hand. "You turned my daughter's life around. You brought her home to her family. *Merci.*"

There was the briefest pause while Armand looked at the outstretched hand, then into the man's eyes.

"You are welcome, sir."

And Armand Gamache shook Monsieur Choquet's hand.

Now it was Armand's turn to stand beside Jean-Guy, as Annie and Reine-Marie stood on the other side of the baptismal font with the minister between them.

The minister was Gabri, specially anointed for the occasion, by himself.

He wore his choir robes, and in his arms he held Annie and Jean-Guy's baby.

"Oh, please," Olivier was heard to pray. "Dear Lord, don't let him lift the baby and sing 'Circle of Life.' Oh, please."

The baby howled in Gabri's arms.

"This is nothing," Jean-Guy whispered to Armand. "You should hear him at night."

"I did. All night."

Jean-Guy smiled proudly.

Gabri lifted the baby up as though offering him to the congregation. "Let us sing."

"Oh no," whispered Olivier.

And Gabri, in his rich tenor, began "Circle of Life," joined immediately by the choir and the congregation, and then by Olivier, in robust, full voice.

Jean-Guy looked at his son and felt, again, a surge of love that left him weak, and strong. He glanced at his father-in-law and saw that Armand had stopped singing and was staring, open-mouthed, straight ahead of him.

"What is it?" whispered Jean-Guy, following his gaze to the back of the chapel. "The cadets?"

Armand shook his head. "*Non.* I'll tell you later."

"Who here stands for this child?" Gabri asked when the song was over. Olivier and Clara stood at their seats.

"I don't know why they didn't ask me," came a querulous voice.

"Probably because you can't stand," said Myrna.

"I can't stand you," muttered Ruth, and struggled to her feet.

Myrna was about to tell her to sit down, but something about the elderly woman made her stop. Ruth was standing straight and tall. Her face forward. Resolute. Even Rosa looked as dignified as a duck possibly could.

Then Myrna got up.

Then Monsieur Béliveau, the grocer, rose to his feet. As did Sarah, the baker. As did Dominique and Marc and the Asshole Saint. As did Billy Williams and Gilles Sandon and Isabelle Lacoste and Adam Cohen and Yvette Nichol and the Brunels.

Jacques and Huifen and Nathaniel and Amelia stepped forward.

The entire congregation stood.

Jean-Guy took his infant son in his arms and turned him to face the men and women and children who would be his godparents.

And he whispered, "May you be a brave man in a brave country, Honoré."

"What were you looking at?" Jean-Guy asked Armand, as they stood on the village green eating burgers off the huge grill Olivier had set up.

A long table had been brought out, filled with salads and fresh rolls and cheeses. Across the green was another, longer table with all sorts of cakes, pies, pastries. Cookies and brownies and candies and children.

Little Zora, in an excited tizzy, ran straight into her grandfather's legs, knocking herself to the soft grass. And looked up at him, in amazement.

He gave his plate to Jean-Guy and scooped her up, kissing her cheek, and the tears that were moments away turned to laughter, and she was off again.

The bar had been set up on Ruth's porch, where the old poet sat in a rocking chair, Rosa on her lap and her cane across the arms like a shotgun. The four cadets got their beers and were deep in conversation.

"What're you talking about?" Clara asked, pouring herself a gin and tonic.

"Ruth says she wants a name for her cottage," said Nathaniel. "She asked me to choose one."

"Really?" asked Myrna. "She asked you?"

"Well, more told me to find one," he admitted. "And told me not to fuck it up."

"So what've you come up with?" asked Clara.

"We've narrowed it down," said Huifen. "It's between Rose Cottage"—she pointed to the sweetbriar roses around Ruth's porch—"and Pit of Despair."

"I dare you," said Clara, laughing, as she and Myrna crossed the dirt road and joined Reine-Marie and Annie, who was holding Honoré and chatting with Gabri.

"A beautiful ceremony, *mon beau*," Annie said, kissing his cheeks.

"*Merci*. I was thrown a little when everyone stood up," he admitted.

"But you covered it nicely by breaking into 'Hakuna Matata.' The King James version, if I'm not mistaken."

Gabri leaned down and spoke to Honoré. "One must always have a song in the heart."

"And an éclair in the hand," said Myrna, lifting hers.

"Sage words," said Annie.

She looked across the village green and noticed her husband and her father walking back to the chapel.

They followed and found the two men standing once again in front of the stained-glass boys.

Reine-Marie slipped her hand into Armand's, then pulled it away.

"You're all sticky."

"That was Zora," he said.

"Of course it was," said Reine-Marie. "What're you looking at?"

Armand was staring at the window, but not at the one boy who always drew their attention. He was looking at one of the other young men.

"He's pointing at something," said Armand.

"Huh," said Jean-Guy, leaning closer. "You're right."

"But what?" asked Reine-Marie. "That, maybe?"

She followed the direction of the finger and saw a bird in the sky above the battlefield.

"Or maybe the tree," said Annie. A single charred evergreen stood askew in the mud.

"I noticed the gesture a while ago, but thought it must be just an artistic touch," said Armand. "But when I was at the front of the church during the baptism, I realized what the soldier wanted us to see. He's not pointing into his world. He's pointing into ours."

He turned, and they turned with him.

"At that."

He didn't tell them that shortly before his death, Michel Brébeuf had made a similar gesture. Pointing above the doorway of his room in the academy, to the frame that could be mistaken for a rose, but was not.

Armand put his hand in his pocket and felt the linen and traced the letters with his finger while the others stared above the door of the church at a stylized stained-glass rose they'd seen hundreds of times before.

They looked and they looked.

And finally—

"My God," whispered Reine-Marie. "It's not just a rose window. It's a compass rose." She turned back to the soldier. "He's pointing at a compass."

They walked closer to it, until Armand told them, "It's really best seen from the front. That's one of the reasons no one noticed before. We were all too close. I only noticed during the baptism, when I stood here."

He stepped onto the dais and they joined him.

The bright June sun was streaming in through the hundreds of tiny panes of glass, stained shades of red and pink and green. It hit the old pine floor of the chapel right in the center of the aisle, creating the cheerful, intricate design of a multipetaled rose. With almost unnoticeable spikes.

The four directions.

"But it's tilted," said Annie.

"It's not tilted," said Jean-Guy. "It's pointed."

"It's indicating a direction," said Reine-Marie. She looked at Armand. "We should follow."

"We should. But not today," said Armand, taking little Honoré in his arms.

The next morning a group set out cross-country. Jacques held the old map, the original, while Armand oriented a compass salvaged from the box of items brought home from the war.

The four cadets were there, as were Clara, Myrna, Olivier, and Gabri. Ruth had decided to stay home.

"I think she's embroidering the name on a pillow," Nathaniel explained to Clara.

"What did you go with? Rose Cottage or Pit of Despair?"

"Another FINE Mess," said Amelia, and Clara laughed.

The troop crossed streams and hiked through forests and fields. They paused at Larsen's Rock, where a cow was once stranded, and rescued.

They climbed over a stone wall and stopped for a drink of water at the intersection of two dirt lanes, where a snowman had celebrated a victory by Le Club de Hockey Canadien.

"Did you notice he's not just celebrating?" said Huifen, imitating the snowman. "He's pointing."

And sure enough, he was. In the direction they were heading.

"You haven't yet accepted a posting," Commander Gamache said to Jacques, as they continued their walk through a meadow of tall wildflowers.

"No. I've been speaking with Inspector Beauvoir and I think I'll take some time away before deciding what to do next."

"Any ideas?"

"The Inspector and I've discussed options. I'm thinking of volunteering in Haiti. And you, sir?"

"Me?"

"In your commencement address, you ended by saying it would be an honor to serve with us. What did you mean by that?"

Armand glanced down at the compass, making sure they were heading in the right direction. The others were fanned out behind. Enjoying the flowers and the bright young green of the trees and the buzz of newborn bees.

Gamache turned to Jacques and smiled. "You'll see."

Armand looked behind him and, spotting Amelia, he waved her forward.

"Here," he said. "You take it."

He handed her the compass.

"But I don't know how to use it."

"I'll teach you."

And he did. Nathaniel and Huifen joined the other two and Armand fell back to walk beside Reine-Marie, letting the four young people lead.

They'd win no races, getting lost a few times before Amelia got her bearings. But finally they arrived, where they all knew they were headed anyway.

To the pyramid on the map. That was not a pyramid at all, but a roof truss.

Their journey ended in the cemetery, now filled with daylilies and wild rugosa roses.

It was Nathaniel who found it.

He knelt beside a headstone, his arms scratched and bleeding from pulling the roses away.

"Look."

There, etched into the granite, was another compass rose. And a flag.

"A control," said Huifen quietly. "For an orienteer to find."

"The last one," said Jacques.

It was over. They'd finally found Antony Turcotte.

The young people rubbed the lichen and dirt from the face of the stone.

"That can't be right," said Nathaniel, sitting back on his heels.

"What is it?" asked Gamache.

Nathaniel got to his feet, shaking his head, while the other cadets remained on their knees in front of the grave.

"We were wrong," said Jacques.

"It's not the right one?" asked Beauvoir.

"Right grave," said Amelia, also getting to her feet. "Wrong person."

There, below the rose and the flag, was the name.

Marie Valois
Died September 5, 1919
Loving Mother of Pierre, Joseph, and Norman
Notre-Dame-de-Doleur

"Not the father," said Reine-Marie, looking down at the stone. "The mother. Our Lady of Grief."

They sat under the Cinzano umbrellas on the bistro's *terrasse*, lemonades and beers in front of them.

After returning to Three Pines, the cadets had taken off, back to the records office. With a new name. And a new mission. And when they had found what they needed, they'd returned.

And now they sat, dossiers in front of them, knees jiggling, just waiting for Clara and Myrna to arrive.

380

Myrna knew where to find Clara. Where she always was these days.

In her studio, painting.

"They're back," said Myrna.

"Almost finished."

"Take your time," Myrna suggested. She wandered into the kitchen, picking up a cookie.

"There," said Clara, getting off the stool and stepping back. "I think it's finally done. What do you think?"

Myrna had been dreading this moment, this question.

She turned to look. And the cookie stopped mid-bite.

"But it's not you at all."

A woman's face filled the whole frame. Staring straight ahead. Facing the world. Meeting it head on. She was pierced and tattooed. She was scarred. And she was scared.

"It's the cadet," said Myrna. "Amelia."

"Yes."

"But it's more than that," said Myrna, stepping toward the portrait, then looking at her friend. "It's the boy, the soldier."

Clara nodded.

She had painted robust youth. Made frail and vulnerable by fear. By the stupidity and cruelty and decisions of old men.

The boy was afraid to die. And Amelia was afraid to live.

But there was something else in that stare. In those eyes.

Forgiveness.

It was hot and the cadets chugged their lemonades.

Huifen looked down at her notebook.

In two weeks she'd be joining the Sûreté detachment in Gaspé, as their most junior agent. But for now she had this, her last assignment and first investigation, to wrap up.

"Marie Turcotte married Frederick Valois in 1893. They lived in Montréal and had three sons. Pierre, the oldest, then twins Joseph and Norman."

Reine-Marie had placed the old photograph on the table beside the map. As Huifen spoke, they looked at Joe and Norm in their uniforms, grinning into the camera and hugging their mother, Clara's home in the background.

Another photograph lay on Reine-Marie's lap. She'd come across it in the archives that afternoon, when they'd returned from the gravesite.

"Turcotte?" said Jean-Guy. "Antony Turcotte was her brother? Her father?"

"We're coming to that," said Nathaniel.

"According to the Bureau of Records, Monsieur Valois was a mapmaker," said Amelia, picking up the story. "Not a particularly good one, but serviceable. Good enough to keep food on the table. He made maps mostly for mining companies. Until one day he walked off a cliff."

"Was he . . . ?" Reine-Marie asked.

"Killed?" said Jacques. "Yes. The next piece of information we found was a record of Marie Valois renting here."

"My place?" asked Clara.

"No, here, here," said Nathaniel, pointing to the ground. "The bistro, though it was a private home at the time, owned by a Monsieur Béliveau."

"I knew he was older than me," said Ruth.

"Not, perhaps, the current one," suggested Myrna.

"I'll see if he's in." Armand got up, and as he walked across the *terrasse*, past the boulangerie to the grocer, he checked his watch.

Past six. It was a warm, still evening, the scent of peony and old garden roses in the air. The sun was still well up in the clear sky and wouldn't set for another few hours.

When he returned, the elderly grocer was with him.

"You're wondering about the Valois family?" he asked.

Armand indicated his chair, and Monsieur Béliveau bowed slightly and sat.

"Did you know them?" asked Nathaniel.

Monsieur Béliveau's somber face broke into a smile. "I'm not quite that old."

"Told you," Myrna whispered to Ruth.

"But my grandfather knew them. He owned this building at the time and rented to Madame Valois. She was a widow, I believe."

"Yes, with three sons," said Huifen. "She must have been memorable, for your grandfather to tell you about them."

"She wasn't," said Monsieur Béliveau. "And neither were the boys. They were just regular kids. What was memorable was what happened to them. All three died on the same day. At the Somme. My grandfather said he could still hear her wail, years later. Just the wind through the pines, my grandmother would tell him. But he insisted it was her."

Reine-Marie looked at Armand. How often had they heard that howl from the forest?

"Why didn't you tell us all this before?" asked Huifen.

"Because you were asking about Antony Turcotte," said Monsieur Béliveau. "Not Madame Valois. I'd never heard of Turcotte."

"Well, where does he come in then?" asked Gabri.

"After her sons were killed, Marie Valois went to live in Roof Trusses," said Jacques. "She died just after the war."

"Spanish flu probably," said Myrna. "Judging by the date on the head-stone. It killed millions in 1919."

"Why would she leave Three Pines?" asked Gabri.

"You've never been a mother," said Reine-Marie.

"He's been a mother—" began Ruth.

"Ah," said Jean-Guy, holding up Honoré, his little feet dangling. "Not in front of the baby."

"She didn't leave," said Monsieur Béliveau, and all heads turned to him.

"*Pardon?*" said Clara.

"Madame Valois. She didn't leave Three Pines. At least, she didn't mean to. Not forever. She kept renting the place from my grandfather."

"But, Roof Trusses?" said Olivier, not sure how to form the question.

"She wanted to get away," said Monsieur Béliveau. "But just for a while. I think it was too painful for her here. But she always planned to come back. This was her home. She left most of her things here."

"Including that," said Myrna, pointing to the old map that had been placed on the table.

"But if all the boys were killed, how did the map get back to their mother?" asked Clara.

"It didn't," said Armand. "This map never left. It was made after the boys were missing in action. Before she left for Roof Trusses. In case."

"In case?" Jacques asked.

"In case they weren't dead," said Reine-Marie.

"This whole village is one big orienteering exercise," said Jean-Guy. "The map, the stained-glass window, the compass rose."

"She made them each a map, to take with them," said Armand. "So they could find their way home, and then she made another, so they could find her."

"You mean she commissioned the maps," said Huifen. "Antony Turcotte actually made them. The man in the toponymie office was certain. He must've been her father, or maybe a brother or uncle."

"No," said Gamache. "I mean she made them."

The cadets, confused, looked at him, then at each other.

"Marie Valois was Antony Turcotte," said Gamache. "She used her maiden name when she started making maps."

"I don't understand," said Huifen.

"Probably a good thing that you don't," said Myrna. But she understood. "Back then, a hundred years ago or so, women weren't encouraged to have jobs, and they sure weren't encouraged to have a profession."

"So they often took men's names," said Clara. "Painters did it. Writers and poets often used men's names. She might have learned mapmaking by watching her husband, and then discovered that she was far better at it."

"Not the first wife to excel at the same profession as her husband, but have to hide it," said Myrna. "The men often took credit for their wives' work."

Huifen looked perplexed. It was, to her, inconceivable. And ancient history.

"So you're saying all those maps—" began Huifen.

"Were done by Marie Valois," said Gamache. "*Oui.*"

Amelia was nodding. "Monsieur Toponymie said that no one actually met Antony Turcotte. It was all done by correspondence. No one ever knew."

"How sad, then," said Reine-Marie, "that after mapping and naming all those towns and villages, Marie Valois finally had one named after her. But not for her work as a cartographer. But because of the enormity of her grief."

"Notre-Dame-de-Doleur," said Armand.

They looked at the photo of the smiling farm woman, between her tall sons.

"But assuming what you say is true," said Olivier, "why did she take Three Pines off the maps of Québec?"

Reine-Marie brought out the small sepia photo. Older even than the one already on the table.

They leaned toward it and saw three grinning boys, children, covered in dirt, their boots resting on spades, and in front of each was a sapling.

"They planted the trees," whispered Gabri. He hadn't meant to whisper, but that was all that came out.

"The others blew down in a terrible storm," said Monsieur Béliveau. "Two fell and one was badly damaged. Gilles Sandon's great-grandfather cut it down. Made the floors of the bistro and bookstore with them. The village was devastated by the loss, my grandfather told me. But one morning they woke up and those saplings had been planted. They never knew who did it."

He and the others looked across the village green to the three pines. Strong and straight. And still growing.

"I think it was just too painful a reminder," said Reine-Marie. "So close to losing her sons. So Madame Valois took the village off the map before sending it in to the toponymie department. It might even have been a spur-of-the-moment decision. Erasing the village, as though she could erase her sorrow."

"But as Monsieur Béliveau said, she always meant to come home again," said Armand. "To return to Three Pines. And return the village to the map."

"Then why didn't she?" asked Gabri.

"She died before she could," said Reine-Marie.

"Of the flu," said Myrna.

Of grief, thought Reine-Marie. And heard a small moan from the forest, while on the village green the three pines swayed and played, reaching out their branches to touch each other.

"*Velut arbor aevo*," said Amelia.

"As a tree with the passage of time," said Armand.

The next morning, Armand and Reine-Marie got up just as a soft blue appeared in the sky. The morning was fresh and mild, and dew was dripping off the lady's mantle and the roses and the lilies. With Gracie on a leash and Henri running free, they walked across the village green to the three pines.

"Ready?" asked Reine-Marie.

"Not quite," said Armand, and took a seat on the bench.

Just as the sun rose, so did he.

He walked over to the pines and chose a spot. Then he put his foot on the spade.

"Can I help?" came the familiar voice.

He turned to see Jean-Guy, a little bleary after a night comforting his crying child.

Honoré was in his arms. Sleeping now that Papa was awake.

Armand smiled. "*Merci*, but no. This is something I need to do myself."

Not because it was easy, but because it was difficult.

The sun rose higher and the hole got deeper, until finally he stopped and picked up the box that had sat in the basement for too long.

Opening it up, Armand saw again the report. The one with his parents' names. Honoré and Amelia Gamache. Killed. By a drunk driver.

Armand reached into his pocket and brought out the handkerchief. He traced the embroidered letters with his scarred finger, then he placed it in the box.

Putting the top back, he lowered it carefully into the hole.

The police report had one other name. Of the boy.

Robert Choquet.

The young man, all of sixteen, had been given a suspended sentence. And gone on to live his life. To get married and have a family.

One daughter.

Whom he named Amelia.

ACKNOWLEDGMENTS

I think the main thing I need to acknowledge is that this book has only been written because of the extreme kindness and patience and help of our friends and neighbors.

Michael has dementia. It has progressed, marching through our lives, stomping out his ability to speak, to walk, to remember events and names.

Dementia is a marauder, a thief. But every hole it drills has been filled by our friends. By practical help and emotional support.

It's not all bad. Far, far from it. There's clarity, the simplicity of living in the moment and knowing what really matters. Kindness. Company. Gentle care. We laugh a lot, and God knows there's plenty to laugh about. And there are moments of deep peace and contentment.

I have never met a braver man. When diagnosed he told me he wanted to be open about it. To tell people. Not to hide away, ashamed. Afraid of being judged or shunned or embarrassed.

Michael has met his dementia with humor and acceptance. With gratitude for all that he has. While he can barely speak anymore, he smiles all the time, even in his sleep. He loves massages and food and friends. And Bishop, our golden. And he loves me. I can see it every day.

Michael and I have found more kindness since his diagnosis than we ever knew existed. From friends. From strangers. But also from colleagues. From publishers and editors and publicists. From booksellers and librarians. And readers.

Like you.

You can imagine that writing a book in the midst of all this could not be done without help. Physical and emotional.

First among the people who have made *A Great Reckoning* possible by lifting so many other weights is my assistant and great friend, Lise Desrosiers.

I honestly, Lise, don't know what I would do without you. I love you.

Thank you to her husband, Del, for coming over when things fall apart. To Kirk and Walter, our first friends out here and foundations in our lives. How many times have you lifted my spirits and actually lifted Michael when he's fallen? Strong backs, strong hearts.

To Pat and Tony, for caring so deeply and being there over so many years. And for taking care of Bishop when needed! Thanks to Linda Lyall, who manages the website and sends out the newsletter and does so much more.

Thank you to Andrew Martin, my U.S. publisher at Minotaur Books, for removing the deadline from the books and not forcing me to write. Or to tour. For understanding and always sending love to his buddy, Michael. Thank you, Andy. Thank you to Hope Dellon, my astonishing editor, for being a great friend and writing just to see how we're doing. And for making *A Great Reckoning* so much better with her notes and insight.

Thank you to Sarah Melnyk, my publicist, for holding the world at bay and not insisting I do anything unless it works for Michael and me. To Paul Hochman, who built the virtual bistro at the Minotaur site, and who knows from experience what we are living.

Thank you to Jamie Broadhurst in Canada, for being a friend first and colleague second.

Thank you to my UK publishers, Little, Brown—and David Shelley and Lucy Malagoni.

To Louise Loiselle, of Flammarion Québec, for stepping back while stepping up.

Thank you to my agent, Teresa Chris, for starting and ending each conversation by talking about Michael.

Thank you to Michael's incredible caregivers, Kim and Rose and Daniel. Without you, our lives would fall apart. How do Michael and I even begin to thank you for your care, your kindness? Treating Michael as a beloved brother/father/friend. Bless you.

To Dr. Dominique Giannangelo, for always making time for us, in person and over the phone. For being steady and calm and compassionate.

To Tony Duarte and Ken Prehogan and Hilary Book. Hilary, by the way, also provided advice on some legal issues in *A Great Reckoning*. Thank you, Hilary!

It would be impossible to list all the friends and neighbors who have stood beside us, but let me mention just a few. Lucy and Danny, David and Linda, Joan, Cotton, Wilder, Cheryl, Deanna. Michael's sister Carol in London.

Richard Oliver. Rosemary and Rocky and Honora. And our beautiful, magical new village of Knowlton, Québec. *Merci, mes amis.*

To Michael's sons, Michael and Victor, who phone and visit whenever they can. And while their father can no longer tell them he loves them, they see it in his eyes and know they are loved.

And to my family who visit and write, Rob and Audi, Sarah, Adam, Kim, Mary, Charlie and Roslyn.

Every day when I tuck Michael into bed, I bend down and whisper in his ear that he is a wonderful man. Handsome and kind and generous. Brilliant and brave. I tell him how proud I am to be his wife. And that he is safe. And he is loved.

Then, over the past year, thanks to all the people I mentioned here and so many others not mentioned, I'd go into the living room and sit down at the laptop. And be in the company of my other friends. Armand, Reine-Marie, Clara, Myrna, Gabri, Ruth, et al.

I wrote *A Great Reckoning* with the peace of mind that comes with knowing I too am safe and loved. And not alone.

Noli timere, dear friend.

3567405664 8323